Mill Song

ALSO BY WILLIAM HARRY HARDING

Young Hart

Rainbow

Holt, Rinehart and Winston | New York

William Harry Harding

Mill Song

GRATEFUL ACKNOWLEDGMENT TO

DIANE MELENDEZ, GAYNELL C. HARDING,

AND JULIAN WILSEY,

WHOSE RESEARCH ASSISTANCE

HELPED SUPPLY THE FACTS FOR THIS FICTION.

First published in January 1985 by Holt, Rinehart and Winston,
383 Madison Avenue, New York, New York 10017.
Published simultaneously in Canada by Holt, Rinehart
and Winston of Canada, Limited.

Library of Congress Cataloging in Publication Data
Harding, William Harry.
Mill song.
I. Title.
PS3558.A62344M5   1985   813'.54   84-4527
ISBN: 0-03-070547-9

First Edition

Design by Elissa Ichiyasu
Printed in the United States of America
1   3   5   7   9   10   8   6   4   2

ISBN 0-03-070547-9

FOR JANE AND JOSEPH HANSEN

AUTHOR'S NOTE

They are gone now, the silk mills of Paterson. Their brick remains, but the mills are gone. So are most of the people who worked them.

My grandfather worked in those mills most of his life. He used to say the mills made the sound of men sweating.

I never worked in the mills, not a single day. But I heard them, too. And each time we started walking back home, my grandfather would sing.

whh
temetal

Book One

Home

1

So cold.

But home would be colder.

The silent, brittle wind on his face and ears kept him from talking, from saying thanks to the driver of the Buick, who had been filled with enough holiday spirit to stop for a lone hitchhiker standing with a duffel bag in a bank of rotten snow, just west of Buttzville, near the ice-worn Delaware Water Gap.

The light at the corner of Market Street and Railroad Avenue blinked green. The Buick sped away, spitting slush and rock salt. For the last hour and a half, the bald man behind the wheel had talked about the industrial detergents he sold and the great pies his wife baked, pies he couldn't wait to taste after a month on the road. Apples in brown sugar with cinnamon, thick-cut peaches in heavy syrup, fresh blueberries, all steaming and oven-fresh in flaky crust. Phil could smell them. Hitchhiking always made him hungry. Only this time he didn't have enough in his pockets for a meal and a bus ticket, too. This time wasn't the same as the others. This time was the end of the line.

And home would be colder. The furnace would be off, maybe the electricity. Nobody lived there anymore.

Street lamps along Market wore silver trees and green and red wreaths. Spanning the street, lines of colored lights held stars and bells that swayed in the breeze. Near the Alexander Hamilton Hotel, the office Dad had worked in had become a sandwich shop: Torpedo. Phil put his duffel bag in his other hand and watched a fat man behind the counter slice cold cuts and slap them over shredded lettuce on a hero roll. No customers. The fat man was making his own lunch.

The window bore no trace of the old gold letters, TRENT & COMPANY. The hand-carved wooden door had been replaced by glass. A bell at the top of the door clinked sadly, as if to discourage customers and warn the sandwich maker. The shop smelled of onions. Where the stock-market electronic tape board had been, giving up-to-the-minute quotes from New York above the desk Dad used to sit at, stood arcade games. The place felt small, not big enough for the leather couches and glass tables that had once made it cozy. For an instant, he was sure he had the wrong place.

"You got money?" The fat man had a mouthful of sandwich. "Otherwise, you get out of my shop."

Phil dug into a pocket of his jeans. Reflected in the store window, he could see how bad he looked: wild hair that hadn't been washed or even combed in a week, muddy pants and boots, a parka so worn the padding was leaking out, a face full of stubble. In that window, he saw the same bum the owner of Torpedo saw. He fished a five-dollar bill from his pocket and held it up as if showing I.D. to a bartender. All the money he had left. Enough to make the fat man grin and say, "Got a special on the capicolla today. That's the Sophia Loren up there."

"Up there" was a plastic sign with plastic letters describing each torpedo sandwich. Each was named after a movie star. An Italian movie star. Roast beef was Frank Sinatra. Add cheese for a Frank Sinatra Deluxe.

It couldn't be the same place.

But the door to the rest room still had the brass sign on it. Phil had given it to Dad five years ago, because that door had been unlabeled and people had gone in there, not only customers but people off the street, and they had used too much toilet paper, clogged the pipes, left paper towels on the floor, and sometimes they forgot to flush. Dad didn't know what to do about it, didn't have the heart to do anything about it, but it bothered him, he talked about the messy, smelly rest room as if he were the janitor, and knowing Dad, he probably had cleaned that place as often as the janitor had, and so one summer day Phil had come in unannounced with the sign and a screwdriver, and while Dad leaned across his desk for a better view and while customers pretended to watch the stock tape but watched Phil out of the corners of their eyes, the sign went up, and because it read PRIVATE, nobody ever went in there again.

"Hey, you okay?" The fat man came out from behind the case of cold cuts and cheese. Mustard stains on his apron. "Not going to pass out on me, are you?"

Phil waved, stuffed his cash into his jeans, and walked out. The sad bell rang again, a dull clap of cheap metal. It made him wince. The slow wind made him shiver. Feeling the shop owner's eyes on his back, he crossed the street.

He cursed Uncle Chuck for using the insurance from Dad's death to open a new office in the Ringbrook Mall, where there was, according to Uncle Chuck, "a better clientele and more of them." Dad's kid brother had probably been right, and right, too, about Paterson being a dying city. It had probably been the smart thing to do. But Dad hadn't wanted to, and Dad was smarter than Uncle Chuck. Dad had loved this Paterson office.

The dispatcher at the bus depot said the old 84 line had been discontinued. A year and a half ago. No buses between Paterson and Ringbrook anymore. "Nobody from Ringbrook bothers with Paterson now," the dispatcher said. "They got all those malls out there."

On the board behind the desk: a listing of times and routes. From this dingy waiting room, littered with Styrofoam coffee cups and paper plates just big enough to hold a Danish, you could go to New York, Trenton, Philadelphia, Baltimore, Washington, D.C., even Florida, but you couldn't go ten miles northwest to Ringbrook, not from here. Phil crumpled the money in his pocket. "So how do I get there?"

"New York first," the dispatcher said without looking up. "Then the One-ninety-two out of there back to Ringbrook Mall East. They run every forty minutes."

It was going to take two hours and cost six dollars. And the dispatcher didn't look like a man who would loan anybody a buck.

Even to Florida. Mom was down there in her new condo now, away from the winter and snug with the flowered wallpaper she raved about on the phone the few times he called her. That condo in Tampa had been a smart investment, she and Dad had talked about it as a retirement place before he died, and what else could she have done with all the money she kept getting from his share of the business? Mom was playing tennis these days. And she was the one who used to ask what *inning* the football game was going into so she could time her dinner. No matter how many times Dad or Phil told her baseball had innings and football had quarters and halves, she never got it. She bought her condo and began swatting tennis balls before the estate was settled.

He didn't know how he got on Clark Street, but when he saw the chain bordering the parking lot by the courthouse and the YMCA, he knew why he had come this way. Dad used to park his Dodge, even his Lincoln here, in the corner nearest the post office. Same spot, all those years. There was a dented Ford station wagon in that spot now. The Lincoln never had a dent in it, not even a scratch. It wasn't even a full year old when Dad died. He hadn't had time to break in his dream car. Uncle Chuck had no trouble getting the Blue Book price for it.

"Damn them." Phil punched the chain. It clattered against iron posts. His hand hurt. He couldn't stop shivering. He couldn't remember feeling more alone. That Christmas week three years ago, he had taken the bus up from Princeton on vacation, met Dad at the office, come here to this lot, to that parking space where some rusting suburban wagon now sat, and the two of them had driven home smiling and joking and it had been the best Christmas ever, with the best tree and the happiest eggnog toasts and the whitest snow, and three days later Dad was dead and Christmas would forever be a funeral.

But he was home. Or nearly there. To put his life in order, to do now, finally, what Uncle Chuck and Mom had done so quickly and so easily: put Dad's death in the past and get on with the business of living.

A woman in a gray coat unlocked the blue station wagon. The engine coughed clouds of exhaust, the car backed up and swung toward the exit on Ward Street. Phil stared at the empty parking space. "I tried," he said, and saying it, here where Dad's car belonged, he felt relieved, as if that parking spot had been waiting to hear his voice for a long time. Only those weren't the right words. Maybe it didn't matter what the words were. Maybe what mattered was he was here to say something, anything.

Why had it taken him three years to come to his senses? If he had come to his senses, why did he feel dazed and undone, as if he were about to enter the courthouse to hear his sentence—"a term of life in the suburb of Ringbrook"—and accept his doom—"no parole"—knowing the taste for escape had been beaten out of him by fear, the same fear he had seen on every face between here and California and back, the fear of being poor, worrying this country like a plague, making everyone greedy, making them bastards because they were so afraid not to be, so afraid of what would happen if they weren't.

The fir tree near the courthouse steps had lights twisting around its branches, lights waiting for dusk to go on. The courthouse had a nice, heavy door. Phil rubbed his hands, sore from the cold, and pulled the door open.

2

Maxie Nash said he didn't mind driving through Ringbrook on his way home to Willowbend. "Easiest way up the mountain in this weather anyway." The round little lawyer offered a thick hand— "So you're Hank's kid?"—and a smile—"The city's not the same without him"—and an apology: "I have to stop at my office before we leave, and check my phone machine. My busiest time of year."

This plump, black-eyed man, who wore a dark suit that didn't fit, who looked to be in his forties, who called Dad "Hank" even though no one had ever called Dad anything but Henry or Mr. Trent, this man wore mittens. When he put on his black topcoat, those black wool mittens made him look like an overweight, out-of-condition boxer on a comeback, in boxing gloves and a robe, stepping into the ring, still believing in miracles.

He owned a red Fiat sedan. The heater didn't work. The radio, he said, had never worked. Something was wrong with the front seat, it kept jiggling back and forth whenever he braked or shifted gears or moved to get comfortable. He double-parked on Main Street and raced to a narrow door between two big store-front windows. On one window, in black block letters edged with gold: M. H. NASH, ATTORNEY AT LAW. On the other, red script: MAXIE'S—MUSIC FOR ALL OCCASIONS. Horns honked, traffic crawled by, and in each passing car window an angry Christmas-shopping face snarled behind snow-streaked glass, making Phil feel like a criminal. Finally, the round little man came out and got back behind the wheel. He was smiling. He took Main down to

Broadway, then over the Passaic River and a left onto Union Avenue.

Nothing had changed here. Old three-family houses and old stores huddled together, with nothing to do but test another winter and the snowmelt that would follow it. A skinny man in an apron swept the sidewalk in front of his grocery store, and the slow rhythm of his rail arms on the wide push broom said this grocer was accustomed to his task and in no hurry, there were plenty of winters still to come for him and his broom.

"So—what?—you're out hiking or camping?" Maxie said. "Your car break down?"

Phil shook his head.

Maxie Nash didn't mind not getting an answer. He kept smiling. "Your father was so proud of you. Had all those photos behind his desk. Hey, wait, didn't he have one of your trophies there, too?"

A small gilded statue of a batter twisting with the force of his swing, bat still in hand. The plastic stand had a strip of brass taped to it, engraved with Phil's name and *Yankees—1970 Champions*. In that office, that trophy never got dusty. He grinned and said, "Little League."

"You were some ballplayer. An all-star, right?"

In that instant, he could remember every kid on his team and the positions they played and how the Yankees just couldn't lose that year, they were the best, and how good it felt to be part of the best, and how long ago that was, how long since he had felt part of anything. "Yeah," he said.

"Me," Maxie told him, "I couldn't hit. Not even a softball. I used to hate guys like you." A laugh came out of his mouth in a cloud in the cold car. "Your father was my first client, you know. Actually, my second client. My mother was the first. She had me draw up her will. Nothing wrong with the original, she just wanted to give me some business. . . ."

The Fiat turned off Union onto Ringbrook Avenue. Iced logs and parts of wind-wrecked trees floated in the dark river. New houses lay up ahead, where forests of elms and maples used to stand. The gentleness of the rolling hills was gone. It was flat here now, bulldozer-flat, and bright with new paint and aluminum siding and Christmas lights on new shrubs. Where old trees once grew, newly staked trees now stood in the hope of one day giving shade to lawns and branches for swings to children.

". . . So I started singing." Maxie Nash laughed softly. "'Jingle Bells.'"

Someone had put a traffic light on the corner of Ringbrook and Willowbend avenues.

"And I knew I was running the risk of being thrown out of court," Maxie Nash was saying, "but, what the hell, I had to do something, the jury was going over to the D.A. And it's the holiday season, right?" He pushed in the cigarette lighter, put a Marlboro in his mouth. He probably believed the Marlboro ads, saw himself on horseback in Wyoming snow, rugged and independent and somehow at peace with nicotine and the Big Sky. How in the world could Dad have gone to him for legal advice—even for something simple, like a quitclaim? It didn't make sense. Nothing was a trifle to Dad.

"The judge only let me get through one stanza"—Maxie Nash pulled out the lighter—"but by then I had half the jury singing along with me." The lighter coils were gray and cold. He shoved it back into its socket and patted his coat pockets for matches. "You should have seen the judge's face when the jury returned a not guilty. Beautiful." He didn't find matches. He slid the unlit cigarette into his coat. "Never been out to your house. You just shout when we get close."

The duck pond was frozen over. Ducks and a few geese rested near bare trees at the far bank. They would be in Florida now if their wings hadn't been clipped. They cut off the foot of a runaway slave, didn't they? They tamed with blood. Always.

The shopping center was all lit up. The parking lot was crowded. Fredo's was still there. Piles of sand had been dumped along the side of the road every fifty yards to be there when drivers needed a shovelful under their tires for traction, and the sand looked cleaner than the banks of snow.

The lights at 329 Ringbrook Avenue were on. Automatic timers to discourage burglars while Mom was down in the sun? At least the electricity hadn't been turned off. The furnace could be switched back on in a second.

"This is it," Phil said. A yellow Corvette stood in the driveway.

"Looks like they're waiting for you." The lawyer who had just sung his client to freedom looked happy. Those lights made him happy. "My best to your mother. Never met her, but . . ."

The duffel bag felt heavy. "I'd ask you in, but"—*but there isn't supposed to be anybody in there and I don't know what the fuck is going on here*—"but I'm not sure there's anything to drink."

"I have to get ready for my gig in Verona anyway."

"Thanks for the ride."

"Don't mention it. Take care now."

The door slapped shut, little tires spun, then grabbed, and the red Fiat started away, building up speed on a short flat section of blacktop, speed it would need to climb the twisting hill road that had once been an Indian trail and was now called Snake Hill Road, unless the new people responsible for the new traffic light had changed that name, too. No one who spent a lot of money on a house would want to live on a street called Snake. It was probably Winding Lane now.

The house looked bigger. Set back on a long lawn of snow, it wore new white paint and new blue trim. The shutters used to be green. New black wrought-iron railing framed the front steps. He looked through a side window of the car in the drive. Leather driving gloves were draped over the gearshift. Uncle Chuck's new toy, for sure. Was he living here now? No, not possible. He liked his apartment too much. He liked being alone with secretaries and medical assistants and coeds too much to move in with Mom.

Ice that had melted today was beginning to freeze again, making the walk sticky. He opened the glass storm door and moved his key toward the lock. He stopped. He pushed the doorbell button. Someone had fixed it: chimes that hadn't worked in ten years sang behind the solid maple door. Nothing stirred inside. He leaned toward the big living-room window. Between panels of blue curtains, he could make out lights on a Christmas tree. Had Mom rented the place out? Who would rent it just for the winter?

The door opened. She wore a velour robe. Red. Her hair was the color of champagne, and curly. She had forgotten to put on lipstick, but the rest of her oval face was freshly made up. A small noise, the sound of a startled wren, escaped her mouth. Her dark eyes got wide. "Philip?"

". . . Mom?"

3

She felt warm and she smelled of nutmeg and eggnog. She didn't even get the door shut before she started crying. She kissed his bristled cheeks, she held him close and rubbed his back, stroking the parka she had given him so long ago she had probably forgotten it. She hugged him, and he knew she was happy. A lifetime of hopes and fears about her child was alive in her arms again. And he had not changed. Holding her and being held by her could still make him cry.

Years ago, the all-star second baseman for the Ringbrook Yankees had come home to this foyer, to these strong arms, his upper lip a mass of hardened blood because he had collided with another player while trying to stretch a double into a triple. He hadn't cried, not then and not when they put ice on his lip and gauze to stop the bleeding and not when, forced to sit on the bench for the rest of the game, his lip had begun hurting as if on fire, and not even during the ride home after the game. But as soon as the door closed and he was home and in Mom's strong, healing arms, he couldn't stop crying.

The rug was new. Chocolate-colored and thick. She had been so proud of her hardwood floors, what had made her cover them up?

"I don't believe you're home," she said. "Thank God you're all right."

"I'm fine." A dull pain shot through his lip. Every time Phil smiled, a thin crease of skin showed under his lip, because the doctor had known Mom so well and had told her what she wanted to hear: she didn't need to worry, her son wouldn't need stitches, the wound would heal. And it had. A little imperfectly, but only Phil and Mom ever noticed the change in his smile. Uncle Chuck never saw it and Dad couldn't find it even when he looked for it. "You look great," he told her.

She held him at arm's length. She laughed. It made him laugh, it always did. "You look . . . tired." And she hugged him again.

A man in a blue bathrobe walked out of the den with a whiskey glass full of eggnog. He stopped by the fireplace, leaned on the mantel, grinned, and sipped his drink. A trace of white clung to his mustache.

Mom must have seen him, too. Her back got stiff and she didn't know what to do with her hands anymore. She rubbed them together.

The man in the robe kept his square grin. Above his head, over the fireplace, three dinner plates hung on the wall: all Dad had left of his mother. The plates wore a fuzzy blue design that didn't go with anything else in the room. But they were there. Still. The man in the robe probably hadn't noticed them. His hand came out straight, like a dagger. "You must be Phil. I'm Ed."

Phil stared at Mom.

"Ed Vance," she told her new rug. Her cheek twitched. She glanced up, her eyes like a frightened puppy's. "My . . . friend."

Her friend had a strong handshake. And dirty fingernails. He smelled of the kind of hand cleaner auto mechanics used. "You're all she ever talks about. Wonderful you're back."

She put her palm flat on Phil's cheek. "Don't be angry at me." Eyes still wet from happy tears now glistened with worry. "I'll put some coffee on," and her hand was gone and she was through the living room and into the kitchen before he could tell her he didn't want coffee.

"Maybe he'd like some eggnog." Ed had a deep voice. "A little rum to warm him up."

She didn't want to hear. She wanted to make coffee. She wanted to crawl into the coffeepot and hide there.

"Christmas cookies by the TV. Help yourself." Ed fiddled with the sash of his robe. "We were just watching Perry Como. He's in Europe this year."

The lights in the den were off. The flickering glow of the TV in there was as faint as the sound of Perry Como singing "O Holy Night." "You watch TV in the dark?"

"Julie!" Ed called. "Phil said the same thing I did! About the lights!" He leaned close to Phil. "Told her it was bad for the eyes."

She dropped a piece of silverware in the·kitchen, probably a spoon.

"She's a little nervous." Ed scratched his cheek. He needed a shave. "Worried how to tell you about me for a long time."

A long time?

"I said you'd understand, no problem."

Such a silly grin. The thick mustache only made it worse. Phil grinned back. "I don't understand. Problem."

It made Ed blink. "Hey, you ever drive a 'Vette? Keys are on the table if you want to take it for a spin."

"How long?"

"Well, as long as you want, I guess. It's got a full tank."

"How long have you been seeing my mother?"

"Oh." He laughed again, a throaty sound, as though he were gargling. "Let's see, it was the tenth of April, I think." A shout: "Julie, it was the tenth of this April we met, wasn't it?" She didn't answer. "Tenth of April"—Ed nodded—"I'm sure of it. Church bazaar."

She didn't go to church. Over the years, she had tried her best to go, but when she went with Dad he made her laugh—he judged the quality of the sermon by checking his watch and counting down the seconds until the Ringbrook Rocket, Mr. Duggin, the druggist, launched himself into deep sleep—and when she went alone she got lonely. The last time she had gone alone, she had been forced to sit next to Mr. Duggin, and when that round head began to nod toward sleep, Mom had struggled to keep her laugh inside and had almost wet her pants. If she had gone back to church, Mr. Duggin must have died. Phil said a silent prayer for the dead druggist. He said it smiling.

"Have a seat and unlax." Ed's arm found Phil's shoulder. "Probably worn out from your trip. You fly back?"

He stepped away from the man in the robe. "I thumbed."

"Coffee in a minute." Mom came out of the kitchen and went straight to the tree, an artificial tree, not the lush blue spruce or wispy Scotch pine Dad used to lug home, not a tree at all but green plastic arms stuck in a brown plastic trunk, odorless. She had probably wanted one like this for years, maybe always. It was clean and neat: no needles to vacuum. She began moving Christmas ornaments from one spot to another, keeping her back to Phil, keeping busy.

"The tree's fine," Ed said. "Come and talk to your son."

Her shoulders sagged, her arms fell to her sides, her voice broke: "He hates me."

The words stabbed. But they made Ed laugh. "Nonsense. He never hated you. You never hated her, right, Phil?"

She turned and for a moment she looked like a little girl on Christmas Day who had just broken her new doll, the one she had wanted so badly. "He hates me now."

He didn't belong here. Not even here. He had intruded. He should have known it would be like this. He should have known everything would change. He studied the plush new rug. It felt better than the old hardwood. "Mom, I don't hate you. I don't know how to do that."

She rocked on her heels, then steadied, then ran at him, clung to him, but she didn't feel like Mom anymore.

"What'd I tell you." Ed fed a cigarette into his mustached grin. His lighter was gold. He smoked Camels. He was an auto mechanic for sure. "Best present you could give her, Phil."

Her arms weren't strong and she wasn't warm and she didn't feel safe.

"I better fix myself something to eat," he said, "before I drop."

"No, I'll do it." She took his hand and led him toward the kitchen. So many presents under that tree. She didn't know that many people. "If you only knew how long I've waited to fix you a meal."

The mistletoe Dad always hung over the kitchen doorway wasn't up this year. Phil felt relieved. He let her pull him toward the smell of fresh coffee.

| 4 |

The old kitchen table that had been big enough to serve dinner on was down in the cellar, she said, with a sheet over its mother-of-pearl top. The new kitchen table was a small circle of glass, barely big enough to hold coffee cups and a sugar bowl. The chairs were ice-cream-parlor iron. They hurt his back.

"I never actually said I would buy it," she told the creamer. "But it is pretty, isn't it?"

She meant the yellow Corvette. She didn't drive on the turnpike or the parkway because she didn't like to go that fast, and she didn't drive in snow because she was afraid to, and she couldn't parallel park because no one had ever shown her how, not in a way that made sense to her, and she didn't even like cars because they were a nuisance—there were insurance papers to go over every six months and the rates kept changing, there were tires to check for air and dipsticks to check for oil levels and batteries to check for water levels and, worst of all, there was waiting in line at the inspection station every year to get a sticker on her windshield saying the car was okay to drive for another twelve months—and this woman was thinking about buying a Corvette.

"It's pretty," Phil told her, his smile too wide for him to drink coffee with. "But it's a lot of car."

"It's an automatic shift," she said.

"She drives it very well." Ed patted her hand. "Very careful."

"It steers like a dream," she said. "And the brakes! All you have to do is touch them and *bam*, you're stopped."

"Maybe you should test-drive a Ferrari," Phil said.

Ed laughed. "Dry sense of humor. I like that."

"Just like his father." Mom sighed, stirred her milky coffee. "I know it's silly, Philip, me and a car like that. I knew it was silly when I first sat in it. But Ed didn't think it was silly." She smiled at his mustache. "He made me feel it was perfectly natural for me to consider buying his car."

They were holding hands. She looked happy. She wasn't going to buy the Corvette, she just enjoyed knowing she could, knowing one other person—and a man at that—thought she and the racy sports car were meant for each other. Phil couldn't see her behind that wheel, in those bucket seats. He didn't want to. He didn't want a mother who wore driving gloves. He pushed back from the table. "I need to get some sleep. Okay if I use my old room?"

"Darling, you don't have to ask to use your room. That's what it's been there for, all these years." She stood, carried his cup and saucer to the sink. "I'll put fresh sheets on."

"I can do it."

"Well, you'll need the electric blanket. You know how cold it gets up there."

"I can take care of it, Mom."

"It's in the attic, you wouldn't even know where to look." She switched on a hall light and started up the stairs. "I'll only be a minute."

He smiled at her voice. He smiled at Ed. "'Night."

Ed grinned. "Glad you're home. Means everything to her." He gathered his robe and stood. "See you in the morning."

Phil swallowed, blinked, drew a deep breath, and got out of the kitchen and onto the stairs as fast as he could.

At the far end of the long hall closet, the little wooden door to the attic hung open. She was in there, going through pillowcases stuffed with sheets and blankets. She didn't need a flashlight. In there, she could see in the dark. He opened the door to his room.

It wasn't his room anymore.

The light blue walls had been painted light green. His banners and pennants and posters were gone. The old bleached wood book-case held books now, instead of baseball trophies. College text-books. His. His closet was full of her winter coats. His clothes hung in the back, covered in dry-cleaner's plastic. She had finally thrown out his sneakers and his spikes.

He sat at the desk by the window that faced a neighbor's lawn. The dark green curtains matched an oval throw rug on the hard-wood floor. In the top drawer of his desk: a dry ball-point pen in the shape of a baseball bat, stacks of baseball cards held together by rubber bands, and his old box camera. They didn't make cam-eras like this one anymore, and they no longer made film to fit it. But he wouldn't think of throwing it out. It had been a birthday gift from Mom and Dad, the same birthday Uncle Chuck had given him a bigger, better camera. Phil traded that camera to a friend for a new baseball and bat, and every time Uncle Chuck saw the pictures Phil had taken, the plump man grinned and said, "That's a damn good camera, might even get one for myself." It had always made Dad laugh because he knew about the trade, knew which camera Phil had kept. Every time Phil picked up his camera, he could hear that quiet laugh. Now he set the camera back where it belonged, grateful Mom hadn't found time to clean out the drawers. Yet.

"How do you like it?" She came in with an armful of sheets and blankets. "It's so friendly now, isn't it?"

It looked like the inside of a key lime pie. "Yes," he said, sliding the desk drawer shut. "Friendly."

"Everything I took down from your walls," she said, her back to him, "is in a box in your closet. With your trophies." She turned. "They catch so much dust." She pulled the green-and-white-striped bedspread off the bed, dropped linens on the mattress.

"Mom, I can do that."

"I want to do it." She found the fitted bottom sheet, checked it for holes. Her hands went lame. Her chin sank to her chest. She was crying.

He put his arms around her. She made fists, sat on the unmade bed. "I didn't want you to come home like this. I wanted it to be . . . better."

He tried to think of something to say, something to make her feel all right, but he couldn't. He stood there and watched tears stream down her cheeks.

Ed made those tears. Ed being here, in her life, her life without a husband. It was wrong for her to cry about that, wrong for Phil to let her cry about it. But part of him liked that she was crying, was glad she was in pain. He hated that part of himself. He knelt to her, took her hands. "Everything's fine."

She shook her head. "I'm not in love with him. There are times I can't stand him, he's so . . . loud." She sniffed. "And it has nothing to do with your father."

"Mom, you don't have to explain. Not to me."

"He was a wonderful man, Phil. But he was no saint."

She wasn't wearing her wedding ring or the engagement ring with the small perfect diamond Dad had said one of his clients had given him as payment instead of money. And because he had that little gem, Dad had felt he had to do something with it, so he had thought about it and decided the best thing to do with it would be to give it to Mom and get engaged, and if that client had not given him that diamond, if that client had just paid the regular way, in cash, Dad used to say with his best smile that he truly wondered if he would have ever gotten married. Dad used to say the second luckiest thing in his life was getting that small stone. The first was Mom. Phil couldn't remember the last time he had seen her hands without those rings. The last time would have to have been down at the shore, maybe ten years ago. She wouldn't wear her rings in the ocean.

"I keep thinking," she was saying, "that I've changed because

I was angry at him. I'm still angry at him."

"Because he died?"

She pulled her hands free, turned sideways on the bed, pressed her lips together. "Philip." His name came out like stale wind. She blinked to clear her eyes, stared at him. "Philip, your father had another woman."

|5|

It stood there, in the pale December light, like a box of worn brick, three stories high. One tree, a naked elm, grew at the far side of the parking lot. In back, a smokestack rose fifty feet above the roof, a slender cylinder of brick with a name painted in white down the face of the column:

Z
O
R
Z
O
L
I

The river ran along one side, cascading down a slope of man-made steps that had once channeled the soft waters of the Passaic into the dye room of this mill, back when silk was king and Paterson was its throne.

It was a nightclub now. And a restaurant. And the bottom floor was a video arcade, so that shoppers in the malls across the highway could deposit their kids here and then go shop. Christmas lights outlined the door and windows, ran along the roof. Centered on the front of the building between the second and third stories, a small sign: ZORZOLI'S.

She was in there.

According to Mom, she was young, still under thirty. She was pretty—Mom had seen her once when she found the courage to come here for lunch before Dad died. She was a businesswoman, and successful. She ran the mill. She might even own it. She was everything Mom was not, and some things Mom had never been. But she was not the enemy. To Mom, she was just a fact of life, a hard, coarse fact, the kind that didn't fit in with all the other facts. Her name was Louise. Not Zorzoli. Not Italian. Louise something. It was better, Mom had said last night, not to know too much.

Phil wanted to know all of it. Mostly, he wanted to know if it was true.

Ed Vance didn't know why Phil wanted to be dropped off here, and he didn't ask. Mom's car, the small blue Ford Dad used to drive after he'd sold his Dodge and before he got his Lincoln, was in the shop for a tune-up. She had asked Ed to drive Phil to the mall so he could see Uncle Chuck. Ed had been happy to do it, happy to wait for Phil to get ready, even though on mild winter days like this one Ed and his crew could get a lot of work done if they started early. He was an architect and builder. He was a nice man. Phil waved to him and he waved back. Then the Corvette roared up the ramp to Route 80 West, toward Whippany and the rural dream house he was finishing for some lawyer.

The arcade was jammed with kids. Electronic gongs and tweeters shot through the vast dark room. Things were exploding in there—spaceships and rockets, laser beams, demons at warp speed. Six-year-olds barely tall enough to reach the controls steered Pac-Man and Ms. Pac-Man and Pitfall Harry through mazes and jungles and it was impossible to hear a single game, everything got mixed and the din of a thousand chases roared into the main hall and didn't go away until the elevator doors closed and the whine of an electric motor pulling steel cable took over.

Second floor—restaurant. Open daily for lunch and dinner. She would be here. The nightclub on the top floor didn't open until six.

"Not open yet." The man behind the podium at the entrance to the big room didn't look up from a pad he was writing on. "Snack bar on the first floor."

Phil stepped out of the elevator, waited for the doors to close. Everything here was red and white: chairs with red cushions next to round tables covered with red-and-white-checked linen, a red candle holder and a red silk flower in a white porcelain vase on each table, booths padded red along the near wall. The menus in the holder at the podium had red covers. "Is Louise here?"

The man looked up. He had hair the texture of steel wool. It looked fake. "If it's about the vacuum cleaner, she wants it replaced."

The sport jacket Phil was wearing, one of Dad's cashmere blazers from the hall closet, was supposed to make him look like something more than a service representative for Hoover vacuums. He toyed with the knot of his tie. "Where can I find her?"

The man pointed toward red doors at the far end of the room. "Replaced, not fixed. We've had it with trying to repair that thing."

Protecting the red rug, a clear plastic runner led to the kitchen. It smelled like beans back there. He pushed on the swinging door.

Three men in white uniforms worked near a grill, the ovens, and a long Formica counter. Two waiters played cards at a table by the refrigerators. She sat at a table beside a stack of serving trays. She was reading an order form, shaking her head at a man in a gray suit seated across from her. "I don't see," she said, "why the whole tomatoes run more than the puree. We have to process them, they should be cheaper."

"You pay for fresh." The man looked bored. He glanced at his watch. "Take the puree. Who'll know the difference?"

She was shaking her head. Her dark brown hair fell almost to her shoulders and turned in at the bottom. A long, lean face, with a sharp chin. No lipstick. Dark eyes. She fiddled with gold buttons on her red vest. A Christmas vest. Velvet. Against her white shirt, it stood out warm and bold at the same time. The skirt she wore came down to the middle of her calves. It was plaid, green and black, and made of that crinkly material, taffeta. She could have been in a fashion show. She could have won it.

"I want the whole tomatoes for the price of the puree." She handed the three-part form back to the man in the suit. "Otherwise, cancel the entire order."

"Miss Davis, no can do."

She smiled. Perfect teeth. "Paco, some minestrone here. He needs good food to think on." Behind the counter, a fat chef grinned and ladled thick brown soup into a country bowl. Louise Davis set the bowl in front of the man in the suit, put a big spoon in his hand. "We make this with fresh beans, fresh herbs, fresh everything. See if you can tell the difference."

Phil cleared his throat. She turned, squinted: "Yes?"

There was something sharp in her stare, almost angry. He had trouble finding his voice. "It's not about the vacuum cleaner," he said.

"What?"

"I'm not here about your vacuum cleaner."

She studied his blazer as if she hadn't thought he was here about the vacuum cleaner in the first place. She stepped closer. She smelled of limes. "We don't allow"—her voice started to trail off—"visitors in the kitchen." She couldn't stop staring at him. All the sharpness ran out of her eyes, they got wide and shiny. Her jaw sagged. She swallowed slowly. Words leaked out of her small mouth. "You're . . . his son."

It was true, then. All of it.

He shut his eyes, sighed. When he opened them, she was studying his face. He wanted to tell her to stop. He wanted everyone here, the chefs, the card-playing waiters, the food distributor, to stop staring at him as if he had stepped out of one of those space games downstairs and was about to blast them with a ray gun.

"You look so much like him," she said.

She must have seen something in him no one else had ever seen. He looked like Mom. He started to say, "I'm sorry," but couldn't even get that out. The brittle courage that had gotten him here was gone. Maybe it wasn't courage to begin with. Maybe it was pride. Arrogance, really. He had been so sure Mom had been wrong, so positive she had gotten her facts messed up, the way she always did. And now . . . Before his legs buckled, he pushed on the door and didn't breathe until he was on the other side of it and walking toward the elevator.

"No, please." She was coming after him. "Please wait." She caught up with him. He couldn't look at her. She was beautiful, and smart, and full of energy, and probably a great lover, and he knew if he looked at her he would feel the same things Dad had felt for her, that any man would feel. He didn't want to like her or want her, he wanted to forget her. He punched the elevator button.

"Make him take the machine with him, Lou." The man at the podium had iron in his voice. "We want the damn thing replaced, buddy."

She slid in front of the elevator. Her smile looked wet. She did wear lipstick, the pastel glossy kind. "You're Phil," she said in a dull whisper, "aren't you?"

His stomach made a gurgling noise. He saw the elevator doors open, but he was looking at her, taking her in, all of her. His voice cracked. "Did you love him?"

Her smile got soft, so soft he felt he could get lost in there. "I still do," she said.

Something was wrong with his eyes, they wouldn't focus. He stepped past her into the elevator, reached to hit the street-level button. Her hand was quicker. She punched the third-floor button. The doors made a clunking sound. She wasn't smiling anymore.

| 6 |

The top floor was done in black and white, Roaring Twenties style, with a mirrored bar taking up one wall, a parquet dance floor in front of a small bandstand, a big ball of mirror chips hanging from a rafter. In a glass case on the wall: a poster of five wrinkled black men in tuxedos, smiling. The man in the center held a trumpet. The Silky Odell Quartet. Appearing Nightly. Featuring "Little Lord Fountain Roy" Mears on piano. A group of old musicians, making a comeback in a big way out here in Ringbrook, to the wonder of New Yorkers, who traveled forty-five minutes to hear blues from the thirties played by men who had lived them. The white piano on the nightclub stage was wired to an amplifier.

Near the edge of the bandstand, on the bar side of the big room, she opened a black door. A brass sign had been screwed to it: PRIVATE.

Her office came out of a different era, turn-of-the-century or earlier. An antique rolltop desk stood against a wall, next to a micro-computer and printer on the kind of mahogany table Hawthorne might have used as a writing desk. She sat on a davenport in the center of the room. Upholstered in red silk, it was backed by a lowboy table and a standing lamp with a large shade covered in raw silk. She gestured to armchairs arranged in an L around a coffee table that held a telephone, an intercom, and a calculator, each the color of milk chocolate. Their power lines came out of the floor. "The chairs are more comfortable than the sofa," she said.

He sat in the one closest to the big, factory-style windows: tall rectangles of glass, crisscrossed by metal in metal casings. Cushions of maroon silk striped with gold made the set of four chairs look regal. A lyre stood in the center of each chairback, matching the lyres between the legs of the coffee table. The chairs were comfortable.

"I wanted a rug," she told him, "but you can't have one with a computer. Static electricity."

The brown in the floor tiles matched exactly the brown stripes on the pale yellow wallpaper. An oak filing cabinet stood beside another door near the computer. No sign on that door. Probably a back entrance. Or a bathroom. Along that same wall: two oak bookcases, filled with leatherbound books. A small step box stood at the base of one bookcase. Chipped and in need of varnish, it looked too beat-up to belong here. He got out of the chair, walked to the rolltop desk, glanced at all the pictures on the wall: black-and-whites in antique wooden frames. "I didn't come here to make any trouble for you," he said.

"No, I didn't think you would." Her skirt made noises. "Besides, your uncle does well enough in that category."

Most of the photos were of the mill in the old days. For some reason, it looked bigger then. Maybe it was because the trees were smaller. A few photos were of another mill, larger than this one. Old trucks and even horses stood outside the buildings in these pictures. Only one photo had people in it. In front of the main door to the smaller mill, a big man in a gray suit and matching fedora had an arm around the waist of a small plump woman in a dark dress and pillbox hat. Beside her stood a younger woman, looking thin in her skirt and blouse. Next to the man, a little girl in a ribboned bonnet squinted into sun. But smiling the same smile as the round woman. The other woman didn't own a smile. The big man looked as if he had never smiled. His hand was as big as the little girl's head.

No photo of Dad.

"Henry talked about you all the time," she told him. "He was so proud of you."

He turned, as if she had his neck on a string. In a far corner: a hat tree. The only thing on it was a steel-gray fedora with a black silk band. It looked too small to belong to the big man in the photo, but it was the same hat, he was sure of it.

"You weren't at the wake when we got there," she said. "Your uncle said you were out getting something to eat. He wouldn't let us stay." She glared at the phone. "He's not anything like his brother. I can't believe they're actually related."

He laughed. How many times had he thought the same thing? Uncle Chuck didn't even look like Dad. Maybe it was the nine years that separated them.

"You have your father's laugh," she said. "It's so good to hear it again."

He cleared his throat. "My uncle probably didn't want you there because you might upset my mother."

"I don't see how."

"Yeah, well, you think about it for a few seconds." His voice sounded sharp. He drew a breath. He could hear his heart beating. He didn't let his gaze stay on her long. He turned toward the bookcases, nodded at the step box. "What are those little stairs for?"

"So I can reach the vases."

More than a dozen small vases up there. Each held a single bloom. Miniature roses. He didn't know how he could have missed seeing all that color before.

"Look," she said, "I don't mind your uncle barking at me, I'm used to that. But I didn't expect it from you." She studied the plaid of her skirt. "Henry worried that you were too much like him. Too . . . gentle. That was the best thing about him."

"I'm not anything like him." It hurt to say it, but it was true. It hurt less than it used to, especially now, knowing Dad had been unfaithful. He turned back to the photos, as if they were safer to deal with than she was, safer than his own memories. The little girl next to the big man in the hat had hair two shades lighter than Louise's and a face so pudgy with baby fat, it was almost perfectly round, with none of the bone lines or angles in the fashion-model face Louise owned now. But the eyes, even squinting, were hers. Playground eyes. "This is you, isn't it."

"I was three. And a brat."

She was never a brat, not with those eyes, that soft, warm smile. She was an innocent charmer, full of wonder, the kind of child who made parents feel lucky and grandparents feel young. He felt sorry he hadn't known her then. He felt something tender about that little girl he knew, something he could never feel about the woman she had grown into.

She sighed and smoothed her skirt. "I thought you would be working at Trent and Company. I went there looking for you two years ago. Your uncle said he didn't think you were ever going to join the firm."

"You went looking for me?"

She lowered her eyes. Her voice got soft. "I hoped you'd help us. Be an ally, like Henry was." She gripped the thick arm of the sofa. "Your uncle's given me nothing but headaches."

"I'm sorry, but . . . " He wasn't sorry. And he didn't want to know anything else about her. Being here, seeing the photos and the old hat on the tree, he already knew too much. "But you have to understand how painful this has been for my mother."

"Why do you keep bringing your mother into this?"

He punched the side of the rolltop desk. "You sleep with my father, right under my mother's nose, and you think it doesn't mean anything to her?"

Dark eyes widened, then got hard. "Is that what your uncle told you?"

"My mother."

Louise laughed. "And I wonder who gave her that idea." She

stood, rubbed a chill from her sleeve. "I never slept with your father."

He squinted at her, wanting to believe her, not able to trust her. She must have seen that in his face. She looked hurt. And angry. She shook her head. "You really are a terrible disappointment. See if you have enough intelligence to find your way out."

A moment later she was gone. Elevator doors opened and closed. Then the silence of an empty dance floor.

He found a door marked EXIT on the other side of the stage. Cold steel stairs sounded hollow under his feet. The knob of the fire door at the bottom landing was sticky from the small hands of Pac-Man wizards. Down the main hall, a teen-ager in a football jersey chased a smaller boy, both of them zigzagging back toward the arcade. For an instant, Phil hoped the little kid would get caught by number 32 and beaten senseless.

He walked toward a gray sky shining through the glass doors. That gray was Ringbrook in winter. That dead and numbing gray was home.

Book
Two

Nonna Do

| 7 |

The last time he had seen the new mall, it was mud with concrete footings and steel girders rising out of it, like a prehistoric sinkhole done up with modern sculpture. He had liked it that way. Even back then, he had given up hoping the meadows would become a horse ranch again, where for a dollar kids could ride ponies and pretend they were chasing bad guys into a box canyon, even though the ride wasn't a ride, it was a walk, one slow circle around a dirt track, the ponies led by the old man who owned the place. Even back then, he knew those ponies would never come back, so the best he could hope for was that the builders would run out of money and go away before they ruined everything.

Now Ringbrook Mall East was the same as Ringbrook Mall South and Ringbrook Mall North: two-story icebergs shaped like sleek space stations, with roof-top parking and most of the stores underground, where skylights let sun in so trees and flowers could grow, convincing everyone they were at ground level when they were really buried thirty feet down and the air they breathed was pumped in and pumped out, filtered, heated or cooled, depending on the season, and the weather was always fine for shopping.

This complex of malls, just twenty miles northwest of New York City, was the biggest shopping center in the world. At least, it had been, for about three months, until someone in Kansas City opened a bigger one. There had been talk of a Ringbrook Mall West, across the highway by the old mill, to make the complex the biggest again and show the folks in KC they weren't dealing with hicks. Nobody talked about the ponies anymore.

The big directory board had a diagram of the mall's floor plan. Each oddly shaped box was numbered. Trent & Co., the directory said, was in 32B. B for level 2, bottom floor. From the YOU ARE HERE arrow, Trent & Co. was one flight down and six stores on the left. With any luck, Uncle Chuck would be out.

Phil had to go anyway, he had promised Mom, and she had agreed not to call Uncle Chuck to say Phil was home and ruin the surprise. The last thing Phil had wanted to do last night was talk to Uncle Chuck. Worried that Louise Davis was telling the truth, seeing Uncle Chuck was the last thing Phil wanted to do today. But he had to. He stepped onto the escalator.

Piped-in music fit the season: Gene Autry singing "Rudolph the Red-nosed Reindeer." No imitations for this mall. Ringbrook Mall East used the real thing. He smiled and hummed along, but it didn't feel good. Near the bottom of the escalator a fountain tiled in earth colors shot water in a fine spray, close enough to the edge of the moving steps that the fountain looked like the logical end of the trip down—step off and step right in. He laughed.

"Phil?"

He blinked and found the voice calling his name on the Up escalator, just across the rail. A small woman in tan suede. Lovely as ever. Sarah.

"Phil, is it you?"

He smiled and waved, turned to follow her movement as the escalators brought the two of them opposite each other, then drew them away.

"Wait for me by the fountain," she said. "I'll be right down."

She had done something to her hair. It was lighter than he remembered. His palms got sweaty. All these malls and all these people and somehow she had gotten on the wrong escalator at the wrong time, and it was just like her: perfect timing. He should run, while he could. He couldn't. He stood by the fountain rim, obedient to her as ever, as if nothing had changed in so many years.

She twisted and pushed her way past other shoppers on their way down to the lower level. She was smiling, her cheeks bright in the unnatural light. She ran at him, her suede boots soft on the tiles. "It really is you!" She kissed his neck, squeezed him hard. "For a minute I thought I was hallucinating."

"You look wonderful." He meant, You feel wonderful. He held her at arm's length. She did look wonderful. Even the thick brown smear over each eyelid didn't ruin her face. "I thought you were a permanent New Yorker."

"Home for the holidays."

"Me, too," he said.

She put a cold palm to his cheek. "The last letter you wrote me was from Elko, Nevada. It wasn't even a letter."

Elko, Nevada, was no place to be in winter. Two winters ago, he had stayed there before pushing on to California.

"A postcard," she said. "With a picture of a dumb Holiday Inn on it."

"All they had." Actually, they had other postcards: side view of the dining room at night, front view of the swimming pool at noon, head-on view of the lobby at check-out time. The postcard he sent her was the best. If he had it to do over again, he would send her the one of the lobby now. "Sorry."

Her suede jacket was as soft as her skin. "I tore it up, I was so angry at you. Then I taped it back together." Her eyes shone bluer than he remembered. Maybe all the brown she was wearing set her eyes off more. She blinked and hooked his arm. "How's your mother? She was so hard to reach, I just gave up after a while. Is she still down in Florida?"

He shook his head. "Home for Christmas."

"Oh, I didn't know. I sent her card to Tampa."

He would have done the same thing.

"Well?" Sarah was staring at him. "I've been waiting more than two years to find out what happened to you. Tell me."

"Oh, that."

She grinned and shook her head. "You *are* going to tell me. You know I can get it out of you."

Sarah Young could get him to do anything, just anything. Always. He nodded and found he was laughing with her.

"I was just doing some last-minute shopping before going to lunch." She held a plastic bag from Lord & Taylor's. Some people hadn't begun shopping for Christmas yet, but it was the last minute to her: she was always ten steps ahead of everybody else. "You're coming with me."

For a moment, he was ready to tell her he couldn't because he had to see Uncle Chuck. Then he knew that in her he had found the perfect excuse—reason—not to see his uncle. Even Mom would understand. "Sounds great."

"We'll walk." She led him back to the escalator. "Very slowly. I don't want you to leave out anything."

He reached for her shopping bag, but she shifted it to her other hand. "I'm so glad you're back," she said, and she laced her fingers through his. "I missed you."

He had stopped dreaming about her. He didn't know how to tell her that. He didn't know how to tell her he had gone for months without once thinking of her, that he had all but forgotten her, that he had stopped loving her.

"Okay," she said, "I still live in the East Village and I still work for Rozen Cosmetics. I'm in charge of tri-state marketing now. My mother's fine and my little brother graduates high school this year." As if Phil were her little brother, who by now had probably outgrown his baby face and shaved every day, she steered him around the directory board and down the long lighted corridor of shops all dressed for Christmas, a holiday slogan or a Santa Claus or a snowman or a reindeer in every window.

Phil had never liked Bruce Young. He had never found a way to talk to the kid without winding up wanting to strangle him. Waiting for Sarah to come down had always meant sitting with Bruce in the living room, listening to that foul-mouthed little creature describe what he thought Phil was going to do to Sarah that night: "Gonna suck her tits, right?" or "Gonna stick it to her good, right?" The trouble was, the little son of a bitch was accurate. And that's why Phil always felt like strangling him.

"Now, you don't get another word out of me," Sarah said, "until you've told me everything that's happened to you since you left."

"Long story," he said.

"I've gotten very good at long lunches." She grinned. "Part of my job. But don't worry, the service at Zorzoli's is so bad, we might not get waited on before dark."

He stopped. Rudolph the Red-nosed Reindeer, Gene Autry said with a big finish, would go down in his-tor-eee. "I have to see my Uncle Chuck."

"You'll like Zorzoli's."

"I hate Italian food."

"Since when? Besides, nobody hates Italian food. Not even the French." She wore her playful smile. "I was only kidding about the service."

A Salvation Army Santa rang a bell by a collection pot a few stores down. Through the speakers, Little Jimmy What's-his-name started singing "I Saw Mommy Kissing Santa Claus." Phil stared at the tassels on her boots. "There has to be someplace else we can go."

She shook her head and sniffed a laugh. "You're still impossible."

And she had him walking toward the fake Santa Claus and the truck-wide doors at the end of the corridor of shops. "It's quiet and comfortable"—she pulled back a jacket sleeve to glance at a small gold watch—"and we'll have almost an hour there alone"—she pressed her side against his—"and I promise if you hate it we can leave."

He stopped walking, took her hand, rubbed her fingers with his thumb. "I'm not really impossible, am I?"

Her face got soft, her eyes glistened as if she loved him again, as if she had never stopped. "You were always the most possible."

He tried a little smile. She took his face in her hands, kissed him: she said hello the same way she had said good-bye. She put her head against his chest. In another instant she might say, "I'm here for you," her signal that she was ready to be held, touched, made love to, do all the things little Brucie always figured she was doing. Phil couldn't let her say those words. He didn't want to belong to her again. He drew a short breath and said, "It's too early for lunch. I saw a coffee shop near Bamberger's."

She pulled back, nodding. Her eyes were wet. The Rozen mascara she marketed was good stuff: it didn't streak. She smiled, squeezed his hand, then let go. "Just as long as you tell me," she said. "Everything."

8

He didn't tell her everything.

She made a phone call and joined him in a booth at the back of the coffee shop. He asked for coffee. She ordered herbal tea, but the waitress said they didn't have that kind. Sarah settled for hot chocolate.

She already knew about his leaving Princeton with six months left to get his degree, because he couldn't study, couldn't sleep. Uncle Chuck had raged at him. Trent & Co. was a two-man operation. With Dad dead, Phil didn't have the luxury of going after an MBA right after college as originally planned. But he was supposed to finish at Princeton. Uncle Chuck had been counting on Phil to start work in the office that summer: graduate degrees could be gotten at night. Mom had agreed. Any amount of college credits was too much for the personnel manager of the paint factory in Haledon: Phil was overeducated for the job of paint mixer and that would be bad for the other workers. It had been the same story at the rock quarry in Willowbend. He didn't care about the other workers, he wanted those jobs. Finally, he stopped caring about New Jersey anymore.

A blizzard caught him west of Scranton his first day on the road. No cars for hours. His feet got numb. He trudged on toward Towanda. An old station wagon stopped to pick him up. A nun was driving it. She had put the chains on the tires herself and she said he was an idiot to be out in this weather. Sister Paul worked as a nurse in a hospital. It had a chapel. She told him to rest in the pews. He slept. The next morning, another nun, dressed in white, woke him with shouts and shoves. An angry angel. She was the head nun and she told him the chapel was a place of worship, not a boardinghouse: if he wasn't out of there when she came back, she'd call the police. Sister Paul came in a moment later, looking tired from the night shift. She gave him tuna sandwiches and orange juice. She told him the roads were plowed and he should get an early start. She promised God would go with him.

He caught a ride south with a business-machine salesman from Harrisburg, whose favorite expression was "Jesus Fucking Christ." He kept thumbing south, hoping for warmer weather. The South was cold that February, colder than it was supposed to be. He slept in train stations and bus stations to save money. He looked for work, but couldn't find any: no local address, no job, not in these parts, sorry and thank you for coming by.

He got good at shaving without a mirror and he got lucky in Knoxville. A trucker hauling auto parts was headed west. Wouldn't mind the company. Could use a hand unloading and reloading at the end of the line, Salt Lake City. Then a little jog farther west, to Elko, where the trucker had a woman. Phil was welcome to the woman's sister and to a ride back to Atlanta. The woman's sister thought he was cute. The trucker thought Phil was crazy to want to stay in Elko: people sold their souls to get out of there. Phil thought the mountains were beautiful, there was a majesty about Elko. The trucker peed on the ground in front of his cab and said Phil should try Tibet if majesty was what he was after. Tibet or Las Vegas.

Five rides later, he made the outskirts of Sacramento. In a little farm market, he found a 3-by-5 card on a bulletin board: *Help Wanted.* A rancher needed a field hand. Fencing, mostly. Some haying. Hard work, low pay. A bed in a bunkhouse and three meals a day. The other workers had leather faces and iron arms. Lonely men, not wanting to get to know anybody too well, there just wasn't room for that. They weren't movie cowboys: they didn't sleep with their boots on.

He was probably the only person who ever hated San Francisco. Expensive, cold even in late summer, unfriendly. He got mugged. They found the money in his wallet, but they didn't even look for the cash in his sock. They didn't hit hard. He thumbed north that same night.

Near Mendocino he got a job at a general store. The lady who owned it let him sleep with crates in the back room until he could find something better. He tagged goods, took deliveries, swept up. The owner was nearing fifty. Her husband had left her a long time ago. She wasn't sure if she kicked him out or if he just split. She said it worked out to the same thing. Her name was Vera and she came to the back room one night and stayed. She kept coming. She had a daughter in town. One night, the daughter came. Phil got out of there before the trouble started.

The Green Valley Country Club in the foothills east of San Luis Obispo needed workers. It was new and the golf-course superintendent wanted flowers by the parking lot and trees along the fairways. Phil drove a gas-powered cart and planted annuals and cypress seven hours a day. He slept in the golf-cart garage the first week, listening to the hum of electricity recharging a hundred batteries. He moved into the ladies' locker room the same day he was asked to clean it. It had a sofa in the lounge area and no women ever came to the locker room after dark, they must have been afraid of the place at night. For the next few months he saved his money, and by the anniversary of his first year away from home he had learned to hit golf balls with a five iron borrowed from the pro shop. He went looking for an apartment close by. Before he could find one, he was told enough flowers and trees had been planted, the course had to cut back on labor. They gave him two days' notice. He took towels from the ladies' locker room and headed south.

Los Angeles wasn't even there the day he drove through. Smog and haze hid buildings and mountains. More traffic than he had ever seen. A sugar truck had overturned, leaving a mound of white powder on the freeway. Like ants, cars crawled by. An old Chevy burned at the side of the road to Riverside. The owner stood fifty yards in front of the flames, just shaking his head. Nobody stopped. The young trucker Phil was riding with said it was a light day.

Riverside was there, he could make out the low skyline. The trucker stopped at a construction site near Corona. Phil helped him unload six crates of bathroom hardware. The man who signed for the load was alone. The big house he was building was framed and partially roofed. He looked tired. He said if Phil could help him get the toilets and tubs in the right places, he'd pay a full day's wages. Nonunion scale, of course. The builder had no use for unions.

His name was Gary Simms. He was fifty-five. He looked older. He built "spec homes." "Spec" for "speculation"—would anybody buy? He built them by himself, only bringing in a few hands to help raise the walls. He'd been doing it that way for twelve years, making a good living. He couldn't work as fast anymore, he had fallen through the roof—"Not off it, mind you, I'm not that stupid"—and crushed a shoulder. A minor inconvenience. But if somebody wanted to learn the trade—all the trades—Gary Simms wouldn't mind having that somebody along with him now, as long as that somebody was honest and hardworking and had something that resembled a brain in his head. They got the tubs and toilets and sinks in the right places. Phil slept on the jobsite that night, studying stars through holes in the unfinished roof.

Gary was a good teacher. A better friend. He let Phil live in one of the houses he hadn't sold yet. He bought Phil tools and a pair of work boots with steel toes—"Only kind worth shit." He had a six-pack of Coors ready every day at quitting time. He loaned his GMC pickup to Phil, told him how to get to the beach. He took Phil to Disneyland and Knotts Berry Farm and went on all the rides with him, even the roller coasters, which Gary had been wary of all his life—"Not afraid, mind you, nothing to be scared of." He took Phil to the Angels game at the Big A in Anaheim. He took him to the Western Regional Little League tournament in San Bernardino. He took him to meet his mother in a nursing home in Riverside, and on the way back, he had tears in his eyes when he said, "She thinks you're my son."

It took over a year and a half to build three houses and sell one. Depressed market. Depression. Interest rates were too high. The cost of borrowed money was eating Gary up. He couldn't stay in business if he didn't sell his houses. He said he wasn't worried. Good houses sold regardless of the times. They were good houses. They weren't selling. The rough times only brought Phil and Gary closer. Like father and son. And Phil knew if he didn't leave soon, he would never leave this man. There would come a time, and soon, when he wouldn't know how.

He went to the bank and talked to the manager about restructuring Gary's loans. The manager liked the loans as they stood. The loans were out at 21 percent. Gary couldn't afford a partner these days. Gary couldn't afford a sandwich. Phil withdrew everything he had in a savings account at that bank: $8,000 from wages and $17,000 from what Gary had decided was Phil's share of the house that sold. He had the cashier's check made out to Gary D. Simms.

He left the check in Gary's toolbox. The night was warm. He caught a ride east within an hour. He fought tears in the car and worried that the driver would think he was crazy. The driver thought Phil was beautiful. Phil got out at the next light in the desert town of Indio.

A gang of kids found him asleep in a field outside of Coachella. They didn't hit him at all. They held a knife to his throat. They found the money in his sock. They left him his driver's license and wallet and walked away laughing like jackals.

A camper bound for the caverns near Carlsbad, New Mexico, picked him up the next morning. Teen-agers. The camper had been a gift from parents. They fed him bean sprouts, trail mix, and citrus wine that tasted like fruit slush and was guaranteed not to rot his liver or give him a hangover or do anything except pump vitamin C into his blood. The wine made him sick. They dropped him off in Las Cruces and said they hoped to see him again, if not in this life, in another.

He found daywork at a Quality Inn in Van Horn, Texas. In Dripping Springs, he painted a shed that looked like a small barn. He got picked up for vagrancy in Temple, and escorted out of town in a souped-up police car the deputy must have picked out of a *Smokey and the Bandit* catalog. He finally got out of Texas and felt winter blow into the river land below the Ozarks. In Memphis he bought a bus ticket for as far east as his money would take him. Not far: Asheville, North Carolina. He stole a five-pound bag of peanuts from a truck-stop gift store and caught a ride north to Pittsburgh with a man who was towing a used car and was tired of doing all the driving. The man didn't want to stop for anything but gas. He had brought his own food, and he didn't offer Phil any of it. The peanuts were stale.

Pittsburgh was cold and Altoona was colder and coal dust on the snow in Hazleton made him think the world had ended. On foot in the mountains at Stroudsburg, he prayed for his Pennsylvania nun to come find him. The industrial-detergents salesman in the Buick found him first. Phil told Sarah about the pies the man's wife made. Sarah put her hot chocolate down. "It sounds like a movie."

"There won't be a sequel."

She put her hand on his. "At least now you know who you are."

He had left because Dad had told him, "Don't think you know how people live, you can't learn that in college. You have to work beside them, live how they live. When they come to you with their money, you have to know how important it is." Deathbed words. Phil had traveled to find out how people live and he hadn't found out much.

"You're going back to Princeton," Sarah said, "aren't you?"

He nodded. He was going back to a place he could learn something. Then he'd be as ready as he would ever be to work for Uncle Chuck, to do what Dad had done his whole life: "The job isn't to make anybody rich, it's to keep them from going broke."

Sarah was leaning out of the booth, waving. She couldn't want more to drink, she had already finished three hot chocolates. He turned. A giant of a man was coming his way in long, smooth strides, muscles stuffed into a striped jacket and white turtleneck. He was smiling.

Sarah kissed him. "Guy Ullis, this is Phil Trent. A long-lost friend."

The big man had powerful hands. He frowned at Sarah. "I got your message at Zorzoli's. What's with this dump? I thought we were having lunch. Alone."

"Guy plays for the Giants." She sat him on the bench on her side of the booth. "He's a nose guard."

The New York Giants. Football. Not in Yankee Stadium anymore, but in the Meadowlands of East Rutherford, New Jersey. Somehow, that would never seem right.

"What do you do?" Guy asked him.

"Nothing."

"Nothing?"

"I'm independently unemployed."

"Phil's had a tough time." Sarah moved closer to the big man. "We used to go together."

The giant squinted. Phil swallowed: "Ah, a long time ago."

Sarah grinned. "It's all right, we have an open relationship."

"You never told me about him," Guy said.

"I just didn't get to it yet."

What was Sarah doing with this ox?

No.

He wasn't going to fall into that trap again. It had taken him too long to climb out of it, years of struggle to stop seeing in her qualities that didn't exist, to stop hoping so hard those qualities were there that he had injected them into her personality himself. How many times had he redefined and softened her cruel remarks to friends? How often had he rebuilt her naïveté into innocence, something charming, to be treasured? He had even learned to congratulate her vanity as the best proof of how special she was. He had protected her, defended her, apologized for her, nourished her—he had gotten so good at it, everyone, even Mom, had come to believe Sarah was perfect, and everyone, even Mom, had begun wondering what a perfect woman like Sarah could see in Phil—and in the end he had invented her.

He could have kept a psychiatrist busy with that one for years. The truth was simpler. Harder, but simpler. Sarah was beautiful, exciting, and willing. And love, back then, centered on sex. He had been in love with her that way. He hadn't wanted to be in love with someone who wasn't perfect. He had known that now for a long time, yet he still had trouble facing it. To believe it was to have been a fool. All those years.

He was sweating.

"I don't like the idea," Guy said, "of you having lunch with ex-lovers."

"We're not having lunch." She inched away from him. "And I never said we were ex-lovers."

Phil checked his watch. Dad's watch. If he had taken it with him three years ago, someone would have stolen it. "Hey, look at the time."

Sarah pouted. "You could join us."

"He said he has to go," Guy said.

"No, he did not." She looked into the small eyes in that rock-hard face. "We were lovers."

Something was smoldering behind those little eyes. The skin above Guy's collar got tight. Phil slid out of the booth and was about to lie and tell Sarah how good it was to see her again, when she took his hand and said, "I'll call you."

"You will not." Guy punched the table. A saltshaker toppled.

She squeezed Phil's fingers. "Will you be home tonight?"

Phil bent to the table. "Sarah, it's my first full day back here. I don't want to spend it in the hospital."

"Don't be afraid of him, he's harmless."

"Yeah, totally." Guy said it with a grin.

"You touch him and I'll never speak to you again."

Shaking his head, Phil pulled his five-dollar bill from the tens and twenties Mom had put in his wallet this morning. He left the cash on top of the check, tried to smile for Sarah one last time. He couldn't say good-bye, he just held up a hand, turned, and walked out.

By the time he passed Bamberger's windows and found the escalator, he stopped sweating. Through hidden speakers, the Chipmunks sang "Winter Wonderland." But he was sure it wasn't the music that was making him laugh.

| 9 |

She was sitting on one of the white leather couches, reading the *Wall Street Journal*. Not reading it, paging through it. She was as surprised to see him as he was to find her here. She jerked her head toward the doors to twin offices in back of the receptionist's desk: "He's in there. Hiding."

"He's lunching with a client, Miss Davis." The woman at the desk was over fifty. She looked dumpy, dressed all in gray. If Uncle Chuck had hired this woman, maybe he wasn't chasing coeds anymore. "I really don't expect him back at all today."

"Coward," Louise said.

Phil stepped to the desk. "Are you sure he's not here? I'm his nephew, Phil Trent."

"Oh, yes." The receptionist's glasses made her gray eyes look bigger. "Your mother phoned to say you were coming in. Mr. Trent asked me to apologize. But he'll be at your house for dinner tonight." Her smile was lopsided. "He's so happy to know you're home."

He was in there.

One of the doors behind the desk had a nameplate on it: CHARLES A. TRENT. The other door was blank. "Okay if I look inside?" Phil said.

The receptionist tried her smile again. There was nothing wrong with her mouth, she just wore too much lipstick. "I don't think he'd like that."

"'I don't think he'd like that.'" Louise mimicked her, then

slapped the newspaper on the table in front of the couch. "Who cares what he'd like?"

"Miss Davis, please. I'll have to ask you to leave if you can't keep your voice down. What if a client came in?"

"I'd tell him exactly what I thought of that miserable little man you work for."

Big dull eyes behind bifocals pleaded with Phil. "Customers come in all the time to watch the stock-market tape, especially during lunch hour."

Block letters and numbers moved across the electronic board high on the wall. Chairs had been placed in front of it, making that section of the office a little theater. A computer stood nearby, so clients could get quotes on any stock and not have to wait for the tape. All the furniture in here was modern. Not anything like the old Market Street office. Not cozy.

"If I don't see him today," Louise was saying, "I'll be back tomorrow." She squinted at Phil. "I'm not about to let him get away with this."

An office was waiting for him behind the blank door. One day, his name would go up there. He walked to it, opened it.

"Mr. Trent. Please." Filing cabinets and a few cartons sat on a blue rug. This was storage space now. It looked small. It didn't smell new. He reached for the knob on Uncle Chuck's door.

"I already tried that," Louise said. "He locked it."

"He is not in the office." The receptionist worked her frown into a smile for the two men who walked in. They nodded at her and went straight to the computer by the chairs. By the look of their suits, they didn't need to know what the market was doing: they would make money anyway. "I don't want to have to call security," she whispered.

Phil sighed and walked around the desk, leaned on the arm of the couch nearest Louise. "I'm sure he has a back door to his office, so he can go in and out without anybody knowing. He's not in there."

Her eyes got hard. Her fingers made fists. And suddenly, Louise looked ready to cry. "I've always hated him. But until now, I've never felt good about it." She blinked, and her stare went cold. She stood and glared at the receptionist. "Tell him I'll be in to see him tomorrow morning. Tell him he should have his lawyer with him."

She tugged at her vest, looked at Phil, then looked away. "I'm sorry for your mother. But if she believes—well, then she deserves the pain."

She slipped past him and out the door.

The receptionist raised her eyebrows. "Running that place is too much for her. Your uncle has tried to get her to understand that, but—"

Phil walked out. He caught up to Louise a few stores down. She saw him out of the corner of her eye, but she wouldn't look at him. She kept walking. "Please," she said, "don't say anything."

He matched her stride. "How about sign language?"

She fought a smile and lost. Still, she wouldn't look at him. She blinked and said, "He would never wear that tie with that blazer."

He lost a step. "I'm not him."

She stopped. She turned. She looked at him. In another second she would be checking her watch, telling him she had to get back to her restaurant, and he couldn't think of anything to say to stop that from happening.

Then he saw Guy the nose guard lumbering straight for him, giant fists swinging at his sides, a sneer on his face and something hot in his small eyes. It made Phil swallow. He said, "Oh, shit."

He thought about running. Louise must have thought he was crazy. She cocked her head, squinted at him. He couldn't get his legs to work. He couldn't swallow anymore.

But the nose guard kept walking, his eyes not seeing anything or anyone. He went by in a hurry. And he didn't look so big anymore. Maybe it was the way he let his shoulders sag. He disappeared down the wide hall, just another body in a crowd of shoppers.

Louise stepped closer. "Are you all right?"

He felt clammy. He rubbed his arms. "Yeah."

She checked her watch. Her lips moved, but only a sigh came out. She put her purse in her other hand. "Before I do anything about your uncle, I'd like you to know the truth."

She had tiny red marks at the bridge of her nose. She must wear glasses. "I'm listening," he said.

She shook her head. "All you'd get from me right now is anger." Another glance at her watch, another sigh. "I have to clear things at the mill first, then we can go see my grandmother." She started walking. "She'll tell you. Henry was like a son to her. A good son."

Near a shop that sold nothing but silk flowers, she glanced at him and said, "Your tie is fine."

He smiled back at her. He didn't feel cold anymore.

10

He had heard about this section of Ringbrook, but had never been here. It was as old as Paterson, and once a part of it. A pocket of land, it stood surrounded by the little mountains of three towns—Totowa, Haledon, and the southern tip of Willowbend—and faced the Great Falls entrance to the city. Even the road that led to this small island of homes belonged to another township. No town had wanted this piece of real estate. Ringbrook had gotten stuck with it, by default. It was one of Paterson's original immigrant encampments, a Dutch settlement first, later a Germantown, then an Irish ward, an Italian neighborhood, now mostly Puerto Rican. It was called Little Notch. Some of the streets here had cobblestones showing through worn macadam.

She parked her noisy Datsun at the curb in front of a white bungalow with a wide porch. The lace undercurtains on the square windows looked yellow from years of sun. She led the way up a slate walk lined with rosebushes someone had pruned to look like little trees. She didn't use a key on the storm door or the front door. She just turned the knob and walked in. Who in his right mind would leave a door unlocked in Paterson?

A living room stood to one side of the hallway, a staircase to the other. Straight ahead, a parlor. All the furniture here looked as though it had come from Louise's office. Maybe it was the other way around. He studied an oil painting on the wall just inside the door: a rural landscape in summer, everything in final bloom.

"Damn it." Louise put her coat in a closet off the parlor. "She's been baking again."

The smell of fresh bread came from an open kitchen in back of the parlor. He followed her into the living room. More paintings. Some were watercolors. Most were landscapes like the one in the hall. A few were of storms. A set of four portraits had been grouped together behind a boxy overstuffed couch: old black faces, without smiles.

"My mother did all of these." Louise sat in a wing chair facing a console television. "She was just getting good when she died. Would you like something to drink? All we keep is anisette."

He shook his head. The couch was hard and the back was too straight. He crossed his legs and waited. He had gotten good at waiting these last three years. He had had a lot of practice.

She didn't move or say anything for what felt like a long time. In this light, filtered by old lace, she had soft edges, and in some places, no edges at all, just hair blending into shadow, an elbow merging with the line of the chair, almost as if some parts of her were being erased. Finally, she blinked. "I never did very well in math at school."

He nodded, thinking he must have missed something she had said either in the car or just now. He uncrossed his legs, leaned into the arm of the couch. It was harder than the back.

"Your father said I had lousy teachers." Her smile got wide. "He made it all so easy to understand, I've been a whiz at it ever since. I'll bet you were good in it, too."

Math was one of his strongest subjects. Dad had made the numbers and the figuring easy to understand, and his shortcuts made homework a breeze.

"And then there's this." She touched a small stuffed animal on a footstool by her chair. A white baby seal. "Henry won it for me on the boardwalk. Throwing baseballs at milk cans, I think."

Not possible. Dad couldn't throw a baseball hard enough to knock over a milk can.

She held the seal in her lap as if it were a live puppy. "He said it was the only thing he had ever won at those games. That just made it even more special." She returned the seal to its footstool throne. "I was twelve when he gave it to me."

"Louisa?" A shrill voice called from upstairs. "Home so early?"

She glanced at her watch, called to the stairs, "Put your robe on."

"I have the heat up, no?"

"You have a guest." Louise shook her head, then sighed and leaned toward the couch. "Henry meant the world to her. If she knew what your uncle . . . " She stared at her lap. "Please, don't say anything to hurt her."

Slippered feet hit the stairs. Through the arch to the hall, he could make out a blue robe coming down the steps, a slender hand on the banister. He stood.

The little woman who walked into the living room had white hair and dark brown eyes. Her hands were lumpy and spotted by age. She stopped near the TV, took the kiss Louise gave her, tied her robe sash, and stepped closer to the couch. She had wrinkles around her mouth, but the rest of her face looked young. Maybe the light in here was playing tricks again.

"This is Henry's son," Louise said, "Phil."

The old woman squinted. "Henry's boy?"

Phil swallowed dry air and nodded.

She put her palms together, shut her eyes. When she opened them, they were wet. She took three quick steps, hugged Phil, kissed his cheeks. She smelled of sleep.

"I'll get us something to drink," Louise said.

"Nonna do." And the little woman shuffled toward the parlor, then turned and smiled. "I pray one day you come back." She had the same warm smile Louise owned. "Sit. Nobody stand in my house."

He kept looking at the spot she had just left empty, trying to figure out what she meant by "come back." He had never been here—he would have remembered the place, especially the paintings on the walls—and he was sure he had never met the old lady before. Maybe Louise had told her that Phil had left town. Maybe that's what she meant by "come back." Maybe she was just senile. "She's the woman in the photo," he said. "In your office."

Louise's skirt crinkled against the seat of the chair. "I grew up calling her Nonna Do because that's what she said every time I tried to do anything for her—like wash the dishes? *Nonna* means 'grandmother' in Italian." She aimed a slow smile at the kitchen. "She'll insist you stay for dinner. She's a wonderful cook. We use all her recipes at the mill."

He fingered piping on the couch arm. "I'm not sure I can."

"You have to. You owe your father that much. And her, too."

Nonna Do came back with a wooden tray that held a bottle of clear liqueur and three shot glasses. She set the tray on a side table, filled the glasses. "We make a nice toast." Her fingers looked brittle, but they were steady. She had been heavier once: her wedding band had thread wound around the underside to keep it from falling off. She handed out the anisette. "Louisa, you say."

"He wants you to tell him about Henry and Pop-Pop." Louise stared at Phil, raised her glass. "To the truth."

The old woman cocked an eyebrow as if confused, then shrugged and clinked her glass against the other two. *"Salúd."*

Book
Three

Silk City

1915

It wasn't paved with gold. It wasn't even clean. America was smokestacks.

Great clouds, as dark as the burning coal that made them, spewed from brick chimneys one hundred feet tall. Those round red towers got ever narrower from base to top, like giant fingers of a woman's hand, so slender and graceful any sculptor would have been proud to have carved them. Letters had been painted one below the other down the full height of the tallest chimney:

M

A

S

T

E

R

It was the right one. The one he had come so far to find.

In places here along the river, summer sky leaked through, as if winking in the smoke. So different from the pale color of his home sky, this blue was dark and cold. Even in the late June heat, America's sky made him shiver.

And cough. His best suit of clothes, his only white shirt, his only tie, would be grimy with soot in less than an hour if he stayed outside on the streets. He wanted to go back to his mountains in Campania. He fought tears. He cried too easily. His father had told him that and his mother had said nothing to dispute it.

Twenty years old and he still cried like a little boy. The Americans would laugh at him. It was a mistake to come to this filthy place.

From his jacket, he took the letter his uncle the mayor had written inside the train station at Avella. He had read the short note hundreds of times—on the train to Naples, on the boat across the Mediterranean and the Atlantic, on the hot island in the harbor where the Americans kept everyone from everyplace, on the train from New York to here, Paterson—and by now, he could recite the words, but he could no longer enjoy them. By now, reading the letter only meant more waiting. He would be glad to get rid of it, as grateful as he had been months before to receive it. He matched the letters on the paper to those on a sign nailed to the mill: MASTER DYE & FINISHING. He crossed the wide street, his note bending in a breeze off the water, and opened the front door.

The skinny woman at the desk inside asked him the same thing every officer had asked at every point in his travels: "Your papers?"

He reached for his wallet, then stopped. He would not show this woman his papers. She didn't wear a uniform. He held out the letter and tried to sound like the mayor: "Mr. Galli, please." Not a question, an order. "Give orders to those who take orders for a living," the mayor had told him, "and ask questions only of those who give the orders." The woman squinted and snatched the letter from his hand. Her eyebrows got busy. She shook her head, as if she couldn't read Italian. She must have been able to, because she handed back the letter without looking up and said in an accent he could barely understand—Piedmontese?—"Upstairs in the office."

The stairs had not been swept. Halfway up, noise from machines came through the walls. At the head of a long hall, he found another desk, but no one sitting behind it. He knocked on the first door. Inside, someone grumbled. He turned the knob and walked in. "Mr. Galli?"

Salvatore Galli didn't get out of his big chair. He wasn't fat like the mayor. He had a young man's body with an old man's face. He took the letter. He read the signature first, and his surprise turned into a sour smile. He studied the rest of the letter, and that smile did not get better. Finally, he folded the note. "So, August Zorzoli, what is the service your uncle claims you did for my niece?"

It had been a long time since August had heard anyone speak the dialect of his home. It made him smile. It made him want to like this man. He cleared his throat. "I escorted her home one night, when some soldiers were giving her trouble."

"You are a hero, then? All of Avella cheers you?"

He shook his head. He had done nothing more than take the girl by the arm and lead her out of the town, and the soldiers had been too drunk to follow or want to, those soldiers had thought the whole thing called for another drink.

Galli's shoes had been freshly shined. His palm smacked the little table beside his chair. "What was she doing out at night?"

"An errand for your sister."

The thin man laughed. "My sister could have sons if she married right." He eyed the letter again. "Your Uncle Carlo is not the mayor of Paterson. I don't have to do this."

Even when his uncle the mayor was asking a favor, it sounded like an order. He had been the mayor too long. August nodded at the man in the chair and turned to leave, happy he didn't have to put that letter back into his pocket and protect it any longer.

"You read and write," Galli said, "like all the Zorzolis?"

The Zorzolis had been the town recorders ever since records were kept, and in time, the townspeople had become dependent on the family for everything from deeds to wills, and a Zorzoli had been the mayor as long as anyone in Avella could remember. Even Zorzoli women were taught to read and write. It used to be a town joke. Now it was only an oddity, of no real importance. "Our language," August said, "and some Latin for the law."

That smile again, as if those thin lips had touched wine

too young to drink. Small hands unfolded the letter, carefully, thoughtfully. "I have two sons. A few years older than you, I think. My mill goes to them. They must agree before I give you a high position here."

"I only ask for a job."

Galli waved the note. "I'm not the stupid man your uncle the mayor thinks. You work for me, I use your talents." He let his arm drop, and his smile showed yellowing teeth. "And Galli pays you what you're worth."

He pushed out of his chair, told August to wait where he stood, and went out and down the hall. It was hot up here. Through a dirty box window, he could make out the summer river, low and full of silt. Moments later, Galli came back. He fingered the letter. "My wife will like to keep this."

August made a shallow bow—his father's gesture anytime a woman was mentioned in conversation. It made Galli cock his narrow head. He pocketed the letter, stepped to a low desk in a corner, moved papers to uncover a tin box. Paper money inside, and coins. He picked out a large circle of silver, put it in August's hand. "You get paid by the day, like everyone else. Go see the girl downstairs, she'll show you the work. You have somewhere to sleep?"

The money felt warm. He shook his head.

"You sleep here, then. She'll find you a spot." The old man turned and went back to his desk. "Find someone to teach you to read and write English and you'll get two dollars a day instead of one."

August couldn't move. He opened his hand, saw the shine of silver. Paid already, and he hadn't done a minute's work. It wasn't possible. He couldn't find his voice to say thank you.

"Be quick, Zorzoli," Galli told him without turning around. "Go earn your pay."

He ran down the stairs, eager to find paper and pen to write home and tell everyone, especially the mayor, about America, knowing they would never believe him.

It wasn't even work. It was numbers. And names that looked impossible to pronounce: Lawrence-Massachusetts, Harrisburg-Pennsylvania, Chicago-Illinois, Poughkeepsie-New York. It was like stealing. A dollar a day.

And the English everybody spoke was not the same language they wrote. One could be learned from anyone—mill workers, cooks, even children—or from books with drawings in them to show what the words meant in Italian and in English, and how they should sound. But the written language could be learned only from someone who knew how to read, write, and speak both English and Italian, because all the books on how to read and write English were in English. There must have been such people, but no one knew where to find them, no one had any use for them or the money to pay them.

For bills and orders, Galli had made up a system that got around the written language: he numbered the colors of his dyes. If the written order called for silk in "champagne beige," it was still color 08 to Galli, no matter what the Americans called it or how they spelled it. Simple. And it worked. There would not be a need to learn how to read and write English, only a need to copy the letters and match the numbers.

August got good at copying and matching, good enough to convince Galli that his new worker had learned to read and write the new language. August got a raise. Another dollar a day.

The corner of the upstairs hall of the mill Galli let him sleep in was fine for sleeping, but not for living. Inside of a week, August found a room in a house on River Street, twenty minutes by foot from the mill. The woman who owned it, Mrs. DeMatto, cleaned it daily, changed his sheets weekly, fed him twice a day, and for a small additional charge, washed his clothes once a week. The room was brown, with one small window facing the street. The curtains came from the mill, a gift from another worker who had lived here before he moved out for something bigger and better. This room, with its cot and chair and standing wardrobe, was bigger and better than the corner of the house August had called his own in Avella: this room had a door.

He kept his silver dollars in a box on the floor of the wardrobe. By winter, when the hot breeze off the street turned cold, he knew he would have to buy another box or a bigger one. He solved the problem by going to a storefront downtown where, for a fee, they would take his silver dollars and send them back to Avella. Galli had been doing it for years with no problems. August handed the clerk sixty dollars and the clerk gave him a receipt for fifty-four dollars that would be sent to Ferdinandi Zorzoli of Avella and should arrive within four months. August sent a letter to his uncle the mayor, advising him to watch for the money, but not to tell August's father or mother it was coming. It was to be a surprise. The letter would only take two or three months to reach the mayor. August couldn't wait to read the proud man's reply.

On the shiny table in the hall, catching light through lace under-curtains, his name stood out on an envelope from home. The mayor's handwriting was as bold and careful as ever. Black lines from the post office ruined the large stamps. The letter felt dry, almost brittle. He worked a finger under the flap, pulled out the note.

The money had arrived safely, much sooner than expected. It had come at a time his mother would need it. Ferdinandi Zorzoli had died in his sleep. Avella mourned him. If August had any more money, he should send it to his mother. And if he had enough money, he should return home, where he was needed.

He took the letter up the stairs, unable to see the words. He saw his father dead in bed, his mother's steady tears, the priest and his cage of incense, the mayor leading the march to the grave. He saw his mountains. He wanted to go home, but knew he could not, it cost too much. If he could save enough, it would be better to bring his mother over here. America had been her idea. Her dream, for the last of her four sons. America did not have wars. Young men did not die there. But she would not come. He could beg her and she would not come. She would not leave the spot beside her husband's grave empty, she would fill it with her own body when the time came. His father was dead and August knew he would never see his mother again. This is what the mayor's letter meant.

He stared down at the black street the snow had broken, listened to the spring river race away from the rumble of the Great Falls. He wondered why he couldn't cry.

1928

The woman who cleaned his office did too good a job: she scrubbed the windows so hard, she broke one of the glass panes. She worried he would fire her. He was, after all, the boss.

His official title was Manager of Operations. He had chosen it himself, after seeing it in a newspaper. Old man Galli, who was out sick most of the time now, hadn't known what that title meant, but if August Zorzoli wanted to be called Manager of Operations, that was fine. Titles were cheaper than raises.

August taped a piece of cardboard over the broken window. Summer light fell on his long desk and the stacks of papers he had to get through this morning, and it made the small photo on the dull brick wall look shiny: his mother in her bridal gown, trying, but unable to find the smile he remembered her giving to children, flowers, and cool nights when the cooking was done. His uncle the mayor had sent the picture more than three years ago, along with the rest of his mother's things—what was left of them after family and friends in Avella took what each felt was owed him. Those few things, including the rosary she was never without, remained in a box. Only the picture came out. The rosary should have been buried with her. August could not forgive his uncle for the oversight.

Beside the photo: a long frame holding his naturalization papers. It made him grin. It was a duplicate certificate. He had told the clerk in city hall that he had lost the original. The original was in a small safe in his bedroom. August worried someone might steal it if he hung it on a wall. He was willing to let thieves have the duplicate. And he was worried someone might come to his rooms at night and try to arrest him if he could not show them his papers. Some Americans hated Italians. He had read about those people in the papers that came by train each day from New York. Last summer, those people had executed Vanzetti because he was Italian. They had executed Sacco because he was Italian and poor. It made sense to have papers both here in the office and in his rooms. It made sense to be able to show such people he was an American.

"Augie, we close down in an hour." Ernie Galli smiled in the open doorway. His hair was wet from the heat of the dye box, but the extra starch made his shirt look fresh. "Pop wants everybody there before noon."

"Not like last year." Mike, the little brother who was twice as big as Ernie, wasn't smiling. His leather apron was dirty. So were his hands. The rolls of silk he cut and loaded onto trucks would have to be checked. Again. "I'll blow the whistle five minutes early."

"We quit," August told them, "when the run is over."

"Pop never cared about finishing the run on the day of his birthday picnic." Mike edged past his brother and stopped just inside the office. "You want our workers to go union? Just because we promise them a little something and then don't come through?"

He sat at his desk, pulled a set of papers to the center of the blotter. The workers would join Dyers' Local 1733 regardless of what Galli gave them. Ernie knew that. Ernie was the smart one. Mike didn't listen to him anymore. And he was still young enough to think he could do what he pleased and get away with it. Maybe he could in the new mill towns of Pennsylvannia, but not in Paterson. Paterson was too ripe for unions, too perfect. It was here the first real labor strike in America took place, two years before August had arrived and long before Mike Galli was ready to cut and ship silk on his own, and every year that walkout got celebrated like a saint's feast day with the Paterson Pageant. One day soon, Local 1733 would take over this city. And Mike Galli would be running this mill. He would ruin everything. Unless his father kept his promise and made August a partner.

"I'll speak to Salvatore today." August liked being able to call Galli by his first name. It was something the brothers could not do. "Ernie, the dye box will overheat without silk running through it."

The elder son nodded and headed down the hall, past his father's empty office. Mike sneered and inched closer to the desk. "He's the best dye-box man in the city, and you tell him his business? You never worked a day down there."

August didn't look up. He was thinking about Vanzetti, so well read, such a noble bearing. Like Uncle Carlo the mayor. Not a man who would rob or kill a payroll guard. Why couldn't everyone see that? "Look at your hands. Your silk will have to be checked for dirt. Have it ready in fifteen minutes."

"It's already wrapped and loaded!"

August looked up. Slowly. He smiled his uncle's dry smile. It worked. It pushed Mike Galli back, turned him, sent him down the stairs, angrier than ever, but knowing who was boss.

The order form on top of the papers on his desk was from the state capital in Trenton. Blue silk, for drapes. Color 03: navy. When August had first come here, America's president had been a man who had lived in the same governor's house where silk from this mill would soon hang. It had to be an omen. Today, then, he would make old man Galli a man of his word: he would make Salvatore Galli take the money and sign the papers. Today, August Zorzoli would become a partner.

A wide porch ran along the front and one side of the oversized white bungalow. Fire-red and orange azalea bushes bordered the big lawn. The petals felt wet. Someone had just watered. His mother had loved flowers, especially roses. His father had brought her pink roses once. She had cradled them in her arms and cried. In this country, everyone had enough water to waste some on flowers, even thirsty ones like roses. His mother would have liked it here.

He squinted from sun off the azaleas. Such a fine house. And a good neighborhood. Little Notch was even nicer than the Riverside section of the city, where August now rented the top floor of a two-family house on East Eighteenth Street. Five rooms, all to himself. Still, he missed Mrs. DeMatto's cooking. His new landlady, Mrs. Cimoli, was from Genoa and she went weeks without making pasta. Her ham was always overdone: she said she was worried about a disease that came from undercooked pork, but her veal was tough, too, thanks to more roasting than it needed. If he stayed there, he would keep losing weight. It was time he agreed with everyone: he needed a woman to take care of him. It was past time he took a wife and started sons. But the only women he knew or was likely to meet either worked in the mill as sewers or worked outside the mill as prostitutes. He had not yet met a woman who could read or write. He had given up thinking he would. He walked toward the smell of salted fish and the sound of voices and music at the back of the Galli house.

Workers in their church clothes filled the yard. Most sipped lemonade, though jugs of homemade wine had been brought. They would not drink the wine until Galli made his toast. August put his gift on a table already heavy with ribboned boxes and neatly folded paper bags, each with a card so the old man would know who had given him what. August had written many of those cards for workers who could not write. His small box wore no card. Galli would know who the box of vanilla chocolate was from.

Mrs. Galli carried a tray of fruit from the kitchen to a long table near the dancers and the Victrola. She wore a polka-dot dress. Not silk. Rayon. It made her wide body look wider. She handed the tray to a young woman in a sun hat, then checked pastries sitting in white paper wrappers on pans of cracked ice. One worker spotted August by the presents. Then another saw him. Whispers started, elbows poked sides, fingers went to lips. All the talking stopped. It made Mrs. Galli jump. She turned. August made a shallow bow. She grinned and held her arms out to him. She smelled of fresh sugared cream. He took her hands, kissed her cheeks. The voices in the yard came back to life.

"How is your Salvatore?"

"Resting. So tired these days. But better than last year."

"I must see him. Before the party."

She nodded. "I'll have to get him ready. You know how vain he is—still. You eat." She reached across the table, took the woman in the sun hat by the wrist. "Beata, feed him some baccalà." Her hands came close together and she pulled them down in front of her in a straight line. "Like a stick." Then a whisper close to August's shoulder: "Her father's Lorenzo The Barber down the street. From Campania. Here two years. Pretty, no?"

The woman in the sun hat must have heard it all, and if she was from Campania she would understand the Avella dialect, yet her face stayed tight. She forked chunks of salted cod onto a small plate. Her dark hair fell below her shoulders. She had warm brown eyes. But her skin was pale. There was something wrong with her: she looked sick. August forced a smile and took the plate she handed him. "Thank you."

She didn't speak. Mrs. Galli nudged his side. "No English. They keep her in the house all day." With a shrug of wide shoulders, she marched back into her kitchen.

"*Grazie,*" August said, raising the plate of fish.

"*Prego.*" The young woman didn't look up, she busied herself with the pastries.

The baccalà tasted heavy. He set the plate on the table and picked up a cannolo. The rummed filling inside the canoe-shaped crust was almost too sweet with almond paste. He finished it in three bites and reached for another.

"You eat dessert first?" She was smiling now, wide lips in dark shade cast by her hat brim. "Not good for your stomach."

He let go of the pastry, picked up the plate of baccalà, stared at it.

She covered her laugh with a pale hand. "I'll fix you a nice sandwich. You like provolone?"

"If it's no trouble."

He watched her stuff chunks of dry cheese into a thick roll and wondered what village she was from. Her dialect was close to his, but she spoke so fast, she must be from Naples or a town close by. Neapolitans were always in a hurry with everything. Except wine. "Your father cuts hair?"

She handed him the sandwich. "Manfro's on the next corner. Everything is new. Two chairs."

He buried his smile in the sandwich. She was proud of her father, proud that his business was so good he had to hire another barber just to keep up with the customers. "You should eat something yourself."

She shook her head. "Not in this heat."

"Over there"—he pointed to a red and white beach umbrella by the grape stake fence—"you would be cooler."

"I promised Mrs. Galli I would serve."

"But your health—"

"My health is fine." Her eyes got hard, color flushed her cheeks. Maybe there was nothing wrong with her. Maybe she just didn't like the sun. She ladled water from the melting ice onto the lawn. "The pastries will get soggy this way." She glanced over her shoulder at the workers. "You'd better take your sandwich to another place. They won't come to the food if you're here."

He stopped in the middle of a bite. It was true. They were afraid of him. Because he paid them. Because they worried he might not pay them one day. They felt about him the same way people in Avella felt about his uncle the mayor: few would dare speak to Carlo Zorzoli without permission, and when they did speak, they asked for permission to do even the smallest things, like move a fence or bring an extra cart to market. His swallow tasted sour. He put a cannolo on his plate beside the fish, bowed to the barber's daughter, and carried his plate and sandwich toward the clothesline in the corner of the yard nearest the house.

A kitchen window slid open. Mrs. Galli stuck her head out. "August, come in now. He wants you to bring his chair outside."

He looked around for a place to leave his food. Ants would find it if he left it on the grass. Mrs. Galli would make him eat it all, even the baccalà, if he brought it inside. He was still turning when the barber's daughter slid the plate out of his hand. "You are too sad to be an American," she said. "Like my father. A professor back home. There are no schools for him here."

She took the sandwich, put it on the plate. She smiled and gave him the cannolo—"I'll save you one more"—and a moment later she was back at the food table, serving workers. He wondered if, after he wheeled the old man out and the birthday toast was made, the professor's daughter would like to dance with the new one-quarter owner of Master Dye & Finishing.

1936

The special contract looked like a long letter, the kind his uncle
the mayor still sent twice a year—on Christmas and Easter—but
it felt heavier. It was a piece of law and it seemed to gain an ounce
or two each time he picked it up. It had big words in small print.
English words. He didn't know what some of them meant.

His father-in-law the professor had studied it. He had even
mentioned it to the Irish lawyer who still lived nearby and came
into the shop once a week for a trim and a shave with hot towels.
The professor said the contract was fine. But he had never met the
new owners of Master Dye & Finishing, had never spoken with
Mr. Burns to see his eyes jump sideways as if something were
always startling him, and the professor had never heard the sharpness in Mr. Townsend's laugh. The professor knew the words. A
real barber would have known the men.

Cold air slipped into the bedroom through an open window.
Little Notch, August had learned over the last three years since
moving from his rooms on East Eighteenth Street, got colder than
the city. It lay in a hollow, backed by low mountains, and when
winter came, winter could not get out. Beata had stopped telling
him how sleeping with the window open was a good way to catch
pneumonia and, worse, that it was a waste of heat. She wore a
flannel nightgown to bed now and she dressed the baby in wool.
She had stopped going downstairs in the middle of the night to
warm herself at the stove. She had even stopped trying to shut the
window or stuff the opening with towels while her husband slept.

He chose a red tie from the wardrobe. It still looked new, as if it had just come out of the box Galli had given him on the old man's last Christmas. August had wanted to wear it to the funeral. Beata made him wear a black one. Today, nothing she could say would stop him from wearing the red tie.

It was a special contract because it was different from the one the Galli brothers had signed in the spring. They had sold their 75 percent ownership of the mill outright—for $50,000, enough money for both of them to live handsomely off just the interest—and there was nothing in their contract about keeping their jobs, though they had what Mr. Townsend and Mr. Burns called "an understanding" about that. The new owners had three other mills, all in Pennsylvania, yet they had not personally supervised even one dye room for a single day. They claimed they never fired workers who had been on the payroll at the time of the sale, and they never asked former owners to leave. It was Mr. Townsend's idea. He called it "zero turnover." He always smiled when he said it, and he said it a lot.

The special contract was August's idea. It meant that everything would stay the same for him: he would keep his 25 percent share of the mill and its profits, keep his job for life. It had taken more than half a year to draw up. It had been worth fighting for. He finished the knot of his tie, shut the window, and carried his suit jacket downstairs.

His wife was not in the kitchen and his daughter was not in the nursery next to the bathroom. That room had originally been a closet. Whoever built this bungalow had been smart about everything but that. The room was too big to hang clothes in, too small to be a sitting room, and so convenient to the kitchen that it was always cluttered, tempting pots and pans, flour, beans, and canned goods to be stored inside. It had been easy to make it into a nursery, needing only a small window for ventilation, and some paint. It stood directly below the master bedroom. No cry went unheard, and there were nights August swore he could hear the baby turn in her crib, the soft swish of wool against linen as clear to his ears as the sound of traffic on the avenue three blocks away. He had painted it yellow—one can of paint, one day to do the whole job—because blue was too dark and pink was too hard on the eyes and because he had wanted his wife to know he truly didn't care if the baby came out a girl or a boy, he would take either as a blessing, and the yellow paint said that. The yellow on the walls said he had loved the baby long before he had seen or held her. That yellow said he was a good father.

He found whiskey for his coffee in the sun porch behind the kitchen. Through the big window by the stairs to the cellar, he could see them in a corner of the yard, bundled up against the cold and huddled near her fig tree. They wore mittens Mama Manfro had knitted. They unfurled burlap, began wrapping the little tree as if it were a newborn child. It was the same age as Millie, but already five times as tall. It had given eight figs in its three years—August was counting—but Beata promised it would give bushels of fruit soon, all it needed was time. And a burlap coat each winter. And more fertilizer than her roses got, and more water, too. But it made her happy. It gave her hope and the chance to do something other people couldn't—grow fine crops of figs in a hostile climate—and she needed that now, when she could no longer do what normal women her age could.

They got the burlap over and around the tree, then began sewing the material shut with silk thread. He sipped coffee. The sweet taste of liquor warmed his throat. Seeing them in the yard, not mother and daughter, but two playmates, made him smile. *My girls.* There was a time not long ago he thought he would lose them.

They had named the baby after the professor's father, a noted mathematician in Italy. August was glad she was not a boy. A boy would have to be called Emilio. The girl they could call Millie. She was not strong at birth. The doctor had trouble getting her to breathe, he had to keep slapping her and for a moment it looked as though she would never cry. The doctor could not stop Beata from bleeding. What was for everyone else a simple thing became a nightmare for August, his wife and baby taken out of the house and put in the hospital. The doctors didn't have to do anything to the baby but feed her. They had to take out Beata's womb. They said it saved her life. She said she was dead inside.

They came home together, and Beata stayed in the bedroom, not wanting to see the neighbors who had come to congratulate her and hold the new baby. She said she could not nurse the child. She meant she would not. Mama Manfro found a woman from River Street to do the job. Her name was Annette. Mama Manfro called her "the cow." Her own child, a boy, was two months old. She always fed Millie first. There were days Annette refused to take the money, she had so much milk it was a sin to let it go to waste, and her husband had a job, and in these times, anyone with a job was rich. "You let her go without taking the money," Mama Manfro told him, "she makes claims on the baby later, like a witch." August didn't care about the money or witches. He worried that he had never seen his wife hold her child.

"You don't even pick her up."

"When I get my strength back."

For a while, he believed her. He put the baby beside her, but all she would do was stare at those small fingers opening and closing in the air, never catching anything that belonged to their mother. The doctor said it was normal. Mama Manfro said it would pass. The professor didn't say anything.

In the middle of the second week after Millie had been born, August fired the cow.

He gave Annette extra money and told her not to come back. The baby would not stop crying from hunger. Mama Manfro got hysterical. She said horrible things, curses August had not thought her capable of. She ran to get her husband and promised to come back with his razor.

"You're starving her," Beata told him.

"Not me. You."

She kept silent. Her face got so hard that he was sure she couldn't hear the baby crying anymore. He wanted to slap her. He picked up the child, patted her back, walking around the room with her. Her cries only got louder.

The professor came up the stairs in his barber's apron, short hairs clinging to the hem. His pencil-thin mustache was still black, but the waves on top of his head had gone gray, almost matching the silver frames of his glasses. His wife followed him into the bedroom, her square frame dwarfing him, her face hot with sweat. "Ask him why he wants to kill our baby."

"I want her to have a mother," August said.

"They put you in jail!" She had forgotten to take her hat off. She glared at him and pointed to the stairs. "Run and get the cow before someone else does."

"She gets her mother's milk," August said, "or nothing."

"Lorenzo, make this madman listen to me."

The professor sighed. "This is not our house."

"It's our grandchild!"

The thin man turned and stepped to the door. He stared at his daughter in the bed. "Beata, God is watching." He walked out, and his wife thumped after him, cursing him down the stairs and over the porch.

August put the baby in Beata's arms. "Feed her." He shut the door behind him.

The big woman was still following the professor down the street, yelling at his back. Neighbors stood at windows and in their yards, watching. August climbed down the porch steps, cupped hands to his mouth, and called after her in Italian so everyone on the block would understand: "Old woman, never come to my house again. You are a curse."

She stopped yelling. The professor stopped walking. August nodded at them, turned, and went back inside. He heard her scream in the street. He locked the door. He sat in the living room and waited, eyeing the clock next to the radio. When five minutes had passed since he had last heard the baby cry, he walked up the stairs to the bedroom door. He opened it slowly.

She was nursing the baby and wiping tears with her free hand. She was trembling. "It will kill Mama if she can't see her grandchild."

"When she learns whose baby it is, she will be a good grandmother." He smiled. "And you will be the best mother." He shut the door and went back down to the kitchen to make her the Indian tea she liked so much and, suddenly hungry, to find himself something to eat.

Less than a week later, she began humming, usually "Santa Lucia," each time she nursed the baby. From that day on, Emilia had music. . . .

They finished sewing the burlap and stepped back to admire their work. The tree with the sack over it must have looked funny to them, because they started laughing. They held hands and swung their arms, and he was sure they were singing, the clouds coming from their mouths had the shape of a song.

He felt tears roll down his cheek. His two girls had taught him how to cry again. He rinsed his cup at the sink, got his coat and hat, and walked through the parlor and out the front door, tucking the special contract inside his jacket. He would have to walk fast. This morning he didn't want to be late.

They were standing at his desk, looking over ledgers the young clerk took care of. They saw him walk in, but said nothing. They kept studying the figures.

He put his hat and coat on the tree inside the door. "You shouldn't be in my office."

Mr. Townsend, the smaller man, had a fast smile and a barrel chest not even his hand-tailored suit could disguise. "We own the place, don't we?"

August stepped to the door connecting the clerk's office to his, knocked once, walked around both men, and sat in his chair. "You may have a seat."

Mr. Burns shrugged and took out a cigar. "Our best month so far. Got a real winner with that teal blue." He patted his pockets for matches and slid his lanky frame into the chair nearest the desk.

The clerk's door opened. The skinny young man had sand-colored hair and light blue eyes set in the face of a girl doll, so white it looked hard, like china. He stopped just inside the office. "I asked them to wait until you got here, Mr. Zorzoli. They ordered me to—"

August raised his hand. "No matter. Take the books back to your desk. And bring me today's sheet."

The clerk picked up the ledgers. He had a head for figures. He had come looking for a job two years ago, and Ernie Galli had felt sorry for him—his father had died, an old man, too old to be much of a father, and there was no insurance, and there was a mother with a young child, the boy's little brother. Ernie persuaded Mike to try the boy on the loading dock. He lasted two days. On the afternoon round to the shipping bay, August found him crying behind a truck, squeezing the dollar in his hand so tightly his nails dug into his palm. The story the boy told could have been anyone's story: people all over were more than hungry, they were desperate. But what possible use did the mill have for someone who could not lift even a half-roll of silk?

He was still in high school and he got good grades. In spite of everything, he still dreamt of going to college. He wasn't like the others who came only for money, and he wasn't like most of the young ones who dreamt of being a boss. August took him upstairs and showed him the paperwork. Henry Trent could read and write

English. He could do figures almost as fast as August could. He got a new job—at night so he could finish school—and a sack of food to take home. His face was so full of tears he couldn't say thank you.

Henry smiled now and backed up toward his office. "I'll have the inventory done before my vacation's over. If Mr. Galli in shipping ever gets me the rest of the paperwork."

August nodded. Mr. Galli in shipping might become the first former owner to be fired by Mr. Townsend and Mr. Burns. Mike no longer cut silk. He drank too much for that. The next worker he punched would be his last.

Henry's door closed. Mr. Townsend moved to a chair by the wall, but didn't sit. "Our lawyers need the contract today. They have to get it to city hall before the Christmas holidays."

The hall of records in Avella was a basement, cold and lighted by candles. The Zorzolis who worked there had pains in their joints and weak eyes. August had never seen the hall of records in Paterson. He wondered if everyone who worked there looked like Henry Trent.

He drew the special contract from his jacket. "Where it says I can be made to leave," he read from the long paper, "*for cause*—"

"Just legal talk," Mr. Burns said. "We want you to stay on, you know that."

"Who else knows how to run the place?" Mr. Townsend grinned. "Zero turnover, remember?"

August pointed to the sentence. "I want it to say I can't be made to leave unless the mill closes."

Mr. Burns took the cigar out of his mouth, glanced at his partner, blinked. The fight was about to start. August would tell them how much the mill meant to him, how he would not let them take it from him. He would force them to understand.

"You write that in yourself," Mr. Townsend told him, "just the way you said it. We'll initial it."

August squinted. "You say . . . it's fine?"

"Fine." Mr. Burns lit his cigar. "It's fine."

Maybe they were good men after all. This America kept surprising him: it was so easy to get what you wanted, almost too easy. He felt blessed to live here. With his pen, he drew a line through the printed sentence, and in the margin he began writing the way Henry Trent had taught him. He made each letter perfect.

1941

Henry stood at the edge of his big desk, his face hard and cold, a dead man's face. He didn't believe what the letter said either.

The letter said the mill was closing down.

His young eyes widened and narrowed, seeing in those words the same future August had recognized hours ago, when the letter first came by special messenger. The mill would be shut before Henry could finish his third year at the college in Montclair. And he had a girl now, a nice girl from the good side of Paterson, where there was a park with deer and rabbits, and children like Emilia, who had never seen a doe or a buck, could feed the animals lettuce by hand through a mesh fence. He had met Henry's girl at the picnic last year. She was being sent to a fine college in New York by her parents. They must be good parents, educating a girl. She would be a teacher, she said. She didn't mind that Henry was behind her in school. She understood why. She understood Henry. She was proud of him. She was a little sprig of a girl with no chest, and though Henry had surely never mentioned romance to her, Julie Wyatt was at the heart of his plans and she knew it. It made her happy.

The letter said the mill was bankrupt.

It wasn't possible. Last year Master Dye & Finishing made another record profit, as it had each year under the new partners. August's share had been $16,000, more money than he knew what to do with. This year, the books said that sales were up, costs were down: a new record would be set.

The letter said Master Dye & Finishing owed more money than it was worth. And the loans were being called.

"These creditors," Henry said without looking up from the page, "they're the other mills. The ones Burns and Townsend own." He swung his stare toward August. "We never borrowed money from them."

"From the bank only," August told him. "Each time we pay back every cent. This year, too."

"Then it's a mistake."

"I called them before you come in." Long-distance to Harrisburg. Neither Mr. Burns nor Mr. Townsend was there. The lawyer who signed the letter was. He said there was no mistake. He said August should be grateful to Mr. Burns and Mr. Townsend, they had persuaded the creditors to be generous: the mill would be allowed to run through Thanksgiving, now just a week away, and Christmas, so that the workers would have money for food through the holidays. The lawyer said the mill would have to close by April of next year. The week after Easter at the latest. He said he was sorry.

"We make too much money to go broke." Henry made a fist. "The books say it all."

The lawyer on the phone said it could not be stopped, it was "irreversible."

"Unless I buy all the loans." And August had already talked to the bank. He could not get that much money. Even with what he had in cash, he couldn't get a loan big enough to add up to $285,000. The man at the bank downtown said he didn't fully understand the circumstances, but he was sorry to hear the news. The man at the bank had lost a good customer and that was what he was really sorry about.

"I'm telling you, Mr. Zorzoli," Henry said, "there's something fishy here. You should get a lawyer."

The lawyer in Harrisburg said if August tried to interfere by taking this to court, they would sue him personally for everything he had. It was a matter of first lien and second lien and the law said those liens had to be satisfied. The law said Master Dye & Finishing was dead.

"I knew you'd fuck it up." Mike Galli stood in the open doorway. Drunk again. The girl downstairs had probably told him everything. If Mike knew, all the workers knew. He grinned and shook his head. "Ran it right into the ground, didn't you. If it wasn't for Burns and Townsend, we would've been bust long before this."

August took the letter, folded it, then turned in his chair so he wouldn't have to face the man in the doorway. "I did not send for you. Go back to work."

"Work? *You* never worked a fucking day down on the floor. Work, that's rich."

The chair seemed to turn all by itself. August felt the smile grow. "Pick up your pay. And never come back."

Mike Galli laughed. "You can't fire me, Zorzoli."

"You come in tomorrow," August said, "I tell them to throw you out. And this time, they can punch back and nobody will fire them."

"You son of a bitch."

"Your father would be ashamed of you," August told him. "He would have put you out years ago."

Galli stopped coming forward. His head got heavy. He turned as if it hurt to move, as if his bones were broken. He left without a sound, his shoes so light on the stairs it was as though a gypsy had stolen his weight. For an instant, August worried about him. But only for an instant.

Henry sat in the chair near his door, put his face in his hands. He would have to find another job. He would never find a job that paid enough to keep him in college and keep his mother and brother in food. Henry Trent would have to change his plans. His girlfriend might change her mind. "There has to be something we can do."

"If I give you money," August said, "to go to school and live, you would pay me back?"

That head of sandy hair came up slowly. He swallowed, then nodded. "But . . . but what if I can't?"

"You try?"

"Of course, Mr. Zorzoli, you know that, but—"

"You try, then you can." He got out of his chair, stepped around the desk, put out his hand. "We do business."

Henry stared at the hand. His arms got stiff, then began to shake. His lips moved, but nothing came out. He pushed out of the chair, hugged August, his face hidden in a shoulder of silk. He made a cooing sound, like a baby.

August patted the young man's head. He smiled at the picture of his mother on the wall between photos of Beata in the wedding gown her mother had made and Emilia on the day she was baptized. He wondered if the women would mind a picture of Henry Trent hanging beside them.

It could have been spring, the day was so warm. She had opened all the windows to air out the house. She had persuaded him to put on old clothes and come outside to help prune and rake and do all the last-minute yard work she and Millie had been waiting for—no, praying for—a Saturday like this to make possible. He laced his boots and started down the stairs.

The man coming up the porch steps looked lost. He wore a new suit and new shoes. He held a small piece of paper in one hand, a briefcase in the other. He was probably selling something. Insurance? August waved him away with the back of his hand, said those magical words Mama Manfro always used—"Not today"—and turned toward the kitchen.

"Mr. Zorzoli?" The man was smiling now. "Harry Burns sent me. Can I come in?"

August walked to the door, opened it reluctantly, ashamed to be seen wearing clothes that should have been thrown away. The man didn't seem to notice. He stuffed the little piece of paper in his jacket and handed August the briefcase. "Your share of what they got out of the deal."

The briefcase felt heavy. "Deal?"

"You bought in for a thousand, right? So you're being treated good. Remember that."

And he was out of the house, going down the porch steps. At the door to his car, he waved. "Harry says to wish you good luck."

The new blue car roared to life and rolled down the street.

August opened the briefcase. There was money inside. More than $1,000. Much more. He took it to the table in the parlor.

"Papa!" Millie ran through the kitchen, grabbed his sleeve. "Mama broke the faucet and there's water coming out all over the place, it won't stop, you have to fix it."

She didn't come up to his chest, but she was strong enough to pull him a few feet before he stopped her. "A minute," he said.

"No, now!" She was so beautiful, even prettier than her mother, with coal-dark eyes as shiny as those in a church statue. She was perfect. She frowned and put her hands on her hips the way Mama Manfro did when she was giving orders. "Papa, this is an emergency in case you didn't know it."

He laughed. He let her pull him through the kitchen and the sun porch, stopping her only long enough to put the briefcase behind the cellar door. It could have been spring, the air was so warm. He squeezed his daughter's hand and ran with her toward faint screams and the sound of gushing water.

The man from the state put a chain across the door. The lock he used was as big as his hand. His assistants hammered posters onto the boarded-up windows: NO ADMITTANCE. The same signs were going up on the garage across the street, where parts of truck engines had been removed to make sure no one could drive what had once belonged to Master Dye & Finishing. It took one man to open this mill. It took so many to close it.

Workers stood in the street. Many were crying. Soldiers came to watch: this was more interesting than walking around, waiting to be shipped to the war. Their new uniforms caught the hard spring light. His brothers had looked like that, hadn't they? August couldn't remember. But he was sure the smiles were the same. Soldiers always smiled. He put a hand on Henry's shoulder, glad that the army had found something wrong with the boy's ear. God was not so cruel to take both the mill and Henry Trent at the same time. August gave silent thanks that God had made the right choice.

The man from the state put the key to the lock in his briefcase and walked straight to August. "We won't let this rest. I'll see you in jail." He glanced at the soldiers and smiled. "You just got your own personal war, Zorzoli. With me." He crossed the street, yelled something to his men, then got in his car and drove toward the Great Falls.

"Don't let him bother you," Henry said. "It's like those newspaper stories, all fake."

The smokestack didn't look so tall anymore. The padlock on the front door was not fake. It was shiny.

"They're only after you because they can't get to Burns and Townsend." Henry shook his head. He had figured it all out. The $6,000 in the briefcase that had come the day before Pearl Harbor had made it clear. The new partners had borrowed from themselves, in the name of Master Dye & Finishing, kept the money, then used the mill's profits to borrow still more until there was no more money left, they had it all, every cent the mill was worth. They had made a fortune going broke by selling the mill to themselves, year by year. They had planned it that way. They had probably done it before. And now they would sell Master Dye & Finishing, every truck and desk it owned, the buildings, too, only this time to somebody else. They would make even more. "The goddamn frauds."

The man from the state had figured it out, too, and called it by the same name: fraud. He said he would send all the partners to prison. A newspaper said this case would send the man from the state to Congress.

"You'll be late for school," August said. "Go now."

"I have time for lunch. Come with me."

"Every day I leave here at six. Today, too."

"That's over seven hours from now!"

August got coins from his pocket and put them in Henry's hand. "You have a big lunch. Keep your brain strong."

After a moment, Henry sighed. "Well, at least promise me you'll get something to eat."

"I promise."

He took his time leaving. He walked around the workers and never got close to the soldiers.

August took out the pocket watch the workers had given him for Christmas, before the stories came out in the papers saying August Zorzoli was a crook, like his partners. So far, none of the workers had asked him to give back the watch. It had Roman numerals on the face and his name written into the back. It was the finest watch he could imagine owning, better than the solid-gold one his uncle the mayor had from Rome, because the mayor had had to buy that watch for himself.

The workers were leaving now, small groups of them wandering off in different directions. The soldiers were already gone. There was nothing left to see. Ernie Galli walked by, his shoulders worn round from bending to the dye box. He stopped to shake August's hand, and without a word, he trudged down the street in a tired, steady gait, as if he had just finished a day's work and was going home for dinner and sleep, to be ready for tomorrow's silk.

August sat on the folding chair Beata had made him take with him this morning. She knew he would stay. She knew he would sit in the street if he had to. The chair came from the church, and he was to return it on his way home. The slats felt hot from the sun.

He could hear the other mills on the street, making sounds the hammering and the padlocking had blocked out before. Heat hummed in dye boxes, wet silk rumbled on rollers, dry silk stretched taut under the cutter, sewing machines clattered as they hemmed yardage tape to dyed edges, brown paper rustled, twine snapped, trucks rolled, and the smoke pouring out of the chimneys, like the river easing in and out of brick channels, made the sound of men singing in whispers.

He kept listening, now and then looking at his watch, and waiting for the click of the last door closing to send him home.

1947

"A promise is a promise." The soft brim of his fedora felt cold in his hands. "The young men need the work."

"But I need you." Frank Lazzaro spread his arms as if checking for rain. "How about I make you a partner?"

August kept turning his hat. This mill on McLean Boulevard, below the Great Falls and at the bottom of the hills of the Riverside section, had once been a rival of Master Dye & Finishing. Five years ago, the war had taken most of the workers, including both of Frank's sons, and National Silk had needed all the experienced hands it could get. Frank had taken his raillike body out of the owner's office and had gone back to work at the dye box, a job he had left on doctor's orders, though he looked healthier now than ever before: the war had given him an excuse to go back to what he loved. But he couldn't work the dye box and run the mill at the same time. He had needed a manager, and he had said he didn't care what the newspapers had written about August Zorzoli. Beata had said, "Think of the salary," but she had been thinking about her house and her growing daughter, and she would have said anything to get her husband out of forced retirement—and out of the house. August agreed to take the job, but only until the men came home from the war. The men were entitled to get their jobs back.

Little Frankie Lazzaro did not come home. The other son, Julius, did. The wrong son, everyone said. The one who came back was too stupid to get killed: the army let him peel potatoes. The smart one got killed right away: the army let him charge at machine guns. And now Frank Lazzaro was offering more than the job his smart son would have come home to, he was offering the dead son's share of the business.

"Mr. Zorzoli, please. I can't replace you. At least think about it a while."

"I have already stayed one year too long."

"We're making good money here, business is booming. Your share would—"

"No." He stepped around the little man. "No more partners."

The office felt small again, as cramped as it had the first day. He took a picture off the wall. Henry Trent looked handsome in his college cap and gown. He looked happy. August smiled. "I will try to find you a new manager."

Lazzaro said nothing. He sat in a chair by the door and watched the pictures come down, one by one.

There was no room in Henry's office to hang his diploma or even a picture of the girl he was going to marry. The cubicle was walled with shelves, each one jammed with ledgers and stout reference books. No windows. No place for a guest to sit.

"Lazzaro would be happy with you," August said. "He liked you as my clerk."

Henry shook his head. "It's not for me."

"More money than here. A chance to be an owner." He bent to the desk, but didn't lean on it, afraid of disturbing mounds of papers lying everywhere. "These stockbrokers, they make you a partner?"

"It's not that." The young man who had been so neat now stuffed pages into a folder as if he cared more about speed than he had once cared about precision. "There's just no future in silk. The war taught everybody how to live without it."

"Business at all the mills is strong."

Again, the head of sandy hair shook. He was using a cream

these days. It made his hair look slick. It made him look older. "Cheaper fabrics are just as good."

August straightened up. "You would not work for me then, when I start a new mill?"

"Mr. Zorzoli, I—" His mouth got tight. "You have plenty of money. Those investments I put you in, most of them have tripled."

"Trent." One of the bosses stuck his shiny head into the room. "Those quarterly reports were supposed to be on my desk before lunch."

"They're on your desk, sir."

"I can't find them."

"Be right there."

The head disappeared. Henry put on his suit jacket. It hid how skinny he was. "This'll only take a second." He stopped in the doorway, but didn't turn. "Mr. Zorzoli, I think you should just retire."

August grinned. "My new mill will change your mind."

Small shoulders sagged. "You can't get the kind of money you need to open a mill."

"My investments, no?"

"And risk everything?" He slapped a bookcase. "Look, take Lazzaro up on his offer, then."

"No more partners. Except you."

"Trent!"

The way the boss shouted made Henry frown. "I can't, Mr. Zorzoli. Please understand." And he was gone.

August didn't understand. Something was happening to Henry Trent. It must be the girl. She was teaching French in high school now. She would be the one who convinced him to leave the mill and take lower pay from stockbrokers. Stockbrokers were respectable, mill workers were mill workers. Since they got engaged, Henry had not been around so much. And he never brought Julie over to dinner, no matter how many times Beata asked him to. Julie Wyatt didn't want to be in Little Notch. She didn't want Henry to be there. "Young lovers like to be alone," Beata had said. August wanted to believe that. But he was afraid that the girl believed what the newspapers had said back when the war started. He was afraid she was trying to protect Henry from the crook most of Paterson believed August Zorzoli to be. All the talk about a trial had only made things worse.

There was no trial.

The young state attorney said he "lacked sufficient evidence" to win a conviction. He wasn't smart enough to catch Mr. Burns and Mr. Townsend, and he hated that. He called the owners "cheats," and "thieves," and "criminals" and the newspapers printed everything he said. When the mill was sold to a cardboard manufacturer two years ago, the papers reprinted the story of Master Dye & Finishing, and in the retelling the facts got darker, thanks to comments by Mike Galli, who said his father had been "blackmailed into selling Zorzoli a share of the mill" and had died regretting it. Neighbors who had shrugged off the first reports now stopped saying hello. A group of workers at National Silk demanded a new manager. Children in Emilia's school sent her home in tears. And Julie Wyatt became a permanent ghost, the empty space beside Henry at the dinner table, the silence in his eyes whenever he was asked about the future.

August put on his hat. His mouth was dry, his chest felt tight. He walked past the quiet rich men in the lobby and out to Market Street. In alley shade at the corner of the building, his breath came back. He wiped sweat from his brow and started home.

She was a woman now. He had pretended not to notice her changing shape, her newfound grace in walking, sitting, tilting her head. But he could not pretend to ignore what had happened to her eyes: they could quicken like fresh oils on canvas, and in the suddenness of those moments, she wasn't just looking at something, her eyes actually seemed connected to the object, as if she were trying to draw it closer, as if she had the power to absorb it. They were dangerous eyes: men would be hypnotized, women would be jealous. They were his mother's eyes exactly.

"I chose Patrick Henry," she said, "because there's only one biography on him. Easy reading. You want two pieces of bread tonight, Pop?"

"Give him one." Beata spooned a brasciole from the pot and began unraveling the twine from the rolled meat. "And from the center. The ends are too hard. Those bakers, they don't care anymore."

He shrugged and poured wine that came from New York. It tasted sweet. He liked it better than the wine his father made. He drank a silent toast to his family in Avella, what was left of them. The mayor and so many other villagers had died when the war found them. The mayor had probably been hiding with the rest, but they gave him a hero's funeral. In her letter, the mayor's sister said he had the biggest headstone in the cemetery. August knew he would not receive another letter from his home.

"We shouldn't even feed him tonight." His wife kept her stare in the pot and her back to him. "A good job like that won't come again—for us."

Emilia put a piece of crusty bread beside his plate and kissed his cheek. Boys would fight for that kiss.

"Mama can't believe you quit," Beata said. "Even Papa thinks—"

"No business at the table," he told the wine.

She turned, spoon in hand. "We're not eating yet."

He tore off a corner of the bread, put it in his mouth, and began chewing. She squinted at his jaw, then spun back to her pot. "So stubborn. Millie, the man you marry, make sure he's not a donkey."

Emilia laughed. "Ma, if he doesn't want to talk about it, that's not stubborn,"—she smiled at him—"that's just how he feels right now."

"Ah, how *he* feels. And me, I feel like talking, but that's wrong?"

"A new job"—he pushed the bread off his plate—"comes with a new mill."

She stopped stirring the sauce, shook her head, then glanced at the ceiling, as if asking God to forgive her husband for being such a fool. With Emilia's help, she served dinner. She nodded at her daughter, then bowed her head and waited for the girl to say grace. With her first forkful of stewed meat, Beata cocked an eyebrow and tried to conceal a slow smile. "Where is this new mill?"

He swallowed rigatoni, reached for his wine. "Not at the table."

She squinted, angry words burbled in her throat, but a knock at the front door stopped her from speaking. She slid her chair back and walked through the parlor.

"Pop, couldn't you tell her something, just this once?"

"I tell her about a new mill all the time. She never believes."

Henry Trent came into the kitchen, his raincoat still on, his hair wet. Beata got him a towel from the bathroom, hung his coat over the tub, sat him at the foot of the table. Without asking if he wanted food, she put a full plate in front of him.

"A long face." August pushed the wine toward him. "Trouble with your girl?"

He shook his head. "Just tired. Drove the office car out to the country."

"You got wet," Emilia said, "inside a car?"

Henry didn't smile. "I had to walk around."

"Too dark to drive," August told him. "Not safe."

"He has headlights, Pop."

"Let him eat," Beata said, "before he drops."

"Mr. Zorzoli, about this afternoon." He pushed pasta and the shredded pieces of brasciole around the plate. "If you really want to start a new mill, I think I found one for you."

August couldn't speak. He swallowed meat and tried to clear his throat.

"He won't talk about it at the table," Beata said.

"Where?" August asked.

"Out in Ringbrook." Henry sipped wine. "It was set up for weavers, but it's on the river and it wouldn't take much to make it a dye house." He turned his glass. "It's been closed since the war. The price is right."

"How much?"

"They'll take half of what they're asking. My boss wanted to buy it for the land. Ringbrook's a good investment, it has to grow."

August pushed back from the table. "We go see it, then."

"What about your dinner?" Beata said.

He brought the raincoat out of the bathroom. "When he gets back."

"You'll catch your death out there. And what can you see in the dark?"

He kept silent and handed Henry the coat.

Emilia's eyes glinted into the soft light. "I thought it wasn't safe to drive."

August kissed her forehead. "Headlights, no?"

It might have been the hard summer rain or the darkness of the night clouds, but the closer the big car got to Ringbrook, the worse August felt about the mill he had been so anxious to see.

The road was full of holes. Trucks would ruin tires, and tires cost money. But Henry said the county would fix the road, the county fixed the road every year.

And the road was too narrow. Two trucks couldn't pass each other safely. But Henry said a new highway was coming, it would run right by the mill, four lanes heading east and west, connecting the Delaware Water Gap with New York City by way of Paterson. Trucks would not have to use the old road for long.

Ringbrook was so far from Paterson, over six miles. How would workers get out here? But Henry said a bus ran every day from Paterson to Willowbend and back, and Ringbrook was on the way.

If it snowed, no bus could get up these hills. But Henry said the new highway would take care of that. The new highway would have no hills.

"Then you should have told me about this mill long ago," August said, "before your boss could think of buying it."

Henry didn't say anything, he kept watching the headlights fight the rain. When he spoke, his voice sounded far away. "I didn't want you to get hurt again."

August put a hand on the young man's wet shoulder, squeezed, then let go. The car bumped over railroad tracks, then swung off the road and stopped. Henry found a flashlight in the glove compartment. "We have to walk down to it, they have a chain across the parking lot."

The river sounded gentle here, so close to where it started. The chain blocking the lot was rusted. A brick building sat in the hollow off the road. It had a smokestack, but it didn't look like a mill. Three stories high, it looked like a small box with windows. Broken windows.

"Well, what do you think?" Henry fished keys from his pocket and aimed his light at the FOR SALE sign on the front door. "Wait 'til you see the inside. A little remodeling and you're in business."

In the rain, the old brick looked soft. Rocks from young hands had made jagged edges in glass. Weeds grew chest-high near the door. There was no point in going inside. Henry was talking about the remodeling and how long it would take and where the special equipment could be found, but August stopped listening. He heard only the rain and the river: they sounded sad to be here. He pulled his collar closed at the neck and glanced at the smokestack. No name had ever been painted there. He kept staring at the naked brick face, and in the moment he was sure he would never own or even work in any mill again, he began to see white letters appear as if by magic down the long, slender column:

Z

O

R

Z

O

L

I

He blinked, but the letters remained.

"Mr. Zorzoli? Aren't you coming in?"

Against the whisper of the running river, a night bird sang from within the cold brick walls. He started walking toward his new mill.

1955

He liked the blue ledgers Henry had used, but the company that made them had gone out of business. Every year the mill had shown a loss in the green ledgers, though each loss was getting smaller. The green ledgers had no luck in them.

He put this year's ledger back into the rack above the clerk's desk. The new boy was neat, but slow. If Henry were here, the figures would come faster, and Henry would find a way to turn the loss into a profit, even in the green ledgers. But Henry was in his own office now, on Market Street in Paterson, and there was no chance he would ever come back to Zorzoli. He was doing too well as an investment consultant, and his little brother was ready to join the firm as soon as he finished the expensive graduate school in Pennsylvania Henry had sent him to. The new clerk didn't think about going to college. He kept paper clips in a glass bowl, pencils in a cup, pens in another cup. His desk blotter didn't have a stain on it.

"He has to be here." Emilia's husky voice ran toward him from the main office. "He eats lunch at his desk."

She was standing near the hat tree. The young man beside her wore a red-and-gray-plaid sports jacket and no tie. He jangled car keys in his fingers.

"Here," August said, and when she turned, she smiled and hurried over to kiss his cheek. "You surprise me," he told her. "No college today?"

She turned away. "Pop, this is Larry. Larry Davis, my father."

"A pleasure, sir." Larry's smile was too big. His handshake

was too firm. The soft wave in his blond hair looked fake. "Sorry I haven't been by sooner."

He sounded rich.

"Mother will be right up," she said. "She wanted to say hello to the girls at the sewing machines."

So—something was wrong. Beata would never come otherwise. It had to be Larry. He wasn't just another boyfriend. He was probably staying to dinner. August pushed chairs together near his desk—"Sit, please"—and stepped into the hall to look for his wife, and to escape having to look at Larry Davis.

She came up the stairs in her dark blue dress, the one she wore to everything important. But she was smiling. She took his kiss, looped her arm through his, and led him back into his office. "He drove us out in a little car with no roof. The wind felt so nice."

Larry Davis laughed. "It's called a sports car, Mrs. Z."

She didn't mind being called Mrs. Z. and she didn't mind his laugh. She touched Emilia's shoulder, then sat in the chair on the other side of the room. "I told them not to call first. You would only worry."

He sat in his chair, slid a folder to a side of his desk. In that folder: arrangements for next month's celebration to mark the retirement of Ernest Galli, the only dye-box operator Zorzoli had ever had. Hands folded on the desk, he watched his daughter's eyes, hoping to find what was wrong, but she wouldn't look at him. In the long silence, he saw how young she was, how his hair was as white as Ernie's now, and how, when the two men walked to the bus stop together each night, both were winded by the time they reached the crest of the little hill.

"They want to be married," Beata said.

He swallowed the dry aftertaste of morning coffee.

"Nothing formal," Larry told him. "Just a quiet ceremony at your city hall."

"No church?" He glanced at his wife. A shiver ran across her lips. She blinked and looked straight at him with the eyes of a wounded child.

"No, nothing like that." Larry's grin showed perfect teeth. "Too much bother, isn't it? And expensive. Needlessly expensive, don't you think?"

"The priest costs nothing," he said.

"Ah, but the rest of it . . . well, we just don't want that." His hand crept onto Emilia's shoulder. "We want to keep it simple."

If the Episcopal minister at St. Paul's had performed Henry's wedding in Latin, it might have fooled any Catholic. And the church had been filled, the gowns had been beautiful. A bride deserved such a day.

"And the church would make us wait too long," Larry said. "This way, we just get the license and . . . we're very much in love."

Julie Wyatt's parents had held the reception at their home. Only members of the family had been invited. Henry said he had tried to persuade the Wyatts to make an exception and invite the Zorzolis. He said Mrs. Wyatt had told him if she did that, she'd wind up having to invite everybody.

"We want it to be next week, Pop."

She couldn't raise her stare. Neither could Beata. And he knew then what was wrong.

She was supposed to be a professor, like her grandfather, someone everybody would respect. Women taught in America, even at universities. And she was such a fine student, always making the best grades, though before he died, Papa Manfro had said she was lazy, too willing to find the easy way, maybe too smart for her own good. But The Professor had been too demanding, everyone agreed on that, especially when Barnard College sent Emilia a special letter that said she could go there to study history and that she would not have to pay the full tuition. Barnard College did not think she was lazy. August had wanted her to go to Henry's college in Montclair, so she would be close to home, but Henry had said turning down a scholarship to Barnard was as crazy as trying to fly to the moon.

So she took the train every morning into Manhattan, then a subway to the campus. She came home every night the first year, but some nights the second year and this year she called to say she had to stay with friends, she had to use the library or share notes or study in groups because that was what her professors made her do. August had worried about her then, and so had Beata. But their daughter made such good grades, she seemed so happy.

She was supposed to be a professor. She would soon be someone's wife. And though her body didn't show it yet, a child grew there.

From the peaceful look on Beata's face, he knew she had known about Larry Davis for a long time, that Emilia had kept few secrets: the two women were still so close, nothing, not even this, could drive them apart.

"He is not a Catholic?"

"Well no," Larry told him. "But, of course, any children we might have would be raised as Catholics."

That big smile again. They had prepared this, these three, they had sat down together and had gone over everything. Because they were afraid of him, his own wife and daughter. It stabbed at his insides. He drew a breath, let it out slowly. It didn't matter what he said, one of them would have an answer.

Larry told him not to worry about how the new couple would live. They would take an apartment in Manhattan. In fact, they had already found it. It was cute, his daughter said. In a safe neighborhood. Larry's parents would pay the rent, they were rich enough for that and for putting food on the table and buying furniture and for any emergencies that might come up.

The baby was probably an emergency to Larry's parents.

"Your parents know, then?"

"Of course. Father's delighted, says it will settle me down."

Then everyone knew. He was the last one to be told. He had hoped to be the first. His uncle the mayor had always been the first person anyone in the village went to: they trusted him. August leaned on his elbows. "You can live here, in Paterson. She should be close to her mother, in this time."

"They come to us on the weekends," Beata said.

"And it'll save me all that commuting," Emilia told him, "so I'll have more time to study." She couldn't keep her smile. Her eyes got hard and darker: she saw in his face that he knew about the baby. She lowered her stare. "This doesn't mean I won't get my degree, Pop."

He glanced at Beata. Her eyes were shut: she was praying. He forced a smile. "No, of course."

His wife's lips quivered again, then her face got soft. And when Emilia looked up, her eyes were as trusting as the day he took her to the doctor's office and the doctor scared her even more than the pain in her throat when he told her she would have to have her tonsils out. The doctor kept tropical fish in a big aquarium in his office. August told her that a doctor who took such good care of small fish would take special care with children. She watched the fish and their beauty made her stop crying. Years later, while she was still a little girl, she found out Dr. Varocco had died. August told her the doctor was old, it was natural for him to die. She said she knew that. She said she was crying for the fish.

She stepped around the desk and put her cheek against his. "I love you, Pop."

He put a hand to her head, held her face close, and for a moment it felt like Father's Day, his little girl hugging him and Henry standing there with a present and a handshake that would become an embrace, and Beata at the edge of the table, rocking on her heels, so pleased with the love in her kitchen. He couldn't make the feeling last, he kept seeing his daughter's naked body next to Larry, kept counting the nights she hadn't come home, and he remembered the women on Ellis Island, women who had made their clothes as neat as possible as if to find the courage to do what in Italy they could never have done: ask a man to marry. Three women had asked him. Each for the same reason: America took families first, single women last. One woman had offered herself to him, anything he wanted, it would be all right, she only meant to please him, and if she did, perhaps he would want her to go on pleasing him for the rest of their lives. He had never seen her before. He said no and he never saw her again. But he heard sounds that night, leaking through thick cold walls, sounds of a would-be bride using sex to satisfy a man and the rules of America. There had been times in his own bedroom when that woman's face appeared in the dark, her smile so brave he didn't feel he had the right to wish her away. He patted his daughter's cheek and told her he loved her.

Something had happened to Larry Davis's face. Without the smile, he looked kind. The baby would love this man. August stood and held out his hand.

The smile came back, but August ignored it and let the young man pump his hand. As if afraid something could still go wrong, Beata ushered the lovers out of the office, telling them to get the license and the blood tests, and to be home by six o'clock, fresh veal would be ready and it lost its flavor if it had to be reheated.

"Better warmed over, no?" He sat at his desk. "More tender."

From the doorway, she waved the back of her hand at him. "They have good teeth."

He was too old for her. The sixteen years that separated them in age had become like thirty. He was too old for the mill. A younger man would make it a success. The older he got, the younger everyone else became, and more and more, his thoughts were being haunted by images of a faceless boy on the hills of Avella, as if the further he got from his childhood, the more he needed to return to it. He was sure he would see that boy's face one day, and that face would be his.

"So beautiful, both of them." Beata walked to the chair and picked up her purse. "Like in a magazine."

He was too old for his daughter as well. A younger father would have kept a closer eye on her. He was too old to be part of Henry Trent's new life. Married six years and still no baby? And still so skinny. His wife, who now taught in another high school, the one in Willowbend, could not cook well enough to fatten him up? A fine home in Ringbrook, not four miles from the mill, but he rarely stopped by—"I'm just so tied up at the office, but then, you know how it is when you run your own business." August stared at the file with Ernie Galli's name on it, but lacked the strength to draw it toward him. "Tonight, I can be home early."

She put down her purse, stepped in back of him, put her arms around him, the side of her face to the top of his head. "Don't worry. They will be happy."

He could feel her smile. He decided to believe her.

1962

"Pop-Pop, it's leaking on me."

She stood on the wooden steps he had built for her, so she could reach the pots on the table and help him with the flowers. Water from the drain hole in a clay pot dripped off the wood onto her yellow overalls, staining them with specks of soil. At least she had changed out of her church clothes. Still, her grandmother would be furious. At him.

He put down his watering can, set the pot on the concrete squares that served as a floor out here. He stood up too fast, his head felt light. He leaned against the table. "We blame the roses. They take too much water."

"Not that much," she said.

It made him smile. Only six years old and she knew not to rub the stain, that would only grind the dirt into her clothes. Only six and she knew about roses.

He had built this greenhouse for Beata, to give her a place to garden in winter, to let her keep things alive and blooming in the cold. To give her hope. She had never set foot in it. It was two-by-fours and clear plastic that came in a roll and lasted only a year and had to be restapled to the simple frame each spring. She said it was an eyesore.

But it worked. He proved that to her the first year, growing bell peppers inside when there was snow on the ground. The day he brought the first pot into the kitchen to show her the little white blossoms on the young plants, she just shrugged and told him he was lucky. She told him bell peppers gave him gas. The peppers didn't survive that winter—the weight of snow tore the plastic, ice had gotten inside—but he didn't tell her that. He told her he had given the peppers to his workers at the mill. He told her he had eaten one himself and how delicious it had been and how he had not gotten gas. He began growing roses after that. A neighbor had told him roses were almost impossible to kill, all they needed was a lot of water and brutal pruning. The neighbor had been right. August grew roses. They were beautiful. After a fresh snow, he liked to set a pot or two outside for a moment and see the wonder of a rose in bloom on the pure white ground. Those winter roses were the most beautiful.

He grew the roses for his mother and for his daughter, to keep the two women alive in his heart.

"Want me to finish the rest?" Louise reached for the watering can she knew was too heavy for her, he had told her enough times. "The pink ones look thirsty."

The pink ones were Tiffany roses. He had thought of planting them along the back of the yard, where the fig tree cast its shade. Such a big tree, so few figs. He didn't have the courage to ask his wife if he could cut it down. He pulled the watering can back across the table. "We finish together. Get the drops."

She climbed down her steps and found the squeeze bottle of plant food under the table. "Can I do it?"

"You count this time?"

She rattled off numbers in Italian and when she got to *undici*, eleven, he held up his hand and she stopped. She had her mother's smile, so broad with pride. He slid a pot toward her. She aimed the bottle upside down, then glanced at him out of the corner of her eye. "Now?"

He sat in the slat chair, squinted to convince her he was watching, then he nodded. She started feeding the dark drops into the soil, counting each one. So careful with her work. In this room of so much beauty, she was the real wonder.

How could a father not want her? He would never understand

Larry Davis. He didn't want to. He would never forgive him. And he would never forgive his daughter.

"It was that car," Beata had said. "I knew it wasn't safe the first time he made me ride in it."

It was the car. It was Emilia, too.

"He left it in a tow-away zone, with the keys in the ignition." His daughter had put the baby to sleep in the crib that still stood in the old nursery off the kitchen. The walls had needed new yellow paint then. His daughter had needed to come home. "That's how I know. He's not coming back, Pop."

He had gotten his degree and then another one and then had gone to work for his father, overseeing the making of screws— "For sheet metal," Mr. Davis had explained during a tour of the plant, "and we're the only company in the world making these"— and it was a good job, with good pay, enough to move to a better apartment, and still it wasn't enough for Larry. Not even his mother knew where he went, or why. She said he might be "trying to find himself." Mr. Davis said his son was "a damned bum."

Emilia had less than a full year to make up for her degree. She enrolled at Henry's college in Montclair, but after two months, she dropped all her courses and signed up for an art class. She stopped going to that class a month later. But she kept drawing. Soon she was painting: fields with nothing growing in them, then old buildings, crumbling, neglected, but none of these ever pleased her. Finally, she found faces in Paterson to paint, old black women who still did laundry in the bathtub or in kettles on the stove, old black men who relived the past each day with cheap wine. One man, her favorite study, had been a musician with a name August could not help remembering: Silky. "He said he could still play his trumpet," she had announced at dinner, "if he only had a good set of false teeth." She didn't cry about Larry, except in her paintings.

Mr. Davis sent money every month. She put most of it in the

bank, taking out only for necessities and for gas to drive all over the city in that little sports car with its twin bug eyes. She took her two-year-old baby along, though Beata wanted to keep the child in the house—with her, a new playmate—and argued that it wasn't safe to cart an infant around the slums. What if she caught a disease? But Louise loved the outings, especially those to Garrett Mountain, a slice of wilderness against the hills of Willowbend. Louise loved the car. Now the only reminders it had ever existed were the oil stains at the head of the driveway.

The wrecker had told August it would cost $750 to fix the damage to the front end, and more than that to get the car running again. It would cost $25 to let the wrecker junk the car. August stood by in the wrecking yard, making sure the men did what they had promised. When the car was dismantled, fenders thrown on one heap, the chassis on another, he left. He told Louise the car had died in the same accident that had taken her mother's life.

She had left the baby home that day. The policemen said she must have been going over seventy down the hill from Willow-bend to Ringbrook. Snake Hill, they called it. At that speed on that hill, they said, she had to hit something. She hit an old abandoned gas station across from a truck yard. If she had hit one of those trucks or another car, if she had hit a tree or anything living, if she had hit a telephone pole or anything that might have hurt or even inconvenienced anyone, then it might have been an accident.

"Next one, Pop-Pop. Come on, you're so slow."

"Not slow"—he slid another pink rose toward her—"only careful."

The church was satisfied it had been an accident. The priest who had conducted the burial at the new Catholic cemetery near the river had been too sad, too eager for the opportunity of such a tragedy—young woman in the prime of life, a baby dependent on her—as if this were not only proof of God's mysterious will, but proof, too, of the reason priests existed. He made a long speech, the kind the mayor of Avella would have been proud of. He never mentioned the car.

It was the car. It was Emilia, too.

"Well, you better water that one." With her perfect little hand, she pointed to the pot she had just finished. "Or the drops will burn the roots."

He put the pot on the floor and brought the watering can to it. A car pulled up the driveway. She stopped counting the drops and backed down her steps. In the doorway, her arms lifted and fell with a quick breath. She spun and thrust the bottle into his hands. "Pop-Pop, he's here."

She ran.

The car had fins. The name in chrome on the fender read *Dart*. The top of a beachball showed through the passenger's window. Henry Trent caught the little girl in his arms. Still so skinny: he picked at food like a bird too anxious to fly to be bothered with eating. From the car, he took a paper sack and sent her into the house with it. As soon as she disappeared, he took a pinwheel from the seat and brought it to the greenhouse. "Okay to give her this?"

He nodded, then watered the pink rose. "You get red all over, like a langusta."

"Julie had to go to a special teachers' convention in Atlantic City, so we thought we'd make a vacation out of it."

"The boy is with his mother?"

Henry shook his head and lit a cigarette. "Asleep in the backseat, totally exhausted. The convention ends Tuesday, and I had to get home to open the office tomorrow, so Julie'll take the bus back up." He fingered the small pink petals. "These are beautiful."

"Not right to leave your wife alone. You're the boss, take more time off." He started putting drops on the next potted rose. "It goes fast."

Beata came out of the house with a bowl filled with saltwater taffy, each piece wrapped in shiny foil. "Three pounds he brings.

He helps eat it, then." She glanced around the yard. "Where's the boy?"

"In the car," August told her. "Quiet, he sleeps."

Louise ran to the greenhouse and the pinwheel turning in the breeze. The colors made her eyes brighten. "Is that for me?"

"Actually, I happen to know your grandfather has a weakness for pinwheels." Henry bent on a knee beside her, waited for her smile to start shrinking, then: "Actually, sweetheart, it's for you."

She thanked him, she hugged him, she took the pinwheel and thanked him again with a kiss. She showed the toy to Beata, who blew on it to make it turn faster. The taffy got passed around. Even Henry had one.

"Mr. Layton will be in to see me tomorrow." Thin fingers cupped the cigarette. "He'll want to know."

Mr. Layton was a builder. He wanted to tear down Zorzoli and build something better. August set the bottle on the table and moved the pot to the floor. "No business in front of children."

His wife sighed, took Louise by the hand, led her to a round table in the yard. Henry watched them dig into the bowl of taffy. "It's a losing proposition, you'd be better off selling out."

"I make a profit."

"Once. And that was only a profit on paper, because we accelerated your depreciation."

"Too hot for business today." He watered the rose. "Louise, get him a cold drink."

"Nonna do." Beata patted the girl's cheek, then disappeared inside the house.

"I don't want a drink."

"Too late, she brings it."

"Louise," Henry said, "run inside and tell her I don't want anything to drink. And tell her to stay in there, where it's cool."

The screen door slapped shut. August stared at the sun bouncing off the white car. "You keep the boy in an oven."

"The windows are open." He lit another cigarette. "Please,

113

listen to me. Layton's offering top dollar. You could retire in luxury now."

"Retirement killed Ernie Galli, no?"

Henry blew cigarette smoke at his shoes. "You'll never get a better offer."

"Good." It tasted sweet, like that one profit that one year: not figures at the bottom of a ledger, but a sign. And he remembered Ernie Galli's funeral, how sad everyone was: here was a man who had worked all his life, every day, and now, when he had the chance to enjoy himself—he was planning a trip back to Italy—he dropped dead on the sidewalk, scattering the mail he had gone out to get. Mama Manfro, who had prayed she might die in the middle of mass, had the right kind of death: she never retired from her kitchen, they found her slumped over dead at her table, a fresh pot of minestrone on the stove, bread rising in her oven. Everyone was dying, it seemed. Even the mill. "Zorzoli is not for sale."

He drew on the cigarette and said nothing.

At his car, standing on tiptoes to a side window, her pinwheel turning lazy spiked circles, Louise chewed taffy and peered in at the sleeping boy on the backseat.

"Only two years apart." Henry was smiling now. "A shame they don't see more of each other." He touched August's elbow. "I have your birthday present in the trunk."

"Next month, not now."

"I know, but Julie said to give them to you today. She's afraid they'll get broken."

He shrugged and followed Henry, who wore long pants and a shirt even to the beach. He put a hand on his granddaughter's head, then reached in and touched the boy's dark hair. Such long eyelashes. Four years old, but not big. At least he wasn't skinny like his father. His feet had sand on them. In a whisper, he told Louise, "A little angel, no?"

The trunk opened. Inside, old photos, framed in wood. Two were of Master Dye & Finishing when it was still called that.

Three were of the new mill, and one of these had August, Beata, Emilia, and Louise standing in the lot in front of the main door. He picked up that picture first, held it for a moment, then lowered it for the girl to see. "Your mother. Beautiful, no? Like you."

She took the picture and kept staring at it. August set the others on the grass near the walk. He hugged Henry. "I put them up tomorrow, on my wall, next to you."

He held on to the skinny man until the tears he felt had eased. For the first time in years, he felt good about Henry. He had a strong marriage, and he was lucky to have a brother who could be a partner, and a son to leave everything to. Henry would be all right now. "You stay for dinner."

"Can't." He stepped back, closed the trunk gently. "Have to get him home and in the tub."

"We have a tub."

"All his clean clothes are at home. Besides"—he lit another cigarette—"I'm beat, too." He got keys from his pocket. "I'll tell Layton you're still considering."

"No matter. I don't change my mind."

Henry frowned, then nodded. He kissed Louise, slid behind the wheel, started the engine. The white car backed down the driveway. It glinted in the street, then rolled away, its fins vanishing behind the trees.

"You get my picture sticky from the taffy," he told her. "Inside for a rag."

She ran into the house. The sun burned his neck. He stared at the faces of his women in the photograph. Beata looked happy. Louise could only squint that day. Emilia had lost weight, and all the feeling in her face was gone. A son would have had more courage. A son would have fought back.

"Here." Louise put a dish towel in his hand. "But the only smudge on there is from you, when you pointed to Mommy." She turned on a heel of her open-toed shoes and marched toward the greenhouse.

He cocked an eyebrow, put fingers to his chin to hide a grin, then he wiped the glass clean. "Eh, you leave the toy on the ground?"

"I can't play now, I have to do the drops." And she was inside the plastic-covered shed, picking up the bottle, climbing her stairs to the table.

He left the picture on top of the others, picked up her pinwheel, walked to the doorway of the greenhouse. "Go change to good clothes. We see the mill."

"Why?"

"It is time you learned about my silk."

"But the roses, we have to finish."

He smiled and handed her the pinwheel. "Today, *cara*, we start."

1973

It sat on a block of its own, between Market Street and Park Avenue, the front of it facing away from the river. Made of gray brick that the years had tinged yellow, it was called "the old mill" by students for the same reason Emilia and her friends had called it "the sweatshop": it looked like the mills nearby. When Henry went there, it was newer and nicer than the old school in the center of the city. Back then, students never called this place anything but Eastside High.

Running the length of the football field, cement steps that served as bleachers still held the warmth of the afternoon sun. The steps and the field were called Bauerle Stadium, named after a student who had drowned at the New Jersey shore back even before Henry's time. A rich uncle had built the stadium as a memorial, and in that way, Eastside High would always be what it had originally been: a cemetery, rows of headstones August had walked by now and then on his way home from Master Dye & Finishing to Mrs. DeMatto's upstairs room.

He opened the program, offered it to his wife. "You can see from here?"

She nodded and ran a finger down the list of names, lingering on *Louise Davis*, as that finger had years ago, when the name read *Emilia Zorzoli*. She straightened her hat and stared at the field. What she saw down there was anyone's guess, but what she saw made her smile.

The music started. Henry aimed his small camera. People behind him asked him to sit down. He said, "I'll go down to the field for a clearer shot," and he left. His wife and son could not be here. The boy was a baseball player, an all-star again, this time in a league named after Babe Ruth, and he could not miss the game. The boy and his mother would not have come even if there had been no baseball. Henry made excuses for them, but August knew from the way Henry said those excuses that years ago he had stopped telling his family about the Zorzolis. Julie Trent was probably grateful for that. But Henry cared. That was enough.

Marching together in caps and gowns, the graduates filed across the grass toward chairs near a platform, where school officials waited. So many students. He wouldn't recognize the few from Little Notch: he didn't know the children anymore. This would be the last class at Eastside High with children from Little Notch in it. The school district had been changed to go along with the new political districts: Little Notch belonged to Ringbrook now. The new high school there looked like a big garage.

He couldn't find her among the students. He wished he had brought the glasses the doctor made him wear. The glasses gave him headaches. He blinked, but everything far away stayed fuzzy.

"Looks so pretty, no?" Beata said.

He squinted, then nodded. She sighed and pulled his glasses from her purse. Without a word, she put them in his hand. Today was not a day for her usual lecture about how he was not Rodolfo Valentino—and never had been if the truth be known—so no one was looking at his face, he could wear the glasses and actually see something beyond his fingertips and people would not think less of him: "They see how old you walk, you think you fool them with no glasses?" Today she was kinder. He put on the glasses.

In the front row, near the platform, Louise looked more beautiful than any other girl in the class. "She is like your twin," he said, but his wife just elbowed him and told him to be quiet. A moment later, though, she hooked her arm through his and leaned against him. He patted her hand, drawing slow even breaths, hoping he would not cough, because the coughing hurt these days, there was never a time anymore when the coughing did not hurt.

The music stopped, the speeches started. Every now and then, the microphone squealed, as if angry at the words. The guest speaker was a famous writer who had grown up nearby. Pockmarks spoiled his face. He gripped the podium as if he needed it for support. He wrote spy novels and movies. Louise said he used "exotic locales" and never mentioned Paterson or New Jersey in anything he wrote. He talked about freedom and responsibility.

August fanned his face with his hat. He wasn't hot, he was nervous. Louise had not let him hear the speech she would be making tonight. "I don't want anyone to know what I'll be say-ing," she had told him, "because if I can't surprise them, I'll lose all my courage." She was the valedictorian, unlike her mother, who had not worked hard enough to be the best. He squeezed Beata's hand. "You remind her to speak loud?"

"Shh."

He kept fanning his face. Mr. Davis would have been here had he lived. Mrs. Davis wasn't coming. She hadn't seen her grand-daughter in years. Mrs. Davis was always too busy to cross the Hudson. Larry wasn't coming either. He had come back once. Bearded, in old denim, his long hair uncombed, he had come to the house with his teen-age "roommate," a girl more drugged and empty-headed than he was, if such a thing could be possible. He told Louise who he was. She was fourteen then. All she said was, "I thought you would be younger." August told him never to come back. Larry just smiled—he still had that grin, no beard could hide it—and picked up his knapsack and walked away in an easy gait that matched the wave he threw back at the porch before he turned the corner. He was up in Canada now, he and the young girl or perhaps another one younger still. They were living "off the land," growing their food, building their shelter, refusing to use electricity. It was, according to both of them, the good, pure, simple life. One good, pure, simple winter would finish those two off.

The famous writer got loud applause. The superintendent of schools announced the awards. Louise got one for English. She got the last award, too, the one for scholarship. She took her place at the podium. No notes. All these people watching her, and no notes. A shiver ran down August's spine.

"The program is wrong," she said, but she did not explain, and people looked at each other, turned the pages of their programs to find the error, shook their heads. August shut his eyes and prayed for her. It got better. Full of caring, she talked about the school and her classmates, about this being a time of discovery for them, a time for them to learn who they were. It was important, she said, to begin by learning who they had been. She paused long enough to find who she was looking for on the cement steps, then she smiled and said, "The program should say, I am Louise Zorzoli Davis."

He did not try to stop his tears. He took off his glasses. Beata threw a kiss toward the platform, then led the applause. Like a cheerleader, Henry was clapping with his hands over his head, but the rest of the people had made more noise for the famous writer.

The roll call for the diplomas came next, and though the principal had asked parents and friends to hold their applause until the final diploma had been handed out, Beata clapped when they called Louise's name. Finally, the graduating class stood and sang a song: "You'll Never Walk Alone." Emilia's class had sung a different song, but it sounded the same.

Henry came back to his seat, pulling the film cartridge from his camera. "She's something, isn't she?"

"Anything happens," August told him, "you treat her like your son." He made Henry promise he would.

The music started again, and the students walked back the way they had come, tassels switched to the other side of their caps, diplomas in hand. People on the steps began to stand. Those nearby followed a man who said he knew where the punch bowl was.

"You like the speech?" Beata put his glasses back in her purse, dabbed at his eyes with a handkerchief. "She works so long to make you proud."

"The best speech," he told her, and he meant it. He wished his uncle the mayor could have heard it, and hoped perhaps he had. "And you?"

She looked down at the empty field. That smile came back to her face. She spoke in her native tongue, for these words were too important to make a mistake with: "She had only to be born to make me proud of her."

He took her arm and led her up the aisle.

It had been closed for going on six years. He had just passed his seventy-second birthday then, and it had been hard for him to go to work every day, but it had been harder still to find workers with experience, let alone expertise in the dyeing of silk. And it had felt good to close it himself, not anything like the time the state came to shut down Master Dye & Finishing. And it felt good to come here, especially in the evenings, when the air was cool and the river was night-quiet. He found the slat chair leaning against the mill. He sat where he always sat, on the side by the river.

The last thing he had done before closing the mill had been to have men come and put a chain-link fence all around it, to keep out the vandals, to protect the property like wrapping on a present, a present for Louise, when she was ready. That fence said there was something of value here.

"I knew you'd be here," she said. "Without your jacket."

Her voice startled him. And suddenly, the night air felt too cool. He put on the jacket she handed him. "I didn't lock the gate?"

"It was locked," she told him. "I have my own key, remember?"

"You should be at the parties, with your friends."

"I'll go later. I just wanted to drive you home. Nonna Do will be worried."

He nodded. She looked even more beautiful in the fading light. "Someday, they tear it down"—he pointed to new malls being built across the not-so-busy new highway, which was not-so-new anymore—"for that."

She rubbed his shoulders. "They won't tear it down."

"Nobody wants silk anymore."

"It's not that, it's just that they can get it cheaper than we can make it. I explained that to you, remember? Hong Kong, Taiwan?"

"Canada," he said, nodding. Then he sighed. "I pay taxes to keep this. For you. Maybe it's a bad idea."

"Well, you can always sell me your share if you want to get rid of it."

He smiled, took her hand, rubbed the back of it with his thumb. She could have gone to any college, but she chose to go to William Paterson over the hill in Willowbend. She said it was a better school now than the one Henry had gone to in Montclair. She said she would worry too much about her grandmother if she couldn't be home every night after classes. She never said she would worry too much about him. He loved her even more for never saying that. "Stay away from the boys tonight. No trouble."

"I'll be fine."

He waved, erasing her words. "What your mother said, too."

"I'm not her, Pop-Pop." She squeezed his hand so hard it hurt. "Now stop this." Then she put her cheek down on the top of his head. "Come on, I'll take you home."

"I ride the bus, like always."

"The senior partner will get in the car and ride home with the junior partner. That's final."

Two days before he closed the mill, he had papers drawn to make Louise a partner. The fat little lawyer Henry had found worked fast. He did a good job with the trust papers, and he didn't charge much. And she loved the idea, she loved the title. Too much, he thought. So, whenever she called herself "the junior partner," he tested her: Did she know what good silk looked like when it came in? Did she know not only what good dyes looked like, but also smelled like? Did she know when the dye box was too hot, when the trucks needed tires, did she know about payrolls and accounts receivable, accounts past due, and how to keep the workers interested in their jobs—not happy, interested? Did she know enough to be the junior partner? But tonight he was too tired to test her. He patted her hand, folded the chair, put it back against the side of the mill, where he would be able to find it in the dark.

She buttoned his jacket. "You need a haircut."

"No barbers anymore."

"I'll do it for you tomorrow, then. And a nice hot shave, too."

At the gate, he dug into his pants for the key, then stopped. "You lock it this time. For good luck."

She locked the gate. He got into the little car she had bought for herself from the money Henry paid her to type his letters, work she could do at home on Henry's Dictaphone. She was a good driver, the teacher at the high school said so. She loved her car. She kept it clean, inside and out, and she never let the driveway get stained by oil. By the time they reached the railroad tracks at the corner, he was asking her about silk.

The night bird's call sounded far away, but loud enough to wake him. He couldn't find his breath. Not even enough breath to cough. He reached out for Beata, but couldn't find her in the bed. Maybe his arms weren't working anymore. That scared him.

She would be all right. She had Louise. And Henry.

He stopped reaching out. He closed his eyes and waited.

He waited for the boy on the hills of Avella. He waited to see the boy's face.

The boy did not come.

A smokestack came instead. New brick. And the letters, perfectly white:

Z
O
R
Z
O
L
I

His name looked good there. Better than good. It looked right.

Book
Four

Silk City
Blues

11

"E presto."

But Louise told her it wasn't early, it was almost 9:30, the nightclub needed checking on—the assistant manager was given to headaches that made him snap at customers—and Phil needed to be dropped off. It was time to go.

He thanked Mrs. Zorzoli for the meal. She shrugged as if he shouldn't mention anything so insignificant as homemade lasagne, homemade bread, homemade rum cake. "Louisa, the hall closet, you look for Pop-Pop's coat so he doesn't freeze."

"He has a sports jacket."

"Take the coat."

"He won't need it, the car has a heater."

"He catches cold, it's your fault."

"How can he catch cold if he goes from the house to the car and then into the house?"

"Maybe it's too warm in here, the air out there fools his body."

From the sound of it, the two of them could have gone on for hours about coats and cars and colds or any number of things that were supposed to concern him, and yet not once would either of them need to speak directly to him or ask his opinion. It was as if he were watching a play in which he had the starring role, but it was not a speaking part. It made him smile. He took the old woman's hands, still warm from the stove. "I'll be fine."

"I'll lock you in," Louise said.

"Nonna do."

"All right, but don't stand in the doorway and let all the heat out." She put on her heavy wool coat, aimed a whisper at him. "She has to watch her company leave, otherwise it's bad luck." She kissed the old woman. "Watch from the window, okay?"

"Maybe he needs the bathroom before the drive."

"He lives only ten minutes away."

"That air tricks his bladder, no?"

Louise pulled on gloves. A growl escaped her mouth. "Well, do you want to use the bathroom or not?"

He shook his head.

"Some food to take home?" Mrs. Zorzoli turned halfway toward her kitchen. "You have it for lunch tomorrow."

"We have to go"—she slid a coat sleeve back, checked her watch—"now."

"Only takes a minute."

He was laughing, but softly. He kissed the old woman's cheek—it was smooth and held a chill—and thanked her again. She held his face in both her hands—"You make sure she drives nice"—then let go and stood back from the door so Louise could open it.

It was night-cold. He rubbed his arms while he waited for her to unlock the car. The seat was so cold it made him shiver.

And Nonna Do was standing in the doorway, waving.

He waved back.

Louise took side streets down to Ringbrook Avenue, then aimed her Datsun up the long hill. She was going to drive without saying a word, she had nothing left to say to him. But she looked angry. Hard light from an oncoming car painted the angles of her face, stealing its beauty, aging her somehow, making her look like the evil witch in those old cartoons. Then the headlights were gone and in the darkness she got young again.

"Stop staring at me," she said. "I can't drive with somebody staring at me."

He glanced out the window, looked for ducks on the pond. She downshifted to make it up the last part of the hill, then she steered the car to the curb and stopped in front of his house. The lights were on. No Corvette in the driveway. Uncle Chuck's Mercedes was there instead. He had backed in again, he always backed in. It used to anger Dad to see his brother's car pointed at the street, ready to leave even when arriving. Uncle Chuck claimed it was safer that way: backing out of the drive was a good way to have an accident.

He found the door latch near the arm cushion. "I don't suppose you'd like to come in."

She kept silent, her dark eyes focused on something down the street.

He opened the door, turned to get out, then turned again and shut the door. "Me either."

Her head spun toward him.

"I can't ride in cars," he told her, "with somebody staring at me."

Her laugh didn't last long. The motor sputtered. She fed in more gas, but it stalled. She slapped the wheel, turned the key, pumped the gas pedal, the headlights dimming with the whir of the starter.

"Turn your lights off," he said. "More power from the battery that way."

She left the headlights on and kept trying to restart the engine. "I may not be able to drop you off back here until after midnight."

"I can call a taxi." A red indicator light flickered in the speedometer. "Sounds like a dirty carburetor."

She stared at him, a curse just in back of her lips. She turned the key to Off, punched off the headlights. Whatever she was going to say came out as a sigh.

"If you have a flashlight, I could take a look under the hood."

"Why don't you just get out and go inside?"

The house looked warm, and he could imagine Uncle Chuck pacing in the den, Mom leaning back from a kitchen counter, saying didn't she just hear a car pull up outside and "Chuck, would you go check?" and any moment a drape would be pulled back, a head would appear in a window, and a whole conversation would start in there, about did either of them know anyone who drove a car like that and was that really Phil in the passenger's seat and should Uncle Chuck go out to see or should Mom call the police because neither of them recognized that car and it was late and it couldn't be a neighbor's car, all the neighbors knew the law didn't allow them to park on the streets of Ringbrook after nine o'clock, but what if it was a guest of a neighbor, wouldn't it be embarrassing to have the police come then, and maybe it was Phil after all, maybe he was taking his time saying thanks to whoever brought him home, maybe he would get out of that car any moment and everything would be settled.

He was sweating. "I could walk around for a while, I guess."

"Without a coat? You'll freeze." She pumped the gas pedal twice, put her hand to the ignition key. "Just go inside, they're waiting for you."

He couldn't look at the house. "Do you still have the pinwheel?"

Her hand stayed on the key, but her shoulders seemed to soften, rolling inward. Light through the slush-streaked windshield made her eyes look wet. She turned the key. The engine started. "I have to get to the mill," she said.

He shut his eyes, slouched in the seat, pointed up the street. "It's that way."

"Now old Silky finally got enough money for a car, but the state won't let him drive." The fat man smiling into the microphone had thick short fingers. He didn't look like a piano player, he looked like a man who moved pianos for a living. "Finally got enough for life insurance, nobody willing to sell him a policy. Got enough now to buy champagne for all the sweet young ladies, only by the time he gets them primed and ready, he can't remember what to do with the pump."

The audience loved it. The lean man on the stool in the center of the stage either didn't hear what the piano player was saying or didn't care. He held his trumpet in his lap and waited for the patter to end. The whites of his eyes looked yellow. Most of his hair was gone. What remained was the color of dull silver.

"But he can still play that horn, can't he?" The piano player fingered a chord, and when the applause died down, he added a lead-in to a slow, thumping tune, joined by the bass player and the drummer, who had traded his brushes for sticks. "Anybody who remembers this one is too old to be up so late."

The trumpet rose slowly, bony hands guiding it to moistened lips. He didn't seem to take a breath, he just shut his eyes and played. The sound, familiar to everyone by now after more than an hour of listening, still came as a shock: it jumped out of the horn raw and tore through Phil's body, tightening his insides, making him wince from the piercing sharpness, but instantly something smooth ran in behind the first note, blanketing him with unexpected warmth, pulling him toward the next note, another bullet, and the whole thing started over again. That sound had the same effect on everyone else in the room. Silky Odell wasn't playing his trumpet, he was shooting it, and those in the path of that sound became casualties of his talent, the willing victims of a one-man firing squad, an old man with an old horn and enough ammunition to bring an army to its knees.

"They're going to try to record him again." Louise took the empty stool beside him at the bar. "But even with the new equipment, it won't be same as hearing him live."

He nodded and kept listening. Then: "It's like being wounded."

He could feel her smile on his neck. She had the bartender

bring him a refill: King's Ransom, on the rocks, the scotch Dad had taught him to love. He couldn't remember the last time he had had it.

"Did you call your mother?" she said. "I'm going to make enough trouble for your family, I don't want her to think I kidnapped you."

He smiled, but he didn't like it. She made him feel like a child. He sipped scotch and studied the light bouncing off the trumpet. "You're really going to sue him?"

"I'll give him a chance to set the record straight so your mother doesn't have to carry this lie to her grave." She brushed hair from her face, got off the stool. "But your uncle won't apologize, he doesn't have that in him. He really is a first-class shit."

He laughed and swallowed scotch at the same time. It hurt. *"You really are a perfect ass sometimes, Chuck."* Dad had slammed down the phone: something about calling in a margin account when it wasn't necessary, making a client sweat when he didn't have to. *"If you weren't my brother, I'd fire you."*

And she was right: Uncle Chuck couldn't apologize, not then, not now.

"You can use the phone in my office," she said.

"I called her."

The trumpet stopped playing and the fat man at the piano began to sing:

> "They got a downtown,
> ain't got no uptown,
> they got jails for the union Joes.
> They got strike breakers, head breakers,
> every kind of hurt maker,
> scare you right out of your clothes.
> Life here mean paying your dues,
> is how you get the Silk City Blues."

Mom had tried not to sound angry, but she was. She said Uncle Chuck had been "so anxious" to see him, it was "so unfair" to keep him waiting.

> "Got miles of freight tracks,
>   whole blocks of smoke stacks,
>   they got mills working all day long.
> They pay two dollar, each dyer,
>   twenty cash to boss liar,
>   nobody calling that wrong.
> Life here a batch of bad news,
>   is how you get the Silk City Blues."

Uncle Chuck said it was all right, it was even understandable—after all, people got their signals crossed now and then. He was sorry he had missed Phil at the office—"our office, Phil, and it's great to know you're back home where you belong"—and while he couldn't stay at the house and wait any longer, he was glad to hear Phil's voice and know he wasn't thousands of miles away anymore. He didn't ask where Phil was.

> "New York 'round the corner,
>   spit and you be there.
> Train leaving, I ain't on it,
>   only job I know is here—where
>   they got the Great Falls,
>   they got their city hall,
>   they got parks 'long the river run.
> They got white folk and black folk and
>   laws for both, it some joke,
>   you learn to laugh on the run.
> Best check the soles of your shoes,
>   is how you get the Silk City Blues."

Mom asked where he was. He didn't tell her the truth, he said he was at the new mall, looking around. She told him Sarah had called—"It sounded urgent"—and wasn't it "nice" that the two of them had run into each other—and so soon—why, it was an omen, wasn't it? "We had a nice long talk," Mom told him. She told him Sarah was doing "so well for herself." She told him Sarah was coming to dinner tomorrow and Ed was going to let Phil pick her up in the Corvette.

"Life here a batch of bad news,
is how you get the Silk City Blues."

He had his key, he told her, he would let himself in when he got home. He didn't ask why Ed wasn't there. He wondered if she couldn't face Uncle Chuck with Ed on her arm or if it had been Ed's decision to stay away. It wasn't that important, but he felt he should have asked. He said he loved her, then hung up the pay phone in the lobby. A young woman waiting her turn behind him pretended she hadn't overheard. He felt her staring at him when he turned to walk back to the bar. He felt her grinning.

No big finish, just a quiet trumpet getting softer, the stage lights dimming, the piano player speaking in a whisper: "Be back at midnight. Remember who loves you." Applause exploded in the middle of the final, fading chord. When the houselights came up, the stage was empty.

"I'll be leaving," Louise said, "right after I check backstage. You can stay if you like, we get a singles crowd for the late show." A corner of her mouth turned up, warping it. "You won't have any trouble finding a ride. Just tell the first woman you're attracted to that you went to Princeton."

"That doesn't work," he told her.

"In your case"—her mouth got softer—"I think it will."

She started past him toward the stage. He turned her by the elbow. "I went to Princeton."

Her arm went limp, her lips pressed together. But her stare stayed the same, eyes the color of warm chocolate making him want to look at something else, but not letting him. "You're right," she said, "it doesn't work."

And she was walking away, down the long bar and through the stage door. He couldn't stop smiling.

The last time he had tasted King's Ransom was after the funeral. He had planned to finish the bottle Dad kept in the dining-room cabinet. He had trouble finishing one drink. He had put the bottle back and locked the cabinet, and somehow that had felt more final than the burying.

He asked the bartender if he could have another.

"Sure," the tall man said, "but I can't put it on the house unless she's here to okay it."

Phil said he would pay.

12

The new aluminum siding didn't soften the peaks in the roof or the sharpness of the gables jutting into the night. It still looked like a Halloween house. And the post lantern near the front steps still didn't work.

He knocked on the door. A tall teen-ager opened it. Brucie was smiling. He was no longer scrawny, he had some bulk. His hair had been cut short, and impeccably neat, in the style of those politicians who preached moral gospel to get elected, then a few years later got thrown in jail for taking kickbacks. New Jersey was famous for them. He said, "Phil, it's great to see you," and he shook his hand. His voice sounded deeper. And welcoming. It had never been welcoming. He saw the Corvette in the driveway and his smile got bigger. "Nice wheels."

A young woman walked up the hall from the kitchen, spooning ice cream to her round mouth. She smiled. She was pretty.

"This is Amy. We're going together." He led her outside to look at the car. "Phil always was a cool dude."

The living room was the same. He sat on the sofa Mrs. Young called a love seat. It had belonged to her mother. Mr. Young had proposed marriage on it. Above it hung a large photograph in an ornate white frame: Sarah and Bruce when they were both children, backed by their parents. Mr. Young looked happy, not like the kind of man who, even when the picture was being taken, was well down the road to drinking himself to death.

He stared at porcelain birds on the nicknack shelf over the TV and waited for Sarah to come down the stairs, just as he had so many times so many years before. Why had he let Mom talk him into this? He should have refused. But he had slept late and she had been angry: it was bad enough that he had stood up his uncle last night, and now he didn't seem the least bit interested in the business documents she had saved for him to look at, and what on earth was he doing staying out so late when he needed his rest, and it wasn't a good idea to sleep all day, lazy people did that, and when she reminded him about Sarah and dinner, he didn't have the heart to say no.

"Why'd you get it with automatic?" Bruce shut the front door. "Better performance with a four-speed."

"It's not mine. Could you tell Sarah I'm here?"

"She knows. Her window's in front. The Princess sees everything."

She had probably always seen everything, every time he came.

"So, I heard you were kicking around out on the Coast." Bruce sat on the floor, pulled Amy next to him, stroked her neck with his hand. "Man, if I ever got that far, I'd never come back."

Phil smiled. "How's your mother?"

A laugh. "At Bingo, like always. You have to come over for dinner, she'd like that."

In the little silence, he waited for the old Brucie to surface, hoping for it, ready to slug the kid. But it wasn't going to happen. He felt cheated. "How's school?"

Awful, Bruce told him, now that football season was over, and he began describing the high school as if the two of them had been classmates: remember old Mr. Garner, well, last month . . .

Last night, Louise had been quiet, almost sulking when she drove him home. She told him she would let him know how things went with his uncle, if Phil wanted to know. He said he did. She said he should tell his mother the truth about Dad. He said he would. He said he wanted to see her again. She said he knew where the mill was, just drop by. He said, "Your grandmother, too." She said Nonna Do would like that, hardly anyone visited her anymore, all her friends were in nursing homes or dead. She said good-night and drove away.

Sarah came down the stairs, turned for the kitchen. "Oh, I didn't know you were here." She walked to him, beautiful in a charcoal-gray suit that Mom would love. She kissed him.

Bruce smiled and kissed Amy. "Anyway, you ought to go over and see some of your old teachers, cheer them up."

"I have some wine in the fridge." Sarah walked down the hall. "Be right back."

Her brother waited until she was in the kitchen, then he got up and drew Phil into the corner by the armchair. "I should tell you, she's going with this pro footballer. Might be trouble, you know?"

Phil nodded. "Thanks."

"Hey, no problem. Got to look after a friend, right?"

"Ready." She buttoned her coat, cradled the wine bottle to her chest. It was probably her favorite, Montrachet.

"You two have a great time," Bruce said. "I'll leave a light on." He looked ready to hug Phil. He shook his hand. Hard. "Really glad you're back."

Amy smiled and finished her ice cream.

Outside, Phil got keys from his pocket. "He's changed, hasn't he."

A burst of breath came out of her mouth as a cloud. She waited for him to open the car door. "He's still a brat."

She got in. She smiled. He shut the door and the courtesy light went out, she was barely visible now. He savored the moment. Then he got behind the wheel and the big engine roared. He slid one of Ed's old jazz tapes into the cassette player, knowing she would hate the music. He turned up the volume.

They were like army buddies with a lot of catching up to do. She "adored" what Mom had done with the living room. Mom took

the cue and began showing her everything, the two of them traips-
ing around the house, eyeing new furniture in new places, finger-
ing new drapes, admiring new paint and how the color matched
exactly the piping in the new throw cushions. Then they disappeared upstairs, their feet soft on the new carpet. Ed took a smile
and a drink into the den to watch a rerun of "The Dick Van Dyke
Show." It made him laugh. "Ever see this one? Buddy gets fired
and . . . "

Phil watched a few minutes, shared a few laughs. He went to
the phone at the stairs and called the mill. She wasn't there. The
phone book had no listing for Davis. It had one Zorzoli in it. On
the third ring, Nonna Do answered.

"This is Phil."

"Eh?"

"Phil Trent."

"Trent?"

"Henry's boy."

"Ahh. You catch cold last night?"

"No, I'm fine. Is Louise there?"

"In the shed, with the pots."

"Could you ask her to come to the phone?"

"No, she yells at me. She stays inside not much longer. She
calls you soon, all right?"

Footsteps on the stairs: Mom and Sarah had finished the tour
up there.

"Uh . . . I probably won't be here, tell her I'll call her back.
Thank you." He hung up and smiled at Mom.

"I might have wanted to talk to him," she said.

"Who?"

"Your uncle."

"I was making a call."

"Oh." She started for the kitchen, then turned. "I have to sign
those papers and get them to the office. Did you look at them
at all?"

He shook his head.

She shook her head. "He didn't want to leave them, you know. I asked him to, for your sake, so you'd know what was going on with the business."

"How about after dinner?"

"I would have signed them last night, if you'd been here. That would have made everything so much simpler."

"After dinner?"

She sighed and led Sarah into the kitchen. "Chuck draws the papers up himself, you know, without a lawyer. Henry always had a lawyer do it. Of course, I didn't sign anything then, I wasn't a partner." She laughed and bent to the oven. "Chuck calls me 'boss.' Isn't that cute?"

Sarah said that was cute.

Ed said, "Buddy's going to get rehired any minute now. Better hurry or you'll miss it."

Mom came out of the kitchen with a dish towel. "I never get to see my PBS programs anymore."

The phone rang. She picked it up before he could. "That's your uncle now. Hello? Why, yes, he is." She was about to hand him the phone when she squinted, pulled it back, and asked, "Who's calling?"

He took the phone out of her hand. "Hello?"

"Hi." Louise sounded tired. "You wanted to talk to me?"

"Uh . . . I did, yes."

"You don't now?"

He smiled at Mom, but her squint hadn't gone away. "Actually, we're about to have dinner."

"He wouldn't talk to me, you know. I couldn't get over there and his secretary kept me on hold all day."

"I'm sorry."

"So I don't have much to tell you," she said, "except the Christmas roses are almost ready. At least something's working out."

He stared at Mom, but she wasn't going to leave. He took the phone off the stand and pulled it into the hall closet, found the light chain.

"We'll be eating any second," Mom said.

He nodded and closed the door. Before Dad had an upstairs phone put in, every teen-age call Phil had made or answered had been from this closet, under this light, next to these coats. It made him smile. "Okay, I can talk now."

"Nonna Do made it sound urgent. How did your mother take the news?"

He swallowed stale closet air.

"You didn't tell her."

"I tried," he said. She hadn't wanted to talk about it. She told him she had gotten used to the pain and that he would, too. He told her there was no other woman. She smiled and asked him if he wanted two eggs or three and if he still liked them soft-boiled. "She's . . . difficult."

"She has to know. It isn't fair."

"I'll keep trying." He drew a quick breath. "Are you going to the club tonight? I could stop by later."

"I hadn't planned on it."

"I could come by your house, then. Might be pretty late, though."

"Why?"

"I . . . uh . . . have some papers to look at. Trent and Company stuff."

"No, why do you want to come over?"

"To see you."

There was a hard silence. When she spoke, it sounded as if she might be smiling. "I'm sort of seeing someone these days."

"Sort of?"

Someone knocked on the closet door. "Phil," Sarah said, "the wine?"

"What was that?" Louise asked.

| 141 |

"The wine steward."

"What?"

"We're very fancy. Look, you said 'sort of'?"

"Well, yes."

"Are you sort of seeing him tonight?"

"Well, no."

"Then can I come over later?"

"He wouldn't like that."

"He'll get over it."

She laughed, then cleared her throat. "I don't think you should. Really, it's not . . . well, this isn't what I had in mind, okay?"

He didn't say anything. He couldn't. He chewed the inside of his lip.

More knocking. "Phil, tell whoever it is you'll call her back." No wonder Sarah sounded angry: Mom had told her it was a woman on the phone. *Good.* "Your mother has to get the soufflé on the table. Now."

"I heard," Louise said. "It was sweet of you to call."

Sweet. *Shit.*

"Good-bye, Phil." And she hung up.

He pulled the light chain. Too hard: it ripped out of the socket. He would have to fix it in the morning. He left the chain in a coat pocket, came out of the closet, and replaced the phone. Ed was already at the table, a napkin tucked into the middle of his shirt and draped over his stomach. Sarah was pouring the wine. It was Montrachet.

"I would have done that," he told her.

She glared at him. "Sit. She's going to serve."

Mom carried the ceramic pot out with oven mitts. It steamed under her smile. She set the pot in the center of the table. "Your first home-cooked dinner in almost three years."

He could still taste the lasagne.

"It's so beautiful," Sarah said, "we should take a picture."

It was yellow specked with green, and so airy that the top threatened to crack off. Mom took off her mitts, picked up the serving knife. "Let's eat it before it falls." She gave the first helping to Sarah. The green specks were bits of spinach. She served Ed last. "I hope you didn't give out this number to . . . to some of the people you might have met on the road."

"Just one," Phil said, wishing the limp egg dish were her pot roast, wishing she had never experimented with gourmet recipes, there was no telling what she might cook up now. "But Fidel said he wouldn't call."

The name horrified her, visions of a dirty field worker with missing teeth and a leer clouded her eyes.

"Castro," he said.

Ed laughed with his mouth full. Sarah ping-ed her fork on her plate. "You shouldn't tease her like that. It's not funny."

It wasn't funny and the soufflé wasn't her pot roast and the dining room had a new ceiling, flecks of something shiny in the paint, like twinkling stars.

"I think you should look at those papers in the morning," Mom told him, "before you take them over to your uncle. That way, you and Sarah will have the rest of the evening to get . . . re-acquainted."

Sarah fed soufflé into her smile and said it was "scrumptious."

The living room was dark. Bruce had forgotten to leave a light on. He was in bed by now, she said. He was into weight lifting and claimed he needed extra sleep. But he was just lazy, she was sure of it. Her mother would be sound asleep. There was nothing to worry about. It would be better down here than up in her room: the bedsprings creaked.

He told her he had to go.

"Not yet." She put a hand between his legs, cupped him. She felt what was happening in her palm. It brightened her eyes. "Welcome home."

She kissed him. She unzipped him. She pulled him toward the love seat so she could sit while he stood. She freed him from his undershorts. She licked him. She took him in her mouth.

Reflected in the glass covering the family portrait, what looked like a face appeared on the stairs. A boy's face. It startled him, but only briefly. He grinned, and in a whisper, but loud enough for the stairs to hear—even if the stairs were empty, even if only the stairs heard, that would be enough—he said, "Suck harder."

The Princess said, "Mmmm," and sucked harder.

Her light was on. If her light had been off, he could have cut the engine and watched the house for a little while. But her light was on.

Maybe she was reading. Maybe she was studying up on greenhouse roses. Maybe she was on the phone with the man she was sort of going with.

Her light was on.

So he drove home.

13

Nothing had changed.

The old washer and dryer stood next to a cast-iron sink in one corner. The furnace took up most of the back wall. The wooden chest with his train set in it sat beside a lolly column. There were tools and an old cabinet holding paint cans at the far end, below the last remaining window, the one the masons left for ventilation when they came to brick up the others and stop water from seeping in and flooding the cellar. The old kitchen table stood against a side wall. Old pots and pans sat on it now, none of the lids matching. The mother-of-pearl top still sparkled.

He searched in back of a pile of lawn chairs for the metal file box. A tennis ball rolled out from under the clutter. It was gray and all its fuzz was gone. It couldn't be the same one he used to throw against these cement walls, practicing his grounders, practicing throwing perfect strikes into a square he had chalked on the wall. It still had some bounce in it. It had to be one of Mom's practice balls.

He rubbed the chill from his arms. Still so cold down here, the best part of the house in summer, the worst in winter. He found the file box near a carton of old clothes by the gas main. Inside: copies of tax returns going back ten years, a deed to a piece of property at the shore that had been sold long ago, an outdated list of stocks and bonds in a blue pamphlet called *My Personal Affairs* some bank had given away to its customers, a new box of paper clips, unopened. But no will.

He checked again, just to be sure. The furnace kicked on, its green walls shivering with air it was forcing up the ducts, the gas fire inside rumbling like an infant volcano. How many times had that tennis ball bounced off the wall, slipped under his glove, and hit that furnace? How many times had Mom come down the stairs to tell him to stop, did he want to blow the whole house up? He smiled and shut the file box. He bounced the tennis ball, then rolled it back under the chairs. He climbed the stairs and switched off the light on all the things that hid down there.

She was by the tree, kneeling to the presents, a pad and pencil in hand. "I didn't even send Mrs. Raymond a card last year."

"I can't find Dad's will."

"It's in the safety-deposit box at the bank." She examined another gift tag, sighed, scribbled another name on the pad. "In the same folder as mine. I'll make you breakfast in a minute."

He sat in a chair near the stairs, glanced at the papers in the folder she had left on the desk: the annual report of Trent & Co. Dull stuff, about which bank had been approved to handle company funds (it was always the same bank, every year), where the offices were to be located (wherever the offices were located was where they were to be located), and a host of details like that to satisfy the IRS that everything about this partnership was legal. Mom's signature looked neat and legible. The other signature was a scrawl, the only identifiable letter was the big *T* in *Trent*, crossed with a bold line that became, in effect, all the other letters in the name. "I thought Dad made Uncle Chuck the senior partner."

"Hmm? Well, he does run it."

"But you're the senior partner."

She picked up a present as if to weigh it, then she shook it, squinted, set it down, and made a note on her pad. "I don't do anything, Phil."

"Then why doesn't Uncle Chuck get the lion's share?" He flipped to an inside page of the report. "From the way this reads, he can't even write a check without your okay."

"That's silly, I've never written a single check for the company."

"Mom, it says here you're giving your approval for him to act on your behalf. If you didn't, he couldn't do anything."

She glanced at him, then raised an eyebrow. "I suppose your father wanted it that way. For you."

"If I started there tomorrow it would take years before I'd know enough to tell Uncle Chuck what to do."

With the point of the pencil, she counted the names she had written on the pad. "I'll never get all these in time." She gathered her robe and stood. "Bacon and eggs?"

"I'd like to see the will."

"You were here when they probated it." She walked past him and into the kitchen. "Everything was left to me. In my will, I leave everything to you. I don't see why you need to—"

"I'd just like to look at it. Hasn't Uncle Chuck complained about the setup?"

She shook her head and looked inside the refrigerator. "Did you eat all the bacon?"

"I had a sandwich last night."

"After that big meal?"

"I was hungry. Mom, if I was Uncle Chuck, I'd be mad."

"He never gets mad. Not at me."

"I can't believe he hasn't taken this to court."

She shut the refrigerator door. "Court?"

"He does all the work, you get all the money."

"No, he gets a salary and we share the profits."

He closed the folder, slapped it against his leg. "He gets thirty percent, you get seventy."

"But he gets a nice salary." She put a pot of water on the stove. "I get a draw. You know, if I need money, I can draw it out, against the profits. I could fry some potatoes."

He rubbed his temple. "I'll stop by the bank on my way to the office."

"Then I'd have to call Mr. Leonard and tell him you're coming in. Even then, I don't think he can let you into the box unless I'm there."

"All I need is the key, they'll let me in."

She held up the pad of names. "And I already have so much to do today."

"Just give me the key, I'll take care of it."

"Maybe I should go with you, then." Her face got long. She turned away from the stove. She was crying.

He went to her, put his hands on her shoulders. "I'm sorry, I didn't mean to—"

"It's not you." She turned and put her head against his chest. "It's just . . . Christmas."

She cried hard. But not for long. The water began to boil and she reached for the eggs. He stopped her, and stopping her made her cry again. It hurt to see her like this. He was on the edge of tears himself.

"I don't even go shopping anymore," she said. "I can't. I do it all by phone, they have the nicest stores in Tampa, and all the clerks are so eager to help, but here, oh it's a madhouse." She used the flat of her hand to wipe her cheek. It smeared her makeup. A freckle, maybe a liver spot, peeked through. "And then I worry about the money."

"You don't have to worry about money. The estate—"

"There's too much!" Shaking her head, she sat in a chair at the table as if her legs wouldn't have lasted another second. "I just don't know what to do." She glanced at him as though he had just leapt into the room through a window. Then she started laughing, quietly at first, building to a throaty rasp. "It's terrible, I know. People are starving and I'm worried about having too much." She drew a deep breath, wiped away more tears. "I never had a problem when it was my money, when I was working. I could spend that. But this is his. And yours. I always feel like I'm making a mistake."

"It's your money, okay? And you've done a great job with the house, that's not a mistake."

"It was almost fifty thousand dollars, Phil."

"What?"

"See?" She fought new tears. "If I don't spend it, it only collects interest." She shivered. "When we bought this house it didn't cost fifty thousand dollars."

He looked at the new rug and the new furniture and the new paint and he didn't see fifty thousand dollars. "Why don't you let Uncle Chuck invest it for you?"

"I never understand his schemes, they sound so risky." Her fingers made a fist. "And next month is January and a new calendar year and the end of the company's fiscal year—your father set it up that way for tax reasons—and the profits have to be distributed, that's what those papers are all about. Your uncle says my share will be over a hundred and ninety thousand." She ran her hand along the edge of the table. "That's on top of your father's pension, and that alone is more than I need to live on." She swallowed hard. "Phil, I just know I'm doing something terribly stupid. I paid the government over a hundred thousand dollars last year. Your father never paid that much."

He sat and took a moment to get his breath. "What does Ed say?"

She sniffed a laugh. "He has the same problem. 'You have to go in debt, Julie.'" She mimicked his deep voice. "'Write off all the interest.' We worked so hard to get out of debt." She put her hand on his. Her eyes teared up again. "There was a time we didn't think we could send you to college. I was going to go back to work. I even thought about going into New York, to the U.N., to be a translator, it pays so much better than teaching."

He smiled and stroked her hand. It made her relax. "I get so sad," she said, "during the holidays. Because I miss him so much. Then the new money comes in and I get worried. It's a terrible time of year."

And she was laughing at herself again.

He rubbed the back of her hand some more. "I'll do all the shopping for you, just give me a list."

"No, you don't have to, darling."

"And I'll look into the money and see what I can do."

"No, it's too much for you."

"And I'm going to make you some breakfast now."

"No, I can do that."

"And when I get back this afternoon, you and I are going to have a talk." He put the eggs in the boiling water, the bread in the toaster. "About Dad. And you're going to listen to me."

"I don't know if I can." Her whisper cracked. She cleared her throat. "Set the timer for four minutes, that's how you like them."

"And after that, you and I—Ed, too—are going out to dinner." He set the timer. He smiled. "I know just the place."

She was right, there was nothing in the will. Dad had left everything to her, and if she hadn't survived him, everything would have gone to Phil. While he was there, he glanced at her new will. He was the only beneficiary. He was the executor. He put both wills back into the same folder, locked the box, and went out to the car.

Her little Ford was used to being driven in summer. It didn't like the cold, new tune-up or not. He took the highway out to the malls and parked on the roof. Trent & Co. was empty. The receptionist looked surprised to see him. He gave her the papers Mom had signed and asked to see Uncle Chuck.

He should be back directly, she said: he was up in Bergen

County, closing a deal on an apartment complex for a client. He told her he would take a look at the files while he waited. She said she wasn't sure he could. He said he would keep everything in order. She said, "But Mr. Trent might not like it." He was about to remind her that he was Mr. Trent, too. Instead, he told her that Uncle Chuck wanted him to learn the business, it was Uncle Chuck's idea that he start with the files, Uncle Chuck would be angry at him if he didn't: he was only following orders. She smiled and showed him the file cabinets, told him if he needed any help just ask, no one was likely to come in before lunchtime anyway, and if he wanted coffee, she would get it for him. She said her name was Mrs. Frolen.

The file cabinets stood in the room that would be his office. It was warm in here, too warm. He took off his jacket, draped it on the doorknob. He started looking for files dated 1980, the year Dad died.

All the manila folders in the first drawer were filed under names of clients. Most of them were small businesses: shops in the malls, service companies. A few were industrial giants, like Tiptoft-Weck, a pharmaceutical house near Singac. The second drawer held tax returns for clients with names from A to K.

Voices in the outer office stopped him. He came out expecting to see Uncle Chuck. Maxie Nash stood at the reception desk, a freshly lit cigarette in one hand, a briefcase in the other. "But UDC sent me over here," he said.

"You can wait for Mr. Trent if you like." Mrs. Frolen wasn't bothering to look at him anymore. "I'm sure he can resolve this."

Maxie Nash exhaled cigarette smoke, rubbed the side of his head. His tie had bold yellow stripes, a summer tie. "I'm due in court in an hour."

Mrs. Frolen smiled and answered the ringing phone.

"Problem?" Phil said.

The little lawyer never got the cigarette to his lips. His eyes widened. He grinned and offered his hand. "Say, you look a hell of a lot better than you did when I drove you home. You working here now?"

He shook his head. "Coffee?"

"Can't. Hurts my vocal cords." He pulled up a sleeve and checked his watch. "Could I give you a document so you could show it to him? All we want is an explanation."

"Sure."

A long piece of paper came out of his briefcase. "See, they didn't lower the interest rates when they should have, so we'd like to know why." He offered the paper, then pulled it back. "Maybe we could make a copy."

Mrs. Frolen didn't want to, but she made a copy. Maxie put the original back into his briefcase. The clasp on it was missing. "He knows my number, so have him call me. And, I know this is asking a lot, but I'm supposed to meet a client here, only a case came up in court and I can't, so could you tell her I have to cancel? It'd save me some steps."

"Sure."

"Hey, that's great." He glanced at his watch again, then turned for the door. "I really appreciate it."

The document was from UDC, Union Development Corporation. It was addressed to Louise Davis, care of Zorzoli's.

"Wait a minute." Phil walked to the door. "What's this?"

"I told you, they should have lowered the rates, it says so right in the original agreement." The round lawyer must have seen that Phil didn't understand. He took a drag off his cigarette and said, "The one your father drew up, when the loan was made. Look, I have to go, I missed breakfast."

And he was striding up the mall, his short legs stretching for extra distance, his shoulders bouncing with each step. He didn't stop to crush out his cigarette, he just dropped it in an ashtray and kept moving.

"One day," Mrs. Frolen said, "he ate his lunch here." She shook her head and pointed across her desk. "On that couch."

He took the document back to the file cabinets. There was no folder for Zorzoli's. The folder for UDC was fat and crammed with papers. He reached in to get a grip on it. Then he heard a new voice in the outer office. It made him smile, even though he didn't mean to. He left the file drawer open and stepped out to meet his uncle.

14

He looked better than ever. His face was still full, a little pudgy really, but he had lost some weight. And he wasn't parting his hair anymore, it had been cut in a natural style that allowed it to fall where it wanted. He hadn't lost his smile.

"My God in heaven—Phil!" He hugged him, slapped his back, hugged him some more. "Mrs. F., this is my nephew. Handsome devil, isn't he?" He didn't wait for the receptionist to answer, he draped an arm around Phil's shoulder and led him into his office. "I was heartbroken when I missed you at dinner. Ah, Phil, it's just wonderful you're back. And for Christmas, too. That means so much to your mom. She's looking okay, isn't she?" He held up a hand and walked behind his desk. "I know, that guy she's seeing, he's not too easy to take, but you have to remember, she's been through a lot, my brother dying, you roaming all over creation, hardly a word from you to say you're okay, so it's natural she'd get a little desperate, you have to give her some latitude there." He sat in his chair and leaned against its high back. He smiled. "You look terrific, just terrific." He shook his head as if to clear it. "Look at me, I'm ready to cry. Ah, Phil, this is wonderful. So how does it feel to be home? Great, right?"

Everything in the office was modern and sleek. Chrome and glass. The lithograph hanging near his diplomas was an orange and red Calder, big enough to be a tablecloth. Even the leaves of the plant in the corner looked polished. "It's great," he said.

Mrs. Frolen came in with coffee and a stack of messages. She smiled at Phil on her way out.

"If I had you here"—Uncle Chuck switched on the desktop computer—"just think of the work we could get done." He waved the messages, swigged coffee. "Buys and sells, nickel-dime stuff, they take more time than they're worth. Your father's idea, the discount brokerage business. I've been trying to phase it out." He swiveled the computer screen toward Phil. "Ever work one of these? Nothing to it, just use the codes."

He glanced at the first message, fed the computer the stock-market symbol for the stock, the number of shares to be traded, the client's account number. Every time he touched a key in the keyboard, it sounded like a drop of water hitting an empty plastic bucket. In a few seconds the screen changed. He touched more keys. The screen changed again. He pointed to the last number on it. "That's the confirmation number, we need that to make sure we made the trade. Want to try one?"

"I might mess it up."

"No, I'm here to make sure." He handed him a slip of paper from a stack. "That's GenCorp, used to be General Tire and Rubber, the symbol's GY."

Phil leaned to the keyboard, set the notice Maxie had left with him on the desk. "Is this the account number?"

"Yeah." Uncle Chuck picked up the long document. "What's this?"

Phil told him.

"Well, what's he bothering me with it for?" He snatched the phone and buzzed Mrs. Frolen. "If that lawyer Nash comes back, tell him we don't hold the note anymore. Send him over to UDC." He hung up and dropped the document into his wastebasket. "Pain in the ass, that guy. Well, come on, get the information into the computer."

He stepped back from the machine, handed back the slip of

paper. "I don't think I'm ready for this."

"I told you, there's nothing to it. Okay, watch me do this one"—
his fingers sped over the keys—"then you try the next one."

"Uncle Chuck, about that loan—"

"What loan?"

"The thing on Zorzoli's you just threw out."

"Okay, the computer's ready for you to tell it buy or sell." He
glanced at the slip of paper, punched keys, waited for the screen to
catch up to him. "That loan's not our business anymore." He
smiled and tapped the screen. "And there's our confirmation
number."

"Maxie said Dad drew up the original loan."

"Maxie? Oh, Nash, yeah." He started working on the next slip
of paper. "Yeah, Henry got us into that mess, I got us out. Dis-
counted the note for cash. We're all clear of it. Good thing, too,
the restaurant's in trouble." He nodded at the screen, punched
more keys, went to the next message on the stack. "I bet you could
master this in less than an hour."

"He said something about interest rates. They should have
gone down?"

Uncle Chuck's eyes stayed dull. He shrugged. "It has nothing
to do with us."

"Maxie said UDC sent him over here."

Those eyes got hard. He squinted at the screen, then picked up
the phone, punched numbers. "See if you can do this one." He
handed Phil a slip of paper, then spun his chair toward the window. "Dick? Chuck Trent. Listen, the lawyer for the Davis woman
was in today. About the note. He said you sent him over . . . well,
somebody at UDC did. Stupid fucking thing to do. . . . Well get
on it, will you? I don't have time for that clown." He glanced at
the computer screen, brushed Phil's hand away, punched some
keys, covered the phone mouthpiece. "You put the account number in last." He smiled and took his hand off the phone. "No, he

won't go to court. Look, call him and tell him you think interest rates are edging back up, so you can't drop his rates now. Tell him you have to wait and see . . . of course . . . I can give you all the statistics you need. Just don't send him back here, I don't like lawyers in my office." He said some parting words and hung up, then smiled at the confirmation number on the screen. "I told you you could do it." He handed him another slip of paper. "Here, earn another commission."

The phone buzzed. He answered and listened, his face getting longer each second. "I'm in conference." He hung up and watched the computer. "DR is the symbol for that stock."

The phone buzzed again. He glared at it before picking it up. "What? . . . Impossible . . . okay, okay." He hung up. "That's good, Phil, thanks. Listen, I have to get these trades in. Think you could go out there and help Mrs. F. get rid of a pest? Just say I can't be disturbed. Be polite, understand, there may be clients out there. Then come back in and we'll get this stuff out of the way and have lunch."

"I was hoping to get some time to talk to you. About the papers Mom signed. I brought them in."

"Oh, good. Yeah, we can talk at lunch, plenty of time."

Phil turned the doorknob. "Do you keep the file on Trent and Company in with the others?"

"Huh? No, in here." He nodded at the bookcase in back of him, mostly hidden by his desk. "We can cover everything. Remember, I can't be disturbed, okay?" He smiled. "You look terrific, kid. Just terrific. Have to tell me all about those California girls, okay?"

A smile came through all by itself: there hadn't been any California girls, not really, but the idea of them still made him smile. Then he frowned. There should have been California girls, he had missed his chance. He opened the door and walked out.

Arms folded, eyes hard, the pest stood rigid near the desk.

Then shock hardened that small frame even more. Then something else set in, something fast and hot, something dark like fear. Louise didn't look happy to see him.

He told her his uncle couldn't be disturbed. He told her he was supposed to get rid of her. He told her he had been thinking about her, about her grandmother, too. He told her he would like to buy her a cup of coffee.

She told him she wasn't going to leave, she was meeting her lawyer here, she was going to settle this matter, and today. She didn't say anything for a few moments, then she stared at him and her eyes got softer. "You look tired."

"He's not coming. He's in court."

"Who?"

"Maxie. He's your lawyer, right?"

She nodded, squinted, crossed her arms. Her green sweater made wrinkles.

He grinned. "He told me to take you out for coffee. He insisted on it."

Her smile was small. "I don't drink coffee. Neither does he."

"He was in a hurry."

She shook her head slowly. And her smile got bigger. Then she checked the wall clock, leaned on the desk, put her face close to Mrs. Frolen's: "Tell him he's had all the chances he's going to get. I'll see him in court." She straightened up, tucked her purse under an arm, and started for the door. "I have time for tea," she said.

He beamed at Mrs. Frolen. "Tell my uncle to have lunch without me." He caught the door as it was closing after Louise, then he turned back to the desk. "And tell him I got rid of the pest."

He caught up to her in three steps. She glared at him. "Pest?"

"My specialty," he said.

She fought a smile and won. Suddenly, a laugh shot out of her mouth. She covered it with a hand. Shaking her head, she led him up the mall.

The original loan had been for $250,000. She said his dad had wanted to make it interest-free, but he had been worried that the IRS might consider it a gift, so he had charged the lowest legal interest he could at the time, 8 percent. He had a clause put in, a discretionary clause, allowing him to lower the interest rate in the future if the prime rate came down. To do that legally, she said, he had to make the clause read that he could raise *or* lower the rates, again because of the IRS. To protect her further, he had limited the potential raising of the rates to 2 percent in any twenty-four-month period. That had been Mr. Nash's idea, she said. Mr. Nash felt that with that limitation it would be possible to delay rises in the rate and still satisfy the IRS. The loan had come from Trent & Co. Dad had written a check and walked her to the bank down-town to make sure it got deposited.

Uncle Chuck had raised the interest rate the full 2 percent not six months after Dad died. Before he could collect the next monthly payment, he had sold the note to UDC. UDC had raised the rates another 2 percent last year, and again this year. Now that interest rates were declining, the company was not considering lowering the rates. UDC liked getting 14 percent. Zorzoli's was having trouble carrying the interest. Zorzoli's was having trouble, period.

And the collateral for the original loan had been the mill.

"It's very slow this Christmas," she said. "And people are spending less."

He watched her stir milky tea. "You must be the only person who calls him Mr. Nash."

Her face got soft. "My grandfather told me to call men 'mister.' He said it would keep them from getting too personal. He was right." She sipped tea. "Any luck with your mother?"

He fished her list from his pocket. "I'm doing her Christmas shopping for her today, then we're going to have a talk. Then I'm taking her to dinner, at your place."

She looked surprised. "Well, we could use the business."

"I wanted her to meet you."

"Not a good idea. That's not how women work."

She was probably right. He probably didn't have any good ideas. He drank his tea and wished it were coffee.

"I couldn't get to sleep," she said, "after you called."

He smiled and didn't say anything.

"I kept thinking about Henry."

He stopped smiling.

"You have his sense of humor," she said. "Cryptic. Has anyone ever told you that?"

"Everybody."

"Oh. Well, you do." She covered a small laugh. "About the wine steward, it was very funny."

"Thank you."

She squinted at him. "Something wrong?"

He shook his head.

"Sure?"

He pushed his tea toward the center of the table. "I was hoping you might have spent last night thinking of me, not my father."

She put her hand on his. It felt cool. "I did. A little."

When she pulled her hand back, he stopped her. "How little?"

"I don't know, a little."

"Hour? Half an hour?"

"Yes."

"You can't answer an either-or question with 'yes.'"

"Some people can." She freed her hand, stirred her tea again.

For an instant, he was sure she wasn't going to look at him again. "I'm older than you are," she said.

He couldn't think of anything to say: everything he could say sounded wrong.

"Two years," she said. "You know that, don't you?"

"I wasn't thinking about it."

She shrugged. "And then there are all these complications, with your family."

"I wasn't thinking about them."

"Well, what were you thinking about?"

"Me."

"You?"

He nodded. "What's he like, the guy you're seeing?"

She shook her head.

"That bad, huh?"

She didn't smile, she squinted. She looked angry. "You never thought about me, how I might feel in all of this?"

"You told me how you felt."

"Before you called to ask me out? I never told you how I felt before that. You never asked me how I felt before that."

"How could I ask you before I asked you?"

"But you never even thought about how I might feel."

He pulled the cup and saucer back. "It has to be the tea, they put something in it."

"You don't even know what I'm talking about, do you."

"I don't have a prayer."

She let out a grunt. She was angry.

"And I didn't ask you out," he said. "I asked to see you again. I never got a chance to ask you out."

"Well, what did you expect? I wasn't prepared for it."

He leaned low to the table and toward her. "Are you saying you never gave any thought that I might ask you?"

She leaned away. "Of course not."

"You never considered how I might feel after I met you? After I got to know you?"

"Well, no."

"Not one single thought about me and how I might feel?" He straightened up slowly. "Hah."

Her eyes widened and she glared at him like that, twin beacons of brown heat aimed at his center. "You're making fun of me."

"You just don't like your own logic."

"The circumstances aren't the same."

"They don't have to be."

She put her elbows on the table so hard, her cup shook. "But they aren't the same. And that does make a difference. And if you can't see that, I don't know why I'm bothering to talk to you."

He stared at the quartered lemon on his saucer, then at her. "Last night, was it an hour or a half an hour?"

"I don't remember."

A waitress came by and asked if they wanted more tea. He said "no thank you" and so did Louise. The waitress left a check. It was wet in the middle.

Louise picked up her cup, then put it down. "Damn."

"What?"

She pressed her lips together, let out a short sigh. "It was more than an hour."

He smiled. After a moment, she smiled back.

| 15 |

She wasn't coming back, he was sure of it.

He glanced down the mall—she wasn't coming, and she was late, seventeen minutes late, it shouldn't be taking her so long to tell her employees she'd be going out for a while—then he walked back to Bamberger's display window. A mannequin was wearing something Dad would have called a knock-around jacket. It was lighter, but the same style as the one Phil wore. He had found it in his closet. He had forgotten he had it. He buttoned it. The mannequin was wearing a fishing cap, little hooks and feathered flies stuck in the band. The mannequin looked ready for spring. The mannequin looked better than he did. He unbuttoned the jacket.

He used his palm to smooth his hair. His slacks still carried the crease of the hanger. He tried stretching it out. It didn't work.

"They have some nice sweaters." She was back. Carrying a paper sack with Stern's printed on it. It looked heavy. "You look like a sweater person. Sorry I'm late."

"No problem."

"Here"—she handed him the sack—"you can carry lunch."

Lunch was heavy. She didn't speak again until she was out on the mall's roof and unlocking her car door, and when she did speak, she didn't look at him: "I'll have to change how I think about you. How I've always thought about you." She made it sound hopeless. She got in and started the engine.

It was closed, but she told him it would be all right. She left the car by the chain blocking the road and led him up a trail to a picnic area. Metal tables, metal benches, cement barbecues, all set out under leafless trees. It faced a wide meadow, patched with snow and dead grass, bordered by tall firs and the bare and twisted arms of sycamores. She came here a lot, she said. She said Garrett Mountain was one of her favorite places.

There was a thermos of soup in the shopping bag. Cheese sandwiches—four of them, she didn't know how much he ate and she wanted to be sure he got enough—and a tablecloth—that was to sit on, the benches were always cold—and one mug—that was for his soup, she'd use the cap of the thermos—and spoons and napkins. Dessert, she said, was the view.

She took a good-sized bite from her sandwich and said she hoped he liked mustard. He said he did. She smiled, and suddenly she relaxed, as if finding out he liked mustard had made everything all right. It made him grin.

"I keep hoping," she said, "I can get here when it snows. I've imagined what it would be like, taking a walk down there with the snow falling."

Down there, near the end of the meadow and centered as if part of a flower arrangement, stood a winter-struck bush. It looked familiar somehow. He could imagine it whitened by new snow.

She poured the soup and told him more than he wanted to know about Garrett Mountain—it was a "reservation," a preserve for wildlife and plants—and Lambert Castle, a fortress at the east side of the park, someone's wild dream cast in stone, haunted now by dark legends and none of them were true, and it was open to the public during the summer if he wanted to see it.

"I've been there." He could remember a veranda and the high view, but nothing more, except the coldness of the place, the solid coldness that had scared him. "My father took us once."

She nodded and ate her soup.

"You should be a tour guide," he told her.

"My mother knew every inch of this park. Most of her landscapes were done here."

That bush down there had been smaller twenty years ago, but it was the same one he had seen in one of the paintings in her living room, surrounded by dying grass in late summer heat.

"The Y runs a summer camp up here," she said. "I always wanted to go, but my grandfather wouldn't allow it. He wouldn't let me out of his sight." She stared at the meadow the way old people stare at their backyards, seeing years of accomplishment and change and the memories of both muddled with the present view, the future plans. "His English got worse as he got older. Strange, isn't it."

She went back to her soup and back to telling him more about Lambert Castle and Garrett Mountain. He couldn't take it. He kissed her.

She kept her eyes open. She didn't look surprised, just tense. And a second later, when he felt her lips soften, she turned away and laughed, a short burst of air racing toward the trees.

He shrugged and kept looking at her. "If I put my arms around you, do you roll around on the ground in hysterics?"

She caught this laugh in her hand, then let out a long sigh that still had most of the laugh in it. "I'm sorry. I just . . . well, all I could see then was you asleep on the backseat of Henry's car. You were a little boy then. It was . . . funny."

He glanced at the antlerlike branches guarding the meadow. "I thought you were trying to change how you thought about me."

"I am." She put a hand on his sleeve. "You were cute, though, as a boy. With the longest eyelashes. And there was a beach-ball—"

He kissed her again. She didn't laugh. He put his arms around her and she didn't laugh. She shut her eyes. He could taste the mustard on her tongue.

She eased away, as if afraid of bruising him. "Eat your sandwich."

He ate his sandwich, started another. She nibbled on hers

now. Even the way she spooned soup had changed, she was delicate with it. "I'm not seeing anyone," she said, her voice aimed at the woods. "Not even sort of." She glanced at him without turning her head, then went back to her soup, stirring it absently. "I just said that because—it was instinctive, a protective device. It really had nothing to do with you."

"I was hoping he'd be short," he said.

She took his hand, but she didn't look at him. "I don't think that would have mattered."

He put his fingertips to her chin, turned her face. "Maybe if we took a walk, it would start to snow."

She touched his cheek. "I have on the wrong shoes." She smiled and something lit her eyes, and she began talking fast— "There are over six hundred varieties of trees alone in the preserve, and two distinct species of squirrels"—and she kissed him.

It was bigger than he remembered. And whiter, bleached by weather. The last time he had seen it, it bore only one name, one set of dates. Now the tombstone read:

TRENT
Henry R. 1921–1980
Julia W. 1922–

It couldn't have been Mom's idea, some carver must have sold her on the notion—the vulture—and it would have been easy, appealing to her sense of order: why bother her son with the trouble and the expense, why not tend to the inevitable now, this is where she was going anyway. Seeing her name there, seeing the blank patch of smooth granite waiting for a final date, seeing that in the cold made his eyes tear.

"She keeps it so neat," Louise said. "The flowers she puts here at Easter are beautiful."

Mom would be coming here soon, to lay Christmas flowers on the grave. He could see her telling whoever she had do it while she was down in Tampa that she would take care of it this year. He could see her at the florist shop, asking for something the florist would have to make up special, whatever he had ready to go wouldn't do, even if it was practically the same thing she would eventually walk out with. And he saw her name in the stone again.

At the side of the grave, a dried rose lay face-down on frozen soil, littered with the leaves of nearby trees. He couldn't tell what color the rose had been.

"If I'd known we were coming here," she said, "I would have brought a fresh one."

He could hear the river run along the bottom of the hill. "Maybe we could get one."

She shook her head. "If I go back, I'd have to look in on Nonna Do, and then I'd have to stay a while."

"I don't mind."

"I'm not sure I'm up to it. Not after . . . not today."

She laced her fingers through his and led him toward the car.

She was up to going to Snake Hill.

The gas station was still abandoned. Most of the roof had fallen in. Twin pumps, 1920s-style, the kind that needed hand pumping, were cracked and the metal tops were missing. So many cars had smashed into this building, it wasn't possible to find the spot her mother had hit. The county had put up big reflectors on the corners of the place and on the pumps. No car had crashed here in over ten years.

"Someday they'll build something new here," she said. "Then I won't have to come back."

Across the street, a big green dump truck pulled out of a parking lot and headed up the mountain toward the quarry in Willowbend. It made a lot of noise. The cab door wore a bright yellow A.

"I used to hope it would be a house," she said. "With lots of kids. Now I sort of hope the college builds something here, a dormitory maybe." She kept looking at the crumbling walls, the rusted parts of cars scattered near the back. "It's just behind those woods, you know. That side road cuts right through to the campus."

She had taken that road every day, she said, every day for four years. He was about to ask her if she wanted to drive to the campus now when he realized this gas station was the reason she had chosen to go to William Paterson College. He touched her arm, kissed her hair. She didn't try to move away, she leaned against him, tucking a shoulder into his armpit. "Kids play here a lot," she said. "Hide-and-seek. I never had the courage to go inside."

He wondered if he should walk her inside. He wondered if he should do anything. He rubbed her arm. Finally, he said, "Do you ever hear from your father?"

Another truck crawled up the hill and she turned to watch its black diesel smoke stream in the white winter air. "Nonna Do thinks he's dead. She had a dream, he was injured with an ax. In a wheelchair, very weak. Then frozen. No wood for a fire." She studied cracks in the concrete drive. "I never really wanted to see him again. Something must be wrong with me."

He put his other arm around her. "I may not be a reliable judge of that."

She smiled, but she didn't mean it. "It's almost four-thirty. I can't ask Mario to take a double shift. The mill can't afford that anyway."

Being here with her, he was costing her money. He was always costing people money, for hospitals, doctors, room and board, college, even Little League cost money. Even people he hardly knew, like the California carpenter Gary Simms, wound up parting with some of their money because of him. He wished all of them would have invested in somebody else. "I want you to meet my mother. She may even have some money to loan you."

"She won't want anything to do with me." She slid out of his grasp. "She couldn't stand my grandfather. He never said so, but I'm sure of it. It hurt him." She stared at him, her dark eyes cold with certainty. "She won't like you seeing me."

"When she understands about—"

"If she does." A car raced down the hill. It made her shoulders bunch together, as if hit by an icy wind. "Besides, the mill may not be a good investment anymore. Once, I was sure it would be, I planned so hard. It just isn't working out." The car disappeared around a bend, its tires squealing. "It's worth more as a parking lot than a restaurant."

She kept watching the road, as if waiting for the car to come back. Then she walked to her Datsun and got in. She didn't look back.

The rear door of the mill was made of steel and had two dead bolts in it. She got it open. She said she'd had a wonderful afternoon. She wished they could have stayed longer at Garrett Mountain, she hadn't meant to drag him to the cemetery and the old gas station.

"I could come over later," he said.

"It'll be too late."

"Are you working the afternoon or evening tomorrow?"

"I'm not sure yet. I'll let you know."

Something had gone wrong. She wasn't going to let him know. He held on to the door. "I need to know when I'm going to see you again."

Her smile looked weak. She seemed to be thinking of something to say. She gave up. She kissed his cheek, turned, and opened the door wider.

"I drove by your house last night," he said.

Her fingers tightened on the knob, her shoulders squared.

"Your light was on."

She stood there for a moment without moving. Then she began shaking her head, and when she turned, her real smile was back. "I don't know what I'm going to do with you."

She touched his face, withdrew her hand slowly, then went inside and shut the heavy door. He waited until he couldn't hear her shoes on the steel stairs. Then he walked toward the corner of the mill, and before he reached the smokestack, he was whistling.

Mom stood at the sink, dicing potatoes. "Did you get them all?"

He shut the back door. "I had a great day."

"You got all the presents? That's wonderful."

Shit.

He left the key to the safety-deposit box on the little table. "Actually, not all of them, no."

She ran water, stuffed peels into the disposal. "How many?"

"Uh . . . not that many. I thought I'd go back tonight for the rest."

"Well, bring in the ones you got, I'll start wrapping them." She put the potatoes in a pot, the pot on the stove next to a small kettle. Her pot roast was in there, bubbling brown, filling the room with its spicy aroma. "Your uncle called. He was so pleased you came in. He said you were an enormous help." She put a low flame under the potatoes. "Better wash up. Ed will be here any minute. You didn't block the drive, did you?"

"No. Mom, we have to talk."

"Did you find a nice figurine for Mrs. Raymond?"

"We have to talk about Dad."

"Oh, Phil, no. Please, I'm not up to it. I told you how the holidays make me feel."

A car pulled alongside the house, its headlights painting the garage. "There he is now," she said. "We'll eat as soon as he's ready."

"You'd feel better if we talked. A lot better."

The back door opened. "Mrs. Trent, may I come in?"

"Sarah, dear, of course." Mom switched on the disposal. It started grinding. "What a nice surprise."

She wore jeans and a parka. She carried a fruitcake wrapped in clear plastic. It had a pink bow on it. "I just wanted to thank you for last night." She spotted Phil by the refrigerator. "Oh. Hi."

"Hi."

"You'll stay to dinner?" Mom asked.

"Well"—she glanced at Phil—"I'm not sure."

"There's more than enough," Mom told her. "But it's not fancy."

Phil tasted the pot roast behind Mom's back. It was delicious. Sarah took off her parka and said she'd stay to dinner. She wore a fuzzy white sweater. Fake angora. Maybe it was real and just looked fake. "It smells heavenly," she said.

"Sarah can help you bring in the presents. I don't want you dropping anything."

"Presents, right."

"Put them in the den, I'll wrap them while we watch TV."

He turned toward the living room. "Maybe I better wash up first."

The stairs were only four feet away, but he never made them. Sarah grabbed his arm and pulled him deep into the living room, backed him into the couch. She leaned soft breasts in the soft sweater against him. "You didn't even call me." She didn't wait for an answer, she slid a hand between his legs. "And you don't look happy to see me."

He glanced at the kitchen doorway, wondering when Mom would pop out.

"Well, are you?" Sarah's strong fingers teased and threatened him at the same time. She laughed softly and leaned in to kiss him.

The front door opened. Ed looked tired. He blinked at what he saw. "Sorry, bad timing."

Sarah drew back, but not far.

"Ed, is that you? Help Phil unload the car, please."

"Sure." He put his scarf back on. "Let's go before I get too warm."

"There's nothing to unload."

Ed shrugged, and smoothing his mustache with a finger, he headed toward the kitchen. "He says there's nothing to unload." At the doorway he stretched his arms wide. "Hello, Julie."

She came out of the kitchen and brushed past his arms, holding a slotted spoon that dripped gravy on her new carpet. "Oh, Phil—no."

Oh, Phil—yes.

16

Somehow or other, in the mysterious ways things worked in this house, not doing Mom's shopping was the smartest thing he could have done. It gave him an escape route. He should have known that all along.

It had started with anger. Mom was so hurt, she even remembered that Uncle Chuck had told her over the phone today that Phil had broken yet another appointment, this one for lunch, and no explanation had been given, and something must be terribly wrong, it wasn't like Phil to be so careless, thoughtless, inconsiderate—she kept going, but he stopped listening after "inconsiderate"—and if Phil needed help, counseling or therapy, she would be glad to arrange it.

He told her he needed all the help he could get. He was about to tell her about Louise, but Ed took over, moving close to Phil, telling Mom there was probably a good explanation, a very good one. Phil said, "I went to Garrett Mountain."

The look of amazement on Mom's face stopped him cold. She almost dropped the slotted spoon. "But it's . . . there are bears up there."

He told her the biggest animals up there were squirrels.

Sarah had to sit on the couch, she wasn't able to stand anymore. She looked frightened, her bony cheeks took the color of her pink nail polish. Ed drew his hand off Phil's shoulder: "Garrett Mountain is closed this time of year, Phil."

"After that I went to the cemetery," he said.

Mom's face relaxed. She said, "Oh." She asked how the grave

looked, did he think it would be all right if she waited until next week to put the flowers on and clean up around the stone or should she get right out there, tomorrow, she could go tomorrow if she had to.

He told her the grave looked fine. He couldn't tell her about the old gas station or about Louise. It didn't feel good. It felt as though he were betraying both women—Louise, by not acknowledging that she existed, Mom, by making her wait to hear the truth about Dad. Inside him, open wounds festered. And he couldn't do anything about them. His saliva tasted sour. He went to the closet—the damn light didn't work, he hadn't even remembered to fix the chain—and got out a heavier jacket. "I'll go get those presents now."

"What about dinner?" Mom said.

"I'll get it on the road."

"But it's pot roast." And she told Ed and Sarah about the time down at the shore when Phil was only six or so: he had run around to all the cabins in the little seaside park and told everybody that his mother was making pot roast and that it was the best pot roast in the whole world.

It was probably still the best pot roast. But she always made too much, there would be some left over, he could have his share tomorrow, it tasted better warmed over anyway. He got her gift list from his other jacket and kissed her. He told her he would take care of everything.

Ed jangled keys and told him to take the Corvette. Phil told him the trunk was too small, he'd never get all the presents inside, he would take the little Ford.

Mom said, "Sarah, go with him. He might be in too much of a hurry to choose wisely."

Sarah got up and started for her parka in the kitchen. She was smiling.

"I don't think so," Phil said.

Sarah stopped. She stopped smiling.

"You'll love the pot roast," Phil told her. He couldn't keep looking at her, her face was getting too hot. He said, "I'll need some help moving the cars."

And then it happened. It happened just the way he remembered it had always happened. Each of them had a peculiar way of starting it: Ed cursed (Dad had only grimaced), Mom got her coat, Sarah pouted. And then they were all outside, telling each other what to do, what they should be doing, and then cars roared, rolled, they smoked, they backed down the long narrow driveway into traffic that honked at them, and the sound of the horns and the engines and the hard braking made the neighbors' lights go on, and the area around 329 Ringbrook Avenue became a little amphitheater, faces in windows staring at the long narrow driveway. Lined with shrubs and hedges and the nubs of shrubs and hedges that had been run over through the years, lighted by a single post lantern that was no use to any driver, rutted by rain and sleet and snow and the hard summer sun, the Trent driveway always stood ready for the next "I just have to run out to the store for a minute" or "My car won't start, I'll have to take yours" or "I thought the Little League game was tomorrow night." Oh, how he loved that driveway. He had forgotten how much he loved it.

He smiled at it. He waved to it. He aimed the car up the street. He drove like hell.

The new Burger King had a drive-through lane, but it was closed because the power company had dug it up to fix a cable. At the counter, he ordered a Whopper.

He didn't have to wait long for his food. He had to ask for ketchup for his fries. The straw dispenser by the napkins was out of straws. High school kids had taken up most of the tables. They all drank Cokes and ate french fries. He didn't spot one of them eating a hamburger. He found a table against a wall and started his dinner. He told himself this was better than some places he had eaten at, a lot better, and the food was better, too. It still didn't taste good.

And it was noisy.

And in the corner, looking so out of place it was laughable, dressed in blue denim that didn't come close to looking right on him, Maxie Nash sat at a table, carrying on what appeared to be a serious conversation with a pimple-faced kid whose eyes were glazed. The boy's mouth moved—one-syllable responses—and his head nodded now and then, and any moment he was going to fall asleep. Finally, he shook Maxie's hand and left.

Phil took what remained of his Coke over to the table. "How did it go in court?"

The little lawyer's eyes widened. He stood and shook hands. The denim made him look shorter. He had been "interviewing" a young musician, he said, a guitar player. He needed him for the "new sound" he was developing, to satisfy all the requests for rock music he was getting these days, everybody wanted it, even the old-timers, even at weddings. He was waiting for a drummer to show up. The kid was already an hour late. Maxie conducted all of his interviews here because Burger King, he said, was the only place the young kids knew how to find. He said there was a price to pay for everything.

"Do you have any legal documents concerning my father?" Phil asked.

Maxie squinted at the ceiling. "I think he had all those handled by Layman and Pierce. They're in Paramus now. If I have anything, it wouldn't be important." Stubby fingers rapped the tabletop. "What are you looking for?"

"I'm not sure, something to do with Trent and Company."

"I don't have anything on that. Just the Davis loan."

"Well, could I come down to your office and look over what you have?"

"Sure. I'll be there most of tomorrow." Maxie sipped a vanilla milkshake. "What did your uncle say about the UDC notice?"

"He threw it away."

The round man sighed, then checked his watch. "Maybe this drummer can't even find Burger King."

He did all the shopping in less than two hours. What he couldn't find at Stern's he found at Bamberger's. He found a nice figurine for Mrs. Raymond at a shop called That Touch of Class. He had every present gift-wrapped. He paid extra for the best wrapping paper, the best ribbon. He handed extra money to the girls behind the counters so they would wrap his gifts first. He made two trips to the car and got all the presents safely in the trunk. He wondered who Mom was buying argyle kneesocks for. And he was hungry again.

He threaded the Ford through the mall traffic and took a back street under the highway to the mill.

The arcade wasn't so noisy. The snack bar was closed. There were fewer than a dozen people in the restaurant. Well, it was past the dinner hour. The hostess told him Louise wasn't here, she was up in the club. He told her he didn't need a table after all.

Two men sat at opposite ends of the bar, the empty stools between them making the sculptured chunk of polished wood look even longer. A few couples sat at tables in front of the stage. Well, it was early, the first show hadn't begun yet.

The bartender remembered him. The King's Ransom tasted sweet. She was backstage, the bartender said, and yes, it would be all right if he went back there, at least the bartender wasn't going to stop him, that wasn't what he got paid for.

Backstage was a dimly lit hallway with two dressing rooms. One of the doors hung open. Inside, in the dark, Silky Odell sat in a beat-up rocking chair, his eyes closed. On the dressing table: a blue velvet sack, its shape molded by the bell of his trumpet. Phil listened at the other door, but heard nothing. He turned and walked back to the bar.

She was there, near the handrails where the waiters picked up drinks. She had a thin stack of papers in her hands, computer paper, hinged together at the perforated seams, green bars striating each page. She studied the printed numbers as if deciphering some ancient codex. Then she told the bartender he had better check again, the computer said it should be time to restock. The bartender smiled and leaned close to her—too close—and said computers couldn't do everything, now could they. Computers, he said, didn't work so well when business got so slow. Maybe she ought to reprogram it, he told her, or maybe she should try something else. And he was grinning.

"Just check the stock," she said.

"No need." The bartender winked at Phil. "Except you might want to reorder King's Ransom. For your friend here."

She squinted. She turned. Not even surprise registered on her face, not even the hint of surprise. Nothing. She sighed and put the papers under her arm. "I have to run some calculations." And she walked past him and opened her office door.

He followed her. "I have a way with computers."

There was something on her face now. It hardened her eyes. She blinked. She was looking right through him. She had been kinder to the bartender. "Look, I can't talk to you now. There just isn't time." Her face got tight, and what she said seemed to surprise her. "You're . . . in the way."

Inside her office, a light was shining through a doorway at the end of the bookcases. That door didn't lead to the backstairs, it led to another room.

"I've been thinking about it," she said, her voice straining to quiet a trembling in her throat, "and . . . and you're in the way."

The words stabbed. She wasn't talking about just tonight. He wanted to say something that would rid her of her worry, felt he had to say something, but he couldn't. Something stronger was pulling him toward the light through that doorway. He squeezed by her, and at the end of the bookcases, he stopped, not sure he should take that extra step. And he was sure he was going crazy, because he was certain that when he did step into that doorway, he was going to see Dad.

He took that extra step.

It was a small office, half the size of Mom's den. An old desk was backed by an old straight-back chair. A standing lamp gave off a soft glow, its metal shade tarnished green. A low bookcase ran against one wall. It was filled with stout binders, their leather covers dry and flaking. Two documents hung on the wall beside the desk. On the back wall, five pictures hung in a tight arrangement around a silver rosary, its crucifix dangling from the lower loop. He stepped to the desk. The documents were certificates of immigration and naturalization. Four of the photos were of women. One was of a young man in a cap and gown. That young man was Dad.

"This is my grandfather's office," she said. "I like to come in here to think."

She was on the wall, too. A little girl examining the insides of a ripe fig and not knowing what to make of it. She was a beautiful baby.

"It's just the way he left it," she told him. "Except for that hat tree. I moved that out so I could have more room."

The picture frames had been freshly dusted. So had the desk blotter. There was a small yellow rose in a glass vase on the corner of the desk.

"Phil, I don't want to hurt you. I don't want to hurt either of us. This afternoon, I—" The phone beeped behind her. She glanced at a flashing button in the machine—"That's my private line, it must be Nonna Do"—and she carried her computer paper to the coffee table—"She probably wants me to bring home some milk"—and she reached for the phone—"Please turn off the light in there"—and she picked up the phone—"And please . . . leave. For now, okay?"—and she turned her hand from the mouth-piece—"Hello?"

He turned off the light in Mr. Zorzoli's office. He could still see the photographs. Dad looked happy.

"When?" Louise sat in a chair. "I can, yes. Thank you, Pete"—she bit a fingernail—"yes, it was very smart of you to find the number." She hung up the phone.

He sloshed scotch and ice cubes in his glass. "Pete?"

"Mrs. Allano's son," she said. "He found my number on my grandmother's nightstand." She stood, looked around the room, strode to the bookcases, yanked her purse off a shelf. Then she froze. Her lips quivered. "She's in the hospital." She tried to swallow. ". . . Heart attack."

He put his arms around her, waited for her to cry. She let him hold her, her body rigid, her arms straight and heavy at her sides. She didn't cry. After a moment, she stepped back and dug into her purse. She made little noises, frightened noises, and she pressed her lips together. "They must be in my coat." She ran to the hat tree, dug into a coat pocket, came out with keys.

"I'll drive," he said. "Paterson General?"

She nodded and put on her coat, then she walked past the bartender and told him where she would be. She kept walking, her shoes hard on the parquet dance floor, her fists clenched as she went through the exit door and down the steel stairs. Outside, she pinched her coat tight around her neck, left the rest of it unbuttoned. He steered her to the Ford. As soon as he had the engine started, she seemed to relax. He drove out of the lot and turned toward the river. She put a hand on his arm, looked at him, her night eyes tender and, he thought, maybe even glad to see him, and she said, "Thank you."

"She'll be all right," he said.

She looked dazed now and she didn't say anything until he turned off Willowbend Avenue onto Oldwood Road, and then the best she could manage was a whisper to the dark trees along the blacktop: "She's all I have."

She cried.

Book Five

Silk

| 17 |

Lined with benches, the waiting room was no more than a square hall, a door in each side: the street door facing the rest room, ATTORNEY AT LAW opposite MUSIC FOR ALL OCCASIONS. There was nobody out here. He knocked on the door to the law office.

Maxie Nash came out in shirt sleeves, his barrel chest stretching silk against buttons. "Oh, good, I was just about ready to go to lunch." He shook Phil's hand and showed him inside.

Dark paneling made the place look formal. And small. It smelled of the too-sweet flowers in an aerosol room freshener. The little lawyer opened a file cabinet, drew out the last file, sat at his desk, his round head directly below a diploma from Rutgers Law School. "I can't show you anything without my client's permission." The folder was marked *Zorzoli's*. "But what I'm willing to do is tell you what I have, then you tell me what you want to see, then I can see if my client will let you see it, okay?"

"Sure."

In that folder he had a partnership agreement between August Zorzoli and Louise Davis, amended after Zorzoli's death to pass his interest to his wife. There was the loan agreement between Zorzoli's and Trent & Co. There were assorted contracts the mill had entered into when it was still a mill, similar documents for the mill as a restaurant-nightclub, like the lease of the first floor to the arcade and snack-bar owners. There were a few pages from a yellow legal pad: notes.

Phil shook his head.

"Didn't think so." Maxie put the file back. "I checked last

night to see if I had anything on Hank or his business." He shut the file drawer, but it didn't close all the way. "Sorry. Your best bet's Layman and Pierce."

The secretary for Mr. Pierce had been pleasant enough on the phone, but she had been firm: if Trent & Co. authorized Phil to review certain documents, Layman and Pierce would of course make those documents available. The authorization would have to be in writing, preferably notarized and recorded in the county of record—Passaic—and also in the county where Layman & Pierce kept the records—Bergen. The secretary asked how Mom was and said to wish her a Merry Christmas.

"Yeah, well"—thick fingers pulled at the shirt collar, stretching the tie knot—"they did the right thing." He blinked, then leaned forward, elbows on the desk blotter. "None of my business, but can't you get what you need from Hank's brother? He's your uncle, after all."

Phil glanced at his watch. It was still early, but he wanted to leave. He had been ready to leave the moment he had walked in. "You're probably right."

"Sure, go straight to the source."

The bow-backed chair was cutting into his spine. He stood. "Thanks."

"For what? I didn't do anything. You need a lawyer or a band, give me a call."

Phil smiled. "Don't you find it hard, running two businesses?"

The round man shrugged. "The truth is, I'd find it hard running just one." He laughed at the puzzled look on Phil's face. "I started playing professionally in high school, as a favor to my music teacher. He had a lounge group. It was an easy way to pick up extra money. By the time I started law school, I was making two hundred a week, working just the weekends." He rubbed his arm as if he were cold, but it was warm in here, almost hot, old steam radiators putting out more heat than the office needed. "So in the

| 186 |

beginning," he said, "it was for the money. Now it's because . . . well, I'm not a great singer or accordion player. And I'm not a great lawyer. I'm decent at both careers, maybe better than decent. But if I gave up my music, or even my practice, what I'd have left just wouldn't be enough." He stopped rubbing his arm and came around the desk. "That commercial for fried chicken—you do one thing long enough and you get to be the best? It's not true. Buy you lunch?"

"I'm having lunch with Louise."

Maxie squinted. "My Louise? Davis?"

He nodded. He had the feeling she was only meeting him to pay him back for driving her to the hospital last night. He had the feeling the next time he kissed her would be the last.

"Funny," Maxie said, "she never mentioned you. Smart lady. But no sense. I wish I could convince her to drop this thing against your uncle. We'll never get it into court." Small eyes got smaller. "I . . . uh . . . presume you know about that?"

"I know about it."

The round head nodded. "Waste of time. And money. And she doesn't have enough of either." His blotter had circle stains on it, the kind mugs leave. He checked his watch, sighed. "Still, it's a terrible thing your uncle did, if he did it. Anybody who knew Hank Trent would know he wasn't the kind to—to let anybody down."

Phil thought about Mom, how hurt she was, how brave she was. He thought about her name on the tombstone, and suddenly he was thinking about Nonna Do in the oxygen tent, her white hair flattened against the white pillow, a needle stuck in a vein in the back of her hand, a tube in the needle, the doctor saying, "When they're this old, it's hard to predict," but he thought the attack was mild, he thought the medication would do the trick, she was resting "nicely." "She should have been on medication long ago," the doctor had said. "Who's her physician?" Louise

| 187 |

hadn't looked at him, she kept her eyes on her grandmother: "She doesn't like doctors. They scare her." The doctor said, "Mmm," and left.

Phil told Maxie about Mrs. Zorzoli. The little man shut his eyes hard and shook his head. Then he asked which hospital and said he'd get over there as soon as he could. "Tell her how sorry I am."

Phil shook his hand. He put on his jacket and walked out of the office. A skinny young man in worn jeans and a new red sweater sat on a bench along the MUSIC FOR ALL OCCASIONS side of the waiting rom, his legs stretched out, arms folded. He was staring at the wall as if it were a movie screen. Phil turned in the doorway. "Somebody here to see you."

Maxie came out, squinted, then stepped closer to the man. "Can I help you?"

A bony arm rose slowly, and as if hitchhiking, a thumb pointed to the wall in back of the bench. "Got some business with that dude."

"Business?"

"For sure." The young man blinked. Slowly, he smiled. His other hand came up and he began beating imaginary drumsticks on his stomach. "Like he needs me."

The round lawyer squinted harder. "Dennis? I waited half the night for you at Burger King."

The young man's mouth fell open. He grinned. "Hey, radical—you're here!"

Phil walked out into the cold.

She was late.

The wind was up and there was sleet in the gray clouds moving in on the city. It was probably already sleeting in Ringbrook. He buttoned his coat collar and glanced through glass doors at the lobby clock in the Alexander Hamilton Hotel. He wondered if she was coming down Snake Hill and if it was sleeting there. He wondered if she was all right. He wondered if she was right: things were just too complicated.

The trim he had given his hair looked okay. He might have to give himself another trim before he found a barber. Barbers were hard to find, everybody was a hair stylist these days. He stepped away from the doors and peered around the corner into a faceful of wind.

She was trudging up Market Street, her head low, her collar turned up. She was wearing boots. In her heavy gray coat, with her arms folded across her chest, she looked like a Russian. He walked to her.

"I had to park near the post office," she said. She kept walking. No smile.

"How's Nonna Do?"

She looked at him as though he shouldn't be calling the old lady that. "Groggy, but stable." She was walking faster now, in a hurry to get inside the warm hotel.

He turned her by the elbow—"This way"—and led her back down Market Street to Torpedo.

She had the Marcello Mastroianni. He had the Sophia Loren Deluxe. He ordered "to go." He told her this might be the lucky day, it might snow at Garrett Mountain. She said she didn't want to go there. She didn't have the time. He said, "Then maybe we should eat here." She shook her head: even the car would be better than here.

The owner of Torpedo said he was sorry, his hot-chocolate machine was broken. He counted out change on the counter and said, "Merry Christmas." The cheap bell over the door sounded better in the wind.

She set a quick pace and kept her stare on the sidewalk. It was too cold for drunks and winos to be sleeping under the railroad bridge by the post office. She unlocked her Datsun and started the engine before she opened his door. She said she had thought of a place to go, close by. She asked him to remind her to get gas before she drove back to the hospital. She pulled out into traffic, and at the light she turned on the radio. All the news today was bad.

They were wider than he remembered. And louder. The mist they gave off made the air warmer here. She told him not to get too close to the precipice, it was traprock and it would be slippery. In fact, in this wind, it would be wise to stay well back. She used a glove to wipe off a section of bench at the view point. She un-wrapped her sandwich. She watched the Great Falls. She said the winter falls were the prettiest.

And she wouldn't look at him.

She bit into the hero roll and told him Alexander Hamilton had first seen these falls when he was an army colonel. Twelve years later, as secretary of the treasury, he had supported the local So-ciety of Useful Manufactures, which planned to build a city here, along the Passaic. The SUM hired Pierre L'Enfant to design it. He came up with a plan for streets two hundred feet wide, stretching like spokes from a central hub. The SUM couldn't afford the plan. L'Enfant used it ten years later when he built Washington, D.C., along the Potomac.

And she knew about Paterson's firsts: Samuel Colt's first re-volver was made here. The first locomotive, the *Sandusky*, was built here, by Thomas Rogers. John Philip Holland used the river to test his *Fenian Ram*, the world's first submarine. She knew about Garret Augustus Hobart, a big shot with the SUM who served as McKinley's first vice-president. She knew about all this stuff be-cause her grandfather had made her learn it. There was a statue of Mr. Hobart in front of city hall, she said.

He stared at her, at the way the wind played with her dark hair, but she didn't notice. She didn't seem to care. The Lenni-Lenape Indians, she said, called this place Totowa: heavy, falling weight of waters. Her smile was thin. "The Great Falls must have sounded more impressive to Mr. Hamilton and his friends."

He wanted to leave. He wanted to put his sandwich down and walk away, no words, nothing. He put his sandwich down. He couldn't leave. He said, "You're not eating anything."

"I'm not really hungry." She stared at mayonnaise on her fingers. "Phil, I'm sorry about last night."

He wasn't sure if she was sorry for crying or for leaning against him in the hospital room, for holding his hand, for falling asleep with her head on his shoulder for more than an hour, for waking up embarrassed. He wasn't sure he wanted to know: he never wanted to sit beside her like this again, to be this close yet be made to feel as though he wasn't there. He watched a chunk of ice go over the falls. He couldn't think of anything to say.

"What I said about you being in the way." Her head turned slowly, her stare walked up his chest. Her eyes looked tired, and sad. But she smiled. "It only feels that way when I'm not with you." She squeezed his fingers. "It's different when we're together."

And he didn't want to be any other place. "Then maybe you shouldn't let me out of your sight."

She shook her head and sent a cloud of breath toward the falls. "When I sent you home from the hospital, I felt . . . I almost called you to ask you to come back." Another sigh, this one long and slow, and he loved it, he loved the sound of it. "I just can't think now, it's awful."

"Louise . . ." It was the first time he had called her by her name. It made him smile. He leaned close to her and when he said her name again, she turned and he kissed her. She put her arms around his neck and kept kissing him. Until she started to cry.

She pulled away, made a fist, and hit the bench. "I can't get anything done. And I have so much to do. You're always there, bothering me."

"Bothering you?"

"In my mind, yes. I keep thinking about all the problems with . . . with being with you." Her fist came undone, her fingers stretched in the cold. "But when I'm with you, I seem to forget about the problems." She looked at him. She didn't like that he was smiling. Her eyes got hot. She turned away. "You wouldn't understand."

He ran a finger along the shoulder seam of her gray wool coat. "I was wondering, do you think I'll ever get to kiss you indoors?"

She glared at him.

"I'm not complaining," he said, "I was just wondering."

Teeth clenched, she let out a grunt. But she couldn't stop her smile. She couldn't stop her hands from fidgeting in her lap. This sigh ran at the frozen ground. "It's hopeless."

"What is?"

"Everything." Her lips pressed together. She glanced at her boots. "Me." Without looking at him, she put a hand on his arm, as if checking to make sure he was there. "I don't even have you yet, and I'm afraid I'll lose you."

He swallowed and nothing went down. His voice cracked, but he got the words out: "You have me."

18

Something was wrong with the boiler.

It wasn't fair, she said. She had brought him here to be alone with him—to make love, though she hadn't said that, she had only said, "I want you," and the Great Falls had answered for him, and she had driven fast up the mountain to Little Notch, he had had trouble keeping her in sight while following her—and now the house was too cold.

"And what happens to Nonna Do if the boiler quits the day she gets home from the hospital?" Louise cursed the boiler, then she cursed the old house. She got a phone book from its stand under the kitchen phone, flipped through the Yellow Pages, and said, "Damn."

"It's probably just the pilot light." He put the phone book back. "I'll take a look."

"It's fifty years old!" She got the phone book back out. "It could blow up."

He smiled and slid the phone book out of her hands. "My father had one in the basement of his old office. I've known about boilers since I was ten." He kissed her cheek and took his smile through the kitchen and down the stairs to the cellar.

He found the light switch in back of the door. The old boiler sat on bricks in the near corner, a silent figure of steel, copper pipes running out its sides like arms, a flexible gas line, gracefully curved, joining the bottom of the tank like an umbilical cord. On his knees, he pried the access panel off. The pilot light was out. He smelled gas. He turned the gas switch to Off, checked Dad's watch—he could hear Dad's voice from another cold cellar: "We wait two or three minutes to let the gas clear"—and he smiled and searched for matches. He found them on a shelf nearby. Long stick matches, the best kind for lighting boilers. There was a picture of a winged lady holding a torch on the box. He rechecked his watch, then turned the gas switch to Pilot, heard the familiar and strangely comforting hiss of gas through the line. He put a match to the nozzle. Blue fire. He counted to fifteen, slowly—"We let the pressure settle down so it doesn't blow out the flame"—then he turned the switch to On. A ring of blue flames danced above the pilot light, and the burning gas began to rumble. He refitted the access panel, brushed off his slacks, and walked to the light switch. At the stairs, he glanced back at the darkened cellar. There were smiling faces down there, he could feel them. He walked into the kitchen and shut the door behind him.

"Great old boiler," he said. "And oversized for this place. Must get it warm in a hurry."

"Yes." She didn't turn around. Arms folded, she stood in a little room just off the kitchen. It had one small window, with a view of the driveway and a piece of lawn, both getting pelted by sleet now. Above a stack of blankets and quilts on the floor in one corner, a cobweb clung to the ceiling and a dull yellow wall. Facing the window: an open closet, crammed with folded clothes and linens, an iron toy horse on top, as if to weight down the pile. Lamps, most without shades or bulbs, sat on end tables no one had dusted in a long time. Nearby, part of a crib leaned against the wall. In the center of the room, by her feet, a big steel pot caught what little light got through the lace undercurtains. The radiator beneath the window began to hiss. She smiled at it—not at him—and said, "Thank you."

He stepped closer, picked up the big pot, looked for a place to put it. It had a hole in the side. "This pot has a hole in it."

Without looking at him, she nodded. "Her favorite sauce pot. She's waiting for science to figure out a way to fix it."

He laughed. She turned and jerked the pot out of his hands. Then she took a deep breath, blinked at the floor, and let out a soft laugh. "She's something, isn't she." She stroked the pot, set it on top of the linens in the closet. "This was my room," she said. "And my mother's." She turned and looked at him. "This is the nursery."

It was where he kissed her for the first time indoors.

Except for a moment, right after the second long kiss, when she said she should really get some of Nonna Do's things into a suitcase first, Louise was as eager as he was. Maybe more eager. She moved the crib headboard and side rail out of the way, then spread a quilt on the rug. She drew the heavy drapes on the window. She tried to turn on a lamp, but none of them worked. She shut the door to the kitchen. She pulled off her boots, slid out of her coat. She looked at him as though she were disappointed that the best he could do so far was to kick off his shoes. If it had been her, that look said, she would have been completely undressed by now.

That look made him smile. He had expected her to be the slow one. He had expected he would have to coax her out of her clothes. He had expected her to be somebody else. "You're wonderful," he said.

"You're slow."

He watched her pull her sweater over her head. She wore a bra. It was mesh, he could see her nipples through it. She squinted at him. She threw the sweater at him. He caught it, brought it to her—"Excuse me, lady, I think you dropped this"—and took her in his arms and guided her down to the quilt.

The old yellow walls, now golden in the dim light from an old lamp, made her skin look like a painting. Every curve, every dimple and crease, every line of muscle caught a different piece of light, breaking her up into soft bits, making him need to run his hands over every part of her, just to make sure she was still together.

She loved his back, she said, loved the deep groove down his spine, traced her finger down it again and again.

Her breasts were smaller than he thought they would be, almost delicate in his palms, her nipples hard and pointed upward to his lips.

She loved his legs, she said, the way his thigh muscles hardened under her touch. She loved his ass, how it fit her hand. She said she could look at him from the back all day long. He said he hoped his front wasn't too big a disappointment. She wrapped a leg around him and told him to shut up.

She tasted salty and sweet at the same time. She rolled, she shivered, she dug her fingers into his hair and pulled. She cried out and she didn't let go of him.

She made him lie flat. She made him lie still. She made her own rhythm, her breasts brushing his chest and his chin, her eyes closed one minute as if in a trance, then open the next and bright with her fire. She made him cry.

She snuggled against him, held him, kissed his chest. After a while, she started tracing her finger down his spine again. She said, "You're wonderful."

He kissed her hair. "I thought I was slow."

"Mmmm," she said and she rolled him on top of her.

The sleet stopped. The radiator seemed to get louder. Warming slush ran down the steep driveway in slow streams, and for a moment it looked as though all the glue that held the cement slabs together was seeping out. But the lawn looked worse. The lawn looked like a polluted lake, grayed by sewer waste, dying in winter sun. He let the curtain drop. "That stuff will start freezing over soon."

She reached out and touched his ankle. She was smiling. She was lying on her side, her hair a black wave against the quilt. She was more beautiful than ever. "Kiss me," she said. "Then we can get dressed."

He knelt to her and kissed her. He forgot about freezing sleet and getting dressed.

It was her horse. Cast iron. Hand-painted. Brown, once, with a jet-black mane and tail. She said it was the only toy she would never outgrow, and she had known that the day her mother had given it to her. It had a broken leg, an accident with the stairs, and so it was in here, waiting for a welder—not just any welder, she had taken it to several and none of them could guarantee a perfect job, there might be a scar that even new paint wouldn't hide—and finding the right welder was like finding the right man, she said, impossible, "But you keep trying anyway."

The horse's name was Rosie.

Her coffee was awful and he told her so. She said it was instant, there was no way to improve it. He said there was no way to drink it.

Her red flannel robe covered her feet. Leaning against the wall as though she needed it to hold her up, she held the phone in both hands and talked to the hospital. Her eyes got wet. She hung up.

She tasted his coffee. "They're keeping her sedated until later tonight. But all her vital signs are back to normal."

"That's great."

She sighed and nodded. "When her head clears, she's going to be mad at me." She put her elbows on the table, her face in her hands. "I promised her I'd never let them put her in the hospital."

"But she would have died."

"In her own home, yes." She sipped more coffee, made a face—"This is horrible"—and pushed the cup away. "I don't know how I'm going to convince her to stay there."

"Maybe you don't have to." He stroked her sleeve. "They might let her come home."

She shook her head. "They want to keep her there for a few days, to make sure the medication is working. They said the time right after the first attack is when she's most vulnerable to another." She reached for the coffee, then pulled her arms into her lap. "She's going to hate me."

He got out of the chair, stepped behind her, rubbed her neck. "I'll go with you."

She put a hand on his. "I'm sorry."

"For what?"

Her fingers got light, her head bowed. "For needing you."

"Louise . . ." Her name sounded full and new, even here, in this kitchen that had heard her name so often and in so many different ways. ". . . You may be almost as fucked up as I am."

She turned just far enough to glance at him. She squeezed his hand, then let go and turned away, bringing the coffee cup to her lips. She didn't drink, she let steam from the brew heat her face. "You're not even a close second."

He rubbed her neck some more. "That's very comforting—the woman I'm in love with is a lot more fucked up than me. For a while I was worried, but now—"

"You're not in love with me. There hasn't been time for that."

He rubbed harder. "Right. But I'm planning on being in love with you as soon as the basic time period ends." He put his watch in front of her. "When the big hand gets to the nine, I will be officially in love with you."

She turned away from his arm, sipped coffee. "I'd better get those things packed."

"I'll help you."

She stood and started walking toward the dining room. "I don't need your help."

He caught a sleeve of her robe, pulled her back to his chest. "Can I have this dance?"

"Stop it." She pushed free. Her lips bunched up, her skin pinked. "You're not funny." She turned and strode through the dining room toward the stairs at the front of the house.

He punched the doorjamb.

"Quiet," she said. "The neighbors will think something's wrong." She went up the stairs, a flash of red against the dark banister.

"No, we don't want to upset the neighbors—just us." He didn't shout it, though he felt like shouting it. He knew she could hear him. He could hear her, her bare feet on the floor up there, dresser drawers opening. He sat at the table, then got up and walked to the window. He kicked the edge of the stove on his way back to the table. He drank coffee. He thought about throwing the cup through the window. He thought about rigging the boiler so the house would blow up. He thought about going upstairs and having it out with her, in a voice so loud the whole neighborhood would hear everything. He thought about her and he couldn't think about anything else. "It's hopeless," he told the refrigerator. He looked inside, but couldn't find any snacks, only casseroles and sauce jars. No one ate between meals here. Maybe the meals were so good, and the portions so large, no one could eat snacks in this house.

She walked into the kitchen with a suitcase and a frown. She put the suitcase by the table. She went into the nursery, picked up her clothes. Standing on the quilt, arms full of loose garments, she stared at the walls and said, "This will be perfect for her. No stairs to climb, close to the kitchen and bathroom." She turned and squinted at him. "It wouldn't take too long to fix up, would it? Some paint—"

"I'm not going let you hurt me like this," he said.

"Phil, please."

"No."

"Don't, this isn't like you."

"How would you know?"

Her eyes narrowed. "You're acting like a bully. And I don't like it."

He forced a grin, a good grin, nice and wide. "I am going to give you the hardest time you've ever had in your life." He sat at the table. "And I'm going to like it."

Her mouth set hard. "I'm not sure I want you to be in love with me."

"Tough."

She glared and squeezed the bundle of clothes. "Well, I don't want to be in love. With anyone."

He turned the cup by its handle. "Coward."

She came out of the little room, eyes wide and hot. "You're not the first man I've made love to."

He smiled at her—for her—and he felt tears building, tears that surprised him. "Just as long as I'm the last."

Her lips trembled, her eyes got softer than the yellow in those old walls. And her smile was the most beautiful thing he had ever seen. "Oh, Phil" leaked out of her mouth and she dropped the clothes and ran into his arms.

In stocking feet, she was sitting on the couch, all the presents he had bought lined up on the coffee table in front of her. He shut the door and she glanced at him. "Hello, darling," she said.

"Hi, Sarah."

Louise squeezed his arm. "Sarah?"

"Would you be terribly mad at me," Mom said, "if I opened these?" Her fingers touched ribboned bows and foil paper. "Just to look at the gifts? I've been debating it all day."

"Mom—"

Louise pinched his arm. "Who is Sarah?"

"It's not that I don't trust your judgment." Mom tried to smile. "And the wrappings are so lovely." Her smile never formed. Her jaw dropped. She saw.

"Mom," he said. "This is Louise."

19

"Oh, Phil, how could you?"

"I tried to get you to listen to me," he said. "Maybe if you heard it from her—"

"You had no right to do this." She stood and glanced about as if looking for the fastest way out of the room, a hand pinching the collar of her housecoat closed at the throat. "I'm not dressed to receive anyone."

"Mom, sit down."

She turned and started for the stairs. "You should have phoned first."

He cut her off. She glared at him. He had never seen her this angry. Her knuckles were white from clutching the housecoat. She said, "I'll never forgive you for this."

He thought about slapping her. It made his stomach turn. He had been angry with her before, but he had never thought of striking her. He put his hands on her shoulders, drew her close, held her. Her body went stiff, a tremor ran down her spine. He glanced at Louise and, with his eyes, signaled her to the couch. She moved slowly, as if suddenly tired, and she sat without taking off her gray coat.

"All I want you to do," he said, "is listen to her."

She shook her head.

"Her grandmother's in the hospital with a heart attack."

Her shoulders tensed, she tried to turn away.

He tightened his grip. "She was like a daughter to him."

She shuddered as though it hurt to breathe.

"She can show you documents about their business relationship—a business relationship, Mom."

She sighed, and he knew she wasn't listening. She was enduring this, and only because he was making her endure it, and her eyes held a vacant look, as if she had put herself in another place and canceled everything that was happening here. He inched her away from his chest, bent to her eye level. "I'm in love with her, Mom."

For an instant, he thought it had worked, a softness almost made it through her empty stare. He tried a smile and said, "She's the one who puts the roses on his grave."

Her eyes began to water. Then she blinked, and her anger came back stronger than before. She squinted, her mouth set so hard she had no lips at all, just skin. "I want that woman out of my house."

His hands slipped off her shoulders. "And I'll go with her."

She shivered, then jerked her head to the side, unwilling to look at him. Her face got smooth, her cheeks almost rocklike. If she cared that he would leave, she refused to show it. He turned away, half hoping she would go upstairs now.

Louise was sitting perfectly still on the couch, eyes low. She didn't seem to care that he would go with her. He studied the china over the mantel, remembered the day the movers broke all the other plates and cups, remembered the hours Dad had spent down in the cellar trying to glue the pieces back together, remembered the day the insurance check came, the smile on the face of the young insurance broker, the words "I hope this settles the matter," and the look on Dad's face that said the broker was far too young to understand how this matter had already been settled, and the day those plates went up on the wall, part of Dad went up there with them, and he never mentioned them again, though there were nights when he would stand in front of them, a glass of scotch in his hand, and he would smile at them as he had never smiled at anything else. Phil didn't know why he remembered that about the plates now, but somehow those plates were more alive than anything or anyone in the room, even him.

He turned and Mom was still there, still glaring at the stairs. "I'm trying to do this for you," he said. "But if you don't want it, maybe you don't want me."

Her dark eyes lost their focus. She was clutching the collar of her housecoat again.

"Phil, you're hurting her." Louise said it so quietly it seemed to come from nowhere, it seemed to float down from the ceiling like the first flakes of snow from the sky. She rubbed the piping on the arm of the couch. "Mrs. Trent, if I'd known all this time you thought Henry and I were lovers, I would have come myself and told you the truth." Her swallow sounded dry. "It's a lie. His brother is the worst kind of liar."

Mom straightened her shoulders, put a hand on the banister, her fingers tightening on the polished wood as if she were calling up whatever strength she had left. But her eyes were full of fear, like a little girl so afraid to believe what she was so desperate to believe, so frightened to risk believing because it would hurt too much if it weren't really true. A tear started down her cheek, she began to shake. She let out a little cry, spun on a heel, and marched down the hall to her bedroom. She slammed the door.

Louise couldn't lift her stare from the rug. She looked cold. "Please, call me a cab."

"This is my house, too," he said, loud enough to be heard in the bedroom. "You don't have to go anywhere."

She glanced at him, then shook her head and stood. "I'll wait for it outside."

She was moving toward the door. She was really going to stand out there and wait for the cab to pull up. His shoulders twitched. "Okay, I'll drive you, then."

She turned the knob. "They must have a phone in that shopping center, I can call from there."

"I said I'd drive you."

"The walk will do me good."

"It's freezing out there."

She opened the door. It was freezing out there.

He walked to her. "Look, I brought you, it was all my idea, so I'll drive you home." He touched her shoulders. "I want to be with you now."

She wouldn't let him turn her back into his arms. "Stay here."

"I can't. And I don't want you taking a cab."

She stepped out of his grasp and down the first porch step. Then she stopped and turned to face him. "I want you to stay here." She watched her fingers button her coat. "If you care about your mother, you'll see she needs you now."

"And if I care about you?"

Her eyes got calm all of a sudden, as if the sunlight didn't bother them anymore. "Then you'd see I don't need you."

She smiled, actually smiled, and there was relief in that smile. She raised the collar of her coat and started walking down the steps, toward the long, narrow driveway.

He watched her go, not believing she was really going, but every step was making her smaller, taking her farther away. And she was walking faster now. He tried to yell, but nothing came out. He reached back and yanked the door shut, and the hard thud it made sounded better than any yell he could have come up with.

He ran across the front lawn, after her.

She must have heard his shoes crunching the semifrozen ground, but she didn't turn her head. She kept walking.

He caught up to her at the edge of the driveway. "The car's right there." He pointed back up the drive at the Ford, but she didn't look. "I can have you home in ten minutes."

She stepped onto the sidewalk and headed in the direction of the shopping center and the duck pond. "I'm going to the mill."

"Fine, it's closer."

She stopped. "Phil, I need to be away from you right now."

"Wonderful, let's take care of you. What about me?"

She glared at him, the light of the setting sun making her eyes darker. "I did what you wanted me to, I came here. I knew this was going to happen. I should have taken my car."

And she was walking again.

"It's over a mile to the shopping center," he told her.

She walked faster.

"It'll be dark by the time you get there." He took her elbow, slowed her down. "You can't expect me to let you walk around here alone."

"This is Ringbrook! Not Paterson." She swept an arm out in front of her. "There's no one here. They're all inside, hiding."

She leaned away from him, but he held on to her sleeve. "On this very spot," he said, hoping to make her smile, to make her stop, to make her want to be with him again, "six people have been attacked. Brutally."

She let out a sigh. "You're not funny. None of this is funny, so just stop." She slid her arm free of his grasp, shivered in the cold air. "I told her the truth. Now she can believe what she has to." She turned, but before she took a step, she turned back. "Ask yourself why she's so ready to believe Henry cheated on her. Better yet, ask her."

He wasn't sure he wanted to know. He stuck his hands in his pockets, swallowed cold, dry air. "Maybe he"—it hurt to speak—"had another woman."

The hardness in her stare made him feel like a traitor. He swallowed again. "It happens," he said.

"If someone told Nonna Do that Pop-Pop, that my grandfather had been unfaithful, she would never believe it. She knew him too well for that." She touched his arm. "I don't know what your mother's problems are. I only know I don't want to have to deal with them."

Down the street, a car started. He drew a breath, let it out. "They don't have to be our problems."

"I don't even want to think about that now. I'm cold, I'm tired, I'm hungry, and I don't want to be with anyone." She rubbed her hands, fished gloves from her pocket, put them on as though her hands hurt. "I want you to go back. Please?"

"I'm not just anyone, am I?"

She sighed again. "No."

"Then don't run away from me."

She blinked and gazed down the street. "I don't know how to be with you right now."

"Just be with me."

"I know how to be alone, it's how I take care of myself."

"Well, great. You make a terrific partner."

She squinted, first at the street, then at him, and there was something bitter in her eyes, something so dark it looked like hate. "Go home, Phil."

A car came down the street. It was the Ford. Mom sat behind the wheel. She kept her stare straight ahead. She drove fast.

"Shit," he said. "I can't believe this. Where the hell is she going?"

Louise turned—"Maybe she needs to get away, too"—and she started walking.

He watched her go, and for some reason his legs felt as if they were getting weaker with each step she took. "I'll walk you there," he said, but she didn't turn around and she didn't slow down. And the Ford was so far down the avenue, it didn't look like a car anymore, just a dark blob on the dark street. "You can come back and call from the house!"

Louise wasn't coming back. For a moment, he thought he might never see her or Mom again, they might vanish forever as soon as they got out of sight. If she wants to walk, let her walk. Let her wait in the A&P, by the automatic door that would keep opening and blasting her with cold air, let her take a cab, if it ever came, and there was no guarantee it would: Ringbrook Cab Service wasn't reliable, they had one driver—what was his name, the ex-fighter, the guy who showed up drunk when he came to take Wally Peck's aunt to New York because Mr. Peck refused to drive in the city and all the buses were on strike—Zack Ryerson, Bone-Bustin' Ryerson, so drunk that poor Mr. Peck had to send him away, and almost fight him in the driveway because Zack wanted to get paid for showing up, but the former number-five-ranked middleweight was out of shape and he knew it and he probably didn't want to risk getting beat up by a high school science teacher, so when the bluff didn't work, Zack drove off and Mr. Peck wound up taking Wally's aunt in to see the Broadway show. Maybe Zack Ryerson would come to pick up Louise. Maybe Zack would take her to the mill by way of Hoboken. It would serve her right.

Maybe some lunatic would attack her on the way to the A&P. And maybe it *would* be Zack Ryerson who came to get her. Maybe she needed Phil. He wanted to run after her. He forced himself to turn around and walk back to the house. She had done all right taking care of herself before she met him, she would be okay. Mom, too. Neither one of them wanted him. And it wasn't the first time he had been deserted. Sarah had done it. It had hurt for a while, but later he had been glad she had left him. Maybe, in a little while, he would feel glad to be rid of Mom and Louise. He tasted a tear in the corner of his mouth, then felt another run down his cheek. He was ashamed to be crying, on this street, where he had never cried before. He was ashamed he hurt. He quickened his stride and marched back across the front lawn.

The living-room lights were on. Mom must have been in a big hurry to leave, to go wherever it was she had gone, probably to Ed's place. If she had forgotten to turn off the lights, maybe she had forgotten to lock up. No, she even locked the door when she went to throw out the garbage. He dug keys from his pocket and hoped they worked. But he wouldn't mind breaking a cellar window and crawling in that way. Tonight, he wouldn't mind breaking something.

The front door wasn't locked. He tested the key anyway. It worked. He found a package of waffles in the freezer. Ed must like them, because Mom would never buy them: if Dad or Phil had wanted waffles, she would go down to the cellar and fish out her waffle iron, or she would tell them to go out and get real waffles at the Pancake House. The frozen waffles were jumbo size, they barely fit the toaster slots. They had pieces of blueberries in them.

No milk in the refrigerator. He took a beer. Mom didn't drink beer, it made her drowsy. The can was brown and it didn't wear a brand name, it was one of those generic products: all it had on it was *Beer*. He tasted it. Not bad. Too cold, though. She had the refrigerator turned up too high again, there was probably frost on the lettuce in there.

He brought his dinner into the den, turned on the television and sat in the new recliner. He couldn't imagine her sitting in this chair. She must have gotten it for Ed. The corduroy felt cozy.

The early news out of New York was as bad as ever: two broadcasters, anchoring a team of reporters, took turns talking. Everybody was on a first-name basis. And none of them seemed to realize that he was smiling during the recounting of accidents, fires, crimes, and the story of the five-year-old girl who was still missing after three days. The weatherman didn't smile: his radar wasn't working tonight.

Maybe Dad had another woman. A long time ago. And Mom had known about it. So when Uncle Chuck told her about Louise, Mom would have been able to believe it. And no matter how hard Phil tried to convince her otherwise, no matter what Louise or anybody said, Mom would never be able to disbelieve it. Not completely. If Dad had screwed up before, it was all over this time. It was hopeless.

And he must have screwed up before. Mom would never believe he had been unfaithful, unless he had given her proof.

Or else there was something really wrong with Mom, something so wrong that it wasn't going to get cured, not at this stage of her life.

He couldn't finish the waffles. And the beer didn't taste so good now, not even after it had warmed up a little. The front door opened. A chill ran over his forearm. He moved the tray and got out of the chair. "Mom?"

"Julie? I'm home. I parked on the street to leave the driveway clear for Phil."

Ed was smiling.

"She's not here," Phil said.

"Out shopping?" He took his coat and scarf to the closet, reached for the light chain, grabbed only air. "Wonder how that happened?" He shrugged and hung up the coat. "Easy enough to fix."

"She just took off."

He closed the door and blinked. "I'm sorry, what?"

"I don't know where she went. Or when she's coming back." He tried to get the rest of the beer to his lips, but couldn't. "I thought she went to find you."

Ed stared at him, then he stepped into the den, punched off the TV, came back to the couch, moved a few presents out of the way, and sat. "Why don't you sit down and tell me what happened." His voice sounded dull, but full of power. "And why don't you do that, Phil, before you do anything else."

It didn't take long, but it took longer than Phil thought it would. Ed kept silent the whole time, he only moved to put a finger to his mustache now and then. The rest of the time, he didn't even seem to be breathing. Finally, he pulled at the already loosened knot of his tie and cleared his throat. "You should have told me you were going to do this," he said. "I could have helped get her ready."

Phil hung his head and nodded.

"You did the right thing," Ed told him. "But you did it the wrong way." He reached into his pocket and came out with the car keys. He put them on the coffee table. "The left front tire might need air, I was too tired to check. I'll wait here for her."

"I don't know where to look for her."

"Julie can take care of herself. I'm not so sure about your Louise."

He stared at the keys. Had she made it all right to the A&P? Did the cab come? He could call the mill to find out. And if she wasn't there? He ran a hand through his hair. "I don't know what to do."

Ed smiled. "Before I met your mother, I would have gone to my office and found some work to do. Now"—he stood and he lost his smile—"I'm going to fix myself some dinner and be here when she gets back." He walked to the kitchen, stopped in the doorway, turned. "It's not my place to say this, but you won't make any of this go away by running from it again." He stepped into the kitchen and opened the refrigerator.

"I didn't run from it." The words tasted beer-stained and bitter.

Ed peered over the refrigerator door. "You didn't stay." His eyes got smaller. "I don't know what you found out on the road. I hope it was a lot. And I hope you can make it count. But the only thing I admire about you so far, Phil, is that you came home." He blinked, then disappeared behind the door again.

The armchair felt lumpy. He studied the gift-wrapped presents, sure that any second he would get so angry he would smash those boxes. But he didn't feel angry. He felt tired. Far too tired to do anything, to be of any use to anyone. He wondered if Louise would be ready to talk to him now, if she needed him. He wondered if he should be here for Mom when she came home. He wondered what the weather was like in Corona, California, and if the houses he and Gary Simms had built were still as snug as he remembered. Everybody, it seemed, could do just fine without him. The car keys felt warm. He could make it out of the state, he had the money for gas. He could sell the Corvette, somebody would be willing to buy it, even without a pink slip. He could go just about anywhere, all he had to do was start the motor.

Only this time, he wouldn't be able to come back. And no one would want him to.

He didn't feel tired anymore. He felt scared. In his own living room, he was shivering. He squeezed the arms of the chair. He got up and walked to the kitchen. "Does she have keys to the office?"

Ed was holding a plate of leftover chicken. "My office?"

"Trent and Company."

The mustache twitched. He set the plate on the table and went down the stairs to the cellar door. He came back holding a red and blue lanyard. Two keys dangled from it. One of them was shiny. "We had to go there once," he said, "when your uncle was out of town. I forget why. These worked the locks then."

It was the old lanyard he had made for Dad back in the third grade. Arts and crafts: the box stitch. Not a very good box stitch, either, not as tight as it was supposed to be. But because Phil had made it, Dad had put his office key on it and there that key had remained, all those years. That key was dull now, but seeing it, Phil could see the old brass lock, remember the solid click it made. Just holding the lanyard made him smile.

"There's enough chicken for both of us," Ed said.

Still smiling, Phil shook his head and put the lanyard in his pocket. "I've got some work to do."

20

The shiny key on the old lanyard worked all the doors. It was like Uncle Chuck to have every lock keyed the same: less room for error. Phil locked the main doors and turned the light on in his uncle's office.

A little green square glowed in the top corner of the dark computer screen on the desk. Even when off, that computer was ready to take information from another computer. Uncle Chuck probably loved computers as much as he loved women. Maybe more: computers were reliable.

Four stout binders stood on the lower shelf of a bookcase in the back of the desk. Each had gold lettering, *Trent & Co.*, embossed on black leather. He pulled out the first one. He needed two hands to get it on the desk.

In the center of the blotter, a cube of onyx sat on a memo. He moved it out of his way. He saw his name on the note:

A Mr. Guy Ullis (You-lis) called for Mr. Phil Trent re: cash investment. Mr. Ullis = a professional football player (Giants).

The phone number on the memo had a New Jersey area code. It was possible these days to be a New York Giant and never set foot in New York.

Mrs. Frolen's handwriting could have won an award. Below her note, Uncle Chuck had scribbled something, none of it legible, except for "have Phil." Have Phil do something. He studied the note. It didn't make sense.

He opened the binder, began reading. The sound of something scurrying across the floor in the outer office made him look up. Nothing there. This place couldn't have mice, could it? The Market Street office had mice in the cellar, their droppings littered the cement near the old boiler. No mice ever made it upstairs, though. They might have had the sense to stay where they were safe. He slid the big chair closer to the desk and went back to reading the first page, a certification of some sort by Layman & Pierce. The great seal of the state of New Jersey had been crimped on a bottom corner.

"Hold it right there."

The voice made his head snap back, his heart race. In the doorway: the barrel of the biggest pistol he had ever seen.

The gun shook in the hands of a short man, braced with legs wide apart, arms outstretched and stiff. He wore a black hat, the kind policemen wear. He wasn't a cop. The uniform was wrong. Black and gold, lots of gold. The man looked scared. He said, "Hands up. Security."

Phil raised his hands slowly and began to stand.

"Didn't tell you to move." The man sounded scared, too. "You hold it right there."

His teeth chattered. "It's not loaded, is it?"

"Hell it ain't."

"Look, put it away." He was sweating, but he felt cold. "I . . . I work here."

"That why you didn't turn off the alarm?"

"I didn't hear any alarm."

The short man grinned. He wore a name tag, but he was still too far away for the letters to be clear. "Burglars ain't supposed to hear it."

"I'm not a burglar." He tried to stand, but couldn't. His legs were shaking. "Look, this is Trent and Company and I'm Trent."

The squint took a long time forming. "Got some I.D., then? No, don't move." He came closer, glancing over his shoulder every other step, as if expecting Phil's accomplice to jump him. They had both seen too many television cops. But this wasn't TV. The little man with a gold name tag, stenciled black with *T. Lewis*, wasn't Kojak. T. Lewis was scared enough to pull the trigger if Phil sneezed. "Okay," the guard said, "but easy."

Phil stood, gently slid his wallet from a pocket, placed it on the edge of the desk. Stubby fingers swept it up, found the plastic pouch with the New Jersey driver's license in it. Thank God Mom had insisted he renew his license. Thank God she had filled out the forms and sent them in with a check while he was away. If she hadn't—well, she had, that's what counted. He swallowed and watched the short man glance from license to face. Why didn't New Jersey use pictures the way other states did? What was wrong with this stupid state, hadn't anybody bothered to think what a photo on a driver's license could mean?

"Address?" T. Lewis asked, and this time he sounded like Kojak.

Phil gave him his home address.

The guard shrugged, handed back the wallet, slowly lowered the pistol. Then he blinked and the pistol took aim again, even before Phil had let out all of his sigh. "How come you didn't shut off the alarm?"

"Well—"

"See, lots of your bogus I.D.s floating around."

"Well"—*Shit*—"It was a test."

"Huh?"

"A test, Lewis. It is Lewis, isn't it?"

"Yeah. What kind of test?"

"Put the gun away, Lewis."

Miraculously, T. Lewis holstered the big gun. Phil found his voice. "We wanted to see how long it would take"—he read the gold shoulder patch on the uniform—"Ringbrook Mall Security to respond. Your employer was informed in advance, of course." He came around the desk, patted the guard's shoulder. "Nice work."

The guard wore a dull stare: he wasn't buying any of this. Then he cocked an eyebrow and said, "How long was it?"

Phil glanced at his watch. "Six minutes and twenty-three seconds."

Lewis frowned. "Must've been that crowd around Sears that slowed me up."

"No, you did fine."

"I could've cut at least thirty seconds off for sure. See, Sears is selling snowmobiles and—"

"Just fine." He guided the short man into the outer office. "Would you mind turning off the alarm for me, on your way out?"

"Already did. On my way in."

"You . . . did?"

"Procedure, Mr. Trent. Wouldn't want every guard responding, now would we. Leave too many stores unprotected."

"Umm."

"Don't forget to reset when you leave." The short man opened the main doors. "I didn't mean to scare you like—"

"You did your job, Lewis." *Almost shot me, Lewis!* "I'll make sure I say that in my report."

The guard touched the brim of his cap, then glanced at shoppers in the mall, grinned, and said in a whisper, "And you're right"—he patted his shiny holster—"it's not loaded. Boss won't allow it. Don't want no accidents." He set the locks, touched his cap again, and took his proud smile down the mall.

One day soon, maybe even tonight, T. Lewis might draw that unloaded gun on a burglar. If the burglar had a loaded pistol, T. Lewis would be dead. How could the boss of Ringbrook Mall

Security sleep nights? The black and gold uniform got lost in the crowd. It wasn't safe out there. He wanted to run after T. Lewis and tell him that. He wanted to tell him about the mice at Market Street. Wiping fresh sweat from his forehead, he walked back into the office.

It wasn't Trent & Co. anymore.

The small and medium-sized sole proprietorships Dad had built the business on had disappeared from the books, there was no record of them in the first three binders. Those retailers and wholesalers had to go to someone else now for their taxes, their bookkeeping, for the discounting of their accounts receivable to raise needed cash, for the investing of what profits they made so that next year didn't have to be as rough as this year. Most of those small businesses couldn't afford top financial advice. That was why Dad handled so many of them: he gave them what they needed at a price they could pay. He worked as hard for them as he would have had his fee been several times what he charged. And his clients knew that. And they were grateful. And Trent & Co. never had a shortage of clients, there were always so many. Too many, Mom used to say: Dad never got out of the office on time. She used to tell him, at the dinner table, that her father's financial adviser had kept bankers' hours. When he wasn't too tired, Dad would tell her that Trent & Co. didn't represent a single banker. And when he was too tired, he got angry, and he would tell her that Mr. Vandermeer the baker was still working at this hour, he was almost seventy years old and he had been up since dawn. "And sometimes he pays you in cinnamon rolls," she once said. Dad had only smiled and told her, "Phil likes them."

Mr. Vandermeer made great cinnamon rolls. Vandermeer's Bakery wasn't a Trent & Co. client anymore.

Uncle Chuck was handling big corporations, like Tiptoft-

Weck Pharmaceuticals and the plastics giant, Ambinco. He did a lot of business with incorporated medical groups comprising teams of doctors who were each private corporations to begin with. He represented partnerships among lawyers who were corporations, the new hospital, the new chemical plant, real-estate developers, lots of real-estate developers, including Union Development Corp., and the largest auto parts manufacturer on the East Coast. Several of these companies were listed on stock exchanges. Tiptoft-Weck and Ambinco were among the Dow Jones thirty industrials on the New York exchange.

Under Uncle Chuck, Trent & Co. was a gold mine.

In Phil's sophomore year in high school, business had been extremely good, the best year ever, he remembered Dad telling him. Dad had earned a salary of $50,000, plus a healthy pension-fund contribution, and an additional $12,000 from his share of the profits. A lot of that money had come from Uncle Chuck's efforts with new clients. Last year, Uncle Chuck, working all by himself, drew $60,000 of salary, $15,000 in pension-fund contributions, and a profit share of $82,800.

And last year had been Uncle Chuck's worst year since Dad died.

Mom's share of the profits last year had been $193,200.

It didn't seem possible.

And Uncle Chuck was getting other allowances as well, like a leased Mercedes, on top of his fringe benefits.

Trent & Co. had never provided a car for Dad. There had never been enough money for that.

In the last three years, Uncle Chuck had done more business than Trent & Co. had done in the decade before. Servicing just one account, the Tiptoft-Weck executive retirement fund, covered the cost of operating the entire office. Everything else was profit.

Phil shut the third binder, put it back next to the others. One more fat binder remained to be looked at. He wasn't sure he was up to it. He wasn't sure he could take looking at all that money. On the note pad he had been scribbling on, he totaled Mom's income from Trent & Co. profits since Dad had died: $422,700. And that didn't include her share of this year's profits, already approaching $200,000 and earning daily interest at money-market rates, which would be paid in a lump sum at the close of the fiscal year, in January, just one month away.

He rubbed his eyes, dropped the pencil. He wondered who was taking care of the books for the fish market on River Street, the flower shop downtown. Maybe they weren't in business anymore. Maybe none of Dad's former clients were.

He pushed the swivel chair back from the desk and stood, then crumpled the sheet of paper, aimed it at the waste basket. He decided to pocket it instead, to be sure he left no trace that he had been here. He started out of the office.

He got as far as the reception desk. He pulled the note paper from his pocket, flattened it out, read it in the dim light coming through the glass from the mall. He ran back into the office, got out the binder he had just put back, and totaled Uncle Chuck's share of the profits for the last three years: $181,157.

Even with his salary and his pension-fund contributions added, Uncle Chuck still came out making $16,543 less than Mom since Dad died. And Uncle Chuck was doing all the work.

Why would he be willing to see somebody else get most of the money he was earning? Why hadn't he bought her out before he changed the business and started making all that money? She would have sold out, she would have done that for him if he had asked, and her price would have been reasonable, he could have made it back in a year, the way he was pulling down money.

Phil stared at the figures. Mom was costing Uncle Chuck over $200,000 a year. It wasn't like Uncle Chuck to let that kind of money get away from him.

Unless he didn't have a choice.

Phil got out the last binder and began paging through it. He didn't know what he was looking for. He hoped he would recognize it when he found it.

It was in the last binder. All of it.

The last binder contained all the minutes and legal documents of Trent & Co., from its first day of business, when it was just Dad, through today.

It was still just Dad.

Dated 1973, the document prepared by Layman & Pierce restructured the partnership. Uncle Chuck had been bought out by Dad. Uncle Chuck still had the right to a share of the profits, but sole authority over all aspects of the business went to Dad.

Dad had bought out Uncle Chuck for one dollar.

Whatever Uncle Chuck had done, it must have been a masterpiece.

A separate clause penalized either Uncle Chuck or Dad for leaving the firm to go out on his own. The penalty was loss of a share in the profits for the year either man left, and a restraint that he couldn't operate or have anything to do with a similar business or activity in the same territory for five years. "The same territory" was defined as New Jersey and a hundred-mile radius from Paterson that included parts of New York, Connecticut, and Pennsylvania. In addition, all pension-plan contributions would be forfeited under a special "vesting rule" that required each man to stay with the company until he reached age sixty-five or died or became disabled.

Uncle Chuck must have thought about leaving.

Another clause restricted anyone other than Dad from bringing in or accepting new accounts and clients.

Uncle Chuck must have gone after clients Dad didn't want.

The last clause stated that Uncle Chuck waived all right to any claim to the business in the event Dad should die first.

It wasn't like Dad to disinherit his brother.

But it was here. In writing.

And Dad's will didn't mention Uncle Chuck at all, did it. Phil hadn't noticed that until now. And Mom's will didn't mention Uncle Chuck either. Mom must know what Dad knew.

He glanced at the document but, without focusing on it, the letters blurred. He reached for the phone, and for a moment, he couldn't remember his home number.

"She's asleep," Ed said. "She came home about ten, a little frazzled. She doesn't like to drive at night, it's hard on her eyes."

"Where did she go?"

"She didn't say."

He hadn't asked her. He probably hadn't tried to talk to her about this afternoon, either. But she was home. She was safe.

"I was just getting ready to turn off Johnny Carson," Ed told him. "I only watch the monologue. Half the people he has on now, I don't know who they are."

"I won't keep you up." He felt wide awake, not the least bit tired anymore. He wanted Ed to get her up and put her on the phone. He said, "I'm glad she's okay."

"Well, she's got a ways to go until she's okay." He cleared his throat. "I'd let her get there at her own speed if I were you." It was the same tone of voice he had used in the living room, quiet, but full of authority: he gave orders in the form of advice. "Is everything all right with Louise?"

"I don't know. I haven't seen her."

Ed cleared his throat again. "Don't forget to check the left front tire." Then he said good-night and hung up.

It felt cold in the office. Even if he knew where the thermostat was, he might not be able to turn it up: it was probably preset or computer-programmed for maximum efficiency. He put the binder back, stuffed his note papers into his pocket. He got a phone book from the reception desk and punched in the numbers for the mill.

The restaurant was closed. The man who answered at the nightclub said, "Miss Davis is away from her desk. Can I take a message?"

Phil hung up. He paged through the book, but found no listing for his uncle. Mom would have the number. Mom was asleep. He put the phone book back. He flipped through Mrs. Frolen's Rolodex, found two numbers for Uncle Chuck, one office, one home. He punched buttons for the second number. The phone on the other end of the line rang once. A phone machine answered. A woman's voice—not Mrs. Frolen, someone younger, and sexier—said, "This is the Trent residence. No one is able to come to the phone. Please leave your message and the time of your call when you hear the tone. Thank you for calling."

A beep came over the line. He drew a short breath. He couldn't speak. He listened to the hiss of tape recording his silence. He hung up.

He switched off the lights. It didn't get dark in the outer office. Through the storefront windows and the glass doors, light from the mall reflected on all the chrome and leather. He opened the doors, locked them, and walked fast. The mall was empty. He didn't have to dodge shoppers to get to the parking lot before T. Lewis or some other guard responded to the alarm at Trent & Co.

21

He took the long way to Ringbrook Towers.

Past the mill, past the abandoned gas station, past the hospital and through its parking lots, past the bungalow in Little Notch, and finally out Union Avenue at a crawl, hoping to spot her Datsun on its way home, ready to turn and follow her. He didn't see her car anyplace.

He took Route 46 east to Route 3. Most of the cars on the road were coming back from Manhattan. All those headlights made him squint. But he smiled. He could see the grease-stained face of the young mechanic in scuffed boots who worked a filling station in Elko, Nevada. Phil had stopped at the station hoping to catch a ride. "Where to?" the mechanic had asked. "California," Phil had told him. "I hear"—the young man had gazed down the long stretch of empty highway leading out of town—"there's never a time they don't have at least some cars on those freeways." There were cars on the Garden State Parkway, too, Phil could make them out from the Broad Street exit ramp. Someone was always awake around here, there was never a time when everybody slept. He wondered what it would have been like to have grown up in a place like Elko, and if he had, what kind of a person he would be now. Probably no different from the young mechanic: amazed, and maybe fascinated, by what life might be like down the road, but not fascinated enough to take the first step. He took Raymond Street up the hill to Ringbrook Towers.

It was one tower. The other hadn't been built yet, tight money had held up construction. It was supposed to be a twin of the first, another glass rectangle rising twenty-one stories at the very edge of town, where Ringbrook met Montclair. But now the residents of the first tower didn't want the second one built. They didn't want the construction noise, the dirt. They had filed a lawsuit, Mom had told him about it over the phone. The lawsuit, she had said, was just one more thing Uncle Chuck had to worry about: several of his clients were involved in the Towers project. She had always taken such an interest in Uncle Chuck's life. She had always listened to him. She had loved him: a sister's love and sometimes a mother's love, and because he took care of her and the business, a daughter's love. Maybe she had loved him too long and too well to believe any part of what Louise had told her this afternoon. Maybe Louise was right, and it was hopeless.

Three rows of buzzer buttons sat in a panel beside the front doors, a soft light making it easy to read the names and apartment numbers. The top button stood alone, centered over the columns of other buttons: Penthouse, *Chas. Trent.* He pushed it.

No answer.

He pushed it again.

"Yes?" came through the speaker, and the voice wasn't scratchy or muffled, it was pure. Uncle Chuck didn't sound tired.

"It's me, Uncle Chuck."

"Phil?"

"I need to talk to you."

"What's wrong? It's not your mother, is it?"

"No." He sighed and rubbed his arm. "It's me."

"I don't understand."

"It's cold out here."

"Oh. Sorry. You remember the way up?"

Phil said he did. Uncle Chuck explained it to him again anyway, and a buzzer sounded in the big doors. Heavy hinges, silent, hidden. Marble tile in the lobby, video cameras aimed at every angle, taping every move. A bank of elevators filled a wall. One

| 224 |

stopped at the tenth floor, one didn't stop until the eleventh floor, the last one didn't stop anyplace but the penthouse. There was no button for that elevator, it required a key or somebody up there to send it down. He heard it coming. The doors opened. He stepped inside. The doors closed, the elevator glided up the shaft, the whine of its motor like a soft purr in the night. He had never been in the other elevators here, but he was willing to bet they weren't like this one. Every time Dad had stepped into this carpeted box he would tell Mom the elevators in this building didn't go down to the basement, people who lived here and wanted to use the laundry machines had to walk down or ride the freight elevator at the back of the place, it was a terrible design—no, he hadn't said terrible, he had said lousy—and Mom would never say anything, she would just stare at the wood paneling, her face peaceful with the certain knowledge that anyone who lived here would not do laundry. The elevator stopped and Phil was smiling when the doors slid open.

The little foyer had been redecorated. The walls were covered with cream-colored paper now. The big mirror was gone, replaced by a lithograph: pastel circles and squares caught up in a spiral that might have been a tornado. The penciled-in title in the corner by the artist's signature read *DNA*. In an alcove beside the painting, double doors hung from ceiling to floor. Mahogany, he remembered. Solid mahogany, from Nicaragua. He reached for the brass knocker. Behind him, the elevator doors closed, the elevator made a clicking sound, as if it had just been turned off. It made him shiver. A door to the penthouse opened, making the sound jar lids make when first opened and the air runs out.

Uncle Chuck was wearing a red kimono. The sash was black. "It's almost one o'clock."

"I tried to call you, your machine answered."

The door opened wide. "Are you in trouble or something?"

"I just want to talk to you. About the business."

"The business? Jesus, can't it wait 'til tomorrow?"

Phil shook his head and walked in. Uncle Chuck shrugged and shut the door. "How can it be the business? You don't know anything about the business." He walked down steps, past a big sectional couch, a playpen couch, that dominated the sunken living room, its corduroy made even softer by the lacquered tables all around. The skyline of Manhattan glowed through the wall of windows, the lights playing on the black cabinet Uncle Chuck opened. "Oh, I get it, it's about that football player. You take scotch, right?" He didn't wait for an answer, he put ice in a glass, poured scotch. Glenlivet. Better than King's Ransom. He poured himself a brandy. "Well, I think it's great. Not even in the office an hour, and already you're bringing in new business."

Phil took the scotch and sat in the armchair next to the couch. There was a balcony outside those windows: one white wicker chair facing the railing and New York. "It's not about that."

"Well, anyway, it's just great." Uncle Chuck sat in the middle of the couch, raised his glass high, then sipped his drink. His feet were small, the skin looked pink. "Hope one of his friends is the quarterback. Those guys, the running backs and wide receivers, too, they're the ones making the big bucks. We get them, we're talking millions. That's why I want you to tell him I'll be handling everything."

He tasted the scotch. It warmed his throat. He tried to find his voice.

"You'll tell him about that, right?" Uncle Chuck leaned forward on the fat cushions. "And maybe he's got buddies on other teams. Or in other sports. Could be just the beginning."

"Uncle Chuck—"

"And we'll do a great job for those fellows, set them up for life. Just have him come into the office." He put the snifter in his lap, the folds of red silk swallowing his hand. "Or tell him I'll run out to the stadium, or to his place, whatever he likes."

He couldn't look at his uncle's smile. He looked at the lights out the window. They seemed farther away now. "Why did you tell Mom that Dad and Louise Davis were lovers?"

The smile got smaller, but it didn't disappear. "Because they were."

"No, they weren't."

He fiddled with the sash of his kimono. "This isn't the time to go into any of that. It's old shit, anyway."

"Not to me." He stopped squeezing the scotch glass, afraid it might break in his fingers. "God damn it, why'd you do it?"

"I don't like that tone of voice." He leaned forward, held the snifter in both hands. "Look, I know this is hard on you. But I had to tell your mother. To protect her. And you. He might have tried to divorce her. You have no idea what a bastard he could be."

"No, I don't."

Uncle Chuck shook his head and stood. He walked in back of the couch, stared at the distant lights. "This is the reason you get me up at one o'clock? Jesus." He glanced at Phil, shook his head again, then turned back toward New York. "I loved him, too, you know. That doesn't change who he was."

"They weren't lovers."

Thick fingers gripped the couch, then relaxed and rubbed the corduroy. "She made him crazy. He got crazy with me, and with the clients I brought in. It was embarrassing, Phil." His eyes were smaller than before, but brighter. "It was—" He made a fist, hid it behind the couch. "Crazy doesn't begin to describe it." He was glaring. "He bankrolled her out of company funds. A quarter of a million bucks to decorate a piece-of-shit building that was worth twice that much torn down, even then. You have any idea what that land's worth today? I could find you fifty developers who'd give their balls to have it." He sipped brandy, pulled his sash tighter. "She used him, Phil. She knew how he felt about running out on her grandfather. The guy was a crook, for God's sake. But Henry still felt bad about running out on him."

He put the scotch down. "He never ran out on anybody."

Uncle Chuck drained the brandy, rubbed his stomach, stepped to the liquor cabinet for a refill. "I knew we'd have this talk one day. And I expected it to be rough." He walked back to the couch. "You don't have to like what I'm telling you. But you do have to hear it." He took a long swig of brandy. "Miss Davis will get what she deserves, you can count on that. She'll be a charity case by next Christmas."

"Not if I can help it."

"Oh, terrific. Now she gets the son in the act. You got a couple of hundred thousand to tide her over? Or maybe you're going to wait tables for her." He waved his hand as if to erase his words. "Look, there's nothing you or anybody can do. That property is taxed on its value and there's no way she can come up with that kind of money and pay off her mortgage, too. Somebody's going to take it from her, probably for a song."

"Union Development."

Uncle Chuck squinted. "They hold the mortgage. If they want her, they've got her." He moved to the end of the couch, sat on the arm. "You're mad at me because I'm telling you the facts? There's going to be a mall where that mill stands. And it's going to connect to the new mall, with a ramp right across Route 46, the state highway department's already approved it, for Christ's sake. It's going to make millions for its owners, and Louise Davis isn't going to be one of them." He leaned closer. His kimono rustled. "If you think you can stop that, you should go into business selling miracles."

The scotch felt too cold to drink. He turned the glass in his fingers. "If it's worth so much, why'd you sell the mortgage? Why not hold on to it yourself and—"

"Because I wanted to dump it. Along with all the rest of the junk we were involved with." His sigh sounded like a snort. "You want to talk about Trent and Company, we'll have lunch at the office tomorrow. You want to talk about this Zorzoli shit, I'm going to bed."

The scotch tasted fine. "You dumped all the old clients?"

"They couldn't afford our fee, we had to stop working their accounts." He crossed his legs. "That was all nickel-dime stuff anyway. A waste of time. Your father's idea of financial services was prehistoric." He reached out and patted Phil's shoulder. "But I'm glad your mother filled you in on what we're doing now. She's making a bundle these days. Can't spend half of it." He laughed and took a quick swig from the snifter. "And now that you're back, you can help me talk her into some tax shelters so she doesn't have to give Uncle Sam half of what I make for her. We can get her into the second tower here. Just a couple of obstacles left to clear before—"

"She doesn't know anything about the business." He stared at that round face, but he couldn't keep his focus on his uncle's eyes. "I went to the office tonight."

"You what?"

"I found the agreement Dad made you sign, about restructuring the partnership. What did you do to make Dad force you out?"

Uncle Chuck was already up the steps. At a table by the dining room, he grabbed the phone and punched in numbers, paced the hall while he waited for an answer. "Yeah, hello, Charles Trent of Trent and Company. Send one of your guards to my office and have him wait there for me." He breathed heavily. "I don't give a shit what your manpower situation is. I'll be there in fifteen minutes." He slammed the phone down, drained the snifter. "Jesus, Phil, what the hell's the matter with you? I've got over three million bucks in negotiable securities in the safe and you go and open the fucking office."

"I locked it."

"Why didn't you just tell me what you wanted to see?" He walked into the bedroom, left the door open. "Jesus, what a dumb stunt."

Phil stood. "I said I locked it."

A dresser drawer opened in there. Something metal hit wood.

"Damn it!" A closet door groaned, hangers clattered. "I can't believe you could be this stupid."

"Have the guards check it, you'll see—"

"Oh, sure, the guards. They got twenty-watt bulbs for brains." Something heavy, like a shoe, bounced on the rug in there. "What am I supposed to tell my clients if they want to trade those securities tomorrow, my nephew forgot to lock up so you'll have to wait for the insurance before you can get your money?"

He wanted to shout back something, but he didn't have it in him. He stared at the open door. It had been a mistake to come here. He should have known. He knew he didn't want to be around when Uncle Chuck came out of that room: things would only get worse. Louder and worse. He left the scotch on the table.

There was no elevator button to push up here either. He found the door to the stairs around the corner of the wall with the DNA painting on it. The stairwell wasn't heated. The metal railing was too cold to touch. It was a long way down.

The mill was closed. In back by the smokestack, a lone light shone on the parking lot. Just looking at the empty asphalt made him tired. Too tired to drive to Little Notch. Too tired to do anything but go home. He gunned the big engine and took the fastest way, out Pompton Road to the highway and the Ringbrook Avenue exit ramp.

Not a single light on in any house on the street. Wally Peck's father didn't work late in his garage-workshop these days. He might not be the neighborhood Mr. Fix-It anymore. Wally Peck's father might be dead. Phil parked in the driveway and let himself in the back door. He used the kitchen phone to call Louise.

Nobody answered in Little Notch.

He started up the stairs to his room. Something made him stop. He turned. He heard breathing, in the living room. It couldn't be a burglar. A burglar would have run out the front door as soon as he heard the door open. He inched back down the stairs, toward the sound.

Not a burglar. Mom. Asleep on the couch, no pillow, a woolen afghan over her, cobalt blue. It must be new, he had never seen it before. Her glasses lay on top of a book on the coffee table. The presents were gone, she had moved them someplace else.

He didn't know whether to let her sleep or wake her so she could rest in her own bed. Did she come out here a lot these days, to read and then fall alseep? Did the nights give her trouble? He wanted to tuck her into the afghan so it wouldn't fall off. He wanted to kiss her. But he didn't want to wake her, so he backed away and walked toward the stairs.

She cleared her throat, smacked her lips, and said, "Phil?"

He peered over the couch. "Sorry, I didn't mean to wake you."

She raised the afghan and sat up, rubbed her eyes. "I must have dozed off."

She had been waiting up for him. No one had done that for him in a long time. And she was the last person left who would ever do that for him. He kissed her.

She held on. She stroked his hair. "Ed said you were worried about me. I'm sorry. For everything."

He drew a breath from the dark room. It smelled of pine needles. "He thinks I ran away three years ago."

"You're home now."

"I'm here, yeah."

She let go and pulled back. "It doesn't feel like home anymore, does it." Biting her lower lip, she glanced at the plates on the wall, at the tree. "I want to believe what you and, and Louise . . ." Saying the name made her stop. She swallowed. "I don't know why I can't. Maybe I don't want to enough." She struggled to keep from crying. "I feel so small."

He put the afghan around her. "Did he have someone else? Ever?"

She shook her head, then put a hand on his and smiled at him.

"She's very pretty. And if you care for her . . ." She let out a high-pitched sigh, almost a yawn. "It took courage for her to come here." She put on her glasses, stood, and folded the afghan, smoothing it out with the flat of her hand. She placed it in the corner of the couch, stared at it. "I don't know what I'd do if I lost you, too."

He rubbed her arms. "I wasn't trying to hurt you."

She nodded, then turned and kissed his cheek. "I'm sorry I can't be who you want me to be. I seem to be disappointing everyone these days. Even me." She put a soft hand to his face. "I'm not going to open the presents you picked out. I shouldn't have even thought about doing that." She picked up her book—"Get some rest, darling"—and walked down the hall.

He wanted to tell her that the presents didn't matter. He wanted to tell her what he had found at the office, about his meeting with Uncle Chuck. He kept silent, watched her go into the bedroom and close the door.

The last time anyone had waited up for him, it had been Dad. Dad had been angry: "Do you have any idea what time it is?"

"You didn't have to wait up," Phil had told him.

"It's four A.M."

"Dad, when I'm at college, you don't know what time I get in at night. Or what I do. If you trust me when I'm away, why can't you trust me when I'm home?"

Dad had stared at him for a moment, his face perfectly still. Then he had blinked and gotten out of his chair. "You know, the last time I felt this foolish was the first time you beat me at chess." He had smiled and hugged him—"Make sure the house is locked before you go to bed, son"—and he had walked down the hall and into the bedroom, his slippers making a kissing sound against the hardwood floor.

Phil started for the stairs, then walked through the kitchen and made sure the back door was locked. He looked in the refrigerator: nothing ready to eat, everything in there needed cooking. There was frost on the lettuce.

He picked up the phone, punched in the number for Louise in Little Notch. If she wasn't home, he could take a shower and get clean before he tried calling her again.

She answered on the fourth ring.

22

"I'm fine," she said.

He didn't say anything.

"I was at the mill for a while," she told him, "then I went to Verona to see Mr. Nash between sets. You've never heard him sing, have you."

"No."

"It was a fiftieth wedding anniversary. He had them all dancing."

"I saw my uncle tonight."

She didn't say anything.

He moved a chair from the table and sat. "He says it'll take a miracle to keep you in business."

She sighed into the phone. "We had twenty-two people for the midnight show."

Twenty-two people could get lost in a room that big.

"I think he's right," she said.

He kept silent for a moment, then told her, "My mother said you showed courage coming to the house today. I think that's her way of saying she's sorry. It's a start, anyway."

"I don't feel very courageous." She sighed again. "Mr. Nash is drawing up a power of attorney for Nonna Do to sign. In case she . . . in case she gets worse and I have to do something with the mill."

"I thought you ran it and—"

"She inherited my grandfather's share."

He listened to her breathe. He got out of the chair and paced the tiled floor. He couldn't think of anything to say.

"How angry at me are you?" she said.

"I'm too tired to be angry."

"I wanted to call you, but I couldn't call your house, not after—are you too tired to come over?"

He smiled at the thought of being with her—even if she didn't need him now, she wanted him—and of making love to her. But his temples began to throb, and out of nowhere came the knowledge of what she was really doing with the power of attorney: "You're going to sell it," he said, "without letting her know."

This sigh was short and fast. "I may have to."

"'May'? I don't hear 'may.'" He stared out the kitchen window. The clear night sky made the backyard look bigger than it really was. Someone had taken in all the lawn furniture, even the wrought-iron table that Dad had left out every winter. "You've already decided to do it."

When she spoke, her voice was soft. "Every cent she has is in the mill. I can't let her lose everything."

"What happens when she finds out?"

"She never really cared about it"—she swallowed part of a sigh—"it's only another mill to her. I just don't want her to think—I don't want to upset her. Her heart might not be strong enough."

"What about yours?"

She kept silent. Even her breathing got quieter.

"There has to be some way," he said.

"A new loan," she said. "A bigger one, preferably interest-free. And that would take a miracle."

He sat down again. He tried to think.

"We can get a lot of money for the property," she said. "A lot more than if we tried to keep it and lost, and the state had to auction it."

He squeezed the phone. "Don't do it."

"Phil, please."

"It's what my uncle wants you to do. He'll be licking his chops. One of his clients is UDC." He stood and put the chair back. "He's changed the whole business."

"I know"—she made a clicking noise—"but—"

"It's like giving him permission to do it." He let the kitchen curtain fall back against the window. "To do whatever he wants."

"Hospitals cost money," she said. "So do private nurses."

"So find a way to turn the mill around."

"I have tried." She grunted into the phone. "The taxes keep going up every year. And business is falling off, I can't keep up with the interest."

"You can lay some people off and—"

"Don't tell me about my business. I've already laid off workers, I've cut every corner there is. Silky's band has been on half pay for over a year." She swallowed and her voice went flat. "And I haven't taken any salary since March. It's just no good."

The phone felt heavier. He switched it to his other hand. He stared at the coffee maker on the counter, the empty carafe waiting for the automatic timer to turn on the machine and have coffee ready for Ed when he got up. He wanted to tell her it would be all right. He wasn't sure it would be.

"I ruined it," she said. "If I keep fighting, I'll just lose."

"Damn it, you have to fight."

It got so quiet on the other end of the line, it was as if she weren't there anymore. Finally she said, "I can't."

He could see that new mall, sprawling across Route 46, connecting to the other malls, and he could see the bricks from the smokestack piled by the river, rubble waiting to be carted away. It wouldn't take any courage at all to let that happen. "What time are you going to the hospital?"

"I'm meeting Mr. Nash there at ten." She must have moved a chair, something heavy groaned across the floor. "Would you come over if I told you the boiler went out?"

"Yes. But . . ." He didn't know how to tell her how disappointed he was in her. He put the keys to the Corvette next to the coffee maker, where Ed would be sure to find them. "But I have to get some sleep. I'll see you at the hospital."

She didn't say anything for what felt like a long time. Then she said, "Okay," and hung up.

The buzz of the phone line hurt his ear. He wanted to go to her. He stared at the keys on the table, thought about moving the Corvette and taking the Ford, thought of her body, her lips. He thought of having to tell her that she was doing the wrong thing, she was quitting, and that he didn't know how to love her tonight.

He walked out of the kitchen and up the stairs. His room felt warm. The shower he was going to take could wait until morning. He set his alarm for 9:00 A.M.

A wheelchair stood empty near the nurses' station on the second floor. The door to 219 looked heavy, but it swung smoothly on big hinges. A white curtain had been drawn in an L from wall to wall, concealing the first bed. Louise was standing at the foot of the far bed, taking a nightgown out of a suitcase. She wore jeans and a dark sweater. It made her look skinny. She smiled at him, then held the gown up for the old woman in the bed to see.

"Ah, the warm one." Nonna Do didn't seem to have enough strength to nod. Near her head, a bag of clear fluid hung on a stand, a long tube coiled around it. The veins on the back of one of her hands looked black, probably from a needle that had been connected to that tube. "You brought my slippers?"

Louise took a pair of powder-blue slippers from the suitcase. They matched the gown. "Phil's here to see you."

The way she said it—a matter of fact, of no more significance than "It might snow today"—and the way she stood her ground and made no effort to come to him, made him realize that she felt as distant from him as he felt from her. There would be no kiss of greeting, no embrace: she wouldn't initiate it, and he couldn't, he was too disappointed in her, and angry at her because that disappointment had kept him up most of the night, she wasn't the brave, determined fighter he had made her out to be, wanted her to be, maybe even needed her to be. It felt like Sarah all over again. And it was his fault, he had set himself up for this, just as he had before, and it would only be a matter of time before the distance between them got so big there would be no way to cross it. Standing there, without moving or saying anything, she was leaving him. It was like watching a dream being erased. This time, he thought, it would be better—safer?—to let her go, without a struggle. He had felt sure that once he was with her again he wouldn't feel this way. But he did.

He stepped closer to the bed. There was an orange on the nightstand. The old lady's hair had lost its shine. Her lips were dry and cracked. She looked at him, but he was sure she didn't know who he was. He rubbed her hand and said, "How are you feeling?"

"Cold," she said.

"You'll feel better once we get this on." Louise started drawing a curtain around the bed and whispered, "She thought she died." He moved back, out of her way. She took the blue gown and a pair of woolen socks behind the curtain. Sheets rustled. She mumbled and her grandmother groaned. It hurt to listen.

The door opened. Maxie Nash came in carrying a briefcase, the cold sticking to his coat. He walked straight to Phil, shook his hand. "Good, you can be the witness." He put his case on the chair against the wall, dug into files. "She's not sleeping, is she? I've got a million things to do this morning."

"Now somebody else?" Nonna Do's voice leaked through the curtain. "Too many, we wake Mrs. Cohen."

"There." Louise opened the curtain. "Do you want me to brush your hair?"

"The poor woman." Nonna Do stared at the curtained bed

across the way. "Gallstones, and nothing they give her stops the pain."

Louise nodded at Maxie, then rummaged through the suitcase. "I know I packed your brush."

"Nobody sees." She sighed. She put a hand to her hair, patted it. "Louisa, my doctor, he looks like Perry Mason." She glanced at the orange on her nightstand. "He brings me this. From his boy in California. Home for Christmas."

Louise couldn't raise her head. She fought tears.

"You eat something today?" Nonna Do squinted at her. "I'm only here a few days, no worry. I'm home soon to take care of you, eh?"

The head of dark hair shook slowly. She drew a long breath. "Mr. Nash, please. She needs her rest."

"Right." The little lawyer flipped through a set of documents, got a pen from inside his jacket. "Mrs. Zorzoli, Louise asked me to draw this up for you to sign."

"I make my will already."

"It's not a will." He swung a tray on wheels in front of her, put the papers down. "Sign here, both copies."

Bony fingers took the pen. Her dark eyes narrowed into slits. "Louisa?"

But Louise couldn't look at her. She stepped to the window, traced a hand over the sill as if testing for wet paint. "It's just in case . . . in case you're here for a while."

It made the old woman squint harder. Maxie cleared his throat and said, "All it does is give your granddaughter the power to take care of things for you."

"She needs a paper?"

"Legally, yes, she does."

In the little silence, the pen did not move. Phil felt his hands clenching into fists. She looked so frail. Maybe the truth would be too much for her to take. He loosened his tie, moved the briefcase off the chair, and sat. "I think she should know."

Louise turned and stared at him. Maxie shut his eyes and pursed his lips. Nonna Do cocked her head.

"And I think," he told Louise, "you should tell her."

This silence was longer than the first. The old woman glanced at the ceiling. Her lips moved as if in prayer. She sighed and said, "The doctor tells you something?"

Louise shook her head, folded her arms, stared out the window. "You're going to be fine. A little rest.and—" She spun toward the chair. "Why are you doing this? You're making her worry."

"Look, wait a minute." Maxie held up a plump hand. "Mrs. Zorzoli, this is a power of attorney." He tapped a document on the tray. "By signing it, you appoint Louise to be in charge of everything you own. She can act just as if she were you. That's what this means."

"Louisa?"

She turned back to the window. "That's what it means."

Phil glanced at Nonna Do. She was staring at him, waiting. He studied the floor. He couldn't do what he had come here to do. He couldn't tell the old woman that her granddaughter was going to sell the mill. He had thought it would be easy. "I'm sorry," he said and he got out of the chair and started for the door.

"What would Henry say?" Nonna Do wasn't staring at him anymore, she was looking off into space as though trying to read something far away.

He couldn't move. What would Dad say? *"Cut your losses while you can still afford it."* Or something like that. Dad was good at cutting losses, he was good at everything that kept people from going broke. Maybe that was the best advice: it was just a building and some land, it had a certain value one way and another value another way, and Dad would opt for the higher value. He would probably say, *"Ride the horse in the direction it's going."* And for the first time in his life, Phil felt glad that he wasn't Dad.

He walked back to the nightstand, picked up the orange. It felt soft, better for juicing than for eating. He stared at Louise, hoping she would turn from the window and face him. "Tell her," he said.

Her shoulders twitched. She crossed her arms. "Henry would tell you I'm only trying to protect you."

"Tell her about the mill," he said.

"His mill?" The old woman glanced toward the window. "Louisa, they come to close his mill?"

"Damn you." She said it not as a curse, but as if all the strength had run out of her. She leaned on the windowsill. A tear started down her cheek. She tried to say something, but nothing came out.

Maxie shook his head and stepped to his briefcase, fiddled with the broken clasp. "You can get one of the nurses to witness it. We can record it any time." He got mittens out of his coat and headed for the door.

"I was hoping to talk to you," Phil said, "about Trent and Company."

The little lawyer kept moving—"Make an appointment"— and walked out.

The door shut without a sound. Louise wiped her cheek with the flat of her hand, then she turned and rummaged through the suitcase. She found the hairbrush. She sat on the edge of the bed, the brush in her lap, her eyes on it. "I tried, Nonna Do. I tried so hard." She glared at him, her eyes wet and dark, but she couldn't hold the stare. Her head swung back toward the window, she pressed her lips together. "I didn't want you to know what a mess I've made of everything."

The old woman studied her, then began picking lint out of the sweater, a smile building with each pinch of bony fingers.

He put the orange back on the nightstand and stepped around the bed, wanting to go to Louise, rub her back, hold her, smile for her the way her grandmother could. He didn't have it in him. He sat in the chair and shut his eyes, and for a moment, it felt like hiding.

Louise told her.

She didn't blame Uncle Chuck or Trent & Co. or UDC or the Passaic County tax assessor or the state of New Jersey. She blamed herself. She had run the business into the ground. She hadn't been smart enough or worked hard enough. She hadn't been right about anything. "If we don't sell it soon," she said, "they'll take it from us. It comes to a lot of money."

"How much?"

"About three hundred thousand, after the loan gets paid off."

"So much? For a small mill?"

Louise nodded. "It's worth millions to the developers."

"He only pays—I forget how much, a little bit, no? Nobody else buys."

"Anybody would buy it now," Louise said. "They can lease the land by the square foot."

"Then we do the same, no?"

"Nonna Do"—she got off the bed and stood in front of the window—"they don't want the mill."

Phil leaned forward in the chair. "They'll tear it down. And build something bigger, a new mall."

The old woman glanced at the papers and pen, then slid the tray toward the wall. "I take my nap now."

"I need you to sign these." Louise came back to the bed, her hands shaking. "I need to be able to take care of you. I can't do it any other way, don't you understand?"

Nonna Do closed her eyes and inched the sheet up to her neck.

"You never gave a damn about it," Louise said. "What do you care if they tear it down?"

Thin lips turned down, eyebrows moved together, but the eyes did not open. "No shout. Mrs. Cohen——"

"You didn't want Pop-Pop to buy it, he told me that himself." She ran a stiff hand through her hair. "Even Henry wanted him to get rid of it."

"Sometimes I'm not the best wife." Eyes still shut, she wet her lips. "Now my August is gone, I always must be the best wife."

Louise let out a muffled scream. She glanced at the papers on the tray and made a fist. She looked at Phil and grunted. She strode across the room, ripped her coat and wool cap off wall hooks, and marched out.

The old woman was staring at Phil. And smiling. Then she turned her head and shut her eyes.

He left quietly, hoping Mrs. Cohen behind the white curtain had slept through it all. He found Louise waiting for the elevator by the nurses' station, hands jammed into coat pockets, her eyes hard. She pushed the Down button a few times. Her eyes got harder. She didn't try to speak, and he was grateful for that.

He leaned against the wall. "Before you slug me, I want you to know I'm not going to leave it here. I'll talk to my uncle, and to UDC. About the loan."

"Oh, wonderful." She jabbed the Down button a few more times. "You're such a hero."

"Louise——"

"And so stupid!" She yanked her cap out of a pocket. "They won't even let you in the building. Don't you understand anything? You can't talk to those people, they don't care." She was wringing the woolen cap as though it were a wet face cloth. "Even if they lowered the interest rate now, I still can't pay the taxes."

"You can get a new loan for that."

Her nostrils flared. "On our cash flow? Don't be an idiot." She flashed a cruel smile. "Excuse me, you can't help that, can you."

He sighed. He punched the Down button. "Where are the UDC offices?"

She stared at him, shook her head. "Across the highway, on the north side of the malls. Please, don't do any more. I can't afford your help."

The north side of the malls across the highway used to be a tomato truck farm.

"I may have to go to court now," she said, "and have her declared incompetent." Her eyes got wet, her lip trembled. "God, I wish I could hit you."

He put a hand out to rub her arm. She stepped back. The elevator doors opened. An orderly wheeled an old woman toward the desk. She had a dull stare and spit leaking out the corner of her mouth. The orderly was smiling: "Here we are, Mrs. Lane, bet we're just in time for lunch."

Louise watched the wheelchair go down the hall. She glared at Phil, her face tight, her skin flushed. She punched him, a clublike blow, her fist pounding his chest. She readied another blow, the same fist held high like a hammer, but her arm sagged, the fist fell on nothing, and she stormed past him, ignoring the waiting elevator, pushing through a door marked STAIRS.

He stood there, unable to move. His chest didn't hurt, but after a moment he rubbed it anyway. Behind the desk, a nurse was trying not to look at him. He heard the elevator doors close. He pushed the button, but it was too late. And the orderly was coming back up the hall, taking long, hard strides and pushing the empty wheelchair as if trying to get a soapbox racer up to speed.

Phil turned and headed for the stairs. Halfway down, his chest began to hurt.

23

The rows had been so straight and neat, wood trellises running to the horizon, green vines leafing in the sun, and all those tomatoes like heavy balls on a Christmas tree. One Saturday long ago, Dad had driven him out here, on the way to a Little League game. The man who owned the farm had needed advice on a new piece of heavy equipment that would enable him to put all of his two-hundred-plus acres in tomatoes. He had two sons, both about Phil's age. They wore jeans and work boots. Instead of a major-league emblem, the patch on their ball caps read *Ortho Fertilizer*. They didn't smile at him or speak to him, they studied his uniform as if confused by the lettering across the front that had begun to peel off because of too many headfirst slides, then the boys went down the long straight rows with hoes and shears. The bigger boy stopped to pick up a rock and hurl it toward the distant tree line. He had a good arm. The road had been gravel then, and the small white house stood only a few feet back, no grass anywhere. There had been an outhouse, Phil remembered, with tractors parked nearby. It hadn't smelled good and he had been afraid to use it. He had been glad when Dad said it was time to go.

There were no more tomatoes. The UDC building, all six stories of it in gleaming steel and glass, sat in the center of a land-scaped lawn, young trees casting leafless stick shadows on the long asphalt drive and parking lot. Big tracts of land behind the building had been leveled by bulldozers. Giant culverts littered the scraped earth. Red letters on a wide sign read FUTURE SITE OF but the winter weather had already stolen the rest of it.

He locked the car. Where would a retired tomato farmer go? Florida? Maybe the man hadn't gone anywhere. Maybe he had died. His sons might be playing men's softball on a field lined with palm trees, collecting their interest checks each month, happy to have escaped the snows and the long seasons of planting and harvest. He walked up a ramp to glass doors.

The lobby looked like a space station, stainless steel and tinted glass catching sunlight. A directory stood near the bank of elevators. The first four floors held offices for doctors, lawyers, accountants, real-estate and insurance companies. The top two floors housed UDC. Every office on the directory was called a suite.

He studied the names on the UDC side of the board. Uncle Chuck had called someone here named Dick. Or Rick. That man would be a big shot, Uncle Chuck wouldn't know any middle managers. The senior vice-president in suite 602 was Richard Jenkins. It was worth a try.

"They won't even let you in the building."

A standing sign in the center of the hall read 1ST THRU 4TH FLOORS with an arrow pointing to the elevators on one side, UDC with an arrow pointing in the other direction. Just in front of the UDC elevators, another standing sign waited: UDC EMPLOYEES SHOW I.D., VISITORS CHECK IN HERE. A security guard in a gray uniform stood near the sign, watching Phil approach. He put a hand to the brim of his cap and said, "Can I help you?"

"I'd like to see Mr. Jenkins."

The guard nodded and pulled a phone out of a wall bracket. "Your name, sir?"

"Phil Trent."

He pushed buttons on the phone—6–0–2—and cleared his throat. "A Mr. Trent to see Mr. Jenkins." He squinted, then glanced at Phil and covered the mouthpiece. "You did say Trent, didn't you?" Phil nodded and the guard turned back to the phone. "Trent, that's right. Okay." He hung up, got a pass from a podium near the sign, and punched the lone elevator button in the wall. "Sixth floor, sir. The suites are clearly numbered."

The pass felt cold. One side read *Visitor*. On the back, small print spelled out rules and regulations, and what authorized use of the pass meant, and that the pass was the property of UDC. He turned so the guard wouldn't see him grin. A man in a brown suit strode past the sign, flashed an I.D. card. The guard nodded. Elevator doors opened. The man in the brown suit got in ahead of Phil and punched the fifth-floor button. Phil punched the button above it. The only other buttons read *Lobby*.

The ride up was quick and silent. The fifth-floor foyer had white walls emblazoned with a red UDC logo. No one got in the elevator. The doors closed slowly. He put the visitor's pass into his back pocket and leaned against the thin metal wall, feeling the vibrations of the car as it started climbing again.

Well, Louise, they let me in the building.

The sixth floor was done in cream, softening the red in the UDC block letters. The hallway stretched in two directions, with corners on either end. He followed the small wall signs—there was nothing else on the walls, no pictures or artwork—and found suite 602 at the back of the building. A potted fern stood outside the door. There was another just like it in front of an office farther down. He turned the knob and walked in.

A secretary sat behind a chrome and glass desk. She had blond hair, cut like a boy's, and her sweater clung to her breasts and body, showing a roll of flab at the sides of her waist. She turned from her typewriter and smiled. "Yes?"

"I'm here to see Mr. Jenkins."

She crossed her legs, her skirt hiking above her knees. She had thick thighs. "Did you have an appointment?"

"No, I just—"

"Then I'm afraid he won't be able to see you today."

He reached for the visitor's pass. "But they told me to come up."

"From personnel?" She drew her finger from the appointment

book. "I'm sorry, but he's in conference the rest of the afternoon. If you have anything that needs his signature, I'll make sure he gets it."

He shook his head, hoping to clear it.

A door to an inner office opened. A man with a thin face stuck his head out. "Is he here yet?"

"No, sir," the secretary told him.

"Well, hold my calls and show him right in. And think of something to tell Levinthal."

The door shut. The woman turned, got a bottle of Liquid Paper from her desk, twisted the cap free, then she leaned close to the paper in the typewriter.

Phil put the pass on her desk. "Would you tell him Mr. Trent is here."

Her eyes jumped from the pass to his face. "Pardon me?"

"Phil Trent. The guard just called you."

"Phil Trent?"

He nodded, then squinted. She squinted back. She punched a button on the phone, swallowed, and said, "The gentleman outside is Mr. Phil Trent." The phone clicked dead in her hand.

The door opened again. Mr. Jenkins came out smiling. He wore a blue suit with a blue polka-dot tie. He was as tall as a basketball player. He offered a big hand. "You're the nephew, right?" He laughed and winked at the secretary. "We thought your uncle was paying us one of his surprise visits." He ushered him into the office. "Couldn't figure out why he didn't just come up unannounced." He shut the door and gestured to a chair by his desk.

The chair was leather. There was nothing on the sleek mahogany desk, not even a pen set or a clock. Not even a blotter. Jenkins eased into a high-back chair. "You know, he speaks of you often. You've been traveling, I understand."

For an instant, Phil thought of saying, "I've been running," but he nodded instead.

"Well, it must be good to get back home." The tall man had a deep crease running down the center of his forehead, from the hairline to his eyebrows. "You know, I played golf with your father once. Years ago, at North Jersey, I was in investment insurance then." He folded his hands in his lap and leaned back in the oversized chair. "He wasn't much of a golfer, was he. But he could putt. Rolled in a fifty-footer that day. On the greens, he was deadly."

The walls were covered with architectural drawings, framed in hardwood: shopping centers, malls, apartment houses, office buildings, a train and bus station in Newark, a new manufacturing plant in Pennsylvania. They all looked the same.

"Is there something," Jenkins said, "your uncle sent you over for?"

"He didn't send me."

"Oh, I see." But the tall man didn't see. He squinted. "Well—shoot."

Phil leaned forward. The leather groaned. "I wanted to talk to you about the loan on Zorzoli's. About lowering the interest rate."

"I don't understand."

"My father lent the money to help out the owner, it wasn't supposed to be a hard-and-fast business deal."

Jenkins toyed with a cuff link. "Have you discussed this with Chuck?"

"I'd like to see the interest lowered to its original rate."

"Look, Phil, it is Phil, isn't it?" His arms were so long, they covered the full width of the desk. "I don't handle that. Not directly. Prime land, though. Underutilized."

"The original rate," Phil said, forcing his eyes to meet Jenkins's, "was eight percent."

The tall man pulled back into his chair, put a hand to his chin. He wasn't having any trouble keeping his stare squarely on Phil. "We're not in the business of subsidizing restaurants."

Out the window, behind the swivel chair, gray clouds inched

across the sky. More cold air, maybe some snow. Phil rubbed the padded-leather arm. "There's a problem with the property taxes. Anything you could do to cut down the interest would be a big help."

"I see." And he kept staring, and this time, he wasn't confused. A buzzer sounded someplace in back of him. He held up a finger, then swiveled the chair and picked up a phone. He listened for a moment, then said, "I'll be right out." When he turned the chair back, he was smiling. "We'll have to cut this short, I have a meeting now." He stood, and it seemed he had grown taller. He buttoned his jacket and stepped around the desk. "I can get someone to show you around the offices. We have some exciting projects on the boards."

Phil stared at his shoes. He didn't want to see any more tomato farms that had been transformed into concrete and steel. "Who does handle the Zorzoli loan?"

"I'd have to check on that. Propably our collection department. But they'd only handle the processing."

"Somebody must set the interest rate."

"I'll be happy to look into it for you."

There was no point talking to this man, this man could keep him going in circles forever. He got out of the chair and shook his head. Hard fingers settled on his shoulder and gently steered him to the door.

A small, runty man wearing thick glasses stood near the shiny desk in the outer office. He held a briefcase to his chest.

"Come right in, Mr. Levinthal," Jenkins said. Then he aimed a softer voice at Phil. "Nice of you to stop by. Give your uncle my best."

The small man brushed by. The office door closed with a soft click. The secretary picked the pass off her desk. "You can turn this in to the guard in the lobby."

He took the pass, ran a hand along its laminated edge. "Why do you have these things?"

"Our investors appreciate how careful we are." Her smile put a dimple in her cheek. "Have a nice day."

Tapping the pass against his palm, he walked out. It would have been better if they hadn't let him into the building. He could have gotten angry at them then, and they would have remained invisible, without faces or hands or smiles. He felt as sterile as the walls up here. They could use some graffiti, the next time he came he should bring crayons. Better yet, gangs of ghetto kids could be bused here to do the job right: transportation, spray paint, and lunch courtesy of UDC, a story every radio and TV station would love to air—heartwarming, decent, flavored with syrup. "Shit," he told the empty walls. Now even his jokes were going sour. Head low, he made his way down the long, bright corridor.

A green box of a car stood in the driveway. He parked at the curb: whoever had come to visit Mom would probably be leaving soon, and Phil didn't want to have to come back out and move the car. He didn't want to have to come back out for anything, he wanted to stay inside where it was warm and drink eggnog and eat Mom's Christmas cookies and put everything else out of his mind.

The green car hadn't been washed in a while. On a grimy fender, a handprint no bigger than a child's stood out so clearly it almost looked like a decal. He opened the front door and walked in.

Seated by the tree, legs crossed Indian-style, revealing knee-length argyle socks, Sarah tidied the ribbon on a small package. She glanced at him, then turned back to the tree. "I've been debating whether to leave this here and come back another time."

In the kitchen, the refrigerator door shut. Ed came into the living room with a sandwich and a can of beer marked *Beer*. "Oh, good, you're back."

"What are you doing here?" Phil said.

The mustache twitched. "Having lunch." He studied the path he would have to take between Sarah and the couch, then he turned and walked toward the front door, taking the long way around to the den. "I took most of the day off to take the 'Vette in and have that tire checked."

Phil took off his coat. "I forgot to look at it last night, sorry."

"I wanted the wheel pulled anyway, to see if it's out of round. But then your mother said she'd take it in on her way to drop off her gifts, so I guess you could say I'm lounging around here with nothing to do. She should be back soon." He stepped into the den, set the plate on a table by the big chair, and came back to the doorway, beer in hand. "It would be nice if you took her to the cemetery. Or at least went with her." He smiled and disappeared in the den. The TV clicked on. Channels got changed, bits of voices and music from each station running into the next.

"Could we go somewhere," Sarah said, "and talk?"

He shrugged and walked into the kitchen. "Have you had lunch yet?"

"Not hungry."

A plate of cold cuts sat on a middle shelf in the refrigerator. He got bread and mustard and started making a sandwich at the table. "Is that your car?"

"My mother's." She stood in the doorway, twisting the plaid ribbon on the package. Then she held it out. "Here. For Christmas."

He put the knife on the plate. "I didn't know you were going to do this."

"You don't have to get me anything." She set the gift on the counter, crossed her arms. Her fuzzy sweater made noises. "Have you talked to Guy yet?"

He shook his head. The box on the counter probably held cologne or aftershave. He could get her perfume. He didn't know which kind she used. "I don't think I can help him. I don't even work there."

"But you will." Her smile was small. "It would mean a lot to me if I knew he was being looked after."

He put slices of meat on bread. "Trent and Company may not be the best place for him."

She didn't say anything for a moment, she just shuffled her feet, uncrossed and crossed her arms. She sighed. "We may be married."

His arms got heavy. Even now, when he didn't want her, when he didn't want to think about wanting her, the idea of her marrying someone else made him pause. But not for long. He smiled at her. "Congratulations."

"Thank you." A whisper, spoken to nervous hands. "Phil, about the other night . . ." She shook her head. "I didn't mean to give you the wrong idea."

You didn't.

"When you didn't call," she said, "I knew I had."

He blinked at the cold cuts and the mustard jar.

"You always called," she told him, "except when you were afraid. Afraid of getting too close. Afraid I'd hurt you again."

He swallowed air. A shiver coursed his shoulders.

"I shouldn't have made us get together again," she said. "I just couldn't help it." She was staring into the dining room, a tear starting down her cheek. "You never let yourself hate me. No one's ever loved me like that."

He stepped toward her, ready to hold her and tell her he had let himself hate her, he had hated her as well as anyone ever had.

"Please, don't come too close," she said, and there was fear on her face, fear he was going to hurt her. She crossed her arms. "I can't see you anymore," she told the refrigerator. "Not the way we used to be. I can't even trust myself to be alone with you." Slowly, her gaze found him. "Not until we can be friends. And nothing else." Her eyes were big and wet. "I don't want to keep hurting you. Or me."

The same reflex that had made him wince at the thought of her marrying someone else now made him angry that she didn't want him for a lover anymore. It passed quickly, too, but before it had, he remembered the first time he kissed her—in back of the gym at Ringbrook High. She had just come in from a field-hockey practice. He had been waiting for her. The sight of her sweaty and breathless, and in gym shorts, made him pull her close and kiss her hard. She slapped him even harder. Then she broke into a laugh and kissed him in front of her teammates and her coach, kissed him as he had never been kissed before. And when she was through, he was the sweaty and breathless one, and she was gone, into the locker room, and when she came out a half-hour later, he was still there and she knew he would be and nothing was ever the same after that.

All along he had thought—without really thinking about it, it had stayed in a corner of his mind, not fully formed, just lurking there—that it had cost Sarah hardly anything at all to be the way she was, there was no danger to herself in stealing the shine from a lover's eyes and then brightening his stare, in deadening his voice, then making him shout, in causing him to fill with passion, even fear, in putting her hands around his soul, tasting his surrender. But it had cost her a great deal. She didn't sleep untroubled, the thoughts and visions of her victories with men did not satisfy, she was not invulnerable, and on empty nights, without a lover or her wars, she did not reign over anyone or anything, not even her dreams.

His smile felt deep and sad. "We can be friends."

Another tear rolled down her cheek. "You were my first love."

She had forgotten about Wally Peck's brother, Stu, who had been a senior and a track star when Wally, Phil, and Sarah were freshmen. But Phil had been wrong, so wrong about her in so many ways—maybe he had been wrong about her and Stu Peck. Maybe the only thing Phil had been right about with Sarah was that she hadn't loved anyone until him.

She drew a deep breath, tried to smile. "I'm glad I waited. I might not have been able to get up the courage to do this another time." She touched his arm—"I have to go"—and turned and walked into the living room, where she found her coat. "And please, see what you can do to help Guy. He's so worried someone will take him for all he's worth. And if he gets injured, he'll have nothing left." Her smile had changed, it was flatter now. "I told him he could trust you. I always could."

He wanted to tell her he didn't trust Trent & Co. and he didn't trust himself. He couldn't find the words.

The phone rang. He picked it off the kitchen wall bracket. It was Mrs. Frolen from the office: "Mr. Trent? Mr. Trent, your uncle, would like to speak to you."

Sarah blew him a kiss and walked to the door. She didn't stop to turn and look at him. The door shut with a quiet thud.

"Phil? It's Uncle Chuck. What the hell is going on?"

There was no chance to answer.

"Dick Jenkins just called me, said you were in to see him, said you told him we wanted the interest rate dropped on the Zorzoli loan."

The present Sarah had left reflected its own bright image in the counter tiles. "I told him *I* wanted it lowered."

"Jesus, what are you doing?"

"I was trying to get the interest rate lowered, Uncle Chuck."

"What right have you got to bring my office into this?"

"I didn't."

"The hell you didn't. Why do you think he called me?"

The front door opened. Mom walked in, and as she started to untie the kerchief on her head, she spotted him in the kitchen doorway. "Was that Sarah?"

He nodded. "Uncle Chuck, they're not going to do anything about the loan. I failed, okay?"

"What's my car doing out on the street?" Mom said.

"I want you to come right down here," his uncle said. "I don't know what sort of game you think you're playing, but I've had it. First you leave the office unlocked—"

"I locked the fucking office."

"Phil!" Mom said.

| 255 |

"Phil," Uncle Chuck said, "don't you talk to me like that. Now get your ass down here, I mean you don't stop to blow your nose, understand?"

Phil let out a sigh—"Don't wait up"—and he hung up the phone.

"No matter what you think of him," Mom said, "you shouldn't use that language."

Ed came out of the den, the beer can squashed in his fingers. "What's all the commotion?"

"He's swearing at his uncle."

Ed's eyelids lowered halfway. He grinned. "Tragic."

"Stop it," Mom said. "Both of you."

The phone rang.

"It's him," Phil told her. "He wants to chew me out for hanging up on him. You want to talk to him?"

She shook her head and retied the kerchief. "I can't, not right now."

The phone kept ringing. Phil smiled across the room. "Ed?"

"I'll pass." He ran a finger over his mustache and stepped to Mom and offered to help her out of her coat.

She pulled away. "I have to get my car in off the street."

"I'll do it," Phil said.

But she was already at the door. "And someone please answer that phone!" She pulled the door shut and walked out.

He sighed at the phone, reached for it.

"No need." Ed came in and pushed a switch on the bottom of the phone base. The phone stopped ringing. "It's just a bell silencer. You can still make outgoing calls." He got another beer from the refrigerator and made his way back to the den. "They're showing a rerun of the Rangers in Toronto, if you're interested."

Phil didn't want to watch men on skates punch each other and break open heads with hockey sticks. He wouldn't know who to root for. And he was tired of being on the losing side. He went back to the table and built a triple-decker.

24

She took a long time moving the car.

He put the mustard and cold cuts back in the refrigerator. The radio on the counter by the coffee machine was tuned to WPAT, an "easy-listening" station, now in a holiday mood: Bing Crosby sang "White Christmas." The chair near the kitchen window held a chill. Elbows on the table, he bit into the sandwich.

The front door opened and shut, Mom walked to the closet out there, hung up her coat. She came into the kitchen rubbing her hands. A white Peter Pan collar stood out against her charcoal sweater. She didn't look at him. She opened the refrigerator. She moved jars—"The mustard belongs on the door, not on the shelves"—and came out with the plate of cold cuts. She had done something to her hair. It was a lighter shade, and shorter. The sides had waves. "There's less than half a tank in my car."

"I'll fill it when it gets down to a quarter," he said.

"Don't talk with your mouth full." She slapped meat on a plate, found a can of nuts in the cupboard. "I may need the car tonight. Please don't make any plans for it."

He swallowed and said, "Okay."

She put the cold cuts back in the refrigerator. She looked stiff, as if she had been outside too long. She turned off the radio.

"Are you okay?" he said.

"Of course."

"New haircut?"

She glanced at him, her face blank. "Yes."

He nodded and smiled. But before he could tell her he liked it, she turned and picked up the plate and the nuts. She started through the doorway, as though considering taking her lunch into the den, where Ed and the TV sat, then she swung her head toward the table, eyed the empty chairs on either side of Phil. She turned back to the counter and began eating.

"Are you sure you're okay?" he said.

Her hand fell flat against the tile. "Yes. I'm fine."

"Was something wrong with one of the gifts I picked out?"

"How would I know? They didn't open them, it isn't Christmas yet."

He put down the sandwich. "Mom?"

"What?"

"Why don't you sit down."

She rolled a slice of boiled ham into the shape of a finger and bit off a piece. "I'm fine here. It's better for my digestion."

He squinted at her back. He took his sandwich to the counter and, standing next to her, took a bite. She glared at him out of the corner of her eye. She finished the slice of ham and rolled another.

"How long before I feel it working?" he said.

"What?"

"How long before I feel I'm digesting better this way?"

"Philip—"

"A couple of minutes? Half an hour?"

She drew her hand back from the plate and turned her head toward the living room.

He leaned against the counter. "You don't suppose standing on one leg helps it even more, do you?"

She spun around, her hand raised as if to slap him. Then she froze, her face got long, her eyes lost their focus. She sighed and went back to rolling a slice of ham.

"Why don't you just tell me what's wrong," he said.

Her fingers trembled. "Nothing."

"Mom, it can't be nothing."

She stopped fiddling with the meat. "Nothing's right."

His arms got heavy, he couldn't lift the sandwich. She took her plate and the nuts to the table, sat in her chair, her back to the counter. She stared at the curtain as though able to look through it at the empty backyard. Did she get this way every Christmas, or was it just this Christmas, because he was home? He wasn't sure he wanted to know. He brought the plate back to the table, sat opposite her, watched her for a moment. He tried another bite of the sandwich. He leaned back in the chair, stared at the curtain. "What happened to the wrought-iron furniture?"

She blinked. "Your father never painted them. They were beginning to rust."

"You threw them out?"

She sighed. "I painted them."

Ed walked in, covering a burp. "You know, there's a fellow at the office who watches hockey because it's the only sport blacks don't play." He tossed a beer can in the wastebasket under the sink. "Doesn't know a thing about the game, he just—well, that's a very nice hairdo."

She didn't mean to, but she smiled. "Thank you."

"And I like that color," Ed said.

"Thank you." She fed a nut to her mouth and kept staring at the curtain.

"Any trouble with the 'Vette?"

She shook her head. "All the tire needed was a new valve stem. I have the receipt in my purse."

"Just a new valve, that's lucky. Did they check the wheel?"

She drew a long breath. "All it needed was the valve stem. They didn't have to check the wheel."

"But I wanted them to check it."

Her jaw set tight. "Then take it down there yourself."

"Julie?"

"The keys are in my purse."

"Julie, what's the matter?" But he was looking at Phil for the answer.

"I'd just like to have lunch in peace," she said, and she got up, "without everybody poking at me."

The doorbell rang, someone rapped on the front door. The door opened. "Hello—it's me." The door closed and Uncle Chuck started through the living room.

Her fingers pulled back from the plate. She glanced toward the footsteps, then at the stairs leading to the back door and cellar.

"Julie, good, you're here." Uncle Chuck pulled off his gloves and frowned at Phil. "Julie, what in hell is going on with your son?"

She turned her head toward the window, held up a hand and wiggled it back and forth.

"He hung up on me." He took off his topcoat and handed it to Ed with a smile and a nod. "He's barging in on my clients and then when I try to talk to him about it, he hangs up on me. Julie, we have to straighten him out."

"Leave her alone," Phil said.

Uncle Chuck pointed a stubby finger. "I'm not talking to you—yet. Julie, I can't run the business if he's going around acting crazy."

She made a fist, rubbed it against her hip. Her eyes narrowing, she faced Phil. "You're turning this into a madhouse." She brushed past him and walked down the stairs, into the cellar.

"Wait a minute, where are you going?" Uncle Chuck pressed his lips together, glared at Phil. "Now do you see what you're doing? You've got me upset, your mother upset—"

"Excuse me." Ed left the topcoat on a chair and went down the stairs, shutting the door to the cellar after him.

"And she's right," Uncle Chuck said. "A madhouse, that's exactly what it feels like to me, too. Do you have any idea who Dick Jenkins is?"

Phil stared at him as hard as he could. "I don't know who anybody is."

"That's right, you don't know a damn thing." He folded his

arms across his chest. His suit didn't wrinkle across the shoulders. "I can't let this sort of thing keep happening, Phil. First the office, then Jenkins. It's got to stop. I'll need your word on that."

Phil looked at the curtain: the sunlight hitting it was almost white. "I won't bother Jenkins again."

His uncle sighed and let his arms fall to his side. "I don't know why you'd want to go about it this way, but in the future, if you want to know something, come to me first."

There was something hypnotic about the sunlight on that curtain, he couldn't stop looking at it. He nodded.

"Good." Uncle Chuck stepped closer, put a hand on Phil's shoulder. "I'll help you all I can, you know that."

"I'd like to know," he said, "why Dad bought you out."

The hand drew back. "It was mutually agreed we'd do it that way."

The curtain seemed to be getting brighter. "You agreed to sell out for a dollar?"

"That wasn't the only provision, read the settlement again. It had to do with taxes and—it's too complicated, you wouldn't understand."

"Why don't you explain it to me"—he turned from the curtain—"so I can understand it."

His uncle's eyes got smaller, his tongue flicked at his lips. He cocked his head to one side, nodded. "Okay. But you have to do more than understand it. You have to accept it." He put a hand in his pocket, stepped to the counter, leaned against it. "There were lots of things about the business your father didn't understand. And what he didn't understand, he didn't trust. I was wrong about him, too, Phil. I thought he'd be pleased with all the new clients I was bringing in, and how much I made for them. And for Trent and Company." He shook his head. "He just couldn't come to grips with it for what it was. He didn't have the training. To be honest, I don't think he had the mental equipment." He held up a hand. "That sounds harsh, I know, but—"

"It sounds stupid," Phil said.

Uncle Chuck let out a sigh and shook his head. "At first I thought I might be making him feel inadequate. He couldn't make the kind of money I could, couldn't interest the clients I brought in." He ran a hand over the tiles, traced a finger down the grouted seams. "But even when I explained it to him, he couldn't make sense of it. He even thought I was making too much money for the company, so whatever I was doing had to be—wrong."

"Was it?"

"Of course not. For Christ's sake, if you're good you don't have to break any laws." He stepped to the table, sat in Mom's chair. "I traded on the foreign exchange, put clients into precious metals, real estate, oil, commodity futures. Henry had no experience with any of that, it was like magic to him. And he was having some personal problems then." He picked a nut out of the can, eyed Phil. "Think what you like, but the Davis woman didn't do him any good." He ate the nut. "I thought, if I fought him on the business, he'd break." He stared at the curtain. "He broke anyway."

The words made him look away, through the doorway and down the hall toward the bedroom where, three years ago, he had found Mom on her knees and screaming, holding Dad's head in her lap. His lips and tongue had begun to turn blue, one arm had stiffened across his chest to clutch the pain beneath his sweater, but the other arm and both of his legs had become rag-doll limp, as if no longer connected to anything: the man on the bedroom floor had looked broken. He hadn't died there—if he had, Mom would have sold the house just so she wouldn't have had to set foot in it again. He had managed to find a way to breathe, he had even managed to talk. But not for long. He had died in the ambulance. So they said. Phil was sure Dad had died halfway down the walk, between the front door and the driveway, his last gasp taken on a stretcher, with the smell of coming snow in the air. White Christ-

| 262 |

mas. They had loaded a corpse into the ambulance, and the siren didn't matter then.

The cellar door opened. Ed went out the back door in a hurry. He looked ready to yell.

"We can go over some files together," Uncle Chuck was saying. "Maybe then it will start making sense to you." He stood and picked his coat off the chair. "You know, I can't forgive your father for what he did to me. I'm just thankful I didn't fight him. If I'd done anything to bring on that heart attack, I'd never be able to forgive myself."

The garage door groaned open out there and closed with a shudder. Phil lifted a corner of the curtain. It wasn't going to snow today.

"I'm going out to Morristown," his uncle said, "to look in on some town houses that were supposed to open two months ago. Nothing very interesting, but if you wanted to come along . . ." He put on his coat, got gloves from his pockets. "We could grab dinner on the way back."

He let the curtain fall back against the window. "I'll pass."

Uncle Chuck shrugged and let his arms drop. "I had great hopes for you, Phil. We all did. Lately, I'm beginning to wonder."

"Me, too."

Shaking his head, Uncle Chuck started toward the living room. "Say good-bye to your mother for me. And try not to upset her anymore." His shoes made a heavy sound on the rug. The front door clicked shut.

The house got quiet. He took a nut from the can. The sound of teeth crunching an almond made him want to stop eating. He swallowed and licked salt from his fingers.

Mom came out of the cellar. "Ed didn't leave, did he?"

"He's in the garage."

She stared through the window portion of the back door. Her

eyes were red. She had been crying. "Did he take a jacket?"

He got out of the chair. "I'll go bring him one."

"I'll do it." She came up the steps into the kitchen, but she didn't try to get past him. She kept her stare on the floor. "I'm sorry for what I said. I guess I'm just used to my own rhythms, of living alone." She looked at him and tried a smile. "I can't think of anything nicer than having you home."

He put his arms around her, drew her close. "I'm sorry, Mom."

She hugged him. "Why am I hurting everyone?"

He didn't say anything, he just held her. After a moment, he kissed her hair and said, "You'd better get him that jacket, it's freezing out there."

She nodded and stepped back, her hands coming together in a ball at her chest. "Maybe you should do it. He might still be angry at me."

"I think he'd rather see you than me."

Her smile was small, but full. She walked to the living-room closet and came back with a parka. "They have these on sale at Stern's, you should get yourself one." She stopped walking and lowered her head. "I threw out your old one."

The laugh started in his throat and made his shoulders twitch. It was so soft it sounded like fast breathing.

"You're not mad?" she said.

He shook his head and kept laughing.

"If I closed my eyes," she said, "I'd swear I was hearing your father laugh."

He stopped laughing.

She bunched the parka to her chest. "Ed thinks you're right. About . . . Louise."

"What do you think?"

She blinked and stared at the window. "I think"—each word was a whisper, softer than the next—"I think I'd like you to be right." She walked down the steps and out the back door.

He turned the phone back on and took the can of nuts into the living room. He sat on the sill of the window overlooking the front walk and munched almonds and cashews, their salt bothering his gums. One Christmas time, so many years ago he had forgotten which one, he had sat in this very spot, looking out at new snow, waiting for Mom to drive him to the dentist and have an abscessed tooth taken care of. There had been a piano in the living room then. No one played it. It had come from Mom's old house. Her parents, much older than the parents of her contemporaries and dead long before Phil had been born, had bought it for her. Every house in her old neighborhood had a piano. All the children on the block, Mom had told him, practiced at least an hour every day. He wondered what that Eastside neighborhood would have been like if all the children played all the pianos at the same time and their music ran down the street like oil. He wondered what he would have been like, what he might have become, if someone had taught him how to play even the simplest song, if he could have made music, just once.

He ate all the nuts. He walked into the kitchen to finish the rest of his sandwich. The phone rang.

Maxie Nash wanted to know if Louise was there, if Phil had seen her in the last few hours, if he knew where she was or could be reached. The little lawyer sounded tired and angry. He said he had some bad news.

Phil squeezed the phone. "It's not Nonna Do . . ."

A sigh came over the line, flat and hard. "UDC just handed me a notice of intent. They're calling the loan."

25

"Can they do that?"

"Not according to the original agreement," Maxie said. "But they've come up with a legal smoke screen."

Phil sighed through his nose. "The agreement won't let them do it, but legally maybe they can?"

"They claim the loan was really a mortgage." He was talking fast. "They call it an 'equitable mortgage' in this notice. And therefore they're entitled to hold title to the property until the loan is satisfied. Cute trick."

"But it's not a mortgage—is it?"

"It was never intended to be," Maxie said. "No title was to be transferred, even in the case of default, that's clear in the agreement." He made a clicking sound. "They don't have a chance of winning this in court, it's just a pressure tactic. They say they'll back off if Zorzoli's pays off in thirty days or agrees to their terms. Merry fucking Christmas, huh?"

He stepped into the living room, then back into the kitchen, but the pacing didn't help him understand what was going on. "Why would they do this?"

"They say they have reliable information that Louise is going to become delinquent on her property taxes."

Oh, shit.

"If she does, the loan is in jeopardy." Maxie wasn't talking so fast now, he was biting his words. "They don't want the state to take the property and auction it to settle the taxes due. There's not a prayer that would happen in this case—her equity is too big, she could borrow against it to settle the taxes, any bank would loan her the money, as long as she was going to sell—but UDC isn't taking any chances of giving somebody else a shot at that land." He drew a quick breath. "Isn't Louise supposed to call you or something?"

He rubbed his chest. It didn't hurt anymore. Probably no bruise. Nothing. "She won't be calling."

"Damn. Well, they sent an offer to buy the mill along with their notice of intent. If we don't accept, or pay off by next month, they're going to take legal action to try to get title."

"But, if they can't win—"

"They don't want to go to court. It's a bluff. They just want her to sell." He made that clicking noise again. "They know she's in trouble and they're trying to make the most of it. Maybe they're worried things can't get any worse"—his laugh sounded sad—"and they don't want to take a chance they'll get better. Obviously they don't want her to sell to anyone else. So my guess is"—he sighed as though he were a judge about to hand out a sentence he didn't agree with—"the minimum they'll settle for is dropping their suit in return for an agreement that gives them the right to match any offer for the property."

"She doesn't have to sign it," Phil said.

"She doesn't have to take their offer, either. But I just don't see how she can refuse."

The garage door opened and thudded shut. Mom would be inside any second: he stopped leaning against the doorjamb. "I went over to UDC today. I think this is my fault."

Maxie kept silent, but his breathing got louder. Finally he started talking: "Look, if you see her, tell her to get in touch with me. They're offering a lot of money, plus a spot for Zorzoli's in the mall they want to build, rent-free for two years and roughly the same square footage as the mill's top two floors. And they're willing to give her partial salvage rights to the building in case she wants to recycle stuff from the old place to the new."

The back door opened. Cold air swept in.

"It's a better deal than I'd thought she'd get," Maxie said. "I should be in the office to around six. Then I'm at the Verona Manor, the Paul Revere Room, from seven 'til whenever. Hello? You got that?"

"Yeah." He hung up. He couldn't imagine Louise saying no to that deal. He couldn't imagine telling her to say no. He couldn't imagine being with her again to tell her anything.

"Darling, are you all right?" Mom stood by the table, holding Ed's hand. She was wearing the parka. It made her look like a kid ready to go sledding, all dressed up in her big brother's snowsuit. She spotted the empty nut can on the counter. "You ate all of them? I'll get you some Alka-Seltzer."

"I've got Pepto-Bismol," Ed said.

He leaned against the doorjamb again. "She's going to lose the mill."

Mom didn't tell him to stop leaning against the wall. She didn't say anything. Ed cleared his throat, but softly, as if he hadn't meant to.

Sweat beaded Phil's upper lip, his mouth felt clammy. "I should have stayed out of the whole thing."

"I'm sure you were a great help," Mom said.

He shook his head. "I'm not in the same league with those guys. They had me for lunch."

"Guys?" Mom came closer. "What guys?"

He stepped away from her, not wanting to be comforted, not believing he deserved to be. "Jesus, what an asshole I am."

"Phil, don't."

"She's right," Ed said. "You won't get anywhere that way."

"I never get anywhere!" He made a fist and thought about slugging the wall.

Her palm found his cheek. "You got home, didn't you?"

He felt weak and worn out, worse than he had the day he got

back. "Everything I do . . ." *Turns to shit.* ". . . Ah, what's the use."

"Maybe you're trying too hard, darling."

"Trying to make up for lost time," Ed told him. "You can't get it back, you know."

He walked past the stove and away from her touch, bent to the cabinet beside the sink, took out a bottle of cheap scotch—the good stuff was locked in the cabinet in the den—and poured himself a glass.

"Phil, it's not even three."

"Let him alone, Julie. He knows what time it is."

He took a swig, stared out the window at the bare branches of a neighbor's elm tree. "Dad always rooted for me, didn't he? Little League, school . . ."

"Of course he did. He was your father."

"If I did things he couldn't do, or never had the chance to do"—he faced her—"that never stopped him from rooting for me, did it?"

"Darling, you're not making sense."

He turned back to the elm branches. "I can't believe he wouldn't do the same thing for his own brother."

In the silence, he drank scotch, then glanced over a shoulder to find her staring into the dining room, her eyes not focused on anything, her hands buried deep in the quilted pockets of the big jacket. He brought the glass to his lips. "Who gets your estate if I die before you do?"

She blinked, but she didn't look at him. "That won't happen."

"If it did."

Her jaw dropped. She turned. "You're not—you don't have something like they thought Wally Peck had."

"Jesus." He tried to clear his head by shaking it and drinking whiskey. "Mom, the point is—"

"One of his friends," she told Ed, "just down the street, got sick and the doctors were worried it was a rare bone cancer. Thank God they were wrong."

"Wally was on dope then, Mom."

"When's the last time you had a physical?" Ed asked.

"Wally Peck?" Mom said. "On dope? Oh, I don't believe it."

He finished the scotch and poured himself another. "The point is, Uncle Chuck has been aced out of everything."

"I don't want to talk about him now," Mom said.

"You don't want to talk about Dad, you don't want to talk about Uncle Chuck . . ." He banged the glass on the counter, whiskey sloshed over his hand. "What do you want to talk about, your hair?"

Ed stepped to her, put an arm around her shoulder. "Phil, there's no call to say a thing like that."

Phil hung his head, nodded. Maybe Uncle Chuck was telling the truth this time. Maybe Dad did break, or changed enough to stop acting like Dad, at least toward his brother. Maybe the best thing to do was to walk away from all of this.

He couldn't. Not until he was sure. And he didn't care what he found anymore, it would be all right, no matter how it came out.

He checked his watch: 2:45. He walked to the cellar door and got the office key off the hook, then came back up the steps into the kitchen. "I know you said you might be going out, but I need your car."

She blinked at the floor. "I'm not going anywhere."

He walked past her and Ed, into the living room, got a coat out of the closet.

"He's all right now, isn't he?" Mom said.

"Who?"

"Wally?"

He shrugged. "I guess so."

"And—" She turned to face him, but didn't raise her stare

from the rug. "And there's nothing wrong with you, is there?"

He put on the coat. "The only sick person I know is Mrs. Zorzoli. And she might outlive all of us."

She looked at him, squinted, looked toward the front windows. Then she stepped to the refrigerator. "You won't be long, will you? I'd like to have dinner early."

"Don't count on me," he said, and saying it made him stop pulling on his gloves. He shut the closet door and walked out.

Mrs. Frolen was turning off the copying machine. "He's not here."

"I know, he's in Morristown."

"Oh, he saw you. Good." She stepped back to her desk. The door to Uncle Chuck's office was closed, probably locked. "He was terribly upset."

"We patched it up." He got out of his coat, dropped it on a couch. "I'm supposed to do some studying here—files, client lists."

"He works so hard." She moved a stack of papers to a corner of her desk. "He was worried you didn't care about Trent and Company."

"I care."

Her smile got bigger. "I'm leaving early today, I should show you how to set the alarm. You have your mother's key?"

He got it out of his pocket, held it up.

"Well then, we're all set." Mrs. Frolen stood and led the way to the alarm.

He had started out using the top of the file cabinets as a desk, taking one file at a time, paging through its contents, jotting down anything interesting on a pad. Now, and for the better part of the last hour, he was sitting on the floor, surrounded by files, each of them open, and he leafed through all the computer readouts, scribbled memos, bills, and notices of transactions as if they were part of one big pile.

There was nothing here.

He didn't understand most of the abbreviations, and almost everything was abbreviated or in some form of shorthand, and it all might as well have been in code. What he could understand still confused him. Some files held schedules of depreciation six pages long. Some clients had traded positions in commodity futures without ever really changing positions, except on paper and maybe in their bank accounts—borrowing against the first deal to get into the second, then borrowing against the second to get back into the first, and then selling the original position and starting the whole thing all over again. A real-estate company in Warren County did over $400,000 in sales and wound up losing more than twice that, its third straight net loss, yet its assets had somehow doubled. Phil had the uneasy feeling that Dad might have had trouble deciphering these files. The files Dad kept on his clients never looked like this. And they never had this much in them.

And Phil didn't know what he was looking for.

He had been through the UDC file several times. Its headquarters were in Delaware and its shares were not traded publicly or listed on any exchange. It was doing close to a million dollars' worth of business every month. It had new buildings and shopping centers going up in five states. It carried a substantial amount of debt, but its cash flow was more than adequate to cover that. It looked like a solid company, the kind old men wished they had some money in and young men wished they worked for.

He stood. A small piece of paper fell from his lap. He picked it up, read it: just a date and an amount of money received. It might have belonged in any of the files. He let it drop, watched it float. He left it where it landed.

At Mrs. Frolen's desk, he switched on a lamp, found the phone book. He dialed the number for Maxie Nash's law office, hoping to get some advice on what to look for. Or some news from Louise. Or maybe just to hear another voice agree that it was time to quit.

No answer. His watch read 4:15. The little lawyer might have stepped across the hall to his other office. Phil hung up and leafed through the Yellow Pages, searching for Music. His fingers stopped. He stared at the fat Rolodex on the desk.

He turned the cards, found the one for Uncle Chuck. Phil hadn't been wrong, there were two numbers listed, one home, one office. The office phone number on the card didn't belong to Trent & Co. Why would Mrs. Frolen have Uncle Chuck's office number in her Rolodex? The Rolodex was *in* the office.

He dialed the number.

On the second ring, a sweet female voice answered: "UDC, the CEO suite."

The best he could do was to mumble, "The CEO suite."

"Hello?"

The Chief Executive Officer's suite.

"Hello?"

Shit. He cleared his throat. "Is Mr. Trent there?"

"Who's calling?"

"This is"—*Hell, why not?*—"Dick Jenkins, down the hall."

"I'm sorry, sir, Mr. Trent hasn't been in today. Have you tried his company's office?"

He hung up.

He stood and the phone book slid off his lap to the floor. He walked back to the files, looked under T. There was no file for Charles Trent. There was a file labeled *CAT.* A thick file. He pulled it out. Charles A. Trent was in there. He smiled.

CAT was on another file in the same drawer: *T&CDBPP,CAT,*

TTEE. The file in back of that one was labeled *T&CDBPP, HT, TTEE/JT*, with the last two letters circled. He grabbed both folders and made room for them on the floor.

The long computer printout said that, among his other holdings, Uncle Chuck owned 1,550 shares of stock in UDC. Trent & Co. Defined Benefit Pension Plan, Charles A. Trent, Trustee, owned another 1,000 shares. Phil was willing to bet that those shares totaled 51 percent of the stock.

He was laughing.

The Trent & Co. Defined Benefit Pension Plan, Henry Trent, Trustee, Julia Trent, Beneficiary, had been worth $681,211.34 the year Dad died. All that money had started in 1956 with a $4,000 contribution on a salary of $20,000. Tax-free interest and continuing contributions that increased about every five years to a high of $18,750 in 1975 accounted for the rest.

A note in the file said that the money had been paid out as a lump sum because the trustee had died before drawing any benefits.

The file had been stamped *Closed*.

According to the W-2 forms on Uncle Chuck's income-tax return for last year, he earned two salaries: $60,000 from Trent & Co. and $135,000 from UDC. Schedules attached to the form 1040 showed he earned an additional $82,800 from his share of Trent & Co. profits and $177,000 in dividends from UDC.

Someone had broken into his apartment last year: he claimed a $2,500 loss from theft.

He listed a fee paid to a tax preparer in the amount of $3,600. The tax preparer was Trent & Co.

At the close of last year, Uncle Chuck's pension fund, started nearly the same year as Dad's on about as much money, was worth $694,700.05.

It owned a farm in western Pennsylvania.

Buried among wrinkled pages near the end of the CAT file: a stock transaction dated 1973. Uncle Chuck had "divested of" 100 percent of the stock in something called First Resource, Inc. The stock had been "journaled" to Richard Jenkins.

A memo stapled to the back of the document wore Dad's handwriting. In pencil.

> *Ltd. partnership w/private investors—some T&C clients, channeled through T&C w/finder's fee to Chuck from 1st Resource. All promissory notes/unsecured: pyramid. Stopped 9/26/73.*

The initials HT had been scrawled quickly, but appeared much darker than the rest of the note, as if more pressure had been used to write them.

Every investor participating in the limited partnerships with UDC was a client of Trent & Co. The files were full of them. Some, like the Tiptoft-Weck executive pension fund, had millions in UDC. Trent & Co., which already took a fee for managing its clients' funds, took a fee for placing the new funds with UDC, another fee for managing them for UDC. UDC took the money and built malls and factories, leased them, shared the revenues with the partners. UDC was returning 16 percent, but at least half of that annual yield was offset by tax-shelter benefits. It might not be pyramiding this time—the new money coming in might not be going to pay the interest on the money already invested. Funds being held for projects still on the drawing board were all unsecured, but some of the investments were backed by real estate and thirty-year triple-net leases. No one had lost any money. Yet. If it was a pyramid scheme, even partially, someone was going to lose some money soon. And Trent & Co. would be in the middle of it.

Uncle Chuck was doing it again, empire building and using Trent & Co. to front for his speculation.

And he was right: he was very good at it.

It might not be illegal this time. But it was wrong.

It could destroy Trent & Co.

It was lousy.

A copy of the Zorzoli's loan agreement was in a manila folder in the CAT file, paper-clipped to three pages of sketches labeled *Ringbrook Mall West.*

The bridge crossing the highway looked like something out of *Star Trek*, a fat tube rounded by a glass covering, connecting the new mall to the others. All the trees in the drawings were young. Maybe architects today didn't know what an old tree looked like. There were access roads and parking lots and a set of one-way ramps at either end of the bridge.

But there was no river.

The architects had forgotten to draw the river.

He laughed so hard, his eyes filled with tears.

He didn't bother to put the files back. He got out his key and walked straight to the alarm.

26

The bartender stopped polishing a glass long enough to wave. His lazy smile said he had not gone on half salary to help out the mill, business was fine as far as he was concerned, just fine. Phil kept walking. He knocked on her office door, tried the knob. It turned. He walked in.

The office stood empty. There was no green square on her dark computer screen. Her computer didn't link up with any other. He knocked on the door to the old office. She wasn't in there, either. The rose in the vase on Mr. Zorzoli's desk looked thirsty. So did the roses on top of the bookcases. Near the old step box in a corner, he found her watering can. He took it to the bar.

For a second, the bartender looked at the can as if considering putting King's Ransom in there. Phil decided he didn't like the bartender. He said, "Some water?"

The polishing rag moved faster inside the glass. "Don't get paid to fill those things."

Phil decided the best job he could have would be to get paid not to like the bartender. "Please," he said.

The polishing rag stopped. The bartender shrugged. He took the can and put it under the tap, ran water. When he handed it back over the bar, his frown said he expected a tip.

"Thanks," Phil said. "Have you seen Louise?"

"She's around."

He grinned—*she's around*—and carried the can back to her office. He watered the rose in Mr. Zorzoli's office first, then positioned the little stairs and began watering the vases on top of the bookcase. He hoped she would come in and find him like this. He hoped she'd be a little angry, only so he could watch her face change as he told her what he had discovered in the files, when he told her there was a chance now, a good chance, that she wouldn't have to sell the mill, that UDC and Uncle Chuck were vulnerable, too, it wasn't just a matter of money now, it was a matter for the district attorney to look into.

She didn't come in. He finished watering the roses. He left the can and the little steps where he'd found them and went to look for her backstage.

Both doors hung open. The fat piano player was in one dressing room, talking to the drummer and bass player. Something about a chord change that would "jangle" the audience, and how a new tempo should play off that chord. The men didn't bother to look at him. And Louise wasn't in there.

She wasn't in the other dressing room, either. Silky Odell sat alone, in his rocker, wearing a red robe that ended where his sock garters began. He was drinking milk. His glance was hard, like his music. He didn't like being stared at.

"Sorry," Phil said. "I was looking for Louise."

The old man lowered the glass to his lap, licked at the mustache the milk had left. He didn't have his teeth in. He said, "You the one she's cursing about?"

Phil stared at the doorknob. "Yeah, I guess so."

Silky nodded. "Best come in. Can't see you so good from there."

A tuxedo and evening shirt hung in the small closet, patent-leather shoes sat on the floor. The velvet sack holding his trumpet lay on the dressing table, beside a jug of milk and two glasses, one of them with a set of false teeth soaking in fizzing water. Thin legs, made thinner by long black socks, nudged a hassock. "Have a seat."

Phil didn't sit. "Have you seen her?"

The robe opened at the chest when Silky reached for the jug. He poured milk into a fresh glass, held it out. "Have some."

"No thanks, you go ahead."

Bony fingers put the glass in Phil's hand. "Have some."

The milk smelled funny. Maybe it was buttermilk. He hated buttermilk. And it was warm. "I'm in kind of a hurry. If you know where she is——"

"Everybody young always in a hurry." He sipped his milk: another small white mustache. "Try that."

He tried the milk. It wasn't buttermilk. It wasn't milk. It was too sweet. And strong.

"Goat milk royale," Silky said, and his smile was gentle, the same kind of smile Dad got looking at his mother's plates hanging over the fireplace.

Phil took another swig. He sat on the hassock. "Do you know where she is?"

"Came in here saying she's leaving."

Phil stood and looked for a place to put his drink. He saw airports and bus stations, train depots. He wanted to go after her. He wasn't sure he wanted to find her. If he had to talk her into staying, maybe she wasn't worth the breath.

"Son, women's saying they leaving every day." He guided Phil back down to the hassock. "You got her so angry, she hurts."

He couldn't look at the old man.

"Probably take her a bit to get through it." Hard fingers pressed into Phil's shoulder. "Give you time to get your act together." He set his glass on the table. "Son, looks to me like you got the girl in love with you. Be real smart and let go of the other one."

"There's nobody else." It didn't sound like his voice, it sounded final. "There never was."

The old man squinted, gripped the arms of his rocker. He must have been sure there had been another woman. He looked lost now. He raised his eyebrows, rubbed his earlobe. "She ain't been in love for real before. Not since I known her. That be since she was two." He nodded at Phil's glass. "Drink that."

The milk tasted even sweeter now. He ran a finger along the piping on the hassock. "It doesn't feel like love. Not anymore."

Silky waited for his guest to take another sip, then he blinked so slowly he seemed too tired to keep on talking. "You got a name, son?"

Phil told him his name. Silky offered his hand. "Wilson Odell."

The hand felt soft, as if the skin had been powdered. And the fingers didn't squeeze, they just lay there, limp, and they slipped out of Phil's grasp in a hurry, as if afraid to be anyplace too long. "Went into New York," Silky said, "to see her rich grandma. For to get money. I tried to talk her out of it." He sighed and touched his ear. "Should've been back by now."

"The bartender said he saw her around here."

Silky swallowed some milk and a laugh. "He sees most of what he ain't supposed to, and none of what he should." He brought the glass to his lips. "Likes the Garrett Mountain. Could be she's gone there."

Phil started to stand, but the black fingers pushed him down. Those fingers were stiff now. They lingered on his shoulder, got softer, then moved back to the arm of the rocker. "Played that mountain once. She tell you?"

Phil shook his head.

"First concert after . . . after being away from it." That smile again. "Had a trio then, bass and drums. This is before we tracked down Fountain Roy. Thought he was dead. Found him living in Bayonne." He eyed his drink. "Being dead would've been better."

Phil's laugh made the old man's smile get bigger. His gums were bright pink. He started the chair rocking. "Played for a bunch of Y kids in this meadow. Louise the only one who liked it.

Said we made the trees happy." He shook his head. "Only thing we done was scare off some squirrels."

He refilled both glasses. "Bought me my teeth, you know. Had them fit special, too, not like some folks." He stared at the teeth in the water glass, then laughed. "Not even twenty and she buys me them teeth. Says I have to play for her then, no way she let me out of it."

He stopped rocking, leaned forward. "I played for kings and queens, son. Even an emperor once. Never so scared as when she made me play for her." He eased back into the chair, sighed. "Didn't have a horn to my lips in twenty-three years. Told her it'd be thin, nothing behind it. All she does is sit there and wait on me to start blowing." His laugh sounded more like a cry, so high-pitched it hurt to listen to. "Played a little 'Is You Is or Is You Ain't My Baby?' for her. Only thing she says when I'm done is, 'Practice.'"

Phil must have laughed too hard. Silky was squinting. "'Course, she kissed me," he said, "so I knew it was all right."

The little piano player rapped on the doorjamb. "Half-hour."

Silky raised a hand, nodded. The fat man walked back down the hall. The rocker squeaked. The old man pushed on the arms and stood. "Special dinner show. Got to dress. Finish that drink now."

Phil drank the rest of his goat's milk royale. Silky took the glass, set it on the table. "Son, how you know with womens is, well, hell. Playing the blues is easy enough, but if you don't feel it all the way, you going to get some of the notes wrong. Feel it right, then even the notes you leave out sound good. Hear what I'm saying?"

He smiled, and it felt like Silky's smile, like Dad's.

"Louise, she's a strong woman." Black fingers squeezed Phil's arm. "Wouldn't do to miss too many of them notes with her."

"If you see her, tell her not to worry—"

"It's for you to do, not me."

"—About the money," Phil said.

The old man let go and shook his head. He fingered the shirt on the hanger. "Close that door on the way out."

It felt muggy in here now. The knob felt slippery. He turned, but Silky wasn't looking at him, he was busy fitting studs into the shirt.

Phil closed the door gently. He drew a long breath. He walked fast.

He didn't see Louise's car in the hospital lot. She might have parked in back, near the emergency room. If she was here. He locked the Ford and walked down the ramp to the main doors. Ed was sitting on a couch in the lobby, munching candied popcorn from a clear plastic bag, watching "Tic Tac Dough" on TV. Two small girls sat near him on another couch.

"What are you doing here?" Phil said.

Ed smiled and raised a hand, then turned to the little girls. "Churchill."

Their heads swung from the man with the mustache back to the contestant on the TV.

"Is Mom here?" Phil asked.

"Churchill?" the woman on the TV said and the game-show host said she was right and the audience applauded.

Ed nodded and said, "Upstairs."

The little girl in the red corduroy jumper clapped her hands. "You should go on that show."

"It's in California," Ed told her. "Too far."

The other little girl hadn't taken off her ski parka. Blue mittens sat beside her. "But you could win so much!"

"What's she doing here?" Phil asked.

Ed offered him the bag of popcorn. "She wanted to see Mrs. Zorzoli."

The woman on the TV would win the game if she got the next question right, and raise her winnings to over $36,000. "See?" the girl in the parka said. "And you're smarter than her."

"Why?" Phil said.

"Because she's already missed one," the little girl said.

He squinted at her, then at Ed. "Is Louise up there with her?"

"She didn't want me to go up." He leaned forward, studied the television. "And I wouldn't know your Louise."

The game-show host read the question smiling: "This baseball pitcher holds the all-time record for most strikeouts. His nickname is Lefty."

Ed rolled a plump kernel in his fingers—"It's Lefty Grove or Lefty Gomez"—and he kept rolling it, trying to decide, both girls watching and waiting for his answer.

"Steve Carlton," Phil said. The girls looked at him. And frowned. He took popcorn out of the bag. "How long have you been here?"

"Since the end of the news." Ed stopped rolling the kernel and ate it. "I'll say Grove."

The woman on the TV said, "Koufax?"

The game-show host said that was wrong, he was so sorry. The correct answer was Steve Carlton of the Philadelphia Phillies.

The little girls watched Ed wince. Then they looked at Phil. They were still frowning.

He ate the popcorn and started toward the main desk and the elevators. Mom came around a corner, head low, one hand stuffing Kleenex into her purse. He stopped, but she walked past him. He caught up to her in two steps. "Is Louise up there?"

She looked up from her purse, eyes wide, mouth open. "Phil, what are you doing here?"

"I'm looking for Louise, I've got some good news for her."

"She isn't here."

"And some bad news for us."

She narrowed her eyes. "I don't think I can take any more bad news." She looked at the painting of the hospital's founder on the wall near the desk. "Your father . . . There wasn't anyone else."

"You talked to her about . . . ?" He cocked his head. "Wait a minute. How is that bad news?"

Her sigh ran toward the painting of the bald man. "When I think of all the nights I cursed him." She got out the Kleenex, but didn't use it. "I didn't talk to her about any of that. I didn't have to."

He took the coat off her arm and began steering her toward the couches. After a few steps, she stopped. She looked ready to cry, and she glanced about as if trying to find a safe place, hidden so no one could see her, so no one could say they had seen Julie Trent lose her poise in a hospital lobby. He turned her by the shoulders to let her hide her face against his chest, but she kept turning. She strode back up the lobby and pushed through a door marked WOMEN.

He stood there for a moment, then he walked back to the couches, draped her coat over a padded arm that had been used as a seat too often, its tweedlike fabric worn thin, the lining underneath stained a dull yellow. "She's pretty upset."

Ed stared at the coat, then looked for her. When he didn't see her, he sighed and let his head swing back toward the television. "She wasn't sure about coming here. She's not too proud of how she treated the Zorzolis all those years." He watched the game-show host smile. "I don't know a lot about it. Your father was close to them for . . . well, since he was a young man, I think she said, and she"—he glanced at Phil, then at the popcorn in his hand—"she made it difficult."

"You're not listening," the girl in the jumper said.

He smiled at her, then eyed Mom's coat. "She was afraid the old lady wouldn't forgive her."

The little girl in the parka cupped a hand to her sister's ear and began whispering.

Phil looked down the lobby toward the rest room. "Maybe that's it, then."

Ed grunted. The little girls began giggling.

"Maybe she's upset," Phil said, "because the old lady forgave her." He stepped in front of Ed, sat on the couch, and waited for the next question to come out of the TV.

He told her in the kitchen.

She listened, but she didn't say anything. She got his dinner out of the refrigerator, put it in the microwave oven, punched electronic squares that beeped and made numbers flash on the display. The little oven started. It made the sound of angry wind.

He leaned against the doorjamb, wondering if he should tell her again. The theme song from *Frosty the Snowman* leaked out of the den. "Why don't you leave dinner to me," he said, "and go join Ed. We can talk about this later."

She got silverware from a drawer. "I don't want to see Frosty melt." She put the silverware on the table and started to make coffee.

"I don't need any coffee," he told her.

"I do." She switched on the machine and got napkins from the holder on the counter. "Will he go to jail?"

Phil crossed his arms. "If it's what I think it is, yes, he will." She didn't turn around. He stepped toward her. "I'm sorry, but I don't think we have another choice." He rubbed her shoulders. "I could try to get him to resign, but I don't know what would happen to the clients. Or the business. It's such a mess now, there might not be any way to get out of it without—"

She turned. "The district attorney's parents used to run the drugstore on Main Street. Your father did their books for years." She smiled. "I think he even helped them sell the building. It's an electronics store now." She moved to the table and put a napkin at each place. There was something wrong with her smile, it was lopsided. "Be sure you remind him of that. I think his name is Daniel."

"You want him to go to jail."

"I want to do what's right." She put her hands on a chairback, squeezed. "Your father spent a lifetime building his reputation. I won't see it ruined by some—" She bit off the rest of it, shook it in her teeth. Then her hands relaxed, her head bowed. "The newspapers will be the worst. And now with television—"

"Der Bingle in five minutes." Ed grinned in the doorway. "And it's all clear in there. Frosty's safe, the kids got the magic hat back."

She stared at him, shivered, turned to the coffee maker and the bubbling sound it was making. "I don't know what to do. If he could fix it, give back the money and—"

"I don't think it works that way," Phil said.

"Julie?" Ed stepped toward her, his old slippers just waiting for Christmas to be replaced by a new pair, a pair that was probably already under the tree. "What's wrong?"

"My uncle," Phil told him.

"What happened this time?" Ed said. "Somebody take his parking spot?"

She slapped the back of the chair. "Go watch your stupid program."

His shoulders sagged, his head lowered. He seemed to be melting. She saw that. She took his hand. "I'm sorry."

He touched her face, and his eyes filled with love for her. This man would forgive her anything. This short, gentle man would be kinder to her than anyone had ever been. Phil wished there were mistletoe over the doorway. It was probably in the attic, it wouldn't be hard to find.

"He's a crook," she said.

Ed squinted across the room. "I don't think you can afford to be wrong about a thing like this."

"What I found," Phil said, "looks like something for the D.A."

"And he's doing it all through Trent and Company." She got mugs from the counter. "It's deplorable."

"Julie, maybe you're still—" Ed touched an end of his mustache. "You may be angry at him for other reasons."

She banged the mugs down on the table. "I could forgive him about that." She got the carafe of coffee and started pouring. "That was my fault. For listening. This is different."

With a sigh, Ed got cream from the refrigerator and sat at the table. He stirred his coffee, sighed again.

Mom moved her mug to the place mat in front of her chair. Then she stepped back and took Phil's hand in both of hers. "Whatever we do, we can't let this ruin your future. Once it gets in the paper, people won't know one Trent from the other."

In the silence, the furnace kicked on. He rubbed her fingers. "I think we'd better take our chances."

"Sounds like you should talk to a lawyer first," Ed said.

She let go and walked to the sink. "It's my decision."

"Maybe he's right, Mom. I can—"

"It doesn't matter." She crossed her arms, stared out the dark window. "I own Trent and Company." Her eyes hardened. "I'm the boss."

Ed blinked, then glanced over the table. Phil shrugged. Together, they smiled at her, and she must have felt those smiles because the hardness left her eyes, her arms uncrossed. She was fighting tears now, as if ashamed of them. She was trying so hard to be strong, and she was losing.

Phil moved next to her. "Okay, Mom. You're the boss."

When she started crying, he hugged her.

27

He had them singing along.

"The Yellow Rose of Texas."

In front of the three-piece band—two young men with guitars and a drummer who might have been sixty—most of the people in the room crowded together on the dance floor, all of them dressed up and grinning, waiting for him to feed them the next line. In his black tuxedo, Maxie Nash didn't look round anymore. Or little. Holding the microphone while his other hand beat a steady rhythm against his thigh, he looked powerful, as if he knew he could make those people say anything. He looked happy.

Phil waved, but the singer didn't see him. He hung his coat on a hanger, walked toward the long, empty tables and the bar. The sign outside the door read HOFFMAN, PRIVATE PARTY, but there hadn't been a Hoffman posted inside to ask who he was or to stop him. A big flat cake with writing on it sat on a table near the band. It hadn't been cut yet.

Like the rest of the Verona Manor, the Paul Revere room had brick walls and big exposed beams holding up the roof. A colonial flag hung near a door marked EXIT, but other than that, there was nothing here to make anyone think of Paul Revere, no portrait, no memorabilia. The Ethan Allen Room down the hall was probably the twin of this one. Phil wondered if the janitors got confused about which room they were cleaning. He wondered if they cared. He moved a chair out of his way and waved again. Maxie wasn't looking at him, he was grinning and pointing at someone in the crowd near his feet.

A sandy-haired man came from the bar and put a drink in Phil's hand and said, "Secret formula." He wore a brown tuxedo that had tan piping around the lapels. His brown bow tie had come undone. There was a lump of something on his trousers: it looked like potato salad.

Phil tried to hand back the drink, but the man just clinked his own glass against it and smiled. "You take a stinger and add lemon juice. Now don't tell anybody. Ever." He walked away complaining about the band.

Some of the drink had spilled out of the glass. Phil held it away from his body and looked for a napkin.

"Leonard's drunk already." A woman in pink chiffon stepped in front of him. She held a glass of champagne and a plate with part of a sandwich on it. She looked about Mom's age. "That's all they do in college now." She shook her head and watched the man in the brown tux cross the room. She might have had her hair done at the same shop Mom went to. She smiled and said, "You're Elvira's boy, aren't you."

"Uh . . . no, I'm not."

It might have been the music, or too much champagne, but she didn't hear. "We're all very proud of you," she said. "It's wonderful how you've dedicated yourself." She frowned at the glass in his hand. "You shouldn't have that, should you?"

He took a step to the side. "I'm sorry, I'm not—"

"And you've come this far." She blocked his path and put her plate on a table. She took the drink out of his hand. "Think what it will mean—to have a world champion, right here in town."

A world champion.

He couldn't stop his smile. For a moment, he wished he could be Elvira's boy. To be the best in the world at something. Anything. For a moment. "Really, you have the wrong person."

"But don't you ever get scared you'll fall and—" She shuddered. "What if your skis hit a rock? You could be paralyzed. For life!"

Smiling wider now, he took the drink back from her, drained the glass.

"Oh, dear," she said.

The secret formula tasted terrible. While she was still staring at the empty glass, he got around her and walked toward the band.

Red and green icing on the big cake spelled out *Happy 40th Anniversary, Deiter and Germaine.* Flowers of colored frosting bordered the cake. It looked too sweet to eat. Had anyone taken a picture of it yet, with the happy couple seated in back of it? He put the empty glass on the table and waved at the band. Maxie saw him out of the corner of his eye, turned, squinted, but he didn't lose a beat or drop a lyric. He waved back and led the crowd to a big finish: "She's the only rose for me."

They clapped for themselves. Maxie nodded at Phil and held up five fingers. Five minutes? Five more songs? The music started. The singer put the microphone back on its stand. He told the audience he had never heard that song sound better. They believed him and applauded again. He picked up an accordion, fitted the straps around his neck. "On this next song," he told them, "I want you ladies to dance with the man who brought you." He sat on a chair and began playing a slow melody.

Phil pulled out a chair and sat. The cake even smelled sweet. He didn't recognize the tune, but it sounded like an old song, one that Deiter and Germaine might have danced to long ago. He tried to guess which of the gray-haired partners was the happy couple.

A guitar twanged a chord.

"I want to see at least ten requests in here when I get back." Maxie was holding up a glass fishbowl. "Make that an even dozen. And if I don't know your song—"

Another chord twanged.

"—I can promise you I'll know one with a lot of the same notes in it."

Both guitars played a loud chord, the drummer beat the cymbals. Maxie left the fishbowl in front of the accordion and came off the stage. "Did you find her?"

Phil stood and shook his head. "It's about my uncle."

"Give me a break. I've got enough problems."

"He owns UDC."

"What?"

"He's been the one all along."

Maxie squinted hard. He got round again. He turned and told the drummer, "I'll be in the lot having a smoke." He led the way toward the door near the old flag.

In the middle of his third cigarette, he held up a hand and said, "Okay, I got it." He turned up the collar of the topcoat he had pulled from the backseat of his car. "You understand, there's not much you can do. Not if you want to keep the business alive."

Phil rubbed his arms. He needed a coat. He couldn't stay out here much longer. He stomped his feet. "I'm not here about the business."

"If all the revenues are tied up in UDC projects," Maxie said, "Trent and Company is finished the day you try to change that."

Even his teeth felt cold now. "I want to know about going to the D.A."

The round head shook. "Your mother's right. The district attorney can't keep it under wraps. Not for long." He blew cigarette smoke into the night. "And if your uncle decided to fight, it'd be out in a minute. Even if he didn't, our D.A.'s a real go-getter. He likes publicity." He flicked the ash off his cigarette. "Look, pretend you'll take it to the D.A. Use it as leverage to get what your mother wants. He'll never know you don't mean it."

Phil shivered and nodded.

"Besides," Maxie told his car, "what if it's not what you think? I mean, it could be legal what he's doing. Unethical, sure, but still legal."

"I don't think so. Listen, I'm freezing—"

"And nobody's complaining. Everybody's getting paid off." Maxie cocked his head and frowned. "There has to be a complaint. Or some evidence of fraud or bilking." He took a drag off his cigarette, held it deep in his lungs, aimed the smoke at the highway on the other side of the dark trees. "Look, it's not my field. You need—a good lawyer." He stared at the pit marks in the hood of his Fiat. "Layman and Pierce, those are the guys you want."

He wanted to put a hand on the little man's shoulder and tell him he was a good lawyer. But he was too cold. "For all I know, they might be in on this."

"No way. They're the best, kid. Your father knew what he was doing when he hired them." He lit another Marlboro off the one he had just smoked. "I want to use this for Louise. If that's okay with you. And your mother."

"It's fine."

"I'll need copies of the stock certificates." Maxie crushed out the wasted cigarette. "Or whatever you've got to prove he owns UDC."

Phil didn't feel so cold anymore. Maybe that was a bad sign, maybe he was starting to freeze. He said, "Sure," and walked back toward the building.

"I could pick them up tonight," Maxie said. "When I'm through here."

He reached for the door. "Sure."

"But you'll have to be there to let me in." Maxie ran up behind him. "It won't be 'til after midnight."

Phil opened the door and walked inside. The room smelled of smoke and perfume. "No problem."

"That's great." He grabbed Phil's elbow, stopped him. "I have to tell you, I'm going to pressure him. Get him to at least with-draw the notice of intent."

The lady in the pink chiffon was standing near the bar. Phil turned his back to her. "Do what you have to do."

Maxie nodded. "You'd better advise your uncle, though. Let him know what you've got on him."

"Won't that mess you up?"

"Look, kid, he might be able to explain things to you so—" He crushed out the new cigarette in an ashtray on a table. "I'm not saying you're wrong. Just don't set yourself up for a lawsuit." He smiled and patted Phil's sleeve. "Even if he's clear legally, I can still use his UDC connection to our advantage, so don't worry about that. Only talk to him first."

Phil stared at the rug. His fingers started throbbing. They hurt. He shrugged.

"No, I want you to promise you'll talk to him first," Maxie said. "Your mother's got the right idea. Smart lady. So prom-ise me."

The drummer and the guitar players were already on stage. Phil nodded.

"Okay, good." The little lawyer took off his coat. "Got to go. I'll meet you as soon as I can." He shook Phil's hand, smiled, and walked toward the accordion. The fishbowl had a lot of pieces of paper in it, more than a dozen. He left his coat on a chair beside the stage and stepped up to the microphone. He held the bowl above his head. "Nice work, gang." The guitars twanged a chord. Maxie dug into the bowl.

Phil made his way past the bar, got his coat, and shut the door behind him. The first muted strains of a new song leaked out of the Paul Revere Room. He didn't recognize this one, either. He started walking.

The copying machine finally stopped humming. A square button in the control panel lit up green. It said *Ready*.

He took pages from the *CAT* and *T&CDBPP,CAT,TTEE* files. Wherever stock in UDC was listed, he made a copy. He put the copies in the bottom drawer of Mrs. Frolen's desk.

He unlocked Uncle Chuck's office, left the originals on his desk. From a thick binder, he removed the authorizations Mom had signed for the coming year. Layman and Pierce might not have a copy of them yet. If something went wrong, if Uncle Chuck refused to cooperate, Phil wanted to be able to use those authorizations as a bartering point. It didn't feel like stealing: Mom had a right to change her mind about who ran the business. She was the boss. He put the authorizations in the drawer with the copies.

He got out the last binder. Seated in Uncle Chuck's chair, he read over the restructuring agreement that explained how Dad had bought out his brother for a dollar. Layman and Pierce would have a copy. He left the binder open on the desk.

He sharpened a pencil. Then another. He wasted more time by using the bathroom off the storage room. On a note pad, he wrote a draft of a new authorization. He used Mrs. Frolen's typewriter. He took his time. He followed the form of the other authorizations. This one he dated today. This one said that for the rest of the fiscal year, Julia Trent and no one else had the authority to run Trent & Co. He read it over for mistakes. He got a pen from a cup on the desk. In the space for the signature, he printed Mom's name, then signed his own, and under it he printed, "Her Attorney-in-Fact." She hadn't given him power of attorney. But it didn't feel like a lie: she had told him to talk to Uncle Chuck and see what could be done. She had told him to do his best.

He went back to the big chair and reread the 1973 agreement. He reached for the phone. He stepped out to get Uncle Chuck's home number from the Rolodex. He decided to use the bathroom again.

He checked the alarm: off. Then the doors: locked. He sat at

Mrs. Frolen's desk, turned the Rolodex. He picked the phone book off the floor and found the number for the mill. He called it.

The man on the other end said Louise hadn't been back.

He looked up her number in Little Notch, called it. No answer.

He put the phone book on the blotter. She wouldn't really leave, she was in New York, just as Silky had said. Maybe she had car trouble. Maybe she parked in the wrong place and they towed the Datsun away, they towed away hundreds of cars every day in Manhattan. Maybe her rich grandmother wanted her to stay the night.

Maybe she had gotten the money. And was celebrating.

In a nightclub.

With a New Yorker.

He didn't care.

He called Little Notch again. The phone kept ringing.

She might have had an accident. No, he wasn't going to think about that. He wasn't going to think about her.

He sharpened another pencil. He didn't need a pencil. He left it on the blotter.

She might have pulled off the highway, so depressed she couldn't drive anymore. She might be parked on the shoulder of Route 3 or off a side street in East Rutherford, feeling now what he had felt on the road: there was so much money around, the signs of it were everywhere—houses, cars, clothes, jewelry, boats, the countryside was oozing with it—and if that many people could have so much, something must be wrong with those who couldn't get their share. The instant he had felt that, he had known why stockbrokers had jumped out of windows. He had known why there were thieves.

And it had made him feel dumb, as if there were a secret to money, a logic it had all to itself. Those who understood it did what was necessary and came out fine. Those who were ignorant of that secret logic did everything they could think of, but unless they were lucky, very lucky, no matter what they did, it was probably the wrong thing and they kept coming out broke.

He turned the Rolodex to Uncle Chuck's card. He put his head in his hands and tried to think of what to say.

Why did some people work so hard—on Christmas or any other holiday, Gary Simms would be pounding nails and installing toilets—only to find they had to work harder to stay even, or close to it? Others made it look easy. Uncle Chuck made it look easy. He was so far ahead, he could play games with his money, he could enjoy playing those games, because even when he lost, he won something, a tax write-off, a capital loss, or an investment credit, all of those angles reducing the income he had to report on his 1040. Uncle Chuck was probably one of those people who figured out how to lose money so he could make more.

Maybe it had always been that way. Maybe the world hadn't changed much since Dad opened the office. Maybe Dad hadn't understood money.

He broke the pencil. He was a fool to stick his nose into Trent & Co. or Zorzoli's or any business unless he knew money, knew its secret. He had the feeling he never would.

Uncle Chuck was going to eat him alive.

He thought about trying the mill again. He dumped the broken pencil into the wastebasket. He picked up the phone, punched in the numbers for Uncle Chuck's apartment. His hand was shaking.

The phone stopped ringing and his uncle said, "Trent."

"It's Phil. I'm at the office."

The sigh on the other end was long and thin. "I thought I told you—"

"I've been through the files."

This sigh sounded like a rasp. "You know, I'm reaching the end of my rope with you."

"I think you'd better get down here. It's about you and UDC."

Except for music playing in the background, the line went silent.

"It's about you," Phil said, "owning UDC."

"You don't know what you're talking about. Those files are confidential. Damn it, Phil, you gave me your word."

"Yeah." He cleared his throat. His eyes hurt. "So much for honor."

Uncle Chuck started talking fast, his voice getting louder. Phil hung up.

He stared at the files all over the floor of the storage room. He wondered if he should use the time to clean up. He tested a couch near the stock-exchange board. He stretched out and studied the panels in the suspended ceiling. They looked so flimsy.

The phone rang.

He closed his eyes. The phone would stop ringing soon. In a little while, he told himself, everything would be all right.

28

The scratching woke him up.

Not mice. A key in the lock.

Uncle Chuck walked in, a white scarf tucked under the collar of his topcoat. Glancing at the alarm box near the copying machine, he closed the door, locked it. "You didn't take your shoes off?" He got out of the topcoat. "That's an eight-hundred-dollar couch."

Phil sat up, rubbed his eyes. He had wanted to say, "Thanks for coming." He said, "Sorry."

The scarf crinkled with static electricity. He wore a green turtleneck and a gray cardigan sweater. He looked ready for the golf course. He carried his coat and scarf toward his office, saw the open door. He saw the files on the floor of the storage room. He stopped. "Jesus."

"I'll put them back."

"This is incredible." Wrinkles creased smooth skin. "I have half a mind to call the police."

Phil stood. It felt cold in here. "Can we turn on some heat?"

"It's on a timer." He stepped to the door of the storage room. "Goddamn pigsty." He shivered, then turned and walked to the reception desk, picked up the phone, listened for the dial tone, hung up. "You have something against answering phones?"

"I wanted to talk to you in person."

He leaned on the desk. His eyes got small. "You got what you wanted."

The cold crept under his sleeves. He stared at the indentation his head and body had made in the leather couch. "Mom doesn't want you to go to jail."

"Jail." Thick fingers rapped the blotter. "You have your old man's sense of humor all right."

The voice sounded like an iron file tearing soft wood. Phil couldn't look at him. "She'd rather see us get out of this another way."

"I can't tell you how relieved I am." His laugh sounded more like a cough. "If this wasn't so ridiculous"—he enjoyed saying that word, he made every syllable a punch—"I'd probably kiss her feet."

Phil's arms were trembling. "I think you're running another pyramid scheme."

"You think? Well, that's important, then. You think so, huh?" He shook his head and walked into his office. "Tell me, what's your fee for this service?" He took a lithograph off the wall. There was a safe behind it. "I might not be able to afford you, though, you being tops in your field and all." He got the safe open, looked inside. Satisfied, he shut the metal door and spun the combination wheel. "I never got advice from a guy who's had his picture on the cover of *Fortune* before."

Phil swallowed and stepped to the doorway. "I went through the files and—"

"Yeah, you told me." He put the lithograph back in place. "And you're so neat."

His legs were shaking now. He wondered how long his voice would last. "Everything that goes into UDC goes through this office."

"That's called an investment channel." The smile looked as thin as wire. "But I don't have to tell you that."

His mouth tasted sour. "There's a lot of money just sitting there, not being used for—"

"As you know"—Uncle Chuck straightened the painting—
"we can't use the funds from an offering until that offering is
filled. That's the law, you see."

"But you are using them. UDC is."

"Really?"

"You're paying out salaries"—Phil stepped into the office—
"and you're paying interest to the investors."

"They're entitled to the interest." That wire-thin smile again.
"As for the salaries, and the overhead, I think you'll find that
comes out of revenues. Ah, but an expert like you probably hates
such oversimplifications."

"The cash UDC collects from investors"—his fingers curled
into fists—"is being treated like revenues."

"You don't say."

"A lot of it is, anyway." He pointed at the storage room. "It's
all there."

Uncle Chuck sat on the edge of his desk. "I can't believe I'm
listening to this."

"And you own UDC." He pointed to the papers on the desk.
"Or are you going to deny that, too?"

"I never deny anything." He reached back, got the documents, glanced at them. "So I own some stock. There's a law
against that?"

"You're the chief executive officer."

He didn't look up from the papers. "And that's against the
law."

With the bottom of his fist, Phil punched the doorjamb behind him. "You're moving the money through Trent and Company to UDC, taking a cut at both ends. Do the investors know
about that?"

"Are they complaining?" He put the documents back on the
desk. "Has somebody lost some money?"

"If they do—"

"If? I don't want to talk about 'if.'" He folded his arms across his chest. "I want to talk about what is. Every investor who's put a dime into UDC has made money. Some of them have quadrupled their investments. Check the balance sheet." He shook his head slowly. "There's nothing wrong here."

Phil turned toward the door. The brass nameplate reflected the overhead lights. "Mom wants you to get Trent and Company untangled from UDC."

"If I did that, there wouldn't be a Trent and Company." He uncrossed his arms. "And I'm not about to consider tearing down what I've worked so hard to create. Certainly not because of some amateurs. I had enough of that shit with Henry."

The nameplate was too shiny to keep looking at. Phil let out a long sigh. "Okay, I'm wrong. We'll have Layman and Pierce come in and go over everything."

Uncle Chuck was smiling. "What for?"

"To make sure it's legal. And ethical."

His smile got bigger. "I hate lawyers."

"If it's the way you say it is, they'll be done in no time."

He stopped smiling. "And when my clients hear I've got lawyers going over the books—that's going to bolster their confidence? They'll feel good about the money they gave me to invest?"

"They don't have to know."

"Oh, they'll know. There's no way they won't know." His fingers gripped the edge of his desk. "I'll have an office full of fucking lawyers, for God's sake. What do I say, we're having a parade?"

It made Phil laugh. "If they find what you're doing is okay, the clients will feel better knowing—"

"It doesn't work that way, kid. They'll pull out just because the lawyers are sticking their noses in." His sigh was short. "And they won't come back in, you can bet on that. All it takes is a little scare and"—he snapped his fingers—"they disappear."

Phil nibbled at his lip. "What if you took the files to their office? Nobody'd know they were—"

"Jesus, you are so fucking dumb." He shook his head and squeezed the edge of the desk. "They'll have to verify holdings, assess values, they'll want to check every goddamn penny. That's how they are. It can't be done quietly. The clients have to sign verification forms."

Maxie was right: Layman and Pierce weren't part of this. Phil couldn't stop a smile.

"Right, it's funny," Uncle Chuck said. "The first goddamn form that goes out in the mail starts a fucking stampede."

The smile grew. "Tell the clients you're doing it as a service, to see if their investments are undervalued."

"Nobody'd believe that, for God's sake. Nobody's that dumb." He tried that smile again. "Almost nobody." He pushed off the desk. "They're already in high-risk positions. And they know that. No risk, no big gain, it's that simple." He put a hand in a pocket. "But they trust me. And I've given them solid performance, so they should trust me. And you want to under-cut that?"

"It's not me. It's Mom. And she owns Trent and Company."

"Yes, she does." He ran a finger over the top of the computer. "And without me, it's worthless." He stared at the back door to the office. "I turn a two-bit operation into something respectable, and she wants me to throw it away? Because she doesn't under-stand it?" He spun around. "For God's sake, she can't even balance her checkbook!"

Phil shrugged. "All she wants is for you to get the business clear of UDC. You can do that, can't you?"

Small eyes got smaller. "You just don't understand what you're asking me to do. Or how difficult it is. Or how long it would take—two years, minimum." He grunted at the floor. "And if I don't do it, she calls in the lawyers, right? And the whole thing turns to shit in a week."

"We call the lawyers," Phil told him. "I don't know about the rest of it."

"What you don't know could fill the Grand Canyon." He sniffed a laugh. He blinked and grabbed the phone, began punching in numbers.

"She won't talk to you," Phil said. "Not now, anyway."

His fingers stopped. He hung up. "So that's it, then. I do it her way or I do it her way. Hell of a position." He threw up his hands, let them fall to his sides. "Okay, sure. Tell her I'll make her happy. I'll throw away a few million, I'll bring the cash flow of this office down to nothing, I'll turn her profits into a loss, and with any luck, I'll have everybody in the financial community laughing their asses off."

Maybe this was a mistake. A big one. He was sweating. "Maybe I could just talk to the lawyers first. If they say it sounds okay—"

"I don't give a shit what they say." Uncle Chuck started walking. He brushed past Phil and turned toward the storage room. "And I'm through fucking around." He gathered up the UDC file. "We're liquidating. Starting tonight. And you and Julie are going to have to live with it. Forever." He carried the file into his office. "And if either one of you tries to butt in, I'll be the one calling the lawyers." He dumped the file on the desk, slid the binder to one side, turned on the computer, picked up the phone and held it out. "Once I start, I'm not stopping. You tell her that."

Phil stared at the phone, the bright computer screen. He couldn't speak.

"And tell her," his uncle said, "I'm drawing up an agreement that says she can't interfere. That means no lawyers until I'm finished." He fed a floppy disk into a slot in the computer. Something whirred in there. Letters popped onto the screen. "I'm not about to work my ass off here and then have her realize she cost herself half a million bucks and try to knife me in the back for doing what she wanted."

"She wouldn't do that," Phil said.

"What do you call this?" He left the phone on the desk,

started typing on the keyboard. "For God's sake, I've seen it before, okay? I've lived through it." He glared at him. "Only this time we're doing it my way." He went back to the keyboard. "I'll have that agreement ready for her to sign in the morning."

"She won't do what Dad did to you," Phil told him.

Fingers stopped playing the keyboard. "You don't know what he did to me, kid."

"I saw his note. About First Resource."

Uncle Chuck sat motionless, watching the letters on the screen. He didn't seem surprised. "He was wrong about that. You have no idea how wrong. And I'm the one, the only one who paid for his mistake." He stared at Phil. "That's not going to happen again."

"Look, let me talk to the lawyers first."

"Hell, no. I'm going to enjoy this." He leaned back in his chair, swiveled toward the fat file. "I'm going to have a hell of a time. In a year, you won't be able to pay the rent here. That ought to make her ecstatic."

Phil studied the floor. His arms felt weak. "She doesn't care about the money."

"Tell me about it. I make her rich, and you know, she never said thank you. She never said, 'Chuck, I had no idea the business could do so well.'" New numbers flashed on the screen. "To hear her talk, you'd think the money makes her sad."

"It does," Phil said.

Uncle Chuck shut his eyes. "Jesus."

"She worries about it," Phil told him. "She worries about her name, too. My name."

"Christ, what did Henry do, clone her?" He slapped the desk. "Hey, it's my goddamn name, too. If the two of you want to think I'm ruining your reputation, that's your fucking problem." His laugh sounded like a duck call. "Without me, you don't have a reputation." He glanced at the screen. "But don't worry, I'll get rid of every cent we've got." The phone started making a strange noise: a squeal. He picked it up and slammed it home to its bracket. "Now get out of here and let me work."

Fingers played the keyboard. Images on the screen kept changing. He was doing it.

Phil started for his coat.

"I expected so much more from you," his uncle said. "I would have shown you how all of this worked. Every detail. You could have learned something."

He stopped walking. He wanted to say he was sorry. He didn't know how.

"Your father didn't want to learn." He must have swiveled the chair, something metal squeaked. "He was happy making next to nothing. I tried to resign, you know."

Phil turned. Uncle Chuck was staring at him, hands folded on top of the file:

"I wanted to get as far away from him as possible. He wouldn't let me. He said I had to stay on, it was like a penance. That's the word he used." He shook his head. "He said he'd call the D.A. if I quit. That's the way he was—no discussion. And he couldn't prove a fucking thing."

"Then you should have fought him," Phil said.

He spat a laugh. "Fight him? For what? So I'm exonerated— which I would have been—big fucking deal." He flicked the edges of papers in the file. "I'm the one with my picture in the paper. People don't care about the facts, they read the damn charges and that's what they believe. That's all they know how to believe, it's a goddamn sickness in this country." He ran a hand through his hair. "Well, this time, I am getting out. All the way out." He stared at the Calder on the wall. "I'm through working with ignoramuses. And I'm sure as hell not going to work *for* them."

Phil traced a finger down the doorway molding. "If there's nothing wrong, then—"

"This is wrong." Uncle Chuck was pointing at the computer

screen. "This is so fucking wrong it's criminal!" He slapped the file, swiveled his chair toward the bookcase. He kicked something back there. He sighed. His fingers started tapping the arm of the big chair. "You know, it would make a lot more sense to do this another way." He swiveled the chair. It didn't squeak this time. He was smiling. "Why don't I just buy her out?"

She had nothing to do with selling the Lincoln or with getting rid of the old office furniture. She hadn't wanted to be involved in moving the office out of Paterson. And she had not been the one who had called the Salvation Army to come for some of his clothes. The cellar was still full of his stuff. Maybe she kept it down there so no one could get at it. Phil didn't know how to tell his uncle she wouldn't sell Trent & Co.

"A lot easier all the way around," Uncle Chuck said. "And faster than . . . than wrecking the business." He leaned back in the chair. "It would put a couple of hundred thousand in her pocket. I'll give her whatever the assets are worth—and something for goodwill." He blinked. "Of course, most of that's my doing, so—" He waved a hand in front of his face. "Regardless, I'll throw that in the pot, too. And before the year is out, she's no longer involved, whatever happens here has nothing to do with her."

He thought about the money she would get. He thought about how easy it would be to sell, just sign a piece of paper and cash the check. Then he sighed. "I don't think she'll go for it."

"We'll talk to her." All the anger had run out of him, replaced by new energy. "I should have done this before, but"—he shrugged and took the floppy disk out of the computer—"the business wasn't worth anything then. I wanted to see her well taken care of."

Maybe he hadn't wanted lawyers in to appraise the value of the business. Maybe it had been easier to use Trent & Co. to build his fortune.

Maybe he had really wanted to see her well taken care of.

"And it wouldn't change anything with us." Uncle Chuck switched off the computer. "The door's still open for you." He stepped around the desk. "Think of what that means—fifty thousand a year to start, in two years you'd be clearing over a hundred thousand. Easy." He stopped just short of the doorway. He was grinning. "We'd still be keeping the money in the family. And when you're ready, I'd offer you a partnership." He laughed. "Believe me, you'd be able to afford it."

Phil couldn't raise his stare from the floor.

"If we gut the company now, you'll have nothing." Uncle Chuck had turned halfway toward the wall with the Calder on it. "I'll be fifty-five in a couple of years, I can retire then, turn everything over to you." He shrugged. "Maybe keep my hand in as an adviser, you'd need that for a while." He put his hands together: they made a soft clap. "That fellow she's . . . seeing. He's got a good business head. She'd listen to him."

She would listen to Ed. Ed would tell her to sell.

"Sure," Uncle Chuck told the lithograph, "it's ideal. She's unhappy with the business, she unloads it. Hell, she doesn't know a stock from a geranium anyway. And then she doesn't have a thing to worry about, no legal problems, nothing."

Phil squinted at him. "She doesn't have any legal problems now."

The thick shoulders turned slowly. He had lost his smile. Something was happening to his face, the skin was going perfectly smooth, all the lines were disappearing. "Phil, it's time you started living in the real world."

29

The real world?

"She owns Trent and Company." Uncle Chuck walked back to his desk. "She authorizes me to run the show, but . . ." He stared at his diplomas. Dad had kept pictures on the wall behind his desk, family pictures, including one of his brother graduating college. "If something was wrong, if the lawyers did come in and found something improper, ultimately she's responsible."

Phil took a step toward him. "That's absurd."

"Is it?"

"She doesn't have anything to do with this."

"In a practical sense, no, she doesn't." He kept staring at the sheepskins. "In a legal sense, I'm afraid she has. More than she could take."

His legs weakening, Phil sat in the chair just inside the door. "What you've done, it isn't legal then, is it."

His uncle put a hand on the swivel chair. "It works."

Phil could see the numbers. They were real now.

"You see, don't you," his uncle was saying, "that it's in her best interests to sell."

The numbers moved.

"Try to understand how much I have on the line, Phil."

Some numbers slid in, some slid out, they climbed over one another, made steps: not a pyramid, a staircase. As long as new numbers slid in, the staircase climbed.

"My share of the profits, my pension fund, all my holdings through UDC." The voice was testing, like a river looking for soft spots in rock. "Like the Towers, or those townhouses I went out to see today. If anyone tried to mess that up, I'd have to fight back. Anybody would."

Phil shook his head. The numbers wouldn't go away.

"And I'd fight back hard."

He could see spaces now, empty spaces under the staircase. There weren't enough new numbers to fill those spaces. Yet the stairs kept growing.

"I'd rather not have to fight." His uncle came closer, put a hand in a pocket of his cardigan. "Until she sells, she's on the line here, too. I wouldn't want to, of course, but if pressed hard enough, I'd have no other choice but to drag her into it."

The numbers weren't there anymore. For a moment, he wanted them back. He stared at the hand in the gray sweater pocket. "She has nothing to do with your schemes. Nothing."

"I work for her. That's something."

He tried to speak, but nothing came out.

"We can make all of this a moot point." Uncle Chuck smiled. "We don't even need lawyers to put the change of ownership through. No sense complicating something this simple." He turned and stepped to his desk, stared at the open binder, ran a hand down the 1973 agreement he had been forced to sign. "And I'll be considerably fairer to her than my brother was to me. I wouldn't use pressure the way he did."

Dad had been right about First Resource. Phil had been right about UDC.

"Not unless I had to," Uncle Chuck told him. "If you want to play hardball with me, you have to understand the rules." His hand moved off the page. He put it back in his pocket. "There's too much money at stake. This isn't the Henry Trent Mickey Mouse Show anymore."

He would do it. He would lie. He would bring Mom into it and keep her there. His flat smile said all that. And in the end, he would find a way to escape—he had probably planned that already, he had probably kept an escape route open from the day he started—and Mom wouldn't be able to escape: no matter how innocent the courts found her, she wasn't strong enough to survive being implicated in this, having her name on an indictment, reading it in the papers, hearing her name called out in court and the whispers that would follow her to the witness stand, to the A&P, the hairdressers—home.

She would break.

"You can go home now," Uncle Chuck said. "I'll get to work on the buy-out agreement. If you like, we can go over it together."

Phil stared at the desk. It blurred. He stood. He walked out of the office. He stepped over files in the storage room. In the top drawer of a cabinet, he found the tool kit. He got out the screwdriver.

She would have to be strong enough.

He would make her strong enough. He would be there to make sure she didn't break.

He walked back to the office and started working on the screws holding the nameplate to the door.

"What are you doing? Phil?"

He got the first screw out, started on the last one.

"Careful, that's made in England. Hey!"

The weight of the nameplate stopped his hand from trembling. "You're right—no more Mickey Mouse." He dropped the brass rectangle on the desk. "And you don't work here anymore."

"Why, you little shit." All the lines came back to his face. His skin reddened. "Who the fuck do you think you are?"

"You're fired," Phil said.

A small fist cocked. Then his uncle started laughing. "Jesus, this is too much. You really think I'm that dumb?" He tapped the binder and laughed louder. "I have her authorizations."

"Find them."

His eyes narrowed. He glanced at the binder, then bent to the bookshelf and grabbed another, put it on the desk, flipped through pages. His fingers stopped. Then his hands relaxed and he looked up smiling. "You stole them?" Another short laugh. "It doesn't matter. Layman and Pierce have copies."

Phil picked up the phone, held it out. "Call them."

The smile disappeared. He squinted at coils in the long cord, his eyes growing darker.

"And while you're talking to them"—he inched the phone closer to the gray sweater—"tell them she signed a new authorization tonight. She's the only one who can do anything around here now."

"She wouldn't do that."

"I'll see you get a copy."

Uncle Chuck blinked. Finally, he sat in his chair. "We had an agreement."

He hung up the phone. "We have a new one."

Sweat beaded near a temple. Small hands closed the binder, put it back on the bookshelf, reached for the other one still open on the desk. "I could take the clients with me." He was trying to smile again. "She'd have nothing."

Phil slid the binder in front of him. "According to this, you have nothing." He turned a page, pointed to the signatures: Dad's and Uncle Chuck's. "And that's exactly what you'll take with you." He picked up the heavy book, stepped back from the desk. "If the clients want to follow you—outside the territory defined here—that's their business." He ran a finger down the document. "But as of now, your salary stops and you forfeit your profits." He shut the binder. "And every cent in your pension fund reverts to the company."

"You can't do that." He was sweating around his mouth now. "It won't stand up in court."

"Probably not," Phil said. "But the seven or eight hundred thousand dollars you're leaving behind will be used to defend our position. That should be enough. Even for a game of hardball."

Uncle Chuck sank deeper into the chair. His head bowed. Watching his fingers toy with a button on the cardigan, he spoke in a whisper: "The Chinese have a saying—you can do anything, except break another man's rice bowl." He looked up, his eyes barely open. "If you can't think of me, for God's sake think of your mother."

"I am." He set the binder on the corner of the desk. "If you're still here in two minutes, I'll call her. Then I'll call the police."

"Phil, listen to me, this is silly."

"And if you try to act on behalf of Trent and Company again"—he turned toward the Calder—"or touch any of the money, if you get within a hundred feet of this office, we'll sue your ass off."

"I'm your uncle, for God's sake!"

He stared at the bright colors in the lithograph. "I'll see what I can do for you with the district attorney."

"None of this has to happen." He was standing. Sweat made his face shiny. "None of it."

"And if you try to involve Mom in any of this"—Phil turned, glared at him—"if you cause her one little problem, I'll beat the living shit out of you."

"Don't you threaten me!" His skin flushed, he started shouting. "I can have you arrested for making a threat like that. And for breaking into these files. I can twist you so many ways you'll wish you never came home."

"What you can do," Phil said, ready to start punching, hoping he wouldn't have to, "is take this with you." He nudged the brass nameplate. "And see if you can lose it."

Staring at the empty stock-exchange board, he wondered how to tell Mom. He couldn't think of an easy way.

He put his head back, shut his eyes. Soft leather welcomed

him, pulled him down, he was sinking into the couch, if he just kept his eyes closed a little longer, if he didn't twitch or move, it felt as though he would keep sinking, until he had disappeared into the padding and springs:

Headline—MAN BECOMES COUCH.

He stopped the smile, fought to keep still. He kept sinking.

And then he wouldn't have to worry about telling Mom, about lawyers, about headlines, he could tell them all to go away.

COUCH TALKS!

The laugh ruined everything. He stopped sinking.

He stood. He couldn't find any indentations in the leather, it was as if he hadn't been sitting on the couch. Not a trace. He wanted to feel for the warmth his body had left behind, but he didn't want to take the chance: the leather might be cold.

He would just tell her. In the morning. With Ed in the kitchen, drinking coffee. He could tell her if Ed were there, it wouldn't be so tough.

It was going to be awful.

Deep inside the couch, a spring made a low, hollow sound. He touched the leather. It was warm.

She might be tougher than he thought, she might surprise him. He might have misjudged her.

Maybe he had misjudged everybody.

He couldn't think of a headline that would say all that in three or four words.

Someone knocked on the main doors.

Maxie. In his topcoat, a dark hand poised at the glass.

"It's open," Phil said.

The little man walked in. "Where are they?"

"Bottom drawer."

He pulled off a mitten. "Uh . . . maybe you'd better give them to me. So nobody can say I took them." His smile drifted toward the doorways to the office and the storage room. He stared at the mess on the floor, glanced at Phil, went back to staring at the files.

He swallowed, then grinned. "Nobody's buried in there, I hope."

Phil laughed. It made his head feel light. He sat on the arm of the couch. His stomach turned. He held on.

She was tough enough. Tougher than he could ever be.

On the way home from Dad's funeral, she had made him stop at a liquor store to buy wine and beer for the people who were coming to the house to be with her and tell her how sorry they were one last time. The man behind the cash register had smiled at the six-packs and the wine bottles: "Stocking up for the holidays, eh?" Phil hadn't been able to look at him. Or clear his eyes. And Mom had seen that. Opening her purse, she had told the owner, "He just buried his father today." The man behind the counter had groaned: "Hey, I'm sorry, I didn't—I'm really very sorry." Handing him money, she had put her gloved hand on Phil's arm. She had just left her husband's grave, yet she could still be there to comfort someone.

If he lived to be ninety, he would never be that strong.

"Are you sick or something?" Maxie said.

He had kept watching her at the house that day, waiting for her to break.

"You want a glass of water?"

"I was the one," he said. "I broke."

Maxie put a hand to Phil's forehead. "No fever. Kid, maybe you should lie down."

He would try to be that strong. It was time someone did for her what she had done for everybody else. It was time someone let her be weak.

He smiled at the round face in front of him. "I need a lawyer."

Maxie listened.

The ash on his cigarette was longer than the part left to smoke. He stared at his patent-leather shoes. Slush had dotted them, taken away some of the shine. "You need better than me," he said.

"You can get Layman and Pierce in on it," Phil told him. "Damn it, I'm hiring you."

He caught the cigarette ash in his hand, dumped it into the wastebasket. He glanced at the storage room, shook his head. He found an ashtray near the couches. He drew a last drag off the Marlboro, crushed it out. "They won't want to work with me." He sighed and cigarette smoke ran out of his mouth and nose. "Okay, look. I'll call them. But I'll just tell them what you want, they'll have to take care of it." He sat on a couch. "You need restraining orders. We can't let him near the accounts, no telling what he'll try."

"I already told him—"

"Get me some paper. And something to write with." He wriggled out of his coat, tossed it to the other end of the couch. "As smart as he is, if he's not legally restrained, he could clean everything out by morning." He took the pad and pencil Phil gave him, started writing. "They'll have to serve the papers on him. What's the address?"

Phil gave him the address.

"Now, where I can help you," Maxie said, "is on keeping the doors open here until we get somebody in to run the show."

"Maybe we should just close it."

"Can't." He kept scribbling on the pad. "No firm's going to take these accounts, not if there's something wrong with them. And they have to be serviced." He started a new page of notes. "Even if we freeze them, which we should. Otherwise, we'll have everybody suing us." He looked up. "Once you get the money problems worked out, you can think about closing the doors. It'll probably take months, though."

"He said it would take years."

Maxie shrugged. "Maybe he's not as good as he thinks he is."

The pencil started moving again, short strokes, lots of dashes.

Phil rolled the chair away from the reception desk and sat. "He said my mother's on the line, too. She owns the company."

"All of it?"

He nodded.

Maxie tapped the pencil point on the pad. "Layman and Pierce will know how to protect her, don't worry. She's the one trying to get everything in shape, the D.A. isn't going to ignore that."

"You're sure?"

"I'm sure about Layman and Pierce." He readied the pencil to the page, then looked up. "If your uncle tries to fight this, it's going to cost a fortune. In legal fees." He held out a hand. "Not for me, understand."

"We can use his share of the profits and his pension fund. It's over three-quarters of a million."

"Please, don't tell me, I might up my fee." He wrote something on the pad. "Okay, we can afford to hire somebody good to take charge here." He glanced at him. "Any chance you could do it?"

Phil shook his head. "None."

Maxie nodded. "I'll see who I can come up with. We'll want Layman and Pierce to do the actual selection and hiring. Now, what about his secretary?"

"Mrs. Frolen?"

"Frolen." He wrote down her name. "She probably belongs to him. Dangerous to keep her."

"But—" He saw her face. He saw her crying. "Maybe we should talk to her, see if—"

"It's better to make a clean sweep."

He drew a long breath. "She knows the files."

The little lawyer glanced over his shoulder at the storage room. "Okay, we'll leave that hanging. Whoever we get to take control will want to pick his own secretary anyway. The best we can do for"—he checked his pad—"Frolen, is to give the final decision to the new man."

Phil nodded.

"Does she have a pension plan here?"

"I don't know."

"Well, I can get into all that tomorrow. It's late." He got up and picked the copies out of the bottom drawer. "You have the originals in a safe place?"

"On the desk"—he pointed at the office—"in there."

Maxie walked in and took the papers off the desk, compared them to the others in his hand. He stared at the green square in the corner of the computer screen. "I've been thinking of getting one of these. How do you turn it on?"

"I don't know."

With a shrug, the round man stepped out of the office. "You have Layman and Pierce on a retainer already, right?"

"I don't know that, either."

Maxie smiled. "Could be you really do need me." He started walking toward his coat.

"Did I do the right thing?" Phil asked.

There was a little silence. Maxie picked up his coat. "The smart thing would have been to sell out to him, then bring action." He started getting into the coat. "The smart thing and the right thing aren't always the same." He found the mittens in a pocket. "I've got to go get some rest. Be on this first thing in the morning."

He wanted to shake the little man's hand, but those hands were full of papers. "Thanks."

"Sure." Maxie walked toward the glass doors. "And thank you." He held up the copies. "Louise needed some ammunition."

Hearing her name made Phil smile. "You were great tonight. On stage."

"Yeah? Thanks." He grinned and pushed through the doors. "'Night."

The doors swung shut. The small black figure started down the empty mall. Phil dug the office key out of his pocket. "Goodnight, Mr. Nash."

| 30 |

So cold.

He thought about turning the Ford's heater back on. It took too long for the engine to warm up: a waste of gas. And noisy, the neighbors might make trouble, call the police. Except for late-night television that the old people in Little Notch kept company with, it got quiet early here and stayed that way until morning. He rubbed his hands, blew into them. He stared at the empty driveway, the dark house. Maybe she had parked on another block, just to fool him. Maybe she was still that angry. Maybe she was really in there.

The porch steps creaked. The screen door rattled when he knocked on it. He opened it, tried the knob of the front door again, hoping he had been wrong the first time, hoping she really was in there and had seen him in the car and had come down to unlock the door and forgive him. The knob didn't turn. He kicked the door—it didn't budge—and cursed it. He had been so sure she would be at the hospital.

He had gone back to the mill, the old gas station, even Garrett Mountain. She had to be at the hospital. But the nurse had said Louise hadn't been back tonight. The nurse had said no, he couldn't go into the room and see for himself, it was past visiting hours. The nurse had picked up her magazine and watched him get into the elevator. The nurse hadn't heard him come back up the stairs.

It had taken less than ten minutes for the nurse to leave the desk and look in on a patient. He had hurried down the hall, into the room. In the darkness, he could make out a sleepy smile on the lady in the first bed and the rising and falling of Nonna Do's chest, the sound of her easy breathing. The orange wasn't on her night table. He had smiled at that. Then he had bent down and checked under both beds. No Louise. He had walked out and up the corridor, angry that she wasn't where she should have been.

"I told you not to go in there!" The nurse had come out of a room farther down the hall, her whispered shout so well practiced he had felt sorry for her, this must have happened to her a lot and she didn't like being tricked, and he couldn't blame her. He had run down the stairs and out into the cold and skidded on the slick pavement: broadside into a lightpole.

His hip still ached. It was probably black and blue by now. And it was her fault. He walked to the back door, knocked. Nothing stirred inside. He looked for her through the window of the nursery. She wasn't in there.

The cold hurt. It stung his cheeks and ears. He walked around in circles on the driveway, thought about shouting, about breaking a window and crawling in to get warm. And if she was inside and making him stand out here and freeze—

He saw a place to get warm: the lean-to of glass growing out of the garage. He smiled.

That door was open.

Old posts had been left in place, but new studs supported the new glass of the greenhouse walls and roof. A gas heater hummed in a corner. It was warm in here. He shut the door.

It smelled of moist dirt and roses. Pots of them lined the floor and worktable. He was surprised she hadn't hung them from the beams. The big block tiles held heat. He moved some pots, sat on the floor, watched stars through the glass. He was glad she hadn't hung flowers from the beams, they would have spoiled the view. A night dial glowed on his wrist: it was past 4:00 A.M. He wondered when she would come home.

She would come home. She had to.

Damn. He had left the drawing of the new mall in the car. He had wanted her to see what Zorzoli's would not have to be. He had wanted to show her how the architects had left out the river.

All the heat in the greenhouse was making him shiver. He could feel his fingers again. He was thawing. But he couldn't swallow. He wasn't going out there, not to fetch a drawing. There would be time to show it to her.

There would be time to tell her he had been wrong.

What she had been willing to do to protect Nonna Do, he had been willing to do for Mom. Louise hadn't taken the easy way. There had been no easy way. There was nothing missing in her. Something had been missing in him.

It had probably always been missing, that's why he had made so many mistakes about everybody.

It might still be missing.

He couldn't be sure. He felt as though he couldn't be sure about anything.

He didn't know how women worked. He didn't understand money. And the weather, he didn't understand the weather, either. And cars, he couldn't fix cars, or lawnmowers, or anything with an engine, even electric trains.

He didn't even know how to turn on a computer.

He would have to tell her that. She would have to know that about him, that the only things he understood were old boilers and how to build good houses. That the only thing he was sure of was that he loved her.

What if she really was at the hospital—as a patient? No, she was a good driver. He wondered if he should find a phone booth and call, just to be sure. He wondered if he felt now the way Gary Simms had felt that time when Phil hadn't come back with the truck until 5:00 A.M. Gary had sat up, waiting, in his easy chair with a reading lamp on, a book in his lap. He had not been reading that book, not the whole time anyway, his eyes were weak and small print gave him headaches. But he had sat in that chair with that book, and when Phil had walked in, Gary had pretended to be reading. "Couldn't put it down," he had said, but he had left the book on the tray table beside his chair and gone to bed not ten minutes after Phil had come through the door.

It would be cold in California tonight, a raw, biting cold that rolled off the mountains, and maybe it would be raining, that ugly, beating rain, so fierce it was a wonder anything survived out there. But it would be warm inside the houses Gary Simms built. Toasty warm, that's how Gary would describe it to prospective buyers. He liked to show his houses in winter, when it was cold and rainy. He liked to show people what a good house felt like.

She had to be all right. She had to come home soon. And he would hear her, even if he slept. He might not hear the wind or the traffic, but he would hear her. He used her work apron for a pillow. It smelled of potting soil. He stretched out, shut his eyes, listened for the sound of her. He drifted toward sleep. He listened hard.

Snow.

Dry, woolly flakes, falling flat on the warm glass, white only for an instant, then beading, running down the clear panes: new little rivers in the hazy light. His watch had stopped. He had forgotten to wind it. But it was morning. And he hurt.

His hip throbbed, he couldn't sit up. His shoulders felt stiff, pain ran across them, out to his elbows. A glass vent in the roof had popped open, its solar actuator must have sensed too much heat. Snow was coming in, dusting clay pots on the workbench, making the small buds still waiting to bloom look furry. He wondered how to get the vent closed.

And someone was standing at the wall of the greenhouse, hands cupped to the glass. He rubbed his eyes.

She was there, staring at him.

She didn't look surprised. She looked ready to run.

He sat up. If she was going to run away again, nothing, not a bum leg or any pain was going to stop him from catching her. He used the worktable to pull himself to his feet. One of his legs was asleep, and his hip hurt worse than before. All those nights sleeping on benches and floors, on rocky ground, and never any pain. Why now? He punched his leg, stomped his foot to get his circulation going. "Louise—" Her name bounced off the glass back. "Wait!"

Her boots crunched the ice-webbed ground out there. She wasn't running. She opened the greenhouse door and stood there, hands on her hips. "What are you doing here?"

"I ran out of places to look for you."

She glanced at the tiles. Her coat looked slept in. Her boots were caked with mud. And it wasn't true what those ads said about long-lasting makeup: her mascara had run, the stuff on her eyelids looked like mold, her lipstick had begun to flake. She put a hand to her hair. "Don't look at me. I'm a mess."

He couldn't imagine what he looked like. Or smelled like. He didn't care. He took a step toward her.

She backed up. "I didn't get the money." Her hand fell to her side. "She was in Bermuda."

He took another step. He was close enough now, if she tried to run he could dive and tackle her. He smiled.

She looked at him. She didn't smile. She stared at the crumpled apron on the floor. "I didn't want to come back."

It made him wince. "I would have found you," he said. But it didn't sound like his voice, it was weak and cracked. Something cold rolled down his cheek. A tear. His lips quivered. If she ran, he wouldn't have the strength to stop her. "I looked everywhere."

She stepped closer, put a hand to his face. He kissed that hand. He could feel his tears now. He drew her close, held her. He cried into her hair.

She clung to him, and that made him cry harder. She rubbed his back, then leaned away just far enough to glance at him. She wiped some dirt from his eyebrow. She smiled. He thought he would never see her look more beautiful. "We should go inside," she said.

He was still leaking tears. He tried to find his voice. "The roses, they're getting snowed on."

She kissed his wet cheeks. "It melts."

Epilogue

Wally Peck's father still had a workshop in his garage, and it was still impossible to walk through there without knocking something over. He said he wouldn't have recognized Phil, it had been a long time since Little League. He said he could fix the horse.

And the weld wouldn't show because he wasn't going to weld it. He was going to drill a small hole in the shaft of the leg, pin and glue both parts together, then fill the crack with resin. When sanded and painted, no one would know which leg had been broken.

He wasn't so sure about the big pot, though. He would try to weld that, but it might look messy. "Has to hold water, so you want it extra strong."

Phil said it didn't matter, as long as the pot worked.

Mr. Peck said it would. He said Wally was married, with two children, and living in Texas, working for an electronics firm. "This horse for one of your kids?"

Phil smiled. He could see every change in Louise's face when she reached under the Christmas tree, found the box, opened it. He said, "Someday."

Mr. Peck scratched his head. He would get to the pot and the horse as soon as he could. The TV in the rumpus room had broken down again and Mrs. Peck needed it fixed before her friends came over for bridge tonight. Phil was welcome to stay and watch, Mr. Peck would be glad for the company.

"I wish I could," he said. Nonna Do was having a birthday party, her seventy-fourth. Her birthday was in March, but she was having it early because she was going home in a few days, and that meant leaving Mrs. Cohen all alone, and Nonna Do was worried that the doctors had found something horrible inside Mrs. Cohen, something worse than the bad gallbladder, something they weren't telling anyone about, it was that horrible, and who knew who would be alive in March—"Even healthy people die these days, no?"—and after all poor Mrs. Cohen had been through, a party might cheer her up—"A party's just the thing, no?"

Yes.

He didn't want to miss it.